RUGGED &
RELENTLESS

RUGGED & RELENTLESS

 HUSBANDS FOR HIRE—BOOK I

Kelly Eileen Hake

BARBOUR
PUBLISHING

ISBN 978-1-60260-760-6

For more information about Kelly Eileen Hake, please access the author's Web site at the following Internet address: www.kellyeileenhake.com

Cover design: Brand Navigation

Published by Barbour Publishing, Inc., P.O. Box 719, Uhrichsville, OH 44683, www.barbourbooks.com

Our mission is to publish and distribute inspirational products offering exceptional value and biblical encouragement to the masses.

 Member of the
Evangelical Christian
Publishers Association

DEDICATION

Every good gift comes from the Lord—and writing this novel was a gift to me. Perhaps because there's a lot of myself in Evie, the heroine. So, first and foremost, this work is for Him.

But after Him come a lot of wonderful people in my life without whose support, encouragement, and reality checks things just wouldn't come out the same. For my writing accountability partner, Steve, who put in the long hours writing with me even a country apart. For Julia, my best friend, who good-naturedly puts up with postponed girls' nights out. For Aaron, my copy editor, who listens to my character questions and always suggests something to have me heading for the keyboard again. . . .

And this one is, most of all, for Tracie, the editor who bought my first novel and came to be a cherished family friend. You'll never know how much your mentorship and love have meant over the years—this book, and all the growth I think it represents, is thanks to you.

Hugs and Blessings,
Kelly Eileen Hake
Mistakes, Love, and Grace!

KEY SCRIPTURES:

Man looketh on the outward appearance,
but the Lord looketh on the heart.
1 SAMUEL 16:7

There is nothing covered, that shall not be revealed;
and hid, that shall not be known.
MATTHEW 10:26

A false balance is an abomination to the Lord:
but a just weight is his delight.
PROVERBS 11:1

PROLOGUE

Maine, April 15, 1886

Y ou don't have to do this, Jacob!" Mama wrung her hands from the doorway to his bedroom, where she hovered a respectful and appropriate distance. Appropriate and distant—amazing how two words could almost sum up a person's life.

"Someone has to." He shoved clothes into the satchel, fistfuls of hardy work material and not fancy churchgoing stuff or business wear. "Why not me?"

"You have a place here! Responsibilities! The business. . ." Mama ticked off answers to what he'd meant as a rhetorical question.

Women. Jake shook his head and stuffed in a pocketknife and his shaving kit and looked around the room for other essentials. With his pistol holstered at his hip, his favorite boots on his feet, and his saddlebags bulging with enough food to see him through a few days, he didn't need much else.

Except. . . He strode over to the bureau, opened his top drawer, and reached until he felt the cool piece of metal he'd thrust back there three months ago. Now he shoved it into his pocket without giving the object a glance.

"Your father needs you to help run the mill," his mother's

litany continued. "Now more than ever with Edward gone—"

He could tell the instant she recognized her mistake. That she stopped talking was a dead giveaway in and of itself, even if her hand didn't flutter toward her mouth as though to capture the name and stuff it back before it could do any damage.

"Yes, Mama." Jake paused to look her in the eye. "Edward's gone." *Good to hear you noticed.* He swallowed the sarcastic comment but couldn't bury the bitterness at its root. "Four months since his death, but no one acknowledges it."

"It doesn't honor his memory to—"

"Remember him?" Laughter, raw with rage, scraped his throat. "But it honors him to pretend he flitted off to another state, leaving Pa in the lurch? It *honors* him to let his murderer go free to live a long life?"

"The way he died. . . Jake, the scandal of it would smear his memory." She shrugged as though in supplication.

"You mean it would smear the Granger name." He swung the satchel from his old bed and went to the door. "I have to go, Ma." Something in him softened at the misery he saw in her face.

"But. . ." Tears filled her eyes and began to spill down her cheeks. It seemed as though the sudden desertion of her only remaining son allowed her to mourn both of them at once, finally crying for the firstborn who'd never come home.

Jake caught his mother in a long hug, not saying he had to go but would come back with Edward's name clean enough to display on the family tree again.

Jake didn't make promises he couldn't keep. And he knew a hug didn't promise anything, but he hoped it gave his mother some small comfort when she'd finally—*finally*—shown sorrow for the things that mattered most to her.

"But. . ." She sniffed, clutching his coat. "What will people *say*?"

Words. Always words, with his parents. *I should have known that's what mattered.* He brushed her hands away. "I. Don't. Care."

"What about this family?" She made a final plea as he slapped his hat on his head. "What about honoring your parents?"

"We have different definitions of honor, Mother." With that, he headed out the door. West, to begin his hunt.

ONE

Charleston, Virginia, May 5, 1886

Sell it." Her sister's voice cracked on the second word. "Tell Lacey to sell it all and be rid of the accursed place forever."

"Tell her yourself." Evelyn Thompson thrust a handkerchief at her sibling but offered no other solace. "Lacey promises some exciting news, and you've hidden inside too long, Cora."

"Mourning, not hiding."

"Lacey mourns for her brother but honors him by pressing on." *But here is another matter. Lord, I can't allow the tragedy of the mines to bury my sister along with her fiancé.* "We must change our plans and see to our futures."

The sodden handkerchief plummeted to the floor in Cora's first show of spirit in weeks. "I told you—sell it. Sell every inch of Hope Falls we own. I'll never set foot in the town that took Braden, and no profit will be made from a ghost town. Tell Lacey to take the offer and not look back."

"You can tell your opinion to Lacey and Naomi in person."

"I can't." The fire in her eyes dimmed. "Evie, please."

The whisper tore into the very foundation of her relationship with her sister. For as long as she could remember, Evie'd sheltered, raised, and comforted Cora. Streams of mopped tears, scores of tended scrapes, hours of hugs invested demanded that she do the same once more. But their lives hung on the outcome of today's meeting.

If I can just get her there! "You can." Evie picked up the soiled handkerchief and thrust it into her sister's hands. "You must."

With that, she summoned the carriage and headed Cora off when she made for the stairs. Instead, Evie thrust a black bonnet atop her sister's head and all but hauled her out the front door and into the waiting conveyance.

The Lyman house sprawled only a few short blocks away—a simple walk the sisters had made hundreds, perhaps thousands of times. But not today. Today, Evie didn't trust her own ability to force her sister through a walk. Today, those few blocks yawned before her, stretched beyond recognition and filled with peril. Thus, the carriage. It wasn't until they sat safely seated inside that either of them spoke.

"I haven't stepped foot in that house since his memorial." Cora's quiet words held no accusation, only resignation.

Evie's stomach wrenched—and not only from the jostle of the carriage, although that would not have been surprising. Any sort of sustained motion managed that unsavory effect. No, this time the sensation traced back to her own insensitivity in forcing her sister to face a lifetime of memories filled with her recently departed fiancé. *It isn't the meeting Cora has been avoiding—it's the house! That should have been obvious.* She gave herself a mental kick. "Forgive me. I hadn't realized the reason you hesitated—"

"Nor did I, to tell the truth. It wouldn't have occurred to me if you hadn't forced me out of isolation." A rueful smile played about the corners of Cora's lips for a brief moment before tightening into grim determination. "We're here."

Fashioned of stately brick and built along Georgian lines, Lyman House graciously watched over the end of a curved street facing an open park. It had, for at least three previous generations, watched over Lymans and seen them prosper. Until Braden and

Lacey broke the delicate pattern. They first bore the misfortune to be orphaned—albeit after reaching their majorities. But the real trouble seemed to be their disregard for more traditional British customs in favor of a thoroughly American spirit of curiosity and adventure.

A spirit Evie and Cora shared. A spirit that led to an impulsive investment in a promising mining town and, ultimately, Braden's death in a catastrophic cave-in.

So the flags flew at half-mast around the grand residence, and the servants wore black and, as they habitually wore black or gray, added a black armband to signal the household's loss. Solemn quiet completely unlike the usual hustle and bustle of the big place shrouded the building.

Too much change in too little time. As she climbed the front steps, Evie fancied the house hibernated; the windows of its eyes and ears no longer flung open to catch the rhythm of the world around it, it slept. She shivered at the notion that it seemed to be waiting for something—much the same way her sister had been ever since word of the Hope Falls tragedy arrived.

Mr. Burk opened the door before Evie so much as raised the knocker, disproving her theory that the house slumbered. "Miss Lyman and Miss Higgins await you in the morning room."

They made their way past the grand staircase, to the left, down the second hallway, and into the third door on the right without any further guidance. The Thompson sisters counted as family, and all the servants knew it. Not one of them would say a word about how, with Braden gone, Cora would never become a Lyman in truth. Not the way everyone always expected.

And if anyone dares show such insensitivity, I'll step on his toe. That should be enough to erase any thoughtlessness until the fool's foot heals. Evie's eyes narrowed. *Slowly.*

"Evie! Cora!" Lacey rushed to greet them, a froth of black fabric swirling about her feet as she sprang from her chair to flood them in hugs.

If the ponderous weight of grief seemed absent in Lacey's effusive embrace, it etched its burden upon her companion. Miss Naomi Higgins, who boasted a mere five years more than her charge, made her way across the room at a more sedate pace. Her thick muslin skirts dragged at her steps, the harsh black of mourning making the premature streak of pure white at her crown even more startling than usual.

"Naomi." Evie placed her hands on her friend's shoulders, exchanging an understanding glance before drawing her close. Although the slightly older woman seemed disapproving, the two of them shared a special bond. Naomi's propriety kept Lacey's exuberance in check much in the same way Evie looked after Cora.

"Evie." Naomi sank into the hug as though allowing herself a brief respite before putting the starch back in her spine. "It's good to see you." She turned to Cora for a somewhat awkward embrace. "*Both* of you."

"Come." Lacey grabbed Evie's and Cora's hands, pulling them to a plush sofa and settling herself between them. "Have some scones or tarts—Cook knew you were coming." Her smile may have fooled a casual acquaintance, but Evie saw beyond the brittle facade erected around a long-standing joke.

The Lyman cook constantly worried that Cora—with her unending energy and impossibly tiny waistline—needed to eat more. At the same time, she respected Evie's position as a restaurateur and never missed an opportunity to impress her. So the great joke at Lyman Place was that if they wanted to eat well, they need only invite a Thompson for tea.

Evie put as much warmth as she could muster into her answering smile and selected a scone—although her stomach still roiled from both the carriage and the difficulties she couldn't keep from her sister. "How could I resist?"

From the look Cora shot her, at least one person knew she could have resisted easily. Evie didn't mind—anything that made amusement flash across Cora's features was well worth the price.

She nibbled at the edge of her scone before putting it down with undue haste. *Really, daily carriage rides might do much to improve my figure. . . .* She shoved the thought back. Now wasn't the time.

With pleasantries out of the way, silence usurped the place of comfortable conversation and laughter. No more would their afternoons be filled with sharing updates from Hope Falls, poring over catalogs for their businesses, and making plans for their eventual trip out West to join Braden.

Wedding plans for Cora's big send-off evaporated like so much spilled milk, and no matter how old the adages about crying being no use, the sense of loss seeped into every niche of their lives. Everything left seemed soured, though Evie refused to say so. *No. We'll make the best of things, just as we did when Pa died. . . .*

Now there was land, interest in a mine to be partitioned off. Decisions to be made about Evie's café and Lacey's general store out in Hope Falls—the businesses in which they'd invested so much on the promise of their new lives. The businesses that now lay fallow in a soon-to-be ghost town. Those dreams kept company with men who'd never made it out of the mines. Lost forever.

"Well"—Naomi cleared her throat—"we can't sit here all day and hope the situation changes." She gave a slight wince at the word "hope."

They all did.

If Naomi could be counted upon to break the ice, that left Evie to keep chopping away at the frigid barrier surrounding their futures. "She's right. We need to discuss what we're going to do, ladies. Where do we go from here?"

"Not Colorado." This from Cora, who looked as though she would have leapt from her seat if Lacey weren't still clasping her hand. "I'll tell both of you exactly what I told Evie—sell it all and good riddance!"

Evie knew the others awaited her response to this outburst, but she held her tongue. This couldn't be her decision. Not only because Lacey held the principal investment, and they'd made promises to their friend, but because Evie felt torn between the two choices herself.

Part of her agreed with Cora. The venture had cost far more than they'd foreseen, wiping out her inheritance and savings. Then it took the ultimate price in Braden's life. Hope Falls. . . even the name, which once seemed whimsical, now sounded a sinister warning. A dark part of her mind, the part that whispered superstitions and imagined phantasms when tree branches scraped windows in the dead of night, urged her to protect her sister and wash her hands of the place once and for all. *Not to be secretly melodramatic,* she chided herself.

Evie focused on the more practical, and thus important, aspects of the situation. With the businesses not up and running and the town defunct, the chances of recouping even a reasonable percentage of those investments were all but nonexistent. And without Braden, Evie needed to think about how she'd support not only herself, but Cora as well. Could she afford to sell out? If they couldn't revitalize Hope Falls, could she afford not to? That's what it all came down to. That's what she'd come to find out. Evie returned Lacey's gaze in silent question, noting the barely perceptible shake of her flaxen head.

"My solicitor assures me that if we sell, we'll lose almost everything we've put into Hope Falls." Lacey bit her lip—most likely thinking about how buying into the town so they could move with Braden and Cora had been her idea. "He also assures me that, with everyone leaving, the chance of recognizing a profit is negligible."

"What does that leave?" Heart thumping, Evie crumbled her scone into a fine powder, where at least it wouldn't cling to her waistline.

"Keeping the land until it becomes a more marketable asset is what Mr. Slurd suggests." Lacey's eyes narrowed. "I disagree. If selling it means we lose everything, and leaving it fallow means the same, we simply must find another way."

"How?" Naomi spread her hands in a fatalistic gesture. Her involvement more limited to a supportive role by virtue of her lack of personal investment, she didn't offer any outright opinions. "I don't see another option, unless another mining company would buy up the entire area."

"There's been an offer, but it's ludicrous."

Evie's fists clenched at the sum Lacey revealed. It wasn't even what she'd paid to begin the café, much less enough for her, Lacey's, and Cora's stakes. Not to mention what Braden left in his will—why, he'd been co-owner of the mine itself. "Shysters!"

"Is there any way to bring the town back?" Naomi's question surprised Evie, who thought her friend would be more in favor of selling out and staying in Virginia.

"No. It floated loose from hell and needs to go back." Cora's voice sounded oddly flat. "There's no saving it."

Or us.

You shouldn't pace. A voice that sounded suspiciously like it belonged to Lacey's mother echoed with her steps. The habit would surely give away her lack of confidence in the plan she was about to propose.

Lacey expected resistance from Naomi but knew she could win over her companion if Evie joined her. Cora, on the other hand. . . She shot a worried glance at her closest friend. Cora would be dead set against the idea.

But we need a solution to our troubles, and this is all that's come up. How can I convince the others to trust in this vision for the rebirth of Hope Falls, when they see it as a place of death?

"We need to redeem it." Lacey reached one end of the room and marched resolutely back toward the settee, where the Thompson sisters watched with wary expressions. Naomi, if it were possible, looked even more leery.

"Do we have some sort of vouchers for the land?" Cora faltered. "I'd thought there'd be more official documents but didn't ask Braden many questions when I signed over my dowry. I trusted him to make the right decisions for our future."

"We all did." Evie patted her sister's knee. "But no one could have foreseen the mine's collapse. No one."

Naomi steered the conversation to less emotional waters. "There are no vouchers to redeem."

"I meant Hope Falls." Lacey fought to keep still. "We need to redeem the town. It's what Braden would have wanted—for us to help Hope Falls recognize its potential and become the success he planned. We owe it to his memory, and to ourselves, not to give up on everything we prepared for."

"It's a town, not a person." Evie's gaze held a measure of calm Lacey envied. "It cannot be made whole again with the mine collapsed and unable to reopen—there's no longer a reason for it to exist. There are other train stops nearby, with Durango and the like."

"We can save it!" Enthusiasm burbled up, threatening a tide of words to drown out the sense of anything she said. Lacey took a deep breath. "It can be saved."

"Towns don't have souls, and even if they did, Hope Falls would be the exception." Cora all but spat the words. "There's no redeeming it. No making it wholesome or eking anything worthwhile from it now."

"Without the ore, there's nothing to sustain the locale." Naomi's response typified the woman herself—cool and logical.

Perhaps Lacey miscalculated. Naomi's analytical mind could be swayed by the economics, and then Evie's practicality might follow.

She curled her fingers toward her palm, thumb picking at her cuticles in a habit her mother would have deplored. Lacey marshaled her points and continued her argument. "That's not true. What Hope Falls now lacks in ore, it still more than makes up in another valuable natural resource with a high demand in today's market." For once in her life, she held her tongue at the right moment, letting that startling tidbit provoke interest. Actually, Lacey bit her tongue to keep from explaining everything all at once, but she wasn't one to quibble about minor details. The main thing was it worked.

All three of the other women—even Cora!—were exchanging quizzical glances and baffled shrugs. Eventually they all focused their attention on Lacey, silently waiting for her to continue.

She couldn't blame them. She always continued, never failed to speak whatever happened to cross her mind. But not this time. This time Lacey would make them ask. Make them invest such simple assets as time, thought, and words into discovering her scheme. It would bring them one step closer to taking part in it. Lacey rather suspected she wouldn't be able to taste anything for a month, but resolutely kept her tongue between her teeth.

"What resource?" Evie—not Naomi, as Lacey expected— broke ranks to ask the question on all their minds.

"Trees!" She almost bounced in her enthusiasm. "The San Juan Mountains are absolutely covered in trees!"

"Lumber," Naomi breathed, understanding instantly. Lacey could have hugged her.

"Precisely. Lumber is in high demand with the supply in New England depleted from centuries of logging. Hope Falls has the supply, and it's situated right on the railroad."

"You're proposing to turn a mining town into a sawmill?" Disbelief tinged Evie's tone, but a spark of interest lit her eyes. "How?"

"We'd need to buy up the surrounding land, but if looking into selling our property has shown anything, it's that we can get it cheaply. Then it's a matter of labor." Lacey hesitated. *This is the part where things get tricky.*

"Hire men, you mean." Naomi raised a brow. "Buying the land and gear to set up a sawmill and hiring men is an expensive venture. You'll need investors."

"Or husbands." Lacey winced. *And I'd done so well up until now!*

"Never!" Cora jumped to her feet. "We won't travel there and make our home without Braden. I won't have it!" Tears blurred her next words, but the meaning remained clear.

Lacey was at her friend's side in an instant. "We'll be closer to him this way, Cora. I want to go."

"No!" She sobbed. "It's too hard. I won't go without. . ."

"If we don't go"—Lacey tried to be as gentle as possible as she spoke the truth—"we're leaving him behind. Not just in the mine, but in our hearts and dreams. Let Hope Falls die, and we've lost the last part of Braden we could have kept alive."

"But marrying another man—it's a betrayal." Cora shook her head. "I can't."

"I anticipated that. But if the rest of us do, we should be able to make a go of it." Lacey's hopes faded at the shock painting Naomi's and Evie's features. "Come now, ladies. Husbands will provide protection, bolster legitimacy to our claim to the land, and, if we do it right, offer the know-how and some of the labor to start things properly."

"It's. . ." Naomi blinked, words apparently failing her.

"Preposterous. Absolute lunacy." Evie stood beside Cora. "Finding investors, perhaps. Jaunting out West to try our hand at converting a mining town into a sawmill? A distant possibility, if only to recoup our investment. But binding ourselves to absolute strangers on a whim? Never!"

"Never say never." Lacey chirped her standby refrain, hoping for a chuckle. Hoping for it to hold some truth.

The Thompson sisters headed for the door, Evie shaking her head. "We'll find another way."

TWO

T hree weeks, endless miles, and dozens of cities populated by hundreds of unhelpful citizens after he started out, the gnawing hole in Jake's gut became a churning chasm. Instead of bridging the gap between himself and his prey, every step he took widened the distance.

He'd made a conscious decision not to travel by train, certain that too many stops and too many opportunities would pass him by. Now, however, Jake's scheme to follow the mysterious Mr. Twyler by taking the personal approach seemed doomed. Sure, talking to people eventually pointed him in the right direction. Eventually. But by the time he got there, Twyler was long gone. Another train stop ahead of him. Another opportunity lost. So this morning he'd parted company with the horse he'd raised from a colt.

Wonder what it says about me that saying good-bye to Honk made me feel worse than leaving home. He pushed the morose thought aside and bought a ticket for Charleston—the best lead he'd wrangled from an uncooperative cardsharp back in Baltimore. When barkeeps didn't remember Twyler's name and local authorities hadn't detained him for a night or two, petty criminals managed to cough something up.

Which just goes to show I've been right all along. Edward didn't get himself killed by some self-righteous drunk he'd cheated at poker. A criminal set him up, then fired a bullet when Edward turned out too smart to swindle. Somehow the vindication didn't seem so satisfying without the proof to show the world. Jake needed proof to still wagging tongues and flapping gums before he could go home.

Soon. He leaned back in his seat and tilted his hat over his eyes. Maybe he'd catch a little rest before he reached Charleston and started the latest round of cat and mouse. *Soon. . .*

Sooner than Jake thought possible, the porter shook his shoulder and stiffly informed him that they'd reached Charleston. The uniformed man's gaze raked over Jake's dusty clothes and trusty satchel, silently accusing the unkempt passenger of angling to ride farther than he'd paid.

Just for fun, Jake pressed a walloping tip into the man's hand as he departed the train. *Why not give him something to tell his family about?* He gave the dumbfounded porter a jaunty wave from the platform before disappearing into the crowd. Who knew? Maybe next time the man wouldn't be so quick to judge by appearances. *And the moon is made of cheese.* Jake snorted.

Appearances, as his parents demonstrated since his early childhood, made the world go 'round. And appearances were part of why Twyler kept evading him. The criminal looked like a gentleman, whereas he—Jake wouldn't call himself a gentleman any longer—looked less than reputable.

Fair enough. Jake didn't feel very reputable as he headed toward the center of town. Main streets were always a good place to find a jailhouse or, at the very least, directions to one.

His latest tip about the poker playoff—sure to draw an inveterate gambler like Twyler—was out of date by a week or so by now. All the same, local police would have had a presence around the big game. Whether they acknowledged it or found it more profitable to look the other way, it served their best interests to make sure no one lost his temper. Or his life. The police were his best chance for meeting someone who'd interacted with Twyler firsthand or who could point him to someone who had.

He ducked into the jailhouse, narrowing his eyes until they adjusted to the dim light inside. Jake made out two cells to the left, one to the right. The right sat empty. Two drunks took up the spots on the left. One snored fit to bring down the building while the other amused himself by alternately twirling his hat atop his index finger and glowering when it fell off.

Promising. Jake headed for the desk pressed against the far wall, where a deputy made an unconvincing show of pretending he hadn't been napping before the interruption. *Men like this are part of the reason why Edward's dead and definitely to blame for Twyler still running free. How many crimes does a man have to rack up before lawmen start recognizing a wanted criminal right under their noses?* Jake eyed the man before him. *Supposed to protect the public, but sleeping on the job.*

Something of his thoughts must've translated into his expression, because alarm flashed in the deputy's eyes, and his hand groped for his holster before coming up empty.

"Looking for your paperweight?" Jake nudged the firearm toward its rightful owner. If it hadn't been such a prime example of modern justice hard at work, he would've smiled. As things stood, he didn't bother to hide his contempt while the other man scooped up the pistol and shoved it back in place.

"What can I do for you?" He slicked back his hair in a futile and far-too-late attempt to look official.

Your job. He swallowed the truth, as he had so many times before. But this time, it wouldn't stay down. "Your job." His words sparked anger in the other man, but it sizzled into shame. *Good.* "I need information about someone who probably came through here for the poker games."

"Lotta men for that, and it's all settled and done with." His hand twitched over his weapon. "Good riddance, I say. We don't need any more of that sort of crowd."

"Greed makes the best men unpredictable." Jake eased his stance to make the man more comfortable. . .and coax more information from him. "I'll bet you had more than your share in here. No town needs extra gamblers sleeping off a few too many or cooling their heels after a disagreement."

"No two ways about that. Which one were you looking for?"

"Twyler's the name. Smart. Well dressed. Average height. Brown hair. Brown eyes." Jake could have rattled off the non-descript list in his sleep. Except for the name, it could describe any number of men, but it was all he had. For now.

"Can't say the name Twyler rings a bell." The only help Jake got from the man was to rouse the snoozing drunk to ask him, but the jailbirds knew nothing more than their keeper. With a shrug, the deputy plunked down and began rummaging through a drawer. He didn't seem the type to keep reliable records, but maybe someone above him kept a tighter ship.

Jake didn't wait long before the deputy surprised him and pulled something worth his time out of the desk. He crossed the room in two swift strides, unable to tear his eyes away from the improbable find now sitting so proudly atop the scarred surface of a desk made from ponderosa pine.

The suddenness of his movements startled the other man, who grabbed the prize and yanked it up against his chest with the fiercest glower Jake had ever seen. And he'd seen many. "Get your own sandwich."

"I'll pay." His hand inched toward where a sizable cookie still lay on the desk, but his eyes never left the work of art the other man held. Generous slices of soft bread—sourdough by the tang scenting the air—lovingly cradled thick slabs of marbled ham and cheese piled nigh unto infinity. Mouth watering, Jake swallowed before speaking again. "Name a price."

"Not for sale." Cruel, he sank his teeth into his lunch with a muffled moan of delight. "Ookin gofu coffee yerself," he mumbled around his mouthful instead of chewing with the appropriate appreciation. He did, however, slap a protective hand over the cookie. So the man had some brains, after all.

"What?" Envy made his question sharp.

"You can go to the café yourself," the hat-twirling drunk translated. "Lucky man, if you do."

"Where?"

"Thompson's Café. One block up and to the north." His hat stopped twirling as he watched the jailer finish his sandwich. A gusty sigh chased Jake out the door. "Wish I could join you."

"I'm going to have to fire that girl," Evie admitted to Wilma as they ran around the kitchen. "But I don't know when I'll have time to find another to take her place."

"She only shows up half the time," Wilma agreed. "With Cora out, we're already shorthanded!"

Evie plowed through the swinging doors back into the dining room, arms loaded with dishes. Unloading them posed no problem—the moment she stepped up to a table eager hands relieved her of her burdens with smiles all around.

Praise the Lord for a booming business. Her own smile rarely flagged, bolstered by those of satisfied customers. *If things keep going so well, we might be able to make ends meet despite the disaster of Hope Falls.*

"Hooo!" Caught up in her thoughts, Evie hadn't paid close enough attention to her surroundings. Even she couldn't say which knocked the breath out of her more—the chair back lodged into her stomach or the stranger who'd stepped through her doors. Not that it mattered much, since either way left Evelyn Thompson standing certain of one thing: *I knew I should have laced my corset tighter!*

But a woman needed to breathe, after all, and her corset couldn't truly control her overly exuberant curves. She had what she privately referred to as an ongoing case of the "sqwudgies," a terrible affliction of squooshy pudginess no man-made device could cure.

So here she stood, squashed between the chairs of two customers who'd simultaneously decided to scoot backward, as the most gorgeous man she'd ever clapped eyes on strode into her café. This sort of thing, she'd noticed, never happened to Cora or the other girls who worked in the dining room.

It was one of the reasons she stayed in the kitchen. *And,* she fumed, tugging herself free and refusing to consider what color her face must be turning, *yet another reason why I have to hire another girl. My dignity can't survive this on a daily basis.*

Somehow she'd pasted a smile back on her face by the time she reached her new customer. "Good afternoon and welcome to Thompson's Café. What can I get you?"

He didn't sit so much as sprawl into ownership of the one vacant table. With a knapsack on the seat beside him and long legs stretched past the table to bracket the chair across from him, he should have looked tired.

He didn't. Everything about him shouted of coiled intensity, from the rigidity in his shoulders to the strong line of a jaw stubbled with at least five days' worth of a beard. One hand seemed nonchalantly half tucked into his pocket, but it was the pocket closest to his holster. His eyes scanned the entire room before coming to rest on her with an absolute clarity she couldn't remember seeing. "Everything."

"Oh." Her mouth went so dry she licked her lips without thinking, and still his penetrating gaze didn't waver. "We aren't the typical café, with only one option. We have roast chicken and potatoes, onion soup and biscuits, ham or meat loaf sandwiches, sugar cookies, and berry cobbler today." She finished the recitation with pride. "So what would you like?"

His brows rose, what might have been a sigh from a less robust man passed through his lips, and his eyes narrowed as though measuring her.

Evie caught herself fidgeting with her apron strings at the thought. Measurements—aside from cups and teaspoons—were the last thing she wanted to think about. But he didn't need to know that, so she put a hand on her hip in what she hoped was a nonchalant fashion. "If you can't decide, I recommend the chicken." It cost most.

"I already decided." A smile broke out across his face. He leaned back and folded his hands across his chest before closing his eyes and practically purring his order. "Everything."

Evie gaped at him for a moment before gathering her wits—and several empty dishes—on her way back to the kitchen. Luckily, the lunch crowd started thinning out about then, and her only other dining room helper—a girl by the name of Lara—had things fairly well in hand.

"Next pot's almost ready," Wilma promised when Evie found the soup tureen dangerously low.

"Perfect. Looks like the rush is slowing down anyway." She filled one of the crockery bowls full of the thick soup, topping it with crumbles of leftover corn bread from yesterday and some of the sharp cheese that went so well with the sweeter flavor of the onion. Grabbing a basket with four biscuits, she tucked a crock of butter inside. "I'll be back in a minute for a plate of chicken and potatoes. . .and I need one each of the ham and meat loaf sandwiches wrapped up." He must want them to go.

Wilma cast a perplexed look over one shoulder and kept working. "Thought you said we were slowing down?"

"We are." Evie elbowed her way through the swinging doors and called back, "It's all one order!" She wished she could see Wilma's expression but chuckled at the thought.

Skirting tables and the more treacherous chairs, Evie reached the stranger. She set down what she'd consider to be his first course, gratified to see him lean forward and pick up a spoon almost before the food hit the table.

"Hat off while you eat—house rules." A thrill ran through her when she set a warning hand on his shoulder. She quickly moved back to gesture at the sign posted on the wall.

"Hats off to the chef," he read aloud, amusement quirking the left corner of his mouth. He slanted a glance toward her. "What if I don't like the food?"

"Then you can take it up with her." Evie fought a smile of her own. "Or the owner."

"Fair enough." He thumbed his hat back until it slipped off an unruly crown of brown hair in sore need of a barber, then placed the article on the chair beside him.

As much as she wanted to wait, wanted to watch him eat his doubts to find them as delicious as anything else she'd mastered in the kitchen, Evie went back to fetch his chicken. And his sandwiches.

Mere minutes later she set them before him with a flourish, smug to see a now-empty bowl and basket strewn across the table.

As Evie reached to collect them, his callus-roughened hand closed around her wrist. "I'll have a talk with that cook now."

It'd been a mistake to touch her. Jake knew it the moment his fingers slid across skin so soft he suddenly resented the fashionably proper, tight cuffs concealing her wrists. The startled widening of her remarkable eyes—gold like the sweetest honey—warned him he'd gone too far.

He could have released her quickly, but that would be akin to admitting his faux pas. Instead, he reached over her arm with his free hand and picked up the now-empty biscuit basket before giving up the warmth of her hand nestled beneath his. "I'm not satisfied." Jake plunked the basket back down as though to punctuate his comment, biting back a grin at the astonishment flitting across her features.

"What!" With the lush grace of a serene Madonna and the

rosy flush of a woman tamping down indignation, his waitress held more appeal than the food she'd brought him. *And that's saying something.*

"You heard me." Jake manfully ignored the smells of herbed roast chicken and potatoes in favor of watching her. He could eat any day—he'd only be in Charleston tonight.

"Dissatisfied, my left foot!" She snatched up the basket, turned it upside down, and shook it as though making a point. "Nary a crumb left to pity a pigeon."

"Yep. I'll discuss it with the chef." He put his hat back on, to really get her goat. "Or the owner."

"You're speaking with her." Her fingers twitched as she eyed his hat, obviously itching to swipe it from his head.

"Chef or owner?" As if he didn't already know. *Owner. No ring. If she's the cook, she'd be married. No way a pretty thing like that with a way around a stove would be unwed.*

"Both." Never had such a sweet smile carried so much grit.

"In that case"—Jake removed his hat in a heartbeat—"you can fix the problem right away."

"The only problem I see is a man who's bitten off more than he can chew." She gestured to the bounty of food before him. "And is trying to talk his way out of paying for it."

"Um. . .Miss Thompson?" the other girl piped up in a thin voice. "He paid while you were in the kitchen."

"Oh." The waitress/cook/owner visibly deflated, curiosity replacing her ire as she focused on him once more. "Then what was wrong with your biscuits, sir?"

"Lots." Now that he knew the identity of the cook, his original plan to compliment her flew out the window.

"Such as?"

"For one thing"—he leaned back, drawing out the time he'd spend sparring with her—"the texture needs fixing."

"Hogwash!" The denial burst out of her with enough force to send the wisps of hair framing her face dancing. "People love my biscuits—they aren't hard, burnt, lumpy, nor doughy. That batch came out the same as they always do—the way my customers like them—light and fluffy."

"Exactly." As intended, his agreement snapped the wind from her sails. *Bewilderment doesn't suit her half so well as exasperation. She's not the sort of woman who's often confused.* Strange how much that pleased him. "Your light-and-fluffy biscuits all but melt in the mouth and leave a man wanting more."

"It's why we serve four per customer!"

"Which brings me to the second problem. In all fairness, it's related to the first. More biscuits in the basket would take care of both." He lifted the basket to emphasize its sorry state—which was, as she'd pointed out, absolutely empty.

"Hear, hear!" A man from a nearby table added his support.

"More biscuits!" another seconded.

Miss Thompson closed her eyes as though gathering strength, and Jake abruptly realized how much his teasing would cost her. *I should have known others were listening—Ma had reason to worry about what others thought.*

"I say you offer a 'bounty of biscuits' option—for an added fee, of course." He raised his voice to make sure this proposition carried. "I'll be the first to take you up on it, Miss Thompson."

"It's not every day I'm served patrons telling me how to run my café."

Jake respected any man who stood his ground, and he'd just found that went double for a woman. They both knew she'd be foolish not to take him up on the offer, but she claimed her territory with aplomb.

"Me, too!"

"Same here!" Three other men took up the chorus of rattling baskets.

It wasn't until she pursed her lips—he suspected to trap a smile—that he noticed their fullness.

Which I have no business noticing. Everything about Miss

Thompson, from the polished toes of her boots, to those tightly buttoned sleeves he'd deplored earlier, to the proud fire in her eyes declared her a lady.

And Jake had left behind his life as a gentleman.

THREE

Evie eyed the stranger causing so much chaos in her orderly café and tried to hide her amusement. Before her sat a tall, rangy example of why that old maxim, "The customer is always right," hadn't made it up on her wall.

But at least he knew when he did wrong and moved to fix it. For that matter, the entire battle of wills led to an extra way for the café to expand its profit. *Thank You, Lord.*

"I'm a patriotic woman," she declared, "so in the spirit of democracy, I'll add the bounty of biscuits to what we offer." With that, she collected baskets and orders, otherwise ignoring the man who'd instigated it all.

"Already have more in the oven," Wilma greeted her when she reached the kitchen and headed for the baking table.

"Conversation carried all the way in here, did it?"

"Bounty of biscuits and all." The two women shared a laugh. "Took me a moment to realize they were shaking their baskets like tambourines though. Wish I could've seen that."

Evie's chuckle went alongside those extra biscuits until she reached the stranger. Then she schooled her features into a completely blank expression as she surveyed the now-clean plate in front of him. Well, almost clean. A few chicken bones littered the surface as he dove into his second basket of bread. "Any complaints about the chicken?" The challenge shot out before she could stop it.

"Just that I ate it so fast, if the bones didn't stay behind, I'd swear it flew by me." He slathered butter on a biscuit, his easy grin nowhere in sight. "I think I'll be changing my order now."

"The cookies are wrapped one with each sandwich," she clarified so if he decided he didn't want them he wouldn't be surprised if she reached for them.

"I figured." One bite demolished an enormous amount of food, but he didn't seem to be enjoying himself as much as before. "I'll need another two cookies—and change my order to a double serving of cobbler."

He didn't look at her the way he had before the bounty-of-biscuits exchange. If Evie didn't know better, she'd say the man outright avoided looking at her at all. Certainly the teasing tone of his conversation switched to all business.

Why? And why didn't I realize how much I was enjoying the way he talked before, until it changed? Evie couldn't very well ask the man, so she set about serving him in this newly constructed silence she found so unsettling.

He ate every bite she brought him—save the sandwiches, which she'd been right in assuming he intended to take with him—without another word. And when he was done, he stood and left with a gesture she'd remember for the rest of her days.

The tall stranger strode to the door, opened it, and turned around. He stood in the frame, silhouetted by the setting sun, and when his gaze met hers, he pointed to the sign on the wall. He made a show of stepping entirely outside before placing his hat back on his head and letting the door close behind him.

Hats off to the chef. Such a small sign of respect, an acknowledgment she'd never thought to see—and it touched her more than it had any right to. Evie was very much afraid she froze in place and stayed that way for an indecent amount of time, staring at the door as though addlepated.

The remainder of the day blinked by, and in no time at all, she'd made it home for the night. Before dark—always before dark. For her own well-being and reputation, as well as those of the women who worked alongside her, Thompson's Café closed earlier than some of her patrons would like. But Evie wouldn't budge on that. *I might not be able to afford losing the business, but I can spare it more than I can spare our safety.*

Regret warred with relief when she reached the boardinghouse where she and Cora lived. Taking rooms with Mrs. Buxton had been meant as a temporary measure. Now, the place she thought of as home would most likely remain such for a long, long time.

When their father died three years before, Evie'd been forced to use her own dowry to keep the household going until she couldn't avoid selling their home. But those proceeds wouldn't last forever, so Evie took her one skill and turned it into her investment. After two years, the café proved itself enough to have garnered a modest savings account and flattering mortgage deal with the bank to fund Evie's part in Hope Falls.

But the grand plan for Wilma to run things in Charleston while Evie went to Colorado vanished in a heartbeat with Braden's death. The bright future of Cora happily married to a wealthy mine owner with Evie and their closest friends living nearby had all been fool's gold. Which wouldn't pay off the mortgage on her restaurant, or even keep rented rooms over their heads.

Just entering their home wrapped a cloak of concern around her thoughts. Worry pressed away the joy she'd found at work, robbing her of any ability to coax Cora back to the world outside these rooms.

It is, she thought, *almost as though where we are becomes a part of us. At home, I mourn for Cora and the promising lives we've lost. In the café, I'm cheery for the customers and proud of what I accomplish.*

So what if we went to Hope Falls? How much worse would things be for both of us, with Cora surrounded by the reminder of what she should share with Braden and me without customers to cook for? The thought made her temples ache.

Even without Lacey's ludicrous mention of hasty husbands, the plan spelled disaster—which was why she and Cora hadn't so much as discussed it in the week since. They'd been right to walk away. *Here, we may not have much, but at least we know its value.* Bolstered, she swept up the stairs and into their suite—to find their rooms filled with visitors.

The small couch held Lacey and Naomi, with Cora—her pale face showing signs of strain—in the only chair. Evie would make do with the ottoman, she supposed, although—

Thud.

With a seat now readily available, the women in the room did the only natural thing—they immediately surrounded Cora on the floor.

"She fainted!" Even Evie couldn't explain why she bothered to remark on something so obvious, aside from the surprise of it. She chafed her sister's cold hands in her own warm ones as Naomi smoothed back Cora's hair and loosened her collar. "She's only ever fainted once before, when—"

Lacey caught Evie's look and nodded, her eyes solemn. "When I told her of Braden's death."

"What did you tell her this time?" No matter she counted Lacey Lyman as one of her closest friends, Evie battled an urge to shake the girl for whatever shock she'd foisted upon Cora.

"Evie?" Cora's voice sounded weak, but her grip would most likely leave bruises on Evie's arms as she struggled to sit up—no mean feat for a woman lying prostrate on the floor in a corset. Little wonder she seemed breathless. "You don't understand."

"Ssshhh, dear. Rest a moment."

"No!" Cora gave a sudden lurch, eyes glittering with a fierce light. "Don't you see? Braden's alive!"

Seems I'm not the only Thompson sister with a secret penchant for melodrama. Evie shook her head.

"No, Cora—you fainted. Things will clear up in a moment." She motioned to Naomi. "We'll get you a drink of water." As she spoke, she maneuvered her sister onto the sofa and propped her against one of the arms, where she'd be less likely to fall.

"Lacey!" Cora all but shoved Evie away in a bid for the other woman's attention. "Tell her!"

"She's right." Naomi's voice whispered in her ear, her closest friend putting a hand on her shoulder as though to brace her for news that would turn their world upside down yet again. "Perhaps you'd best sit down."

Call her silly, but one glance at Cora's wild-eyed expression made Evie reluctant to hear them out. She shrugged away Naomi's hand, using the scant moment it took to reach the ottoman and pull it toward the tea table to seek peace.

Lord, my prayers for Your provision never specified what path You'd choose—it wasn't my place. More than that, it seemed we'd learned that lesson the hard way when all our carefully laid plans for Hope Falls fell apart. But now it's plain to see my sister and I will be swept into something unbelievable. Grant me the faith and strength to see it through and the heart to do so with good humor!

She situated herself on the ottoman, pulled one of Cora's hands into hers, and declared, "All right. Tell me everything."

"I don't know nuthin'." The man shook his head hard enough to bruise his brains. If, that was, someone assumed the down-on-his-luck gambler possessed any in the first place.

Jake didn't assume. Resisting the impulse to get better acquainted with the delectable cook had left him too surly to bother. *The time is long past for me to find Twyler and finish this so I can get back to the things that make life worth living.* "Yes, you do." Jake intentionally widened his stance, an unspoken threat. "Not much, but you know something about Twyler. Spill it."

The barkeep at the saloon where those poker games had been held couldn't tell him much that afternoon, but he'd pointed the way toward the entrenched gamblers who might remember more. From there, persistent questioning and more rounds of whiskey than Jake bothered to count pointed him to this sad excuse for a man.

"Nuh-ugh." A nervous swallow. "He was a mean cuss, but that's all I know. Bad news, but old news, if you catch my meaning."

Seemed Twyler'd been smart enough to cover his tracks, this time. But intimidation wore off in time—and for once, the lag between Jake and his prey might pay off.

"You shared a room with him—where'd he say he was headed?" He casually pulled back the flap of his duster, revealing the holster sitting on his hip. If intimidation worked, he'd beat Twyler at his own game. *I have to.*

"Dunno." A shifty glance from Jake's gun to the street behind him, where no one wandered after dark. No one to interfere. The grizzled gambler started to wheeze.

If the man were younger, in better health, or boasted more fight and less fear, Jake's conscience wouldn't set up a fracas. *But at this rate, I'll be no better than the murderer.*

"Sorry to waste your time." Jake shifted so his coat closed then took a step back to give him more room to breathe. He eyed the man, unable to give up altogether but unwilling to bully the old fellow. *Wonder if cold, hard cash would wipe away the memory of Twyler's threats.* He'd just decided to give it a try when the other man spoke up.

"Durango." Seemed he'd gotten some of his courage back along with his breath. "Dunno where it is, don't care, and don't want to see either one of you again." With that, he pushed back into the saloon, ignoring Jake's muttered "Thanks" with all the dignity of a dethroned king.

For his part, Jake wasted no time heading back to the train station, where he'd leave on the first ride heading toward Colorado.

He settled onto a bench, a man with a ham sandwich—and a purpose.

Twyler was a dead man walking.

"He's alive." Lacey verified Cora's outlandish claim in a single breath. "Braden and two others were pulled from the mines. My brother—" Here, her voice broke. "Is a survivor."

So why aren't you smiling, Lacey? A frisson of foreboding tingled up Evie's spine. *Why isn't Cora leaping for joy? What am I missing?* She looked to Naomi to fill in the gap.

"Along with this happy news, we've received a few other, less joyous revelations today." Naomi seemed to be searching for words. The thoughtful, tactful nature Evie'd always admired chafed today while she waited. "Mr. Lyman's lost the use of his left leg—perhaps permanently. He's also suffered head and back injuries and a broken wrist and can't be moved."

"But he's alive?" Evie remained flabbergasted by the lack of celebration. "Everything else is secondary! This is wonderful!" She turned to her sister. "You still have—"

"He sent word he's dissolving the engagement." Cora's voice had gone strangely monotone and hollow, as though traveling over a great distance. "After his experience, he's reevaluated our situation and decided this is"—she consulted a piece of paper Evie hadn't noticed she crumpled in her hand—"best for all."

"What? That can't be right. . . ." Evie trailed off as Lacey and Naomi nodded that it was, indeed, the case. *Now it makes sense. They're relieved he's alive but stupefied by his foolishness!*

"First I say good-bye because we plan to reunite. Then I get news of his death and struggle to make peace with it." Cora's eyes reddened, but no tears fell. "Now I hear he is alive—but doesn't want me." She didn't make it a question or even an exclamation of disbelief. It sounded almost as though she were making it real by speaking the words.

"That's not true." Evie didn't know how or why she was right; she just knew it with everything inside her. "Braden loves you and that can't have changed." Then it clicked into place. "Head injury? He's not thinking straight and he's been through a terrible ordeal."

"Exactly." Lacey's eyes widened with understanding—and obvious relief. "In fact, with his legs crushed, he might think you want a different husband. It would be just like Braden to want you to be happy, no matter the cost." She all but bounced next to Cora as she convinced herself.

Evie wasn't convinced entirely. In fact, that ordeal and head injury were all that stood between Braden Lyman and her righteous fury over his treatment of her sister. But now was the time to look after Cora, whose color began returning.

"That could be it." Cora blinked a few times, glancing at Evie in something akin to apology before turning to Lacey. "We must go to him."

"Yes. Lyman Place will be put up for sale. Naomi and I will leave before the week is out to oversee Braden's recovery." Lacey looked as though she might say more but stopped herself.

"My engagement still stands, no matter what Braden has to say about it." Cora's chin lifted. "I'm going with you."

Evie's mouth went dry. *Here it is, then. With Braden alive and in need, everyone is going to Hope Falls despite the fact the town will fail. But there's nothing for it. . . .* "Where Cora goes, I go." She answered the unspoken question hanging about the room like the sword of Damocles. "Wilma will hire help and run the café here while I'm in Colorado, as we planned."

"We're in this together." Lacey's smile demanded one in return. "Which is a blessing. There's so much to do, so many things to oversee, supplies we'll need to make this work—"

"Starting with the most important item on our list." Naomi's usually quiet voice rose with a determination demanding their attention. She paused to draw in a deep breath before clarifying. "Husbands."

Silence reigned for a good, long while.

"No, thank you." Evie kept her tone polite. *Perhaps if I treat it as something inconsequential, it will become so.*

Lacey burst out laughing. " 'No, thank you?' " she parroted. "Evie, you sound as if someone offered you liverwurst!"

"Liverwurst, while unpleasant, is fleeting. Marriage binds you to a man for life. It's not something to be undertaken on a whim or with an eye to free labor." Evie shook her head.

"The Bible calls a wife a helpmeet, a partner. These days, women are viewed as secondary. Why don't you think of this as an opportunity to find a man who would be a true partner in all the areas of the life you'd share?" Lacey's words tattled that the heiress had been waiting for a chance to reopen the discussion. More dangerously, her argument struck a chord.

Haven't I given up on the idea of marrying simply because I know it would be the end of my independence, the end of being respected for what I've accomplished through hard work and prayer? What would it be like to share my life with a man, instead of be expected to fit into his?

"We can do so much more than you give us credit for, Lacey." She turned the tables. "You've run a household here and set up a mercantile in Colorado. I've a café awaiting me. Cora will see to Braden, and Braden's claim to the land won't be challenged by the mining company for fear of legal reprisal. Hire a solicitor to see to gathering workers for the sawmill, but don't throw your life in with a stranger!"

Unbidden, an image of the stranger from the café strode into Evie's memory before she shook it free. Now wasn't the time to reminisce over a handsome customer with mischief in his eyes.

"Braden's in no condition to look after us." Cora added her thoughts for the first time. "It must be why he tried to keep me from going at all! With his legs healing, he won't be able to guard and protect us in an untamed land with several men to every woman. It won't be safe for us to live alone, and hiring guards poses the same problem."

Fear bit into Evie at the mere mention of Cora and her friends being unprotected in the wilderness, possible prey to lonely, unscrupulous men. "And Hope Falls is a railroad stop." There'd be no avoiding any passengers—indeed, such passengers would be their only hope for revenue until the proposed sawmill began to turn a profit.

"If any of us had a father, or another brother or two, or even a close male cousin, things would be different." Lacey spread her hands in a gesture of helplessness. "I considered all of this. Husbands aren't something I would suggest except as a last resort. And with Braden in need, I'm more than willing to take this leap of faith."

Of course Lacey would. She'd been the one to dream up this zany scheme! Evie looked to Naomi's better judgment.

"I don't see an alternative. Husbands will offer the personal and financial security we need." The words rang with confidence, but a shadow of pain held out against the hope in Lacey's gaze. "Think of it this way, Evie. In this circumstance, as a landowner and investor, you're in the position to choose your husband instead of waiting for one to choose you!"

Here lay the cause of the shadow haunting Naomi's green eyes. At three years older than Evie's own twenty-two, Naomi ranked as a spinster. So far as any of them knew, she'd never received an offer of marriage before becoming Lacey's governess, then companion, and certainly had not since.

Even now, Naomi didn't own a business or land, nor did she bring a significant dowry to a prospective husband. For her, the notion of choosing a man instead of waiting—always waiting—to be chosen would be appealing.

Evie knew, because she felt the same way. *No man ever chose me, either.* For a moment, she let herself be swept away in the fantasy of choosing a business partner for a husband, standing on the closest thing to equal footing that a woman could enjoy with a man. It had benefits, but somehow left her cold. Still. . .

"I'll do it." For Cora. For herself. For all of them. And as for the husband? *I'll just not think about the fact he didn't choose me and may never have wanted me in the bargain.* She shoved the thought away. No sense anticipating heartache. "Now the real question is how do we find these husbands?"

"Now that I've planned for." Lacey bounced out of her seat. "We'll go about selecting husbands the same way we'd fill any other position."

"Spread word around town?" That was how Evie'd always found girls in need of respectable work when she needed help at the café. The very thought of asking around after eligible men brought on a queasiness on par with riding in a carriage for long distances. A closed carriage. On a bumpy road.

"We can't put it about we're looking for men!" Naomi sounded scandalized. "You'll be ruined."

"That's not what I meant. We won't ask around for husbands." The smile sliding across Lacey's face made Evie's stomach plummet. "We'll hire them."

FOUR

W hat can you be thinking, Lacey? That's akin to. . ." Naomi's voice dropped to a scandalized whisper. *"Prostitution."*

"Pishposh." Lacey waved away her companion's worries. "It's nothing of the sort. Marriages of convenience and arranged marriages make society go 'round, after all. The only difference here is we'll be making the arrangements ourselves."

"To portray it as hiring someone implies he'll be compensated for what he provides. In this case, the groom provides himself." Evie, not surprisingly, took up Naomi's perspective. "So he would be, in effect, selling himself. You can call it whatever you like, but Naomi's right to object."

"By that logic, you're calling Braden some sort of. . ." Cora groped for the words before managing, "Unsavory sellout. He received a sizable dowry upon our engagement."

"That's different!" Evie spluttered.

"Not really." Lacey seized on the opening, throwing a quick smile at Cora. *I knew I could count on her!* "In olden days they demanded a bride price. Money has bought more marriages than love ever could have managed alone. Why not decide what we want from a spouse, gather options, and make our selections?"

42

"Because no matter how you twist social convention to suit your argument, you cannot buy a husband." Naomi lost enough of her reserve to roll her eyes. "And you cannot simply choose what you please and send away for a spouse!"

"Yes, we can." Lacey dug around in her reticule and withdrew the folded paper with a flourish. "If men can send away for wives, there's no reason we can't apply the same principle. Out in Hope Falls, there'll be no one to judge us."

" 'Mail Order Brides.' " Cora beamed in triumph as she read the advertisement. "If that's not sending away for a spouse, nothing is! Better yet, no one calls it prostitution."

"Are you proposing we pen an advertisement to catch the attention of available bachelors?" Humor and curiosity laced Evie's question—far better than the scandalized outrage she'd shown earlier.

"Precisely." Lacey maintained her decorum. Hopping about in victory wouldn't make the others confident about their plan, after all. "We'll telegraph it to all the major papers, who'll run it immediately upon receiving the wired fee. I'll take care of everything once we've written the ad itself."

"So we'll state what we're looking for, and they'll write letters or telegraph us back." Thoughtfulness softened the worry in Naomi's eyes. "We'll read them, choose our favorites, and arrange for meetings. Although. . .what if it doesn't go well?"

"If you don't want to marry the man, send him back." Lacey wanted to be absolutely clear on this point. "Any sign he'd be abusive, any hint that makes you uncomfortable, don't choose him. We need to be mindful of time, but these are our lives. I'd never forgive myself if you rushed into wedding the first bachelor you met simply because you felt forced."

"No—none of us will do that." Evie slanted a hard glance at Naomi, as though demanding agreement.

"Of course not."

I'm glad. Naomi's the one I'm most worried about accepting the first proposal to come her way. She thinks she has nothing to offer—and I don't have long to change her mind. But she'd start that project soon enough. "So, ladies," Naomi mused aloud, tapping her forefinger against her chin, "what does each of us want in a husband? What makes a man the sort you'd want to live with?"

"Or, at the very least, *be able* to live with." Evie's joke shook loose their laughter. "No man's perfect, after all."

"Braden's taken."

"Nice of you to prove your sister's point," Lacey teased Cora. She, of all people, knew her brother to be far from perfect. Cora knew the same—she just needed some time with Braden to remember it! "Let's each list three qualities we'd like to find in a husband. No repeating. Naomi goes first."

"God-fearing, strong character, and appreciation for the little things," Naomi suggested without even needing to think.

"Sharp mind and an easy smile—no, make that a sense of humor. The smile follows." Evie's own smile made Lacey wonder what man her friend was thinking of. "And cares about others."

"I'd say curious with an adventurous bent." Lacey watched Cora add it to the list. "And hardworking. We'll need that."

"But as nice as these sound, they aren't practical enough. Well, most of them." Evie frowned.

"She's right. We'll need to have an age requirement—say, twenty-four to thirty-five?" Naomi shrugged. "Old enough to take it seriously, at least, but not so old they won't work."

"Perfect! We should ask for sawmill experience, too. Someone needs to know what needs to be done to get things started." Evie shifted in her seat, obviously uncomfortable with the idea of beginning a business about which she knew nothing.

Lacey patted her shoulder. "I bought several books about sawmills and logging—even scientific treatises about the types of trees we'll find. At first, we'll need to look after Braden and make more finite arrangements while creating a transport system to the mill site. All that gives us time to learn the ins and outs before the mill goes up and becomes operational." She paused, welcoming the surge of hope and confidence filling her at the thought. "Time we'll also use to meet and marry the men we've asked for!"

"You asked for good things"—Cora tapped her pencil against the table—"but overlooked something rather important."

"What?" All three of them chorused the question at once.

"Something we take for granted until it's gone."

"We can't take anything for granted until we have it," Lacey pointed out. She couldn't let anything ruin this now, when they'd come this far. *We're so close to the greatest adventure of our lives, and there's nothing I take for granted about it!*

"Husbands among them." Evie's wry smile didn't seem to lighten Cora's mood. "Though I don't see how we can take for granted someone we select so carefully. What more could we need?"

"Just one thing." A tear trickled onto the paper as Cora blinked, obviously thinking of Braden as she added one word to their list. "Health."

Braden thrashed against the straps binding him to the bed, fighting against the warm, floating haze of the morphine as it beckoned him back to sleep.

"No!" The protest came out as little more than a feeble croak, rasping past his dry throat. *Confound them!* Didn't they know the waking pain could be borne until he lost consciousness without the drugs? Better that than the fog of the medicine, where memories waited to ensnare him the moment he slept.

Licking his cracked lips, he tried again, but the doctor already seemed far away, the room blurred around the edges. Now the sharp streaks of agony racing from his legs began fading to the bearable ache Braden knew signaled unbearable dreams—but he couldn't stop them any more than he could stop the cave-in....

Hushed voices, words he couldn't make out but understood anyway, brought Braden around the corner to the newest offshoot of the mine.

Known only to himself, Owen, and a handful of others, it promised to be the biggest strike Hope Falls had ever seen. Even in the muted glow of lanterns sulking for fresh air, the vein sparkled with the promise of dreams made real. He lifted the light so Eric could see that golden stripe continuing on into the wall—where they'd not yet excavated.

Safety first. Always.

The geological surveys hadn't been completed, and until they were, Braden wouldn't give the order to proceed. He grinned. We can afford to wait.

Besides, it wouldn't be much longer. He expected to hear back any day now—though Owen urged him to wait until they hired security and half a dozen other unnecessary measures he argued were vital to safeguard the site. Once things went public, his partner insisted, they'd be dealing with claim jumpers.

"All the more reason to get started as soon as we're cleared." Eric's assessment matched Braden's, though he kept his voice low. One tunnel over, workers mined as usual. No need to attract attention to the offshoot.

Approaching footsteps spurred Eric and Braden to move forward, blocking the vein of gold ore from view, until they saw Owen's flushed face. It wasn't unusual for his face to turn red from the exertion of climbing into the mine and traipsing around in thin air—Owen held up more of the business end of things—so Braden thought nothing of it.

"Why are you here?" Dismay sharpened the question to a cry. "Both of you! You shouldn't be here!"

"You're the one who'll attract attention, Owen." Braden tugged the furious man deeper into the tunnel. "Calm yourself."

"No. You didn't listen to me—" Whatever else Owen planned to say was drowned out by an incredible roar as the mountainside was torn apart. Wooden supports buckled, stones tumbled, and dirt rained until it gave way to clouds of dust coating Braden's face, mouth, throat. . .and his very soul.

Cave-in.

While it lasted, he prayed for it to end, but in the silence, he heard the screams, shouts, and cries of injured men the next tunnel over. Oh, Lord. . .what have I led them to? *It wasn't until he heard a moan but couldn't move toward the sound that Braden realized his legs were pinned beneath something. His hands told him it was a wooden support burdened by rock and earth.*

I can't feel my legs. *It didn't seem to matter. He lay, time measured by ragged breaths and unrelenting thirst. His men grew quiet. Braden strained to hear them, but silence steadily won until he prayed for even the screams and sobs from before. . . .*

Light assaulted his vision the moment he opened his eyes, flooding him with reassurance that the nightmare had ended. Braden gasped. He felt his heart thudding from the strain of the ordeal. Felt the leather straps holding him to the bed—tangible proof that the nightmare may be over, but it had been real.

The harsh glare of day taxed his eyes, the only admissible cause for the tears he couldn't wipe away. The doctor ordered his arms bound so he didn't convulse in his sleep and perhaps damage his spine. Or so he said.

Braden knew the real reason. They'd trussed him so he couldn't free himself to begin the work of rebuilding his strength until they deemed him healed enough. He'd heard them talking—confident that the morphine pulled him under long before he'd stopped fighting it—saying he'd never have use of his legs.

But they're wrong. His fists clenched, because if there was one certainty in his future, it was that Braden Lyman would walk out of Hope Falls. *For every man who didn't.*

Even so, he'd never be whole again. He didn't harbor any illusions about that—which was why he'd set Cora free. Braden closed his eyes, refusing to picture her.

She needs better than a cripple who'll at best always have a limp and a chip on his shoulder, he reminded himself. *Cora deserves a man who didn't lose everything when his investment collapsed on top of him. Someday she'll appreciate the choice I made for us both. Now she can have any man she wants.*

Wanted:
3 men, ages 24–35.
Must be God-fearing, healthy, hardworking single men
with minimum of 3 years logging experience.
Object: Marriage and joint ownership of sawmill.
Reply to the Hope Falls, Colorado, postmaster by May 17.

Jake stared at the ad in disbelief for a good minute before giving in to the chuckle trapped in his chest. A second read, and the chuckle expanded to a full-blown guffaw. Obviously, someone with a well-developed sense of humor had far too much time on his hands. Satirizing the way miners and lonely settlers mailed away for brides provided a good laugh.

He flipped through the rest of the week-old paper he'd unearthed from beneath the seat, searching for an addendum to reveal the real reasons behind the ad. The first time, Jake assumed he'd missed the explanation. By the second time he scoured the rag, he'd drawn an altogether different conclusion.

He threw back his head and howled long and hard at the realization the paper somehow left it out entirely. *Without the addendum, there'll be fools who buy into the idea and respond.* The image of the mysterious debutante deluged with marriage proposals made Jake wish he had time enough to track down the printer and discover the author's identity. *Then again, the thing's old enough they most likely printed a retraction in later issues. It'd be interesting to find out....*

The shrill blast of the train's whistle as they pulled into Durango reminded him of his true purpose. *I'll have time for entertainment after I find Twyler.* He set the tattered paper aside and headed for the door long before the train screeched to a halt. He ignored the scroll-worked metal stairs. Why wait when a jump would do just as well?

Jake started walking the moment his boots hit the dirt and

didn't stop until he hit the saloon. The area swarmed with the frantic activity of a booming town—all hurry and hustle with no way to sort things out.

The perfect place for a man like Twyler to lose himself when he got word I'd been tailing him. A grudging measure of—not respect, he'd never respect anything about the man who'd killed his brother and stolen his good name—acknowledgment set Jake's jaw. *The more difficult the prey, the sweeter the victory when I bring him in. Better yet, it reaffirms that Edward wouldn't be taken in by anyone easily. It took a master.*

Jake strode into the saloon, not looking right or left, simply making his way to the bar and plunking his knapsack down. To the casual eye, he'd seem unconcerned and oblivious to his surroundings. Few would suspect he'd taken in the entire place as he opened the doors. He knew which tables were filled, where the piano stood, and which end of the bar he could find the barkeep's shotgun under if he needed it. This last he'd learned from the way the man's gaze often strayed there.

No one would guess—and that's just the way Jake liked it.

FIVE

"I don't like it," Evie announced. "I don't like it one bit."

"We know, dear." Cora patted her hand. "You might have mentioned it a few times this morning already."

"You saw the way they handled it!" She knew she should stop worrying. *Or, at the very least, stop making the others listen to it!* But Evie couldn't help herself. Her fists clenched into balls so tight her knuckles ached. "It was all I could do to keep from marching over there and—" She caught the looks on her friends' faces and amended, "All right, all you three could do to keep me from marching over there." A smile tugged at her, and she gave in. "Thank you, all, for that."

"You're welcome." Naomi answered for the group. "When they dropped your stove, my heart fell right along with it."

"They make it hard work to damage cast iron." Now Evie hastened to reassure them. Her worrying was one thing; her friends' fretting was quite another. *I won't think about the crack in the enamel facing. There's nothing to be done now.*

"Do you know, Evie"—Lacey eyed her as though studying something new—"this is the best you've looked through the entire trip. You've got fire in your eyes and even the color back in your cheeks. Fury becomes you!"

The moment Lacey mentioned it, Evie's color fled. She knew because the clammy sensation that had plagued her throughout their journey replaced the heat of her indignation. For a brief while, the incident with the stove distracted her from the motion of the train. . .and its unfortunate effect on her stomach.

"I do wish you hadn't mentioned it, Lacey." Cora's frown made it clear she'd noticed her sister's improved health and most likely deduced the reason for the change. "She might have not thought about the movement for a bit longer."

"Oh dear. The stove distracted you, and I retracted you. Retracted. . . No, that's not the word. Got you back on track?" Lacey's words tripped over one another and her eyes went big, as they seemed to do whenever something upset her. "On track thinking about the train. . . Oh, I'm making it worse. I'll hush."

"The trouble isn't with you," Evie protested. Although, truth be told, the sudden nervous chatter made the churning worse. Extra anxiety, even someone else's, had that effect.

But the real blame for her internal somersaults lay with the motion of the train. She'd anticipated that it would move forward when she agreed to this venture, but Evie'd convinced herself that modern locomotives would otherwise prove steady and secure. Instead, the rocking from side to side, the tilting turns, and the ever-present assortment of creaks emanating from the train joints and cars themselves churned her as though she were butter. And that wasn't even mentioning uneven tracks, steep climbs uphill, and occasional slants downward.

Hope Falls must be a dream come true, she'd decided early into the trip, *because we live through a nightmare to reach it!*

"We're slowing down." Naomi's announcement put everything else out of their minds in an instant.

Lacey's nervousness disappeared, anticipation making her glow with delight as she peered through the grimy train car window. "Welcome to Hope Falls, ladies!"

The shrill blast of the train whistle punctuated her exclamation as though the conductor waited for Lacey's remark. The train slowed, the slightly choppy tugging of the engine replaced by the stubborn resistance of brakes against metal rails.

Evie's stomach jumped toward her throat at the shift. She tightened her lips as her belly threatened to lose the dry bread she'd forced herself to nibble on for breakfast. When they lurched to a stop—more accurately a long, lurching slide—it took several swallows before she trusted herself to so much as draw a breath.

That she'd bent over as far as her corset would allow escaped her attention until she felt hands smoothing her hair back and more hands rubbing her back as everyone sought to comfort her.

The corset, of course, dug into her hips in a pressing demand that she improve her posture. Immediately. She settled for straightening up as quickly as her testy stomach would allow. In a word, slowly.

How is it that Cora falls off the chair, to the floor, prostrate in a dead faint, and manages to rise easily and with some semblance of grace? Even after days of the "Evie Travels West Diminishing Diet," I so much as lean forward and begin gasping like a landed fish!

She shook her head, rejecting both her thoughts and various offers of help. One deep breath—or at least as deep as her corset and stubborn stomach would allow—and Evie edged into the aisle. Blessedly, the floor didn't move beneath her feet as it had so often over the past days. That made it much easier to smile as she gathered her things and prepared to exit the train car.

She'd made other decisions during the journey—one of them being that, no matter what they found in Hope Falls, she'd smile and find something to be thankful for. After all, Evie believed in living out the fruit of the Spirit. . .and this venture had "lesson in perseverance" written all over it.

For now, though, she needn't look far to find the blessing in the day. *Blessings. . . Surely the fact I haven't disgraced myself by losing any of my meals counts as a minor miracle!*

"Ladies, before we disembark. . ." She paused for a moment at the stunned expressions on their faces. Then she realized everyone must expect her to be overeager to leave the train behind. Evie's smile grew as she continued, "I think it'd be a wonderful idea to pray—thanks for thus far and seeking guidance for what lies before us."

She felt Cora grasp one of her hands and reached out the other to Naomi, who didn't hesitate. They all bowed their heads as Lacey made their circle complete.

"Thank You, Lord, for bringing us here safe and sound." She gave Cora's hand a squeeze, the signal they'd chosen long ago and never abandoned.

"Now we ask for the strength to see this through," her little sister added, joining their prayers together. A brief pause—Evie almost completed the prayer, assuming Lacey hadn't responded to the hand squeeze because it was unfamiliar or she didn't want to—and then Naomi spoke.

"And the wisdom to make the most of the choices You put before us. In Your name. . ." They all joined in saying, "Amen."

"I—I'm sorry. I've never prayed aloud before, and I didn't know you'd want me to." Lacey turned to Cora, still holding her hand, squeezing without noticing. "That's what the squeezing meant, wasn't it? That it was my turn to join in? Such a lovely idea, for all of us to pray together, and I ruined it." Her eyes had gone big again, bright with an unmistakable sheen.

"You didn't ruin the prayer!" Evie took Lacey's hand away from Cora's. "We should have explained, but even if we had, prayer is always a choice. It's never something you do because you're expected to. It's between you and the Lord—and those you pray with or for, depending on the situation. Don't worry."

"But Naomi caught on!" A forlorn sniff followed this.

"We're all here, together. The prayer was about and for all of us, with all of us hoping and loving and thanking. Next time—say, when we begin sifting through the responses to our ad—you can start the circle," Evie suggested. "We'll make it a regular practice. All of us are in this together, after all."

"Oh." A tremulous smile chased away the doubt. "I'd love that. Just think. . .we most likely already have a slew of responses filling the postmaster general's office, just waiting for us!" With the anticipation lighting her face, Lacey led the way out of the train car, into mountain air Evie could almost taste with each breath, now that the doors had opened.

Strange how she'd never noticed how the air hung heavy over Charleston—thick and pungent. Here, the air whispered through the tops of the trees, light and fresh and almost crisp. *If air were something I could bake, Charleston would be dense brown bread, and Hope Falls would be delicate wafers.*

This first impression lasted only so long as it took for the others to disembark. Evie was last to step off the train. Last to set foot in Hope Falls. Last to face the truth of what her new home— what her new life—would be. She looked around.

Closed her eyes. Tight.

Opened them just the tiniest sliver until she realized the only thing she could see were her own eyelashes then flat-out gawked at what lay before them.

It was a mistake to sit in the aisle seat. The others didn't seem as floored as she—and Evie realized why. Watching the scenery pass by only made her more aware of the motion, so she never looked. Even when they stopped or got out at a town, she'd not paid much attention to the surroundings. Hiding her misery seemed far more important.

But the others had. They'd been watching as the train carried them farther and farther into the mountains. Miles away from civilization they'd traveled, deep into the untamed wilderness until they came to that awful, lurching stop in the middle of this. . . breathtaking place Evie was supposed to believe they owned.

As though we could be so presumptuous as to assert ownership over anything so magnificent and powerful as this land. The very idea would be laughable, if it didn't call to her.

Trees peppered mountains mixed with a sky so blue Evie could hardly believe it was the same one she'd lived under her entire life. Clouds the consistency of lovingly whipped cream floated above treetops before disappearing into the distance. The sound of a river rushed nearby, promising refreshment and the ability to make everything they'd need in the kitchen. Well, water along with what she'd brought, at least.

That made her look less to the horizon and more to her immediate surroundings. Which were...somewhat less promising. The mountainside abutting the area beside the town bore silent testament to the collapsed mine in its sparse trees and the way it appeared almost...crumpled. Dust and neglect coated the town. Buildings stood unused. No one broke the tomblike stillness with movement or sound. All in all, it looked exactly like what it was: abandoned.

Until now. No matter what had come before, they were here now. *And we're going to change things.* Evie lifted her chin. *No matter what anyone thinks.*

"I think you're looking in the wrong place, mister." The barkeep swirled a stained rag in a grubby mug. "Looking for any one man in a place like Durango is like trying to find a particular tick on the hide of a mangy stray. Too many of the same kind to try and tell 'em apart. You won't have anything to show for it." He gave a significant pause. "Neither would I."

"I appreciate you taking the time to share your observations." Jake kept his expression impassive, reached into his pocket, and pulled out more than his drink was worth. He slid it across the bar, the smooth glide of gold the most eloquent speech he could give in a mining town. *Could have guessed that, but no use throwing money away.*

"Glad to hear it." The money vanished in an instant, along

with the man's dismissive manner. "Not everyone recognizes the. . .
value. . .of what I can tell them. Never know what you might see
or hear in a place like this, if you know what I mean."

Jake gave a nod in answer, patting his pocket with wordless
promise. "Brown hair and eyes, probably better dressed than most
in these parts." He kept his voice low. "Goes by the name of—"

The barkeep plunked down the mug he'd been wiping with
such force, a crack splintered its way up the side. A warning.
"Funny thing about those observations, stranger. They're best
received at night, when men are tired and relaxing. Otherwise it
might make some folks uncomfortable, you see, to take a good
hard look around and realize others can do the same thing."

"I understand." *I understand the trail could go cold by the time
you work up enough nerve to spill your guts.* "But I'm short on time.
Just point me in the direction—"

"Come back tonight, when you can enjoy yourself." His voice
sounded too hearty, too loud.

The barkeep had outmaneuvered Jake. If he stayed, it'd look
suspicious. More importantly, he'd never get any information
from the man who seemed able to provide it. Left with no other
option, Jake tipped his hat and sauntered out into the street. If
anyone read frustration in the tense line of his jaw or shoulders,
he'd ascribe it to a poor haul in the mines.

Half a day would be unacceptable if Jake had anything to say
about it. Losing even an hour chafed. But Dad's business lessons
held true, and this afternoon Jake would employ his least favorite:
tactical retreat. His old man called it diplomacy, but Jake always
thought of it in terms of battle. Let his father hide behind suits
and smiles, handshakes and shams over coffee or lunches. Better
to be honest about things from the start to his way of thinking.
Business, full of strategies, negotiations, and victories, made for a
battlefield of brains instead of brawn.

Defeat wasn't an option. "Failure," as Dad called it, would not
be acknowledged. He didn't fail, didn't invest in failing ventures,

and most important, he didn't raise "failures" in his sons. To the world, Montgomery Granger upheld that. The three of them ran an extremely successful lumber business, held their heads high in society, and you'd best believe any Granger got whatever he put his mind to. Nothing less would ever be acknowledged, and nothing more need be said.

That is, until Edward went traveling after a supply contract for a new shipping company, and word of his death came to them a solid month after the fact. Dad had something to say to that. "No son of mine got himself killed over a crooked poker game." With that, he turned his back on his weeping wife, leaving Jake to comfort his mother.

His mother collected herself enough for a few choice words of her own. "It's a lie. We don't repeat lies." Jake held his tongue about his mother's penchant for gossip as she thrust the letter at him. "Burn it—make it disappear. This was not our Edward."

Jake took the paper but hadn't destroyed it. At the time, he'd foolishly believed his parents to be in denial over Edward's death, outraged over the implications in the letter. In time, they'd acknowledge the death of their golden boy.

During that time, Jake would investigate the scurrilous accusations against his brother. No one who knew Edward would believe for an instant he would cheat at cards, much less move to pull his gun on the man he swindled.

Problem was time passed. His inquiries turned up no new information—save that the man who'd fired a shot point-blank into his brother's chest hadn't even been arrested—and his parents showed no signs of accepting the fact that Edward would never walk through the front door. Grief could do strange things, and, granted, his parents long ago mastered the fine art of fooling even themselves. But after a month, it became eerie.

As gently as possible, he pressed his mother for when she'd begin making arrangements for Edward's memorial—questions she dismissed as "unnecessary" and "macabre." Broaching the subject with his father resulted in stern censure: "You know better."

Another month of this sort of thing, and Jake decided even his parents couldn't believe Edward hadn't passed on. With the lag in time before they were informed, an entire business quarter had gone by without so much as a telegram from him. More telling, the company he'd gone to negotiate with contacted Granger Mills to implement production as based on their agreement. They had, apparently, paid a full half of the contracted fees to Mr. Edward Granger. Cash.

The day of his brother's death, Jake noticed. He also noticed there'd been no mention of any money on his brother's person at the time of his death, nor had any deposits been made to company accounts. The sizable sum vanished into thin air.

Dad noticed the same—he noticed anything to do with money.

Jake made the only natural assumption. Dad was making investigations of his own into Edward's death, preparing to seek justice for the son who'd never let him down. Meanwhile, mourning would wait. There were too many unanswered questions. Too much to smear Edward's good name when he deserved better.

Jake might have been wrong about his parents' motivations, but that fact remained. If word got out now, people would think Edward to be a cheat, a swindler, and a violent drunk.

Not my *older brother.* Jake clenched his teeth. *Edward truly lived by the convictions our parents pretended. If I'm forced to practice one of his virtues in order to clear his name, I'll be patient. For now.*

 SIX

I t's now or never." *And never doesn't cut it on my menu.* Evie smiled at the thought as she gathered her traveling bag, where she'd tucked her courage alongside the family Bible.

Train workers scuttled about, busy loading water into the steam reservoir or—and this managed to be the far more ambitious undertaking—unloading everything the women had brought with them. Although Evie and Lacey had started establishing their businesses early on, efforts had been abandoned and then redoubled. Mr. Draxley, the mine representative who'd stayed on in Hope Falls and negotiated the sale of the remaining property, helped them send supplies ahead the moment they'd hatched the new plan.

All the same, they were four women with two modest, if solid, businesses and one grand, risky venture to prepare for. That didn't even take into account their plans for marrying and setting up their individual households.

"Packing light" wasn't possible. "Packing light enough not to stall the train engine" seemed a noble goal, to Evie's way of thinking. One they'd accomplished, no less, despite moments of grave misgiving when the locomotive strained up steep inclines.

Only once had their "bare necessities" caused issue—when something with the freight car holding everything snapped and caused it to wobble precariously on the tracks.

Despite dirty looks from some of the men who'd been enlisted at the last stop to transfer the "freight," it seemed this type of thing happened often enough. That realization hadn't settled Evie's nerves—or stomach—much.

Evie kept a close eye on the men as they unloaded her stove this time. True, most of the men were different, but that didn't matter. In fact, the half dozen or so who'd appeared from various places in town struck her as polite and respectful, judging by the way they tipped their hats. What mattered was. . .

"I thought most of the men were. . .gone?" She addressed this to Lacey, whose business contacts made her the expert. Evie was careful not to say "dead." How tactless it would sound to mention the town was supposed to be as abandoned as it looked when they'd first pulled in.

"They were—they are." Perplexed but not concerned, Lacey shrugged. "It looks as though Mr. Draxley started hiring loggers already. I mentioned to him that we'll need several for the initial stages, though I hadn't expected them so soon." As she spoke, more men made appearances—each one offering a friendly wave and a smile along with a dip of his hat.

"I've never seen such bold workers." Naomi gasped as one fellow threw a saucy wink her way. "Mr. Draxley will need—" She hushed as a pale fellow with a twitchy blond mustache bobbed to a stop in front of them and adjusted his spectacles.

"Oh dear, I'm late," a reedy voice fretted. "I'm also afraid I do far better with lists, but I will strive to remember whatever it is you mention, miss." His mustache gave another twitch just before he sank into an overblown bow more befitting a foreign dignitary. "Mr. Draxley, at your service, at all your services. I'm rather afraid I cannot deduce which name belongs to which lady, at this point, but surely that can be forgiven until proper introductions are dispensed?"

He reminds me of someone. Evie pondered who it could be while Lacey made formal introductions. *I can't put my finger on who though.* It tickled at the very edge of her mind but shifted away when she got close.

"Mr. Draxley, would you mind overseeing the unloading of our things? You'll know what to do—everything is labeled either 'mercantile,' 'café,' or 'house.' We've come a long way. . . ."

"That's the house, down there." Mr. Draxley made a vague gesture toward a two-story building closest to the crumpled mountain, obviously too polite to point. "You must long to rest and refresh yourselves. Forgive me for not seeing it sooner."

"I'd like to see my fiancé," Cora broke in, her patience worn to a frayed edge after months of believing Braden to be dead then days of travel. "Immediately."

"You're overset by his experience, but I don't believe you understand the particulars of his. . .condition." The mustache twitched so rapidly Evie began to wonder when it might fall off. "Mr. Lyman wouldn't want to be seen this way. 'Tis unseemly."

"She asked where she could find him." Evie kept her tone even but firm. "I should think it apparent we aren't women to cavil at breaking a few social niceties." She fought to keep a stern expression at the massive understatement.

"I intend to see my brother, so we'll go together." Lacey's declaration brooked no argument. "If you'll just point us to the doctor's office, Mr. Draxley, we'd much appreciate it."

Lips compressed into a thin line, he bobbed his head to indicate a small single-story structure close by.

"Perhaps it's best for the two of you to go the first time," Naomi suggested, as discreet and thoughtful as always. "It's to be expected Braden will tire easily, and he'll be overwhelmed to see you both. Best to keep it to family."

At the word "family," Mr. Draxley's shoulders unhunched, showing him to be less compact than he seemed. "Until Miss Higgins here mentioned it, I didn't consider the matter thoroughly, but Miss Thompson—the other Miss Thompson, that is—does boast some sort of family tie with the Lymans."

"Lacey certainly accepts her as a sister. Cora and Braden would be wed already if not for recent tragedy. A slight delay changes little." Naomi soothed the man's ruffled feathers. Something Evie foresaw would need doing quite often in the coming weeks.

"Of course! I should have seen it right away—Misses Lyman and Thompson would naturally want to see Mr. Lyman directly, after believing him dead and crossing the country to be by his side. Quite romantic of her to show such bravery."

"Thank you, Mr. Draxley." Evie seized the break in his monologue to end it. "It seems they've unloaded everything." The real meaning behind the reminder went unspoken. *Talking doesn't move crates, barrels, boxes, chests, sacks, nor cases to their proper homes. Overseeing and instructing your men does.*

"Excuse me for a moment while I organize things." With another odd little bow—this one not so deep as the first—Draxley hopped to work. The moment he reached the dozen or so men, he straightened his shoulders, raised his voice, and apparently began issuing orders en masse.

The other men slid glances at each other. Eyebrows raised. Gazes shifted to where Evie and Naomi stood watching the tableau unfold. Some men shrugged and looked about to set to it. Others responded to Draxley in low tones, even going so far as to nod in their direction. It looked, Evie decided, like a mutiny about to break loose.

"What is it about men and luggage?" She huffed the question to Naomi, recalling her ire over the stove that morning. "These are big, strong men who'll gladly swing sharp blades at massive trees threatening to crush the life from them, but a few boxes and bags inspire revolt?" *And they claim men are more logical.*

"Not to suggest anything but complete agreement with your sentiment," Naomi murmured, eyeing the colossal heap of baggage they'd hauled along, "but in all fairness, it's more than a few."

"Many hands, Naomi." Evie grinned. "Division works wonders. But where mathematics fails to persuade, a woman has her ways." With that smile still in place, she swept toward the men, adding the last part under her breath so only Naomi could hear her. "After this evening, Draxley will have to fire the whole lot."

"Agreed. They lack a proper work ethic." Naomi beamed and raised her voice as they reached everyone. "Good afternoon."

The transformation almost stunned Evie as, to a man, they straightened up. Literally. Gone were the slouches, sullen glances, and idle hands shoved in pockets. In an instant, grins appeared, shoulders went back, and chests puffed out for all the world as though imitating prize peacocks. Expectation lit their gazes, which remained absolutely riveted on herself and Naomi.

"Good afternoon, ladies." A rumble of voices responded with a haphazard chorus to make even the strictest schoolmarm proud.

Evie blinked. She looked at Naomi, who looked back, as disconcerted as she. They looked again at the men, just to check and see if they were all staring in the same transfixed, expectant fashion. *Yep.* She blinked again—and suspected Naomi did the same, though she couldn't tell. *Maybe I'll ask later.*

Dedicated workers were hard to come by—*devoted* workers almost indescribably rare. Here, before her, stood a dozen men looking at them with the sort of regard she'd only seen reserved for. . .supper. *Or possibly dessert, if a man harbors a sweet tooth.* Her plans to bribe them with the information that some of these boxes held what *could* be a spectacular dinner evaporated in the face of this strange turnaround. Things grew more awkward every moment they stood without speaking. *What on earth is going on here?*

"We sure is glad to see ya," one of the horde spoke up.

"No' expectin' the lassies yet, aye?" another added.

"Leastways, not till the seventeenth," one man said finishing the thought so that the picture began to grow clear.

"But, as someone first mentioned, we're mighty glad you ladies came early!" This reiteration set off a round of nods.

"You're—you're not loggers?" The squeak came from Naomi, but Evie almost would have believed it sprang from her thoughts.

Why wouldn't my thoughts sound squeaky? They'd almost have to right now, since my brain's all but screeched to a halt, and any thought worth its salt would have to be squeezed out. . . .

"Most of us are loggers, some buckers, and Bob and Dodger back there"—the huge man speaking jerked a thumb over his shoulder—"are even high climbers." Hearing his name, one waved as the spokesman completed his recitation. "But we're timber beasts, one and all—just like you asked for in that ad of yours."

Somewhere amid those nonsensical terms lay one simple truth Evie grasped. She hadn't wrestled it into submission yet— most likely never would—but the fact remained fairly obvious.

"Mr. Draxley didn't hire any of you?" She verified, "Every-one came in response to the advertisement we placed, asking prospective grooms to reply *in care of the postmaster general?*" Surely she could be forgiven for placing emphasis on that last part. She'd refrained from adding, "and not in person!"

"He don't seem to care too much, but that were a good way ta give the locale." A bulge in the man's cheek tattled of a wad of chewing tobacco. "We came early to up our chances."

"I believe that's because he—and I'll have to admit we, as well—were expecting written responses to that ad." Naomi didn't shy away from being more blunt. God bless her. "We never imagined you might travel all the way here before we responded."

"Best way to pick a man is to look him over in person," one of the better-looking candidates insisted. "Only natural."

"Well, now that you're all here"—Evie decided to make the best of things—"would you be interested in saving us the trouble of hiring other loggers to do the preliminary work? You'll have room and board and all the food you can eat."

"Evie!" Naomi caught on in a flash. "You're not promising *your* cooking? That's outrageous. You'll work yourself to the bone with those creations of yours."

"They'll work hard, too." Evie beamed at the men then allowed her smile to fade. "Or if not, we'll hire men who will. Besides, I'm going to marry one of the loggers. They should all sample my cooking. It's a fair reward, I think."

"More than fair." The twinkle in her friend's eyes belied her grumble. "Though maybe we should hire others just to have more prospects? I hadn't even considered that, but—"

"Now, now!" Mutters and murmurs among the men exploded into outright protest. "A deal's a deal, missy!"

"You don't lay an offer on the table then yank it away before a man decides whether or not to accept it."

Another frowned at them. "That's not honorable business practice."

Evie made note of him. She liked the sound of his values.

"Especially not if it involves the *dinner* table!" Outrage colored that exclamation, and it evoked the biggest round of agreement yet. "You never mess with a man's meals."

As though I don't already know that. She gave in and grinned. *Looks as though my plan to bribe them with supper wasn't too far off the mark. Meals work in any situation.*

"Should I take that to mean you're accepting the offer?" She widened her eyes as though unsure and waited for the nods.

"We aren't fools, are we, boys?" The spokesman started off the round of verbal agreements, and in no time, they had a deal.

"I'd be happy to make a fine supper for you this very evening, but I'm afraid your first meal will have to wait until we're unpacked, and my stove"—she ran a loving hand along the top of the largest crate—"is in place in the café."

The one who'd mentioned the dinner table volunteered on the spot. "We're more than happy to see to it, ma'am."

"You seemed. . .hesitant. . .when Mr. Draxley made the request." Now was the time for Evie to establish him as their

mouthpiece. He may not be much, but with Braden ill, he'd have
to do.

"We don't work for him," the burliest one explained. "But
we're more than happy to take care of anything for you ladies."

"Anytime." The men hurried to add their assurances.

"Just ask and it's done." They played right into her hands.

"Mr. Draxley might ask on our behalf sometimes." Naomi
spoke the words, sliding a glance at the anxious man and then
looking back to the others with an almost helpless shrug. "If
we can."

"You can do anything you want, ma'am."

"At the moment, we need to discuss our bargain with the
other ladies so we can arrange proper introductions with all of
us present." Evie didn't want to overlook good manners, but
they needed to talk to Lacey. Now. "And then I'm going to fix
something special for our first supper together!"

It was, Jake decided, a meal he'd never forget.

He speared what the cook tried to pass off as a green bean
with the tines of his fork just to watch the limp, grayish thing
slide back to the plate with a faint sucking sound. A glob of cold
potatoes congealed beside them—slightly more appetizing than
the yellowed meat loaf taking pride of place.

He thought it was supposed to be meat loaf. At least they
called it meat loaf. Never mind the fact he'd never seen yellow
meat loaf in all his born days—never hatched any desire to do so,
either. More off-putting yet, the offensive thing boasted a sort of
springy texture when he pressed the fork into it.

Fighting food. By that, Jake meant it was the kind of meal a
man fought to swallow, and the kind of meal that returned the
favor by fighting for its freedom once he'd downed it, then stuck
around to grumble about its defeat for days afterward. He pushed
the plate away in favor of the biscuits.

Bounty of biscuits. The memory of fantastic food prepared by a plucky woman made his mouth water. Jake slathered butter atop the biscuit, hoping for something even vaguely reminiscent of that previous perfection. He bit into it, chewed, swallowed, and reached for his mug.

He wasn't one to judge cooking. Jake couldn't make biscuits himself, so he could understand if they came out a bit burned or underdone or whatnot. *But how in thunder did anyone manage to make one hard as a rock on the outside, lumpy on the inside, and practically the batter itself in the middle?*

Strike one: No edible food. Strike two: No pretty cook— though, in Jake's opinion, that counted as two strikes. If Miss Thompson served this mess to him, he'd have downed it just for the sake of the company. Strike three: The place overcharged.

His hat wasn't budging.

The only thing this place had going for it was the quiet— which first tipped him off the food wouldn't be worth ordering extra. Memories of meaty sandwiches wrapped in brown paper, with sugar cookies tucked atop like sweet greetings, made his stomach growl. He cast another assessing glance at the table before him and ignored his belly for its own good.

Strong coffee and a place to read the papers he'd picked up earlier kept him in his chair—that, and the time he needed to kill before going to get answers from the squirrelly bartender. The man's yellow belly probably matched Jake's meat loaf.

Cracking his first smile since he'd walked into the place, he unfolded the paper and started reading. Then stopped. Jake flipped back to the front page of *Durango Doings,* a two-bit town newsletter he suddenly suspected to be at least a week old.

Today's date stared back at him in smudged black on grayish paper of obvious poor quality. He turned the page to reread the advertisement that caught his eye, certain it couldn't be the same one he'd chortled over from a week-old paper on the train.

" 'Wanted: three men, ages twenty-four to thirty-five. . .' "

He read the first line aloud before shaking his head. Same ad all right. Durango might be out of the way of civilization, for the most part, but with telegraphs transmitting words and the train carrying everything else, nothing could excuse being an entire week behind—even when it came to a joke.

Jake snorted, tossed the rag aside, and reached for the more reliable publication.

He scanned through it, waiting for something to catch his interest. When it did, he just about choked on the grit from his coffee. There, in a prestigious paper, the same cheeky ad stared up at him. No need to check the date this time—he already had.

When an ad ran for several days, in numerous publications, across several state and territorial lines, it wasn't a joke missing its retraction then reprinted in a Podunk town. No.

Jake gaped at the words marching before him, considering them seriously for the first time. *"Object: Marriage. . ."*

"Unbelievable." He didn't realize he'd muttered it aloud until chair legs scraped over the floor.

A fellow diner—who seemed only too glad for a reason to abandon his food—looked over his shoulder and caught sight of what he was reading.

"You just now seeing that?" He poked the paper with a grimy finger. "It's been running in all the papers for a solid week now. At first everyone had a good laugh over it, but now seems like these gals mean business—and some men are planning on trying to take them up on the offer. Strange days, eh?"

"Strange, indeed." Jake set the paper down—atop his plate, so he wouldn't have to look at it. "Makes a man wonder."

"Wonder what the world's comin' to, or what kind of hatchet-faced Methuselah shrews would try to hire husbands?"

Jake chuckled at the way the fellow put it. "Both."

"Way I figure it, they're desperate old maids with tongues sharp enough to cut a man off at the knees. Must be, putting an ad like that in the papers, bold as brass and twice as cheap."

"It's unfair to judge women you've never met." *I suspect he's more right than wrong, but that doesn't make it right to say so.* "There's no way of knowing what they're like."

"Oh, there's a way." The fellow leaned forward far enough to be balancing on two chair legs. "I aim to go and meet 'em face-to-face and see what they have to say."

SEVEN

"Get out!" Braden roared the order when his sister and fiancée ignored him the first time. *No, not my fiancée.* His lungs closed, cutting off his breath the way they seemed to do whenever he overexerted himself. *They have to leave. Now.*

"Braden, we've come all this way to see you." Cora—beautiful, incredible, muleheaded Cora—stepped close enough to place her hand over the sheet covering his. Sweet torture.

Thank God for the sheet pulled up to his chin. They couldn't see the straps holding him helpless as a newborn or a lackwit. And, if he had his way, they never would. He drew deep breaths, fighting for air so he could fight for his dignity.

"We've so much to tell you!" His sister flitted around the room, touching everything, not holding still for an instant. "Why, you'll never guess half of it, absolutely never believe—"

"That you're *still here?*" He needed them gone before they realized the extent of his shame. Before he saw pity and sorrow replace the joy and love in Cora's eyes.

"No, not that." Lacey pshawed. "Stop worrying about that. We're real enough. Not some dream because of what they give you for the pain. Cora and I won't disappear. We promise!"

70

"I won't leave you. Ever." Cora reached over to smooth his hair from his forehead in a gesture meant to be maternal.

She didn't realize the effect her very nearness had—that the movement brought her close enough for him to catch the scent of lilacs and summer so uniquely Cora. She couldn't know that the merest brush of her soft hand against his forehead made him shiver, or that the shiver sent streaks of pain shooting from his wasted legs. *She'll never know. I won't let her.*

"Don't touch me. Just leave." He gritted the words from behind clenched teeth, behind the pain he wouldn't show them. "I don't want you here. Go back home and don't come back."

Cora recoiled as though he'd shot her.

The moment her hand stopped smoothing his hair, his pain doubled. *Coincidence.*

Lacey paid him no heed. "Don't be such a bear, Braden. You've put your fiancée through a lot these past few months."

"She's not my fiancée." He refused to look at her—saying the words was hard enough without seeing what he was giving up. *Yet another reason she has to leave. If she's near, I won't be able to let her go.* Her gasp pierced through him, but he held firm.

"We thought you were dead!" Tears wavered in Cora's voice. "The news devastated me, Braden. When I learned you'd survived, that was all that mattered. Don't worry about whatever else you said. You've been through a harrowing experience. In time—"

"I won't change my mind." He wouldn't turn his head to face her, either, for fear she'd see the truth. It would be all too easy for him to change his mind, to claim her as his own and ignore the fact that she deserved a whole man. *A real man.*

"Neither will I."

"Now isn't the time to be discussing the particulars of your engagement, really," Lacey broke in, hands fluttering as though warding away worries. "We need to discuss our plans."

"The plan. . ." Braden's clenched fists began to ache as he

reiterated, "The plan is for you to *get out of here!*" He raised his voice to a shout on the last four words. *"Now!"*

"No need to yell, Mr. Lyman." Evelyn Thompson swept into the room, Naomi Higgins close behind her. "Our hearing works quite well, thank you. Besides"—she bustled over to lay a bracing hand on Cora's shoulder as she spoke—"we just arrived."

Good. Her sister will take care of her. Braden's hands relaxed a little. *Evie's the practical one. She'll listen.* He'd made a mistake in watching Evie cross the room to Cora, because it let his eyes fall on his fiancée. *No. Not my fiancée.*

Her eyes—her glorious, mismatched eyes that saw straight through him—shone with tears. Her lips, usually curved into the sort of smile a man felt all the way through, pressed together tight, as though damming up a torrent of words. But her hands nearly broke him. He'd ordered her not to touch him, so she'd stopped. Now he saw her hands rested on the edge of his bed, long fingers splayed atop his sheets, stretching as close to him as possible without making contact.

Braden groaned and slammed his eyes shut. *She has to go, Lord. There's a limit to my strength. To any man's strength.*

"It's good to see you, Braden." Naomi's voice pulled him.

"You've all seen him now." Pompous as always, the doctor pushed his way into the crowded room. "That's enough visiting." Choice phrases like "tiring," "overtaxed," and "setback" promised dire consequences if Braden wasn't left to rest and heal in peace.

Strange how the same ominous warnings he'd disregarded, barking orders at the mutinous little man to unstrap his arms, now made perfect sense. Better yet, they shooed the women from the room.

When they left—with every intent to return, despite Braden's orders—the doctor took one look at him and advanced with the morphine. Braden didn't protest. For now, the memory of the mines couldn't be half so wracking as thoughts of Cora crying because she wouldn't listen...

"I couldn't have heard that right." Lacey sank onto a sofa and scarcely noticed the sudden poof of dust. A clear sign of duress, that the fact their current home needed thorough cleaning ranked so abysmally low on her list of priorities.

Somehow she'd thought everything would fall into place once they arrived in Hope Falls. So why was it that, all of a sudden, everything seemed even more complicated? The town seemed far emptier and more dismal than she'd imagined, which meant setting up the café and mercantile and even the mill would be a greater challenge than expected. Mr. Draxley, whom she'd counted as a resource, clearly wouldn't provide much help.

Braden looked worse off than she'd hoped. Worse yet, he'd not been happy to see her. *Ingrate.* She scowled at the thought of all they'd gone through for such an ungracious reception. *My brother needs more than medical attention—he needs to relearn several lessons in manners!*

Because, as disappointing as everything else may be—and there was no "may" about it in Lacey's book—the absolute worst thing about their first day in Hope Falls was Braden's callous treatment of Cora. If Lacey's heart broke at his harsh words and clear wish to never see his fiancée again, she could only imagine how her best friend felt.

Though, judging by the stiff way Cora moved, the absolute lack of expression on her face, and the way she kept blinking, it didn't take too much imagination. Shock, sorrow, and a desperate will not to dissolve into tears seemed about right.

If my brother weren't crippled, I'd tell Evie and let her wallop Braden until he remembered himself!

With all that swirling around in her head, it didn't leave much room for dust balls to loom large. Especially not with Evie telling her how all the men unloading their luggage were going to be trying to marry them. Which made no sense. None at all.

I need a nap. A good lie-down will help sort things out.

"You heard it properly," Naomi chimed in. "Be thankful you weren't there when we heard it from the men themselves."

"Draxley didn't hire them, then?" Cora bestirred herself—a good sign. "I must admit that part makes some sense. He doesn't seem the most effective sort of business manager, does he?"

"In all honesty, he puts me in mind of a rabbit."

"Naomi!" Evie's gasp at the other woman's statement made them all jump. She began to laugh. "Thank you! It's been bothering me the entire time—I couldn't decide exactly who it is that Mr. Draxley puts me in mind of, but that's it. It's as though the White Rabbit from Lewis Carroll's *Alice's Adventures in Wonderland* sprang to life as a man and hopped here!"

"My word." Lacey went into peals of laughter. "Now that you point it out, the resemblance is uncanny. The spectacles. . ."

"Something about the twitchy mustache." Cora chuckled along with them, beginning to rally from the encounter with Braden.

"Weren't his first words something about being late?" Naomi's observation set them off in a fresh round of titters.

There's only so much a woman can endure in a single day without a bracing bout of giggles. Lacey decided that the four of them had been overdue, but the timing couldn't have been better. When they caught their breath, they were far more ready to tackle the situation at hand. Well, situations, but one at a time would simply have to do until they'd settled in.

And cleaned. She beamed as she noticed how the dust had gained importance now that her vexation over Draxley eased. Dust could be done away with, which meant even more progress.

"So the men currently carrying things to the café and mercantile aren't workers. They're prospective grooms." Lacey brought the conversation back to the most pressing topic.

"Both," Evie corrected. "Once they'd clarified their intentions, Naomi and I struck a bargain. Our erstwhile suitors will also be doing the initial work clearing the mill site and so forth in exchange for room, board, and meals."

"And the chance to cut out the competition they might face if other loggers came in to do the job." Naomi sighed. "It seems our earlybirds already expect another influx of men."

No, no, no! This wasn't the plan! The men were supposed to write their responses, and then we'd choose. She grappled with this displeasing sensation of being thwarted for a few moments. *Think, Lacey. What do you do when things don't go your way?*

The answer to that was startling. *Why have I never realized before how rarely things don't turn out as I'd like?* Most likely because she'd never needed to think about it. So she'd think about it now until she came up with a solution. *Ah. . .there. I'll simply turn it around again to work for me.*

"What an excellent stroke of luck!" Her interpretation stunned them all. She understood. Lacey would have stunned herself with such a declaration mere moments ago. "Yes, the unexpected is unsettling, but look at all the benefits of having so many men already here! We won't have to wait to meet them, already have several options, and don't need to feel guilty over those we don't choose, as we didn't send for any of them!"

"Yes, but selecting our husbands was supposed to take several steps and a certain amount of time," Naomi protested. "And, while I'm not saying these aren't fine, upstanding, hardworking men, it's belatedly occurred to me we didn't mention anything about education, refinement, and the like."

"Refinement isn't a requirement to make a life out West," Evie pointed out. "As far as education goes, yes, I noticed their coarse speech, but they know what we do not about the business of lumber. That's what we need—and what we asked for."

Lacey wanted to cheer Evie's speech, but a small corner of her thoughts whispered doubts. *Coarse speech? Lack of refinement? Little or no education? Why didn't I consider that would be the case when we asked for working-class men!*

"Ingenious of you to elicit their help while they're courting.

That way, you don't have to rely on Mr. Draxley to hire workers." Cora raised a single brow. "Better still you bargained for room, board, and meals without any mention of wages!"

"Better yet, they have motivation to work hard to impress us." Evie'd been thinking about this in great detail, it seemed. "And when others arrive—if any other men arrive—they'll have to abide by the same bargain or be forced to leave, having lost face. The men won't stand for anyone not pulling his weight."

"It's obvious which of us is the businesswoman!" Naomi gestured toward Evie with obvious admiration. "I only thought of the basics when you started enlisting them as our workers!"

"There's nothing basic about any of this." Sorrow drew across Cora's face. "This place makes everything convoluted."

"We'll sort it all out." Lacey drew her into a hug. "Braden hurts and his pride put his nose out of joint when you saw him lying there. Give him time. . . And if that doesn't work, you have my permission to do whatever else you feel necessary." *He already deserves it for acting like a fool!*

"I might take you up on that," her best friend warned.

"We all might." From the grim note in Evie's tone, she'd already surmised what sort of reception Braden had given her sister. "But for now, I promised those men supper, and I'll need your help to get it done in time. Besides. . ." Her glance shifted toward the window as she added, "We promised the men proper introductions, so we can all get a better look at them."

"You know you want to get a gander at 'em yourself." The other occupant of the diner waggled his brows in what he clearly intended to be a persuasive manner. The effort failed.

"Doesn't make a hill of beans' worth of difference to me what the three ladies look like." Jake shook his head, suppressing a sudden swell of curiosity. If nothing else, witnessing this strange event would be entertaining—the sort of detour he would've easily made in happier times.

"Ya never know. Could surprise us all and be real lookers. Then you'd regret not tagging along to find out what's what."

"That's a turnaround from 'hatchet-faced Methuselah.'" Jake didn't bother to hide his amusement. "Why the change of heart?"

"Dunno." He scratched his head. "Can't stop thinking it might be a buncha widows with more land than they can handle, not bothering to look for love or money the second time around—just a strong arm and a steady smile. Then I'd kick myself for a fool for not finding out." The fellow suddenly seemed to realize he'd let his inner romantic out in public. "Though it's most likely they've got hairy lips and squinty eyes, o' course."

"Of course." His coffee mug hid his chuckle until Jake knew he wouldn't offend the other man. "But you misunderstood. I meant they can be bucktoothed or beautiful—it doesn't matter."

"In it for the money, then." The flat statement, devoid of any humor, tattled of the other man's disapproval. "Or getting the land out of trust or whatever sort of arrangement must tie things up. Reckon on there bein' plenty of those sorts."

"No. I'm not in it at all. I already told you, Mr.—"

"Klumpf." His companion shoved out a hand for a friendly shake. "Volker Klumpf. Glad to hear you say you aren't after riches. I hadn't pegged you for the mercenary sort."

Let's hope you never have cause to see just how mercenary I can be, Mr. Klumpf. An unlikely concern. True, he'd looked him over with a keen eye at first—same as he did most men. Klumpf seemed about the right height, right age, with brown eyes and shaggy brown hair to loosely match the all-too-vague description Jake worked with. But Klumpf's eager conversation, blithe revelation of his plans, and the gap-toothed smile giving him the air of a good-natured puppy pointed to a conscience so clean it would squeak if anything rubbed it wrong.

Just like when he'd thought Jake might be after the mystery women's money...

If Volker Klumpf's a scheming thief and cold-blooded murderer, I'll eat my hat. He shook the man's hand without reservation. *It might taste better than the meat loaf, anyway.*

"Jake Creed." He'd repeated the lie so often it didn't strike him as false anymore. Jacob Granger didn't exist anymore—traded his family and birthright for a chance to hunt a killer. Jake Creed, the hunter whose belief in justice drove him all the way to Colorado, took Granger's place the moment he left home.

"Glad ta meet ya, Creed. I like the sound of that. . .Creed. Most folks call me Clump. Ain't noble-sounding like yours, but it serves well enough." He shrugged. "Sure you aren't interested in catching the train in an hour and heading up to Hope Falls? We can sneak a peek at the women tonight and see what's what."

"Sounds like an adventure." Jake slapped Clump on the shoulder. "I won't join you, but I wish you all the best."

"Train leaves in an hour if you change your mind." Clump got to his feet, plunked some change on the table behind him, and—there was no other honest word for it—clumped toward the door. Black boots with some sort of heavy sole weighted the man's gait to a distinctive series of thuds. "And if you don't, I hope someday you'll find the woman of your dreams, Creed."

The sudden image of tawny eyes filled with laughter made Jake shake his head. *Not for me.* The comely cook with her mouthwatering dishes and saucy smile could take her pick of men. *I'd have a better chance with one of the hatchet-faced, buck-toothed wantwits who placed this advertisement!*

He eyed the ridiculous thing one last time. A sour smell from the meal buried beneath it made the cream Jake had swallowed in his coffee curdle in his stomach. *A sad day,* he mused, *when a man finds himself plenty of time to kill—and no murderer near at hand to make the work fulfilling.*

The doors to the diner swung open with the sort of shrill creak to make anyone within hearing distance wince. Since Jake now claimed the dubious honor of dining entirely alone, he ignored the sound and focused on the man edging his way into the room.

A slow, nervous shuffle, empty sack bumping against his shins every step, chin tucked low against his chest as he moved in a straight line toward the kitchen in the back, the man's posture screamed that he had something to hide—or something to tell.

Jake's feet hit the floor the instant he recognized the man. An instant before the barkeep's eyes widened and his pace picked up in a bid to reach the kitchen before Jake reached him.

Not something to tell, then. Too late. Jake blocked the broader man's path long before his quarry could hope to evade him. He set himself a wide stance and waited while the nervous barkeep eyed the rest of the room. Once. Twice, to make sure no one else could be watching. Or listening.

The other man relaxed enough to offer a smile as watered down as the whiskey Jake had watched him serve earlier. "I see you found the Down 'n' Out Diner. Hadn't thought to run into you here." Another swift glance around the abandoned place finished the thought—he hadn't expected to run into anyone here.

"I'd never passed through Durango before—didn't know the local spots." Which, of course, translated to: *didn't know to avoid the Down 'n' Out Diner.* "You come here for lunch?" Jake's raised eyebrow left little room for misinterpretation. Having sampled the fare, he knew no sane man would eat here.

"Meat loaf day." A grin broke out across the man's face. "Best sober-up in the world is to force a man to swallow Bert's meat loaf. I stock up on it every week, and let it be known."

"Less trouble on meat loaf day." Jake didn't ask. One glance at his newspaper-covered plate reminded him full well what lay beneath it. The threat might well make men less apt to break saloon rules. "You can have the piece under there."

"Not just meat loaf day." The man snagged the piece from beneath the paper and shoved it into the sack. "Strangest thing about Bert's meat loaf. Keeps same as the day he made it for as long as I've seen. Same sort of bouncy feel but turns white around the edges and darker yellow in the middle. Of course"—he leaned closer as though unwilling to offend a potentially eavesdropping Bert—"smells even worse the longer it sits."

"Glad to give you an extra helping." Jake spared a moment to hope it didn't end any young miner's life. "Now that we're out of sight of prying eyes, what say we talk business?"

"All right, but seems to me you already got—"

"Man goes by Twyler. Average height, brown hair, brown eyes. Would've come through here earlier this week." Jake patted his pocket meaningfully. "Any information you could give me would be well rewarded. Especially where he headed next."

"Wish I could tell you something you don't already know." The barkeep gave a gusty sigh and gestured toward the paper he'd nudged aside. "But you already saw the ad, so you know about as much as I do. Every stranger who's come through these parts and not stayed to mine has gone on to Hope Falls, you see."

"Have any stayed on who fit the description?" He shoved aside the idea Twyler would answer the ad. No self-respecting criminal would follow such a ludicrous course. "Well-spoken sort of man, more educated. Even if he went by another name?"

"Miners come through here all the time, but it's hard work. They're either experienced in mining or they quit in a minute. Someone well spoken and educated would stick out like a sore thumb, and I'd remember him." He gave a shrug. "Best tip I can give you is to go on and try Hope Falls, mister."

Frustration closed Jake's throat. *Twyler won't go to a logging camp to win a bride. It's a fool's mission, and no fool got the better of my brother and evaded me this long. I can't expect to find him there.* He cast a fulminating glare at the paper, the benighted ad mocking him as the know-nothing barkeep sidled around him and into the kitchen. No help there.

It's a dead end. I pack it up and go home in defeat, as good as admitting Edward's a cowardly cheat, or I head to Hope Falls. Maybe someone there will know something worth hearing.

80

"Seems to me it'd be a good place to lose yourself if someone was searching." The barkeep bustled back through, sack bulging and a sly smile stretching his face. "No one would think to follow a man on such a goose chase. Might be just the thing."

"That's—" Jake swallowed the word "harebrained." *So out of the norm it might work—just the sort of thing Twyler might do.* "An interesting notion. Thanks for those observations of yours." He tossed the man a token of his gratitude as he headed for the door, not bothering to acknowledge the man's thanks.

The barkeep—and the sour stench of 'meat loaf' more powerful than should be legal—followed him out the door and down the street a ways. Other people, spotting the sack and obviously knowing what it meant, gave them wide berth.

Morbidly fascinated in spite of himself, Jake had to know one last thing before he left Durango in the dust and boarded Clump's train: "Ever killed anyone with that meat loaf?"

EIGHT

I think I've died and gone to heaven."

The groan following the statement sounded anything but heavenly as Evie wrapped the intruder on the knuckles with her wooden spoon. Hard.

At least this one didn't yelp like number three, or howl like two and four. Compared to those, the groan sounded downright manly. Or, at least, the manliest of the four. The first troublemaker didn't count—Naomi actually gave the swindler a biscuit, setting off the entire problem of loggers popping into the kitchen like so many hopeful ground squirrels.

"No fair!" A distinct note of wheedling entered the fellow's voice while he backed away with one eye on Evie's spoon and one eye on the biscuits. "Kane got one."

"My mistake!" Naomi rushed forward, wringing her hands. "I didn't know the rules of the kitchen, you see, and he asked so nicely, and I didn't realize it would mean all of you would come filing through, wanting to eat before mealtime. I'm so sorry!"

"Don' you be frettin', lassie." The sixth sniffing hopeful poked his head around the door frame. This time Evie recognized the huge redhead. A man of his size couldn't help but make an impression. "Not a one of us have eaten anythin' halfway decent in at least a week, and it's been a good sight longer than that for most. Keeping a dozen strapping men away from a kitchen smelling so fine as this would take a minor miracle."

"Please, missus." Sensing which woman would be weakest to his plea, Number Five zeroed his smile in on Lacey. "I won't tell none of the other guys iff'n you can see your way to sparing another one of them biscuits. You can trust ole Dodger."

"Dodger, you need to learn to take a lady's first answer." The redheaded giant's rumble inspired a flash of alarm, swiftly replaced by determination once Dodger looked at the biscuits one more time and took a deep breath. "I'll leave with you."

"You leave, Bear. I'll keep the ladies company."

"We don't have room for company. We've work to do!" Evie'd gotten caught up watching the byplay for long enough. It was time to reclaim her kitchen. "No men are allowed in my kitchen unless by express invitation. Spread the word, please. Mr. Dodger, I'm a businesswoman, so I'll make you a deal. You're more than welcome to take a biscuit with you on your way out the door." She saw his face light up as he edged toward his prize. She also noticed that the one he called Bear stayed in the doorway, arms folded, shaking his head. *Smart man, that one.*

"Hear the lady out before you take the bargain, Dodge." His warning cemented her good impression of his intelligence.

"What?" Dodger froze, hand hovering over the biscuits, where he'd been trying to decide which looked largest. "She said I could have one, so I'll take one. That's the deal, ain't it?"

"That's the first part. You see, it's a choice I'm offering you." Evie saw Cora's grin as she nudged Naomi with her elbow. "You may take one biscuit now, or you can have supper later this evening. Whichever decision you make, you abide by."

"Or supper?" Dodger asked it the first time. At the round of nods, he exploded. "*Or* supper, she says! I'm not trading an entire supper for one measly biscuit. That ain't fair."

"Neither is you getting something the other men don't." Evie pointed toward the door with her spoon. "Now that you've made your choice, I'll be happy to see you at the supper table. If you'd kindly extend my offer to the others, we can be through with these interruptions once and for all, I'd assume."

"We've been dismissed, Dodge, me-boy." The redhead reached into the kitchen and snagged the smaller man's shoulder. "Let's not hold up that fine supper any longer." With a surprisingly boyish grin, he hauled a still-spluttering Dodger out of the café. "And we'll be sure to pass along the message, ma'am!"

Ma'am, he called me. Evie couldn't help but notice that the first man who caught her eye called her "ma'am" but reserved the more appealing and feminine "lassie" for Naomi. *I should expect more of that. Lacey's so pretty and lighthearted, the men will swarm around her. The only reason she's not already wed is she wanted more adventure than becoming a society wife.*

She chopped carrots while she evaluated the situation. *After Lacey's taken her pick, the men will look to Naomi and me. Naomi first—she's more soft-spoken and would make a better bride than I would.* The mound of carrots grew before her, the series of chops busying her hands and giving ease to her heart as she confronted the plain truth with no frosting. *Not to mention her trim figure. I'm too bossy and loud and plump. I'll be the last of the women left to hire her husband. So as long as there are three I could live with, things will be all right.*

"You're brilliant, Evie." Lacey scooped away the carrots and plunked them into the massive pot boiling atop the stove—far too soon. "That generous 'offer' of yours will keep the men from sticking their noses in your kitchen again tonight!"

"Tonight?" Naomi harrumphed, carefully browning the second round of chopped beef then adding in diced tomatoes to the mixture of meat and onions, as Evie instructed. "That's the sort of threat we can reuse every meal to keep scavengers at bay."

"Scavengers." Cora giggled. "You make them sound like

crows, skulking about, waiting for us to drop something so they can swoop in and snabble it up. Or fight over it."

"Snabble?" Evie pulled the carrots off the stove then pushed more potatoes toward her sister. "You made fun of my word when I made it up, and now you dare use it?"

"Joking about the words you make up is a sister's privilege. Besides, I like the ones you create. They're so expressive and vibrant—just like you are." Cora put down her paring knife to reach over and give Evie's hand a fond pat.

"We can always tell when Cora's repeating an Evie-ism." Naomi's smile took the sting away. "You have a flair with words, the same as you do in the kitchen. Creativity always shows."

Evie shook her head and went to rescue the next batch of biscuits from Lacey's overexuberance. So far, Lacey had committed just about every crime known against biscuitkind. She'd left the batter lumpy then overstirred to correct it. She'd rolled them too thick, then too thin. Left them in the oven too long, and not long enough. This time it looked like overdone batter combined with thin rolling. In truth, the entire scavenger issue hadn't been Naomi's fault. Entirely.

The other three women had been sneaking ruined biscuits out of the kitchen for a while now, and Naomi simply got caught ditching the duds. The bribe she'd used to purchase silence—one of Evie's own biscuits—brought the man sniffing around for more. With others trailing in his wake when he left empty-handed.

"I think snabbling scavenger has the right ring when they first show up," Lacey mused, almost not noticing when Evie shooed her away from the biscuits and set her beside Cora to peel potatoes. She certainly didn't catch the glare Cora shot Evie as her sister pried an already-peeled potato from Lacey's fingers and replaced it with a runty one still wearing its skin.

"No!" Evie swiped the paring knife she'd just put in Lacey's hand and demonstrated again. "Like this. Never move the blade toward yourself. Always keep your thumb out of the way."

"I see." Lacey reached for the knife again and merrily began slicing the skins off half her runty potato. Meaning she took off half the potato along with its skins, of course. "I also see that the scavengers turn to beggars awfully quick."

Evie watched for another moment to make sure Lacey wouldn't lose a thumb or do herself any other sort of injury. She couldn't let her friend near the stove, they didn't have time to waste any more rounds of biscuits, chopping carrots would be far too dangerous, and besides, Evie hadn't planned to feed a small army of men right from the start. Potatoes she'd brought aplenty for Lacey to mangle. It would have to do for tonight.

"You could sell predinner biscuits and make a fortune." Cora's suggestion made everyone stop whatever she did and stare.

"Cora, I've never heard something so absolutely—"

Mercenary, manipulative, downright shameful. Evie finished Naomi's exclamation a dozen different ways even before Lacey beat her to it. *Maybe even a little bit funny, but mostly—*

"Brilliant! I say propose the idea to the next scavenger."

"That's dishonorable. We agreed to meals as part of their payment for the hard work these men will do." Evie rationed the browned, seasoned meat into pie pans as she rejected the plan. "Although I might as well mention we'll need a far sight more food than I brought along—especially if more men show up. Mr. Draxley will need to put in an order as early as tomorrow for an entire array of supplies if I'm to feed a logging outfit from the first day. We already have two stoves, but I'll need the room and storage we discussed right away, too. The café wasn't designed to accommodate the quantity of a log camp cookhouse."

"The men can build on an extra room tomorrow, I'd think."

"Naomi's right—the mercantile is supposed to be stocked with lumber so they can start right away." Lacey added her second potato to Cora's enormous pile and announced with a great sense of accomplishment, "We've finished the potatoes!"

"Great job." Evie winked at her sister, sharing the joke instead of letting it become a sore spot. By then, she'd rescued her carrots from the pot and set the water a-boiling once again. "Now those can boil while you start to mash the others!" Because, of course, Evie saw to it the first ten pounds of potatoes Cora peeled—minus their skins—stood alongside condensed milk, butter, and salt for mashing. She hastily added the other ingredients and toted the still-hot pot over to the worktable for them. *Thank You, Lord, that I brought an extra masher. Even Lacey can't do worse than make a mess of her apron with this task!*

Meanwhile, Evie kept a watch on the minced beef, onion, and tomato mixture as Naomi finished pan after pan, laying it into pie tins to cool and form the thin skin signaling their readiness for the mashed potato topping. Shepherd's pie, alongside the biscuits Evie whipped up in such a frenzy she had already planned on ways to use leftovers the next day, should make those men more than glad to hold up their bargain.

The peas and carrots she'd steam last, to avoid that dreadful cold limp vegetable phenomenon she'd seen too often. Peas and carrots, steamed slightly soft and bathed in butter with a hint of brown sugar, never failed to please her diners. Better still, they cooked quickly and went with almost anything.

With everyone busy and things progressing, Evie sifted a good amount of flour onto a clean wooden surface then put over a third again as much sugar alongside it. With her fingertips, she rubbed butter into the sugar until thoroughly mixed then lightly added in the flour bit by bit, working it until it formed a rather loose dough. She lifted it onto a baking sheet she'd greased beforehand and shaped it into a long oval about a quarter inch thick and three inches wide. Her fork pricked even holes all around before deft strokes of her knife separated the mass into long strips she sprinkled with more sugar.

She readied two batches of the shortbread before the time came to finish assembling the shepherd's pies. Evie set Naomi and Lacey to beating eggs while she and Cora spread fresh mashed potatoes atop the cooled minced meat and vegetables.

A sister could always tell when her sibling had lost patience, and Cora's acceptance of her best friend's inexperience in the kitchen fared far better when both of them stayed outside it. For that matter, it seemed everyone fared better when Lacey stayed away from the kitchen. Evie heard the splat of a dropped egg and reconsidered. *Make that far, far away from the kitchen. Any kitchen, really, but* especially *mine!*

Within moments, the dropped egg forgotten, they had no fewer than twenty-one shepherd's pies ready to brown in the oven. They had the dozen loggers, Braden, the doctor, Mr. Draxley, and themselves. The ladies wouldn't eat one each, but Evie held it was best to make a little more than they expected to need. They glazed each with beaten egg for that glossy sheen Evie considered her signature then sprinkled cheese on top for extra flavor and color.

Naomi kept an eye on the pies, rotating and removing them when ready. Cora steamed the peas and carrots, the sugar Evie'd already browned in the pan adding sweetness so she need only dab butter atop the vegetables afterward. The biscuits stayed warm in covered baskets near the oven, much like they had back home.

"I'll make tea for everyone, if you like." Lacey's offer took Evie by surprise. "Coffee for the men, I'd suppose."

"Have—" Evie groped for a diplomatic way to ask, couldn't come up with one, and simply blurted out, "Have you ever made tea, Lacey? Or coffee? It's not as simple as most think."

"Oh, I know!" Apron filled with more stains than the other three would see in the entire week, Lacey nodded with great confidence. "Tea, chocolate, and coffee were the only things Pa insisted I learn to make for myself. It was useful when we traveled. Particularly if Pa took meetings—I could replenish the coffee without waiting an age in an uncivilized place." She beamed at the evidence of her independence. "If worse comes to worst, I can also drive a team of horses and shoot a pistol. It's all part of being a modern, self-reliant woman, you see."

She's invaded other kitchens? Evie took a deep breath. *Even if only to make tea and coffee, I pity the cook who returned to the carnage Lacey left in her wake.* The other women gave voice to their reactions, too stunned to stay quiet.

"Self-reliant?" Naomi echoed in what Evie knew to be disbelief, but apparently Lacey interpreted it as admiration.

"Your father let you shoot a gun?" Cora's horrified gasp came closer to Evie's own reaction. "A *real* one?"

This elicited a matching gasp from Evie. *When did Cora's priorities become more organized than mine? And, really, what could Mr. Lyman have been thinking, to let Lacey lay so much as a finger on a firearm? She can't handle an egg without chaos.*

"I'm a dab hand with pistols." Lacey's nonchalance could have been comforting, but Lacey managed to be nonchalant about everything from butterflies to a dozen hungry loggers. While she spoke, she took down the grinder, selected coffee beans, and began grinding with an expertise lending credit to her claim. "As a matter of fact, I didn't want to mention it for fear of frightening anyone, but I brought one along for each of us."

Silence filled the kitchen. The familiar backdrop of the stove burners and oven didn't count as noise to Evie as she joined Naomi and Cora in gaping at Lacey. While she gaped, she nudged Cora out of the way and took the carrots away from the heat before they burned, but otherwise, she'd ground to a halt.

"I knew your father took you shooting, Lacey, but he never confided in me about your proficiency." Naomi, as Lacey's live-in companion for the past five years, obviously felt she should have known about this. "Nor did you ever mention it before."

"We agreed it wasn't the sort of thing to make Charleston society look upon me more favorably." A blithe shrug as she took the grounds and began measuring them into drip percolator pitchers Evie herself only recently learned to use. "Our own business ventures, my friendship with a female businesswoman"— she shot a conspiratorial grin at Evie—"and the proposals I chose not to accept already served to make me something of an...oddity, shall we say? We thought it best not to make it known I carry a pistol around in my reticule whenever I travel."

"There's a pistol in your purse right *now*?" Cora's curiosity began to overcome her disbelief and outrage.

"Of course! To be honest, I'd hoped to have the chance to teach you each some level of competence and a degree of comfort with your own before we invited any suitors to Hope Falls." A frown twisted her pretty features. "Perhaps tomorrow, while the men are building the storeroom onto the café, we can start?"

"Absolutely," Evie answered almost before she thought it through. She knew what Cora and Naomi were thinking—the way their jaws all but hit the floor told her they worried she'd lost her mind. "With this many men around, we should avail ourselves of every type of protection at our disposal. If Lacey claims proficiency, I believe her. She's quick to admit when she lacks experience in cooking. I want to learn, and I'd sleep easier knowing you both did, too. Won't you agree?"

She watched their faces while she spoke, but the distinctive aroma of shepherd's pie had her opening the oven, grabbing a dish towel, and pulling out the golden-brown pies the moment she finished. She waited a beat as Lacey set the percolators atop the stove to come to a boil. They exchanged a brief nod—a silent agreement Lacey would teach Evie even if the others didn't agree to join them the next day. Evie then busied herself sliding the sheets of shortbread into the oven.

"Someone should point out the danger of this little scheme. I suppose, as the oldest, I should be that someone." Naomi's eyes sparkled. "Instead, I'm going to be honest and say it sounds like great fun. Learning to handle a firearm should be one of the benefits of moving out West, and there are the safety concerns Evie pointed out to consider. I'll join both of you."

"By now you should all know better than to think I'd miss something like this!" Competition glinted in Cora's gaze. "When else would I get the chance to become a crack shot?"

"There's something deliciously. . .masculine. . .about it, isn't there?" Lacey carefully checked the color of the coffee, judged it too light, and set the percolator pitcher back on the stove.

"Liberating, I imagine, to know you can defend yourself." Evie had reason to be glad she'd put warm bricks in the base of her pie safe—they would keep everything toasty until the shortbread finished. Usually she'd simply send supper out ahead and stay in the kitchen. Tonight—and every night hereafter—she needed to dine with the men to become better acquainted.

"Not to mention invigorating. It's a wonderful thing to have a secret, I must say." Lacey blanched. "Not that I regret telling you three. You're all becoming a part of it, making it an even better secret than I kept before. I love that! I promise!"

"Calm down, Lace." Cora tweaked one of her friend's curls. "We understood what you meant and didn't take any offense."

"Impossible to refuse the chance to learn something men believe only they can master." Naomi's laughter caught on. "Someday, if we have cause to reveal our secret, it will most likely be for no better reason than to wipe a smug, superior smile off a man's face or warn him not to underestimate us."

"Is there a better reason?" Evie kept her reply light but hoped they never ran into a real threat causing them to draw their pistols. *But if we do, at least we'll be ready.*

As Jake somehow knew he would, Volker Klumpf spotted him at the train station and affixed himself like an extra appendage. And also just as Jake knew he would, the man called Clump yakked nonstop from the time he plunked himself onto the train seat to the time it came to a rough halt in Hope Falls.

At least, Jake assumed Clump kept talking. He'd caught a nap an hour in and woken four hours later to find his new friend midsentence. *Call me crazy, but I doubt it's the same sentence I fell asleep to*. Not that he could remember either way, mind.

Twilight bruised the sky as night bullied its way forward, its bluish-purple glow silhouetting a town eerily empty. Lights shone in only two buildings, leaving the rest of Hope Falls to encroaching darkness. Jake frowned. Whatever he'd been expecting, a ghost town hadn't made the list.

He headed toward the closest light, which also happened to be the larger building. Clump's distinctive tread tailed him, but Jake noted at least two other sets of footsteps. He threw a casual glance over his shoulder. *Yep. The two others I marked on the train as heading for the Hope Falls free-for-all.* Good. One of the men matched Twyler's description. It didn't mean much—about one in three managed that—but Jake would keep an eye on him all the same. *Not a bad start for a wild-goose chase.*

With every step he took, his conviction Hope Falls harbored secrets worth uncovering grew. And grew. By the time he opened the doors to the building he now saw marked as CAFÉ, nothing could convince him he'd made the wrong decision in coming here.

Not the dozen or so men glowering at him as he stepped through the doors, muttering about do-nothings who swooped in for supper. Not the strangely familiar sign hanging on the wall: HATS OFF TO THE CHEF!

Motion at eye level drew his gaze toward an opening door in the back left corner, where women bustled through. Each carried platters of food—much to the delight of the men seated at the long tables lining the dining room.

Jake's stomach rumbled its own homage to the mouthwatering steam rising from the savory dishes. The food smelled so good, it almost kept his attention away from the women. Almost wasn't good enough, though he wished he hadn't noticed that the women filing through the door were pretty enough to make the air heavy with competition.

Beautiful women, good food, and an offer too good to be true. It spelled trouble.

The ladies made their way into the room one at a time until four formed a neat row. Finding each lovelier than the last, Jake wondered if this wasn't a terrible idea, after all. Until his gaze followed the line, snagging on a pair of golden eyes wide with recognition.

Then again...

NINE

Evie gawked. She gaped. She was very much afraid she down-right ogled the stranger standing in the midst of her new dining room, looking for all the world as though he hadn't done the exact same thing in her old café back in Charleston.

She scarcely remembered to snap her mouth closed as he lifted a sardonic eyebrow, motioned toward the sign she'd brought all the way to Hope Falls, bowed his head, and swept away his hat just as he had before.

Oh my. . .

"Dibs on the last one." Clump elbowed Jake in the ribs.

"Not on your life." Jake's growl sent the shorter man's eyebrows shooting toward his hairline, but Clump didn't back down. "She's not up for grabs, Clump. There are three women in that ad, and four women standing up front. She's last because she's the chef, not one of the brides-to-be." As he spoke the words aloud, they gained enough weight to send the lump in his throat tumbling back down to his stomach, where it could settle. *That has to be it. Miss Thompson doesn't belong here.*

94

"How would you know?" Clump's jaw stuck forward. "I like the looks of that one, and you didn't want to come along in the first place. I said dibs."

"If anyone's layin' dibs on any of the women, it's one o' us what got here first." A lean man buried in far too many layers of clothes for a logger rose from his spot. "You four hop back on the train before you think to claim what you've no right to."

Cheers and cracked knuckles encouraged them to take that kindly advice. It also made a set of tawny eyes narrow—something Jake knew instinctively boded well for no man. Or, more importantly, his stomach. And his stomach wasn't having the promise of Miss Thompson's food carried out of sight.

"If it comes to that, we were the first four to get here." A swarthier man with an incongruous top hat perched jauntily atop his balding pate rose to his feet and gestured toward his companions. Rumbles of discord couldn't swell to a roar before the fellow held up his hands and continued. "But every gentleman knows that it's the ladies"—here he paused and tipped his hat toward the women before continuing—"who make the final choice. We'd all do well to remember that, before taking it upon ourselves to make others unwelcome where we stay by invitation."

"Well said, Gent!" One of his friends pounded an empty tin mug on the wooden surface of the table, and others swiftly followed suit. In a few moments, even the most hostile loggers nodded their agreement, outdone by their own logic.

"Well said, indeed." Miss Thompson laid down the heavy platter she held on a sideboard while exchanging a knowing glance with the other women. She selected one of the fragrant pies—potpie, he suspected—and made her way over to where the first man tried to muscle them out of town. A man, Jake noted, who numbered among at least half a dozen to bear Twyler's not-so-distinguishing hallmarks.

"Mr. Dodger, did I hear you say a man shouldn't lay claim to something he has no right to?" She held the dish beneath the lucky man's nose, so close he practically salivated atop the golden mashed potatoes Jake recognized meant shepherd's pie.

"Yes, ma'am." He donned an air of wounded dignity.

"Do you know, Mr. Dodger"—Miss Thompson slowly moved the pie back and forth, pretending not to notice every man's eyes following the motion as she spoke—"I absolutely agree with you." With that, she turned and handed the pie to Clump. "Welcome to Hope Falls, sir. Mr. Dodger admits he won't attempt to claim what he has no right to, so you're more than welcome to his supper." A dimple appeared in the recess of her left cheek.

Jake swallowed his laughter at the bereft look on Dodger's face as he mourned the loss of his perfect pie and regrouped.

"Here, now. The deal says I'm supposed to get my meals!" His demand earned him glares from the other women, grins from the men as he dug himself deeper, and the undeserved attention of Miss Thompson as she turned to face him once again.

"We made another deal, Mr. Dodger. When you invaded my kitchen, I told you if you took a biscuit then, you'd forfeit your supper tonight. If you don't recall, I'm sure the man you called Bear will be happy to speak up."

Or lose his own supper. Jake's satisfaction slipped a notch when he realized Bear must be the brawny Irishman seated nearby whose nodding response sent a smile to her face.

"Aye, lassie, that I do. You're free to call me Bear, but just so you know me proper, Rory Riordan is my Christian name."

"I recall saying I wouldn't swap supper for a biscuit!" Righteous indignation colored the response. "I want my pie."

"What a man says and what a man does can be two very different things." Miss Thompson's words struck straight through Jake, almost making him miss what happened next. "Please empty your left jacket pocket, Mr. Dodger, then turn it out."

"That don't make no sense." The man's face went purple.

"The more quickly you humor Miss Thompson, the more quickly we'll serve supper." The woman dressed in the frilliest gown called out this encouragement, prompting the other men to add their demands and yells until Dodger turned out the pocket.

"No, not that one." Her tone brooked no argument. "I didn't say your overcoat, but your jacket. That's the pocket to empty."

The man gave a sigh of resignation and plunged his hand between layers of garments to hold out a blue pocket. Along with a few coins and an impressive amount of lint, a shower of crumbs scattered across the tabletop beneath his jacket—clear evidence.

"As I suspected. You tried to have your biscuit and eat supper, too." Miss Thompson shook her head. "I expect more from any man who works here—and still more from any man who intends to court any of my friends. God-fearing, the ad said. It meant men of character and honor."

Friends, she said. Jake raised an eyebrow at Clump, who didn't spare him a glance. His attention stayed divided between the pie in his hands and the woman who'd handed it to him. Jake couldn't blame the man, but something inside him growled at Clump's all-too-obvious appreciation of Miss Thompson. *Lucky for him it's only my stomach.*

"A man's got to honor his stomach when it growls." Desperation for a fine meal made idiots out of better men.

"Say what you mean, and your stomach won't argue." Jake decided to support the spunky chef's decision. Before another man could beat him to it. "A man's word is his bond."

The Gent and Bear were quick to back him up. Clump was quicker, but then again, he had the pie to protect. Dodger looked ready to lunge for it, but the man next to him grabbed his arm and held him in place, the other men at the table muttering dire warnings about holding up their own meals until it got through his thick head he'd have to abide by the cook's decision. At last he gave a grudging nod and hushed.

"We'd like to welcome you all to Hope Falls." The blond in the fanciest dress spoke on the women's behalf. "First, I'd like to make introductions. I know you're all waiting to eat—which means we have your full attention." They all smiled.

"Ain't that the truth," came one good-natured reply. A few other, more restless murmurs agreed.

"You'd have our attention if you brought nothing but your pretty selves," one slick fellow swore, his smile oozing charm.

Jake decided on the spot that one meant trouble, no matter his blond hair ruled him out of *his* manhunt.

The second in line—a regal lady whose raven hair bore a shock of white—spoke in a low, melodic voice. "Gracious of you to say so."

"Before we share our names, we want to clarify that the ad was correct—only three of us seek husbands." The frilly one spoke again. "My brother claimed Miss Thompson long ago."

Discontent surged through Jake. *I knew from the start she'd be spoken for, at the very least—a woman like that.*

"I'm Lacey Lyman," she continued. "Sister to Braden Lyman, who owns the now-defunct mine and town of Hope Falls—in name only. My brother holds portions of the land and businesses in trust for myself and my friends. The ad mentioned a sawmill. With the mine collapsed and inoperable, we seek to plumb the other treasure of these mountains. That's why you're here, gentlemen, to begin the Hope Falls Sawmill. Three of you will become husbands. It's our hope the rest will stay on as members of the company. Time will tell."

"I'm Naomi Higgins—cousin to the Lymans." The black-haired beauty kept her words short. Something a man could appreciate.

"I'm Cora Thompson." Probably the youngest of the four and third in line, the last name of the ginger-haired woman caught Jake's attention.

Thompson? Did she say Thompson? If he could, he would've perked his ears to hear the rest, on the off chance she was the—

"Fiancée to Braden Lyman, and sister to. . ."

Jake didn't know if she actually trailed off or not. He'd stopped paying attention when relief surged through him. *Another man hasn't laid claim to the feisty chef.* Then reality hit him like a felled sugar pine. *So she wrote the ad along with the other two women—and not a single hairy lip nor hatchet face to be found among them.* Sudden, unfounded rage darkened the room and folded his fists. *What was she thinking?* Well, that much seemed obvious. Nothing. None of them recognized the danger they'd placed themselves in. Four comely women alone in a town full of men they'd *advertised* for?

"Evelyn Thompson." His incomparable cook flashed her dimple to the crowd of men. "It seems silly to say I'm Cora's sister, so I suppose that's all for now. We'll be getting better acquainted in coming weeks. For now, we'll serve your supper. Each night we'll sit at the same table and a different group of you will join us." She gestured toward one of two empty tables, where Jake planted himself without further prompting, putting his back against the wall so he could face the room. "Tonight, we hope each of you will stop by and chat with us for a while."

Jake eyed the men in the room—fourteen of them, all looking pleased as punch. Except the one who'd done himself out of a fine supper by filching a biscuit, of course. None would leave willingly— even if Jake could convince the women to abandon their scheme. *Which would also mean losing my only chance at Twyler.* The evaluation he came up with became more grim by the moment as everyone around him carried on, supremely unconcerned.

Clump reverentially set his pie atop the table and lowered himself in front of it as the women spread throughout the room, distributing pies to each man. Pitchers of hot coffee sat atop each table, alongside sugar bowls.

The engaged Thompson sister placed dishes of carrots and peas on each table for the men to help themselves once they'd dug enough room into their pie tins. She also slid familiar baskets, heaped with fluffy biscuits, onto the tables for the men to pass around. Good thing she doled out four baskets per table of six, or fights would've broken out on the spot. As it was, it came to a near thing. The younger Miss Thompson—the one clearly labeled as "taken"—finished first and joined them at the table first.

Wish the others would hurry up. Jake eyed where a burly logger held up the other Miss Thompson—and her pies—with conversation. Apparently the table with the ladies would be served last, and see the women last. He understood the reasoning behind it. He understood the fairness of it.

I also understand the others will be finished and invading the table the minute the women sit down, and we won't get a moment's peace. Jake squelched a surge of irritation. By the end of the evening meal, he'd know who to look at more closely and which husband-hopefuls couldn't possibly be Twyler.

He couldn't have manufactured a better scenario to scope out the men—or stay close to the women. *Because that's the only thing I can do. I can't stop the foolishness now it's been set in motion, but I can stay here and protect them from the worst of the danger.* Jake cast a glance at Miss Evelyn Thompson, who walked toward his table at long last. *Even if they never notice.*

Aside from those first few moments when she first spotted him, Evie made special effort to ignore the stranger from Charleston. Well, he'd been a stranger in Charleston instead of a regular, but he'd visited her café, so that's the only way she could think of him for now. *I need to stop thinking about him!*

Then Dodger showed the nerve to try to oust the one man she knew she wanted to stay. Evie didn't know why she wanted the tall, rangy stranger with his easy smile to stick around. She didn't have to. All she knew was that the weasely man who'd dared snitch a biscuit and think she wouldn't notice also dared to act like he owned Hope Falls. Her eyes narrowed in preparation to set the upstart in his place—the men needed to know who ran things and respect it. From the very beginning.

Rabbitty Mr. Draxley made it painfully obvious he wouldn't

speak up on their behalf, as he hunched in a corner. The man visibly shrank. Evie noticed that, in his fear that he might be called upon, even his mustache seemed to have lost the will to twitch. A sad sight, to be sure.

The genial Gent spoke up, wisely making the point for her and earning himself an extra piece of shortbread later. Pity for Dodger he didn't take the words to heart—the slight troublemaker still sneered at the late arrivals.

Evie had thought to turn a blind eye toward Dodger's offense. Creating a confrontation on their first night, before they'd established order and the men had a taste of their incentive to make the deal work, seemed a poor idea.

I shouldn't have forgotten this is business. Meals for logging and even courting count as transactions. The others look to me as the businesswoman, and we can little afford to leave a single loophole or let anyone else take a stronger position to negotiate. We're already outnumbered.

So she caught him in his lie and gave away his pie. But not to the stranger. Evie kept very busy being unaware of his presence at the head of the newcomers. She didn't even think about him—thinking about not thinking about him didn't count—until they'd introduced themselves to the men, served supper to everyone else, and headed to their own table.

Where he sat. Directly across from the only seat left.

Cora. Evie narrowly avoided elbowing her sister in payback for the nudge Cora served her earlier. The one that effectively nudged her out of her gaping and brought her back to her senses. *Cora knew about the stranger from the diner, saw my reaction to this man's gesture. Even if she doesn't suspect he's the same one, she's still meddling. Little sisters have no right to meddle.* She took a deep breath and slid onto the bench. *That's reserved for big sisters!*

"The men wanted to wait for you," Cora said, explaining the untouched, cooling plates Evie eyed with some concern.

"Now we can pray together." The somewhat nondescript man

she'd given Dodger's pie to gave an undeniably sincere smile.

"We'd be honored to have you bless the meal, Mr. . . . ." Naomi groped for a name and came up empty-handed.

"Klumpf." Without further ado, he bowed his head, signaling the others to follow suit. "Dear Lord, we thank You for everyone's safe arrival and ask Your blessing on the food before us smelling so good and the hands that made it. Amen."

"Amen," Evie chorused along with the others. She'd taken note of which men bowed their heads before picking up their forks and which didn't bother. Though she allowed some might have prayed before she reached them—particularly the last few.

"Thank you, Mr. Klumpf." Cora passed Evie the vegetables.

"Thank you, Miss Thompson, Miss Thompson, Miss Higgins, and Miss Lyman." Mr. Klumpf raised his fork, heavy with seasoned beef and mashed potatoes, to his mouth and paused in appreciation before chewing. He gave a sigh. "Thank you."

"You're more than welcome, Mr. Klumpf." *I like him.* Klumpf showed a wholesome appreciation for the Lord and good food—qualities she looked for in a potential husband. *He also,* she acknowledged, comparing him to the enigmatic man at his side, *isn't so handsome he'd look for great beauty in his bride.*

While she considered the two men occupying the bench on her half of the table, the other two introduced themselves. Evie heard and forgot them both just as quickly. She'd ask the other women to remind her later that night, when they compared their impressions of the men. To be honest, most of the names hadn't stuck with her so far. Her memory, so fine for recalling the finest details of any recipe she read even once, always failed when it came to putting names to faces. Almost always.

"Now, sir, you have us all at a disadvantage." The way Lacey eyed the stranger from Evie's café didn't sit well.

"Jake Creed." The same slow smile she remembered crept across his face, softening a jaw too strong for most faces. "I'd tip my hat, but I already took it off in honor of the chef. Miss

Thompson—the elder, that is—made it clear she expected a man to bring his manners to her table the first time we met."

So he remembers. Not overly surprising—the female owner of a restaurant was enough of a rarity to stick with most people, and she'd encountered Mr. Creed a scant week ago. *But he also remembered to take off his hat, and his decision that I'm worth it. Or,* she allowed, *that at least my cooking is worth that respect.*

Either way, that fact overshadowed being labeled "elder." Mostly.

Only one thing bothered her. *Creed.* The one thing that saved her when it came to her abysmal memory for names was that, more often than not, people somehow fit their names. Long ago, Evie came up with a theory that, since people couldn't change the names given them at birth, they grew into them. Much the way muffins or jumbles baked into the shape of the tin or mold they were poured into, people adjusted to reflect their names.

So as Evie got to know a person, she knew the name. Take Klumpf, for example. With a broader build, he boasted a low-slung walk, distinctive for its heavy tread. She'd noticed it in the few steps he took to the table and attributed it to the thick-set soles on his heavy boots. Klumpf clumped. Evie matched the man to the name and wouldn't struggle for it again.

Creed? A sense of purpose emanated from him, but the name didn't fit. *After all, aren't creeds statements of belief? The sort of thing usually handed down by those in positions of wisdom or authority?* Chills prickled down her arms as his gaze met hers with the intensity Evie convinced herself she'd misremembered. Somehow, the man before her seemed the sort to create his own system, not wait to be given what he wanted.

TEN

J ake wanted to throw all the other men in the room into a freight car and lock it. Didn't really matter when the train left, so long as the men couldn't get out and tempt him to knock their fool heads together. The lot looked ready to fight over who got to sit in the empty chair at the head of the women's table.

Evelyn Thompson tilted her head, the soft contours of her profile a taunt to any man, forcing Jake to consider the idea he may be just as much a fool as any other sap in the building. If he wasn't already sitting here, he wouldn't have waited in line. Then she smiled at something one of the other men said.

Not the dimple. Jake stopped just shy of cramming an entire biscuit into his mouth to stop a groan. *Protecting the daft woman will be next to impossible if she keeps smiling like that. I'll need more bullets than an army regiment to keep the men away. Even worse once they figure out she's the cook.*

Maybe he'd do better to just snag her and jump aboard the next train himself. Jake pushed aside a twinge of guilt over the thought of the other three but swiftly reasoned it away. The younger Miss Thompson had a fiancé to look after her, who happened to be Miss Lyman's brother and Miss Higgins's cousin. Let him worry about the other three. From where Jake sat, it seemed like they'd hatched the entire crackpot idea and swept Miss Thompson along with them into the lunacy.

He shoveled another bite of shepherd's pie into his mouth, creamy mashed potatoes blending with heartily seasoned beef in such a way as to make a man believe in miracles. *Yep.* Jake eyed the woman sitting across from him, sharing one of those miraculous dinners with her sister. She—and her cooking—was the only thing in this fool town worth saving.

Too bad he'd be up against fourteen—no, fifteen—lumberjacks the moment he tried to take her. Even Clump would fight him tooth and nail. Jake shot a glance at his traveling companion to find the man making calf eyes at the cook. *Especially Clump.*

Even worse, Miss Thompson didn't look like a woman who wanted to be rescued. Which meant he might've been wrong in judging her a woman of good sense. Jake hated being wrong under any circumstance, but for some reason, this rankled more than most. Evelyn Thompson wore the face of an angel, whipped up meals to make a dying man smile, and ran a business of her own with spunk and grit. A woman like that wasn't allowed to plant herself in the middle of the most harebrained scheme ever hatched.

He should haul her out of Hope Falls to prove it. But somewhere in this mess of men sat a murderer. *And I'm not leaving until I find him. Miss Thompson made her choice, and I've made mine. Twyler's who I came for, and Twyler's who I'll leave with. Justice before—*

"Move, mister." Men crowded behind the row of women and glowered at him, interrupting his train of thought. And more to the point, his supper. "You've sat there long enough."

"Excuse you?" Thunderclouds gathered in Miss Thompson's gaze, while the other women merely seemed amused by the show.

"Don't you worry 'bout a thang, miss." A voice near the back piped up. "We figgered out how to make it so's we all get a chance to get ta know ya better, without goin' one by one."

"I ain't movin'." Clump crossed his arms, uncrossed them to snag the last biscuit, and crossed them again. "I'm eatin'."

"You chose your seats before we arrived." Jake set down his fork. "You were served first. We're going to finish our meal."

"You four can finish at another table." A demand.

"We could," Jake agreed, "but we won't." He picked up his fork and started eating again, sending a smile to comfort the now-nervous women. Not that they deserved it. They should've known this sort of thing would happen when they paraded themselves in front of a dozen lonely men, with no rules.

"Then you won't finish at all." A man whose swift movements labeled him a high climber darted forward to grab the smallest man from the train by the collar. His fingertips barely brushed his target before he hit the floor. He sat there for a moment, stunned, before rising to his feet.

"That does it!" Miss Thompson slapped her palms on the table and stood, drawing all attention to herself. "There will be no brawling in my café. There will be no fighting over which men sit beside us, or we won't take our meals with you at all. There will be order, or giblet stew and liverwurst will be the only items on the menu. Do I make myself understood, gentlemen?"

"Oooeee, she's a spitfire, thatta-one is!" Someone with more admiration than brains whistled. "I like that in a woman."

"Seems a mite bossy to me," another muttered.

"I don't care. See how her eyes flash? She's right purty when she's riled," the first one said, defending his choice.

Magnificent describes her better, Jake decided, watching a vibrant rose flush climb her cheeks, her eyes indeed flashing.

"We thought it would be a simple matter for everyone to share a meal then have each of you men stop over and say hello for a moment." Miss Lyman stepped over the bench, the other women following suit until all four stood at the side of the room, in varying postures of disappointment, worry, and anger.

"She's the one I like," a nameless fool evaluated. "Women should look like that—girly and poufy and so forth."

"Poufy!" Miss Lyman patted her sleeves—which, Jake suddenly noticed, were kind of poufy. Apparently she didn't like the term much, though. "I'm not 'poufy.' This is fashionable!"

"I never liked the frilly, fussy sort, m'self," another judged. "But that one in the corner's got possibilities."

"We assumed you could behave as gentlemen!" Miss Higgins scolded, wagging her finger at every single one of them like an irate schoolmarm. "You should all be ashamed of yourselves!"

"That one," another scoffed, "seems kind of priggish."

"Nah. A woman should be prim and proper." The one who'd pointed to Miss Higgins shook his head and grinned. "In public."

"Oh, I see what you mean." Knowing chuckles spread through the room as every man caught the implication that a woman who was prissy in public might be a lot less controlled in private.

Thankfully, the women didn't seem to understand the joke. They were plenty overset, each one blushing and angry.

Good. Maybe they'd rethink the wisdom of their plan. But for now, the men weren't showing proper respect, and it needed to be checked before things got further out of hand. Tonight would set the tone for the rest of this farce, and Jake couldn't let the women be endangered—no matter they'd done it to themselves.

"That's enough." He stood between the women and the crowd almost before he'd decided to move. "These are ladies." Jake emphasized the title and made eye contact with a few particulars whose comments had set up his back. "If you can't treat them as such, I'll be more than happy to escort you to the train."

"Aye, and I'll be doin' the same, d'ye ken?" The giant redhead didn't stand beside Jake. He stood a few paces away so they bracketed the women. His speech wasn't as easy to understand as before—his thickened accent a sign of his ire, most likely—but not a single man could mistake his meaning.

"You don't talk that way about ladies, and you don't act that way around them." Clump plunked himself between the two of them so they formed a semi-solid barrier. "I won't let you."

"Ribald jokes offend delicate ears." His top hat marked the Gent's progress through the crowd as he took a place alongside Clump. "And aggressive postures disrupt peace. It will not do."

Before any others could detach themselves from the fold, Jake decided to put the force of their conviction to use. "Each man who wants to stay, and work, and respect these fine women, sit back down. Anyone else goes to the train. Tonight."

To a man, every single one took a seat. Some grumbled, some looked embarrassed—as though they'd only just remembered their manners—but most seemed amused and even relieved to have order established. Only Jake, Clump, the Gent, and the redhead they called Bear remained standing.

"Do you think. . ." Cora's whisper drew Lacey's attention away from the men standing and, from the sounds, sitting before them.

She couldn't really tell about the ones who might be sitting down, because the four who stood in front of them did an excellent job of blocking her view. *Which isn't what we hired them for.* Lacey let loose a disgruntled little huff.

"They've entirely forgotten we're standing back here while they decide how to run our town?" Evie's whisper carried just far enough for Lacey and—Lacey assumed by the way her cousin sidled over—Naomi to hear. "Yes, I do believe that."

All four of them took a moment to look at the backs of the four men forming a human blockade between them and their beaus. Not a single one turned around or even looked over his shoulder. They just kept glowering at the others—or at least that's what Lacey imagined they did. The backs of their heads didn't really tell her all that much about their expressions, after all.

Funny how all four, different as they were, stood the same way as they took control of the unruly room. Boots planted a little wider than shoulder width apart, jaws thrust forward, arms crossed over their chests in a sort of instinctive male posture that screamed of take-charge masculinity and authority.

Of course, only two of them really managed it with any aplomb. The men on the ends—the great big Irishman and the rangy Mr. Creed whose presence obviously made such an impact on Evie—exerted the power that made the others listen. The one in the top hat, for all his fine manners, couldn't exert enough primal influence to keep a bunch of working men under control. Neither could the stockier Mr. Clump, for all his good intentions.

"They can't forget us!" Lacey whispered back. "Please tell me why are we whispering when we don't *want* to be forgotten?"

"Because those four are taking over our town, and we need to set everyone in his place," Naomi hissed back, her explanation eliciting nods from the others. "We need a plan."

"Mr. Draxley should come to our aid at a time like this." Lacey craned her neck, searching for the businessman in what she already knew to be a futile attempt. Even if she spotted him, the squirrelly fellow wouldn't take a stand for anything.

"We need to just walk up there and start listing rules." Evie's brows lowered in determination. "First rule: We invite who dines with us, and there is no changing that arrangement. I'll go up and say it while you three each make up a rule of your own, and we'll keep on going from there until we're done." With that, she headed toward the line of men still firmly planted in their way, bound to uproot them.

Lacey exchanged startled glances with the other two and scurried to keep up. In a moment, they'd slipped past the men to stand directly in front of them. If they turned around to face the four fellows, they could perform a rollicking Virginia reel. As it was, they stayed where they stood, with the women in front and the men right behind, waiting to follow.

But where are we leading them? She slid a glance at Evie, who'd burst up there with more outrage than solid planning but somehow managed to take her place last out of all of them. *And where is Evie leading us with this little maneuver?*

Evie didn't know where to go. If she went to the right of Mr. Creed, she'd most likely wind up shimmying against the wall. If she attempted to make her way to his left, she'd be squeezing past both him and Mr. Clump—which would be worse for two reasons. First, she'd brush against both men and give either a chance to halt her progress. Second, if Cora tried to go to Clump's right, she'd block her sister. Which left her the wall.

This would be so much easier if I were a slender wisp of a woman, but the element of surprise works wonders, Evie assured herself, striding behind Mr. Creed, darting right, and sliding past. Make that *almost* sliding past.

A fraction of a step, and he stopped her midslide, his shoulder lightly pinning her against the wall for the merest moment while he dipped his head and murmured something for only her to hear. "Stubborn woman." As quickly as he said it, he'd shifted away to let her through, leaving only the memory of the words and the heat where his arm pressed against hers in his wake.

She shrugged it away to stand squarely in front of him—where she could best ignore the man. Besides, her friends already stood in front of the other three, waiting for her to begin taking back control of *their* town. None of them encountered the slightest trouble slipping through. *Naturally.*

"Now that you've each made the decision to stay," she began, "it's become excruciatingly apparent we'll need to establish a few ground rules for how we'll be running Hope Falls. Anyone who can't follow these simple laws is welcome—"

The man behind her cleared his throat in a meaningful, manly sort of way, as though to punctuate her comment.

"No, make that *encouraged* to catch the next train." She gave a bright smile to the assembled men. "I'm certain you can each find it yourselves, but should the need arise, the fine gentlemen behind me are more than willing to. . .assist. . .you in departing."

"Aye, that we will." Rory Riordan's agreement burst from his massive chest with no further prompting, an angry growl showing one and all why he'd been given the name Bear.

Evie couldn't be certain if it was her words or the men who supported them that made the impact, but heads nodded around the room in agreement. Some more willing than others, but she wouldn't quibble about it for now. Results were results.

"First and foremost, there will be no fisticuffs in the café, the mercantile, or on the job." She held up one finger to signify this as the first rule. "Do I make myself clear?"

Another round of nods, peppered with yeps and all rights and even a few why nots, told Evie that she'd made her point.

"Next rule." Cora spoke up. "After tonight, each of us will invite one man to share the evening meal that day. One chair will be open at either end of the table—for two of the four men behind us. This is not negotiable and cannot be changed."

Evie held up a second finger, despite growing grumbles from the men. "If you take exception to our choices, you may leave town or, at the very least, the café for that night. Any squabbles or rudeness, shoving, or other such behavior regarding seating will result in loss of the next meal. No exceptions will be made, and no such behavior tolerated. Understood?"

"The same holds true if you refuse to work or the other men report you are not pulling your weight," Lacey added.

"Or if you lie about your fellow worker in an attempt to belittle him in our eyes or cost him his meals," Naomi finished.

Evie held up one hand, palm open, all five fingers outstretched. "Do we have an agreement thus far, before we continue, or does the crowd need thinning already?" She felt rather than saw the men behind them take a half step forward.

Mr. Creed's breath warmed the back of her neck, the toes of his boots bumping the back of her own in a silent challenge.

She refused to skitter away, instead holding her ground.

No men stood up, protested, or otherwise demonstrated a need to be removed from her café. They were learning. Quickly.

"No disrespect will be shown to these ladies." Mr. Creed started talking behind her, a rumbly reminder that not every man had learned something—and this one needed to stop trying to fight her battles for her before something awful happened.

Like I get used to someone else taking care of things. Evie swallowed a lump in her throat at the thought, horrified by her own reaction as he kept speaking in that low, gruff tone with just enough of a rasp to make it distinctive even when all the men spoke at the same time.

"Unless you offer an arm while walking alongside one or some such reason, not a one of you will lay a finger on any of them." Creed's voice lowered an octave as he issued this directive, the raw intensity sending chills down Evie's spine.

ELEVEN

O ch an' ye be touchin' so much as a hair on any lassie's head
I'll be seein' to it ye canna dance a fankle agin fer certain sure."
Rory Riordan's booming oath all but shook the rafters. His accent
became so thick, it would take Evie's butcher knife to cut through
to the English beneath it, but no one doubted he'd sore regret
finding out the particulars of the Irishman's threat. He sounded
so irate by the very idea of any one of the men daring to sully one
of the lassies, it made Evie want to smile. Rory seemed the finest
of the lot to her.

She bit her lip to keep from ruining the fine impression he
made on the other loggers and, after a swift glance, ignored the
expressions on Cora's, Lacey's, and Naomi's faces. Cora beamed
fondly at the giant redhead. Obviously blood ran thicker than
good sense when it came to her sister. Lacey's eyebrows winged to
meet her hairline. Naomi couldn't seem to stop blinking.

Creed, for all his faults—never mind that Evie couldn't think
of any truly grievous ones at the moment as she knew she could
come up with them some other time—saved them. He simply
kept on spouting rules as if he owned the place. "You'll not take
an insulting tone when speaking to them, nor will you discuss

them with anything other than the proper respect. If any one of them takes exception to something you say, or the way you say it, an apology won't be enough."

"Not hardly," Clump added, cracking his knuckles.

"I daresay we should add that, even if the ladies don't hear something, but any of us"—the Gent gestured toward the four Guardians, as Evie dubbed them—"take exception to what you say, the same will apply. Gentlemen are gentlemen at all times."

"That should be so," Lacey agreed before she must have realized what the men maneuvered to do.

Evie stepped in immediately. "Be that as it may, no men will be made to leave Hope Falls without our agreement." She gestured to the other women and looked the Gent, then Mr. Creed squarely in the eye to show she wouldn't let them push out the others based on their own judgment. "That won't do at all."

"Of course not!" Naomi seconded her immediately.

"But ye need be sheltered when men forget themselves and act like bluidy savages, aye?" Mr. Riordan's speech started clearing up more—a reflection of the lessening tension.

"We'll decide what measures need be taken for what offense." Evie looked around the room, letting her gaze rest on a few particular faces. She remembered which men made the comments to initiate this entire fiasco. *They already think I'm bossy—and I thought the same thing earlier. Why not show them the worst, so only the ones who are truly willing to live with it will bother courting me? At least I'll make sure the others are protected.*

"Normally a lady doesn't point, but since I don't know your names, I'm afraid I'll have to resort to using some sort of gesture to indicate who I mean. Please step forward if you're included." With that, Evie raised her entire hand and dipped her fingers in the direction of the men whose boorish comments had incited this ruckus to begin with.

First, the one who called her a spitfire who looked pretty when angry. *I refuse to be swayed by the fact he called me pretty.* Nevertheless, she found it far easier to single out the man who'd called Naomi priggish, as well as the logger whose incomprehensible joke about public prissiness set off a round of hoots and hollers earlier. The fellow who'd admired Lacey's "poufy" muttonchop sleeves joined the growing group as well. But Evie could easily admit, if only to herself, she took a special satisfaction in calling forth the observer who'd dared judge her bossy before one and all. The slight fellow she'd heard others label a "high climber," who'd tried to muscle the other man out of his seat, rounded out the ranks of those she judged guilty of creating chaos.

"You want us to take these rascals outside?" Clump's voice, just another way his name matched him, came out in low, almost guttural syllables—not unpleasant, but certainly noticeable.

"No, thank you, Mr. Klumpf." Evie had to remind herself to add the *f* at the end of his name, since he'd volunteered his nickname and, worse, Mr. Creed referred to him as such. "Tonight, as the first night with the Hope Falls rules, we'll take a first-step misbehaving measure." She caught Cora's smile as she remembered her childhood and knew what was coming. "My sister will be happy to tell you the cost for your actions."

"Mother died before I left the nursery"—Cora shared more than Evie intended her to—"but I was blessed to have an older sister who helped raise me. Misbehaving brought penalties, but the first numbered among the harshest." She cast a commiserating glance toward the men about to be sentenced. "No dessert."

Poor dullards—it would've been kinder to take them to the train. Jake couldn't help but pity the fools. The hangdog looks on their faces showed they possessed enough sense to recognize what they'd lost. It seemed Miss Thompson hid something of a cruel streak, to make them stay and watch others enjoy whatever she'd baked. *I hope it's those cookies.* His mouth started to water.

"No dessert!" one of them mourned in a low moan.

"Can't we just apologize? This one time?" Another—the one who'd called Miss Thompson pretty when riled—attempted to bargain. That one would bear close watching from here on out.

"What is it? No, wait—don't tell me." The overeager big-mouth who'd commented on Miss Lyman's sense of fashion clapped a hand over his eyes. "I might not be able to bear it."

Jake noticed a satisfied smile tugging at the stern expression Miss Thompson wore. She wouldn't give an inch. *Good. If she backs down, they lose all hope of corralling this group.*

"Tell us!" One of those who'd not lost his share piped up.

"It will be waiting for you when you return," Miss Higgins promised. "Along with fresh coffee for every table."

"Return from what?" Clump asked the question a breath before every other man in the room voiced some variation of it.

"Washing your dinner dishes." Miss Lyman favored them all with a beaming smile. "If you'll step outside, you'll find two barrels by the water pump in the back. The first with soapy water, the second with rinse water. Wash your tins and forks clean and bring them into the kitchen, if you please."

"You want us to wash our dishes?" Someone not-so-bright scratched his head and squinted. "Ain't that woman's work?"

A few grumbles of agreement sounded, but no one outright agreed.

Jake figured no one wanted to lose out on dessert.

"There are twenty people here tonight, and you all believe more will arrive in the next few days. We didn't anticipate so many mouths to feed, and there are other things demanding our attention." Miss Lyman squared her shoulders. "There are men who were injured in the mine's collapse to look after, and other business matters to attend to. The ad asked you to respond in care of the postmaster, and we expected letters rather than men."

Burying his face in the palm of his hand wouldn't do any good, Jake knew, but the sudden explanation for the situation made too much sense. These gently reared women placed that ad naively believing they'd weed through letters to select a small group of prospective grooms, and found a heap of timber beasts waiting for them when they stepped off the train. The mention of men injured in the mine collapse sat heavy in his stomach—it certainly wasn't the excellent supper he'd eaten.

They're trying to save a dying town and ease Mr. Lyman's guilt over the mine collapse. Anger sparked. *No matter his guilt, no matter the men injured, Mr. Lyman belongs in this room watching over his sister, cousin, fiancée—and her sister.*

"My sister struck a bargain to feed you, and we're happy to abide by it." The younger Miss Thompson rubbed the back of her neck. "But we haven't time to take care of everything, and cook, and wash up after all of you. We can either cook or clean, so we assumed you'd all be more than happy to pitch in so you could enjoy real meals and even dessert instead of soup every day."

"I'll do it!" The one who'd first protested was all but drowned out as over a dozen men stampeded toward the door.

Jake beat them all. The way he figured it, Bear and the other three could keep an eye on any stragglers. He'd be in the best position to watch everyone file through the kitchen, past the women. He didn't plan to let a single man alone with them.

It worked. Jake stepped through the back door to the kitchen mere seconds after the women entered, their arms loaded with baskets and carafes. He set down his pie tin and started sweeping stacks of baskets out of their arms and setting them onto the massive wooden worktable dominating one wall of the kitchen. He gave a nod to each of the women then busied himself taking the small butter crocks out of each container and shaking biscuit crumbs into one catchall basket. There weren't many crumbs, but it gave him a handy pretext to stick around—and a reason for the women to let him.

Other men filed through in what became a patterned march. In the back door with a clean, wet pie tin, they stumbled to a halt. Then came the blink 'n' sniff to take in the cheery warmth of the kitchen, layered with the smells of fondly remembered dinner fading beneath a rich, buttery scent Jake couldn't quite place.

Miss Lyman's welcoming smile as she handed them a dishcloth provoked a dazed grin before the fellow dried his dish and handed it to a waiting Miss Higgins, who stacked it neatly on a shelf and tucked his cutlery into a wooden drawer in orderly rows. At that point, the younger Miss Thompson would direct him toward the swinging doors to the dining room and ask that he stand near the entrance to wait for the others.

The elder Miss Thompson laid out bowls on the surface beside him, eschewing any contact with the men as she went about preparing what must be dessert. She spooned a healthy dollop of blackberry jam into the very center of each bowl, working steadily alongside him. The woman most likely didn't realize she'd chosen the safest position, but he appreciated not having to look around to see where she'd flitted off to.

All the while, Jake tucked the crocks of butter into a nook at the side of the door, giving every man a good once-over as he walked through. A few, like those who'd stood up alongside him, or the ones who'd let their mouths talk over their good sense, he recognized. Some passed initial inspection immediately. Several loggers would be too broad in build or too tall for the average height and appearance that thus far protected Twyler. One or two fell by the wayside for red or blond hair or blue eyes.

By the time he'd looked over the entire crew, Jake counted only half a dozen men who might fit the bill. Shame he couldn't number only six on the list of men he'd have to keep an eye on when it came to the women. Jake didn't trust a single, finger-lickin', goofy-grinnin' one of them.

Riordan's sheer size made him a valuable ally, but the man showed signs of being possessive and territorial—which might make him the worst of the bunch later on. The man tried to hang around the kitchen, jeopardizing Jake's position, but without a task to perform and his bulk obviously in the way, he had to leave.

Gent put on pretentious airs, with that overly formal language and silly top hat of his. Jake suspected the man used the hat as a means to further camouflage his thinning hair—telltale smudges around Gent's scalp, ears, and fingertips tattled of careful application of shoeblack. The man must be in his forties to take such measures, Jake figured.

Even Clump presented more problems than help. His friend from back in Durango looked ready to follow Miss Evelyn Thompson around like a besotted puppy, ears perked and tongue hanging out as though begging for the smallest scrap of—

Shortbread? Jake shoved stacks of baskets up against the wall as the chef headed his way with sheets of golden cookies pulled from the pie safe. So *that* explained the rich, buttery aroma wafting through the room. Fresh coffee, which the women put on before the men began filing through, promised a solid counterpoint to the sweetness of dessert. Strong coffee usually swallowed anything else in the air, but even it had the sense to savor Evelyn Thompson's fresh-baked shortbread.

If the men still wandered through, they'd refuse to leave. Jake knew, because he didn't plan on budging from that warm, heaven-scented room until all the women exited before him. Even then, he'd be following to protect his share of that shortbread as much as to oversee the treatment of his makeshift wards.

A man had priorities, and Jake well knew he only boasted three. First, hunt down Twyler and bring the murderer to justice. Second, ensure no bystanders got hurt in the process. This is where protecting the women came in and things got complicated. Their ad gave him the chance to catch Twyler, but it left them in far more danger than that. And third, eat as much of Evelyn Thompson's cooking as possible.

Admittedly, he'd only tacked on the last one tonight, but its recent addition didn't lessen it. On the contrary, he'd given up everything for those first two priorities—it took something mighty important for him to make room for a third. And right now, those fingers of shortbread, made airy by fork holes and delectable by shining crystals of sugar dusting each piece, held his complete attention. Well, almost.

He'd never thought about it, but if someone asked, he'd probably have said such a talented chef would have graceful hands with long, delicate fingers and a light touch. Jake couldn't help noticing Miss Thompson's hands, smaller than he'd realized before, nails trim and neat as she deftly arranged four cookies around the dollop of jam in each bowl. Swift, capable hands used to hard work. They suited her spunk and grit.

The same spunk that brought her out West with a wild plan to find a husband. Suddenly the shortbread didn't smell so sweet. *The same spunk that made her leave safety, slide past me, and lay down rules, taking control of a group of scoundrels. . .*

"Who's that one for?" He spotted a bowl with double the shortbread when she spooned more jam into the center of it.

"Mr. Dodger." She didn't say another word about the matter. Miss Thompson didn't need to. After taking away the man's shepherd's pie—no matter he deserved losing it for thievery and hypocrisy—obviously the woman's soft heart worried the man would be hungry. With a little extra after some of the men had forfeited their dessert, she'd found a way to be kind and stay firm.

Yep. Jake shook his head as he followed the women back into the dining room. *That spunk's going to cause trouble.*

"Braden?" Cora's voice came to him, the same clear memory that helped him through the darkness before. This time, the promise of her tugged him from the mines more easily than ever before.

He struggled from the clutches of drug-induced sleep, fighting through the murky fog beyond the blackness of the mine to crack one eye open. Light pierced his vision, but that wasn't the shock to slam his eyelid shut.

Braden took a ragged breath. And groaned. *It's not enough that*

I have to send Cora away, Lord? Must she bring her sister's cooking? Hunger panged through him at the thought of something other than the gruel and soup the doctor foisted on him for weeks on end—not, Braden suspected, because he shouldn't be eating heartier meals but because the doctor couldn't cook anything else. So whatever lay under that tea towel almost tempted Braden to put his plan to run her out of Hope Falls on hold.

Regret already swamped him for the way he'd treated his fiancée earlier. *It didn't work.* Braden's jaw tightened. *She should have listened. Should have left.* The surge of anger saved him.

"What are *you* doing here?" He barked the question, refusing to open his eyes and witness the look on her face. Refusing to see anything that would edge away the rage and submerge him in the desolation of his current situation. "I don't want you."

Liar. His conscience bit into his battered pride.

"You look at me when you say that, Braden Nicholas Lyman." Tears trembled in her voice, and most likely in her eyes, but he wouldn't look. Cora could be a myth sprung to life, the very opposite of the ancient Gorgon whose glance turned men to stone. Those mismatched eyes of hers, one blue, one brown, held the power to break through the walls any man erected.

If Braden looked, he'd crumble. And if he crumbled, she'd see the pathetic excuse for a man he'd truly become. *Never.* "I don't want to look at you. I don't want to see you."

A strangled gasp, all but inaudible, warned him Cora wouldn't give in easily. "What do you want, Braden?"

To be whole again. To be able to hold you. To know I didn't kill my men. He swallowed. *But I can't have any of that, so I'll settle for* "Your leaving." *So your life won't be wasted, too.*

"You can't have that."

Her words so closely matched his thoughts, he almost smiled. Cora always came close to knowing what was on his mind, if not managing to guess exactly. Any smile died a swift death at the idea of her knowing. . . "Yes, I can!" Braden shouted the words, head turned so he wouldn't see her. "I say you don't belong here. Get out."

"No." She set the tray—which he'd forgotten until then despite the smells still lingering in the room—on some table or other. The thud told him before her footsteps rounded the bed.

"Yes." His hands fisted beneath the sheet, twisting in what he already knew to be a vain attempt to break the bonds holding him. Before Lacey left, he'd have her hire another doctor. That way, something good would come from this mockery of a visit.

"I won't go anywhere until you look me in the eye. You haven't done it once, Braden. Not yesterday afternoon, not now." Her words rushed out in a flood. "You left to come here, and I agreed to it although I missed you. I believed you dead and grieved terribly. When I heard of your survival, I rushed to your side, and by all that I have in me *I will not leave* until you look at me and I believe you don't want me anymore."

Consigning himself to the monster he'd fought since the mine's collapse, Braden opened his eyes. Then opened his mouth. . .

TWELVE

A nd then"—Cora gulped in a great big breath, gathering strength for another round of sobs—"he looked me straight in my eyes and ordered me to leave. To make it clear, he said out of his room, out of the building, and out of Hope Falls. He just stopped short of demanding I leave Colorado entirely!"

"Oh no." Lacey patted her shoulder. "I'll talk to him."

"No." Evie caught Lacey's eye and shook her head. "The three of you go on ahead back to the house. I'll have the doctor walk me back. . .after I have a word with your brother."

Lacey considered for a moment—probably torn between wanting to shake sense into her brother on her own and wanting to protect him from Evie's wrath—before giving a short nod. Not one of them argued as she and Naomi steered a tearful Cora toward the dusty house they'd yet to fully explore.

Evie watched their progress, all too aware of the men currently rushing back and forth between the café and mercantile, hauling supplies.

Breakfast went well—partly because they hadn't joined the men for the meal and partly because last night's rules remained fresh in everyone's memory. Today marked the first time their workforce would earn their keep.

Evie only hoped they were worth the staggering order for eggs, meat, vegetables, and cooking supplies she'd placed with Mr. Draxley. The nervous man balked when she requested dairy cows, but she'd prevailed in the end.

They simply couldn't purchase ready-made butter, cream, buttermilk, and bottled milk to be transported daily on the train, and Evie needed the milk and cream for cooking and baking. Besides, they had plenty of sheds that could be emptied to house some livestock. It would prove a sound investment.

As would the "conversation" she intended to have with Braden Lyman. Evie's eyes narrowed as she watched the other three women disappear into the house—too far away to interfere. She didn't bother to hide her ire as she practically stomped into his room. He'd made Cora cry; now he'd face the consequences.

"I said, 'Go away.'" Braden's words lashed out but missed their target. He didn't open his eyes to see who arrived, only lay beneath the covers, gritting his teeth even after he spoke. The muscles in his jaw worked hard enough to show even beneath the unfamiliar beard now covering the lower half of his face.

"What kind of man can't look a woman in the face when he tells her to leave?" Evie shooed away the doctor, who'd cracked open his study door a bit, and waited for him to close it before advancing into Braden's room. This conversation needed no other participants. Just her, Braden, and his missing conscience.

"Evie." His eyes snapped open, his scowl mirroring the fierce rage she held trapped inside. But not for long.

"You remember me, then. Good." She took two long steps to reach the foot of his bed. "Now you can start remembering yourself, your manners, your promises, your responsibilities—"

"What of your responsibilities, Evelyn Thompson?" His roar cut her off mid-recitation. Well, not quite. She'd hardly *begun*, which made his interruption both rude and poorly timed.

"I'm taking care of them." *Don't ask me how.* Evie knew Lacey hadn't discussed the sawmill scheme with her brother yet.

"You're supposed to look after Cora!" The words exploded from him with enough force to send Evie back a step. "What were you thinking, dragging her to this forsaken place with no one to protect her? I trusted you to keep her safe!"

Oh, Lord. . .he's right. We've bitten off far more than we can chew. Worst of all, now Braden tells Cora he doesn't love her. I can't raise a fallen soufflé, and I can't mend a broken heart, Jesus. . . . Please help.

Fury faded into apprehension—the far more unsettling emotion. Anger had a way of bracing one, powering a person through a storm of troubles with righteous zeal. Unease crept more quietly, filling small spaces between solid plans with doubt and worry.

I've ignored too many possibilities—that Braden might truly not want Cora as a fiancée, that men might respond in person, even Draxley's incompetence. We can't afford not to consider such things or overlook the obvious signals.

Still, some things held true no matter the circumstance. "No." Evie drew a deep breath. "We relied on each other to look after Cora. You trusted me to bring her to you safe and sound; I trusted you to keep her that way once we arrived. I kept my part of the deal, Braden Lyman, and you know it. You know it the same way you know you've broken both your unspoken promise to me and your spoken words to my sister. Your fiancée."

"Not my fiancée!" His head thrashed side to side in vehement denial. "Not mine anymore. You have to take Cora home, Evie."

And suddenly she knew. Evie looked at Braden Lyman's face, eyes wild with a sort of desperation she'd never seen, and felt it as sure as she'd ever known anything. Plain and simple—"You still love her." Her words made him freeze, almost as though the very act of drawing a breath would confirm them.

"I don't want her." When he finally spoke, Evie watched closely, carefully. . .and noticed what she'd overlooked before.

God, grant him the strength to lean on You in his suffering. I can't imagine what it's like to be so trapped. And I have to confront him with the truth, for Cora's sake.

"Here. You don't want her"—Evie took one step with each word, stopping just beside him, where his head rested on the pillow, watching her finish the sentence properly—"here."

His breath hissed in as though she'd hit him. "No."

"Yes." Evie made a broad gesture to include the expanse of the bed. "And this is the reason. I didn't notice at first, but now that it occurs to me, I can't believe I missed it. I'm so sorry, Braden. I can't imagine what it's like to be paralyzed, but Cora will learn of it whether you send her away or not."

"I'm not paralyzed."

He'd been silent so long and muttered the words so low, Evie almost asked him to repeat them. Then decided that would be foolish. "You used to use your arms and hands when you spoke, Braden. Now, no movement at all."

"Straps."

"I beg your pardon?" Evie refused to blush, but the direction of the conversation headed toward the indiscreet.

"With both legs broken, the doctor decided casts weren't enough, so he strapped them down." Braden's words came out curt, as if forced from his chest. He wouldn't meet her gaze. "I dislocated my shoulder, though that went back in place well."

"But. . ." No matter she regretted beginning this conversation, Evie couldn't let the matter drop. "Your arms as well?"

The doctor appeared in the doorway. "So he won't fall while he sleeps and do further damage. There's some concern over the position of his spine. The arm bands are a necessary measure, as otherwise Mr. Lyman always removes the lower constraints."

"He's not a child." Evie rounded on the man. "After being trapped in a cave-in, the last thing anyone needs is to feel trapped by anything else! It's simple common sense."

"Initially we tried rails around the bed, but that was the reason he gave for tearing them off," the doctor spluttered.

"I won't live in a lidless coffin." Braden all but snarled at the man, winning Evie's admiration. *She* would have snarled.

"Surely now his shoulder's healed sufficiently to remove any..." Evie searched for a delicate way to phrase the request and came up with a serviceable "*Upper* restraints, at least?"

"Mr. Lyman has proven he will undo the others, once able. I can't jeopardize the welfare of my patient to suit his whims."

"With all the *visitors* Mr. Lyman can *expect* now"—Evie emphasized the words so he'd know good and well she included Cora in those visitors—"I'm sure he'll find the strength to leave well enough alone in exchange for the use of his arms."

They locked gazes in a silent battle for what seemed like hours, but most likely lasted mere seconds.

Finally, Braden gave a short nod—tacit agreement to leave the lower restraints alone. Evie bore no illusions he'd agreed to their continued presence in Hope Falls, nor did she envy Lacey. His sister was welcome to the task of explaining the grand plan they'd already put in motion—without Braden's permission.

"Cora need never know," was the only promise she made as she left. Evie knew Braden would continue to act beastly in an attempt to run Cora out of town...for her own good. She also knew her own stubborn sister better than to believe he'd succeed. Either way, now that she knew Braden still loved her sister, she'd leave what lay between them just that way. Between them.

If I convince Cora to go home, she'll always pine for the Braden she lost and wonder if she could have nursed him back. If I drag her to Charleston, she'll hate me and run back to Hope Falls the moment my back is turned. Either way, I'd be going back on my promise to Lacey and Naomi, who are relying on me.

The weight of it all pressed into a lump at the back of her throat. *Braden Lyman isn't the only one trapped in Hope Falls.*

Jake caught her coming out of the doctor's office—which took a fair bit of planning, absolute use of the authority he'd stepped into the night before, and above all, a good sense of timing.

He'd kept an eye on all four of the women the entire morning, but especially Miss Thompson. The sassy chef flaunted an independent streak that showed why she shouldn't be left alone.

After a breakfast of sweet buns and bacon to leave any man too contented and agreeable for his own good, the women began making requests. Jake admired their strategy. He even admired the requests. Adding a large storeroom onto the café seemed the order of the day—requiring the men to knock out a door in the only wall not already graced by one to the dining room or outdoors or taken up by the stoves. It also meant utilizing supplies from the mercantile and making the men work together in town, where the women could see if anyone wandered off or caused trouble.

From where Jake stood, it looked like a brilliant piece of planning. Not only did it ensure the women could keep the town stocked and the men fed; it made sure they knew it. A man liked knowing his stomach rated as a high priority.

But as soon as they'd cleaned up after breakfast, the women headed to the doctor's office. Where three waited outside. Only the younger Miss Thompson—the engaged one—went in with a tray of breakfast.

Jake measured off the dimensions of the storeroom, outside. He kept tabs on the situation with the ladies, letting the Gent measure and direct the cutting of the doorway, while Bear directed men in the mercantile, digging out tools, nails, lumber, rope, and other sundries. Clump kept busy emptying the kitchen of anything that might get in the way.

Which meant Jake—and maybe a few of the more shrewd suitors—was the only one to see the fiancée fly out of the doctor's to cry all over the other women in a fine show of feminine hysterics. He got the others working on minor details when he caught some showing too much interest in the spectacle a few buildings over. Jake didn't want them noticing only three women walked back to the house they shared. One stayed behind.

Alone.

Foolish, headstrong woman. Jake bit his tongue and mentally reeled in more colorful concerns for what could happen if one of the rougher fellows caught Miss Thompson wandering on her own. Anyone with the ability to add one to one and come up with two could see the younger sister's distress ruffled the mother hen's feathers. She'd marched right in to cluck at the offender, and she'd find herself in a stew if no one looked after her.

Jake proposed a door on the outer wall of the storeroom, facing the train station, for easier transport. A blithe announcement that he'd get the women's agreement and make sure nothing else needed to be cleared from the path gave him the pretext to hover close to the doctor's office. He managed to walk around the corner just in time to surprise Miss Evelyn Thompson as she exited the doctor's. Alone again, with not even the sense to have the doctor escort her to the house where she'd join the other women.

"Miss Thompson." He offered her his arm before she could recover from the way his sudden appearance startled her. As he expected, she automatically accepted it, slipping her hand into the crook of his elbow almost before registering the action. "Allow me to escort you to the house? I'd hoped for a word."

"Presumptuous?" She muttered the riposte on a breath so low Jake knew she didn't intend for him to hear her.

Laughter shook him as he contained his mirth to paltry chuckles. If he let loose, the other men would head over. "Not the word I had in mind, Miss Thompson." Jake grinned anew over her blush when she realized she'd been caught.

"I should not have said that," she admitted, a rueful smile tilting her lips. For once, her dimple didn't peek out.

"But you don't apologize for thinking it." Jake waited for her to deny it or tack on a hasty addition to her apology.

"Absolutely not. My thoughts are my own, and I won't apologize for their existence." Her dimple sprang into view as she flouted his expectations. "I only regret their escape."

"You surprise me, Miss Thompson." Already shortening his stride to match hers, Jake slowed his pace still more.

"In what way, Mr. Creed?" Her use of the name struck him. After her refreshing honesty, it rang more false than before.

"Few show such candor." Jake debated his next move, reluctant to prove her right, then added, "Or such foolishness."

"Your very comment proves I'm not foolish at all to call you presumptuous." Her hand, which had nestled so agreeably in the crook of his arm, became stiff and somehow hostile. "Merely observant. While I'm grateful, to an extent, for your efforts on our behalf, you take too much upon yourself, Mr. Creed."

"Miss Lyman told us last night the four of you hadn't planned on dealing with prospective grooms showing up in person. The four of you as good as said you can't handle the situation." Jake kept his tone even. "The men took things too far, and it would have gotten worse if someone hadn't stepped in."

"Presumptuous! We didn't say we couldn't handle it!" She gave a little huff. "Nor did we ask you to interfere, as I mentioned before. Reminding the others to behave as gentlemen is something we all appreciate. Taking it upon yourself to create rules for our town is most certainly not!"

"Yep." His agreement threw her off balance for a scant second before he added his final assessment, "Foolish, all right."

She started seething again, her fingers curling into his sleeve like a harmless creature trying to develop claws. Which, in Jake's estimation, didn't land too far from the truth.

"Words don't hold up without action behind them. Same with rules, Miss Thompson. They can't make a difference if no one enforces them. What does it matter who makes the rules, if they're good ones and will be enforced for your safety and the good of the town? I'm going to be blunt here." He stopped, pivoting to face her and tightening his arm against his side so she'd stay put and hear him out. "You four can spout laws until you're blue in the face, but if all you have is cooking to keep a crowd in line, you'll run into trouble sooner or later. Men want things other than food, and out here, there's places with five men to every woman. Why do you think they're all here?"

He paused to let that sink in, to let it register that she stood, alone, with a man she didn't know. "Placing that ad and coming here was foolish. Not admitting you need help now you're all here is foolish. And yes, Miss Thompson, I'm presumptuous enough to warn you about it." *So you can stop the foolishness.*

"It seems, Mr. Creed, that we've reached an impasse." Evie drew herself up to her full, if unimpressive, height. "You want me to stop making my own decisions; I want you to start apologizing."

Never mind the fact I'm very much afraid your assessment is dead to rights. She couldn't really tell if it was guilt over not agreeing with his good sense about the ad and their position or worry over the safety of her friends, but a sharp pain jabbed her side, a sort of stitch beneath her ribs.

"You misunderstood, Miss Thompson. It's not that I want you to stop making decisions." He started walking again, covering the last few steps to the house before leaving her with his final, parting shot. "I want you to start making better ones."

THIRTEEN

T here's nothing worse than letting a man get the last word," Cora fumed, prying open another packing crate as the four women stood in the midst of the parlor. "Nothing at all."

"I couldn't agree more." Evie nudged a traveling case toward the pile they'd designated for "upstairs." "First, there's the matter they think they've bested you." *Insufferable, arrogant dictator, he is. Handing out orders right and left.*

"And once you know precisely how you want to respond, to put him in his place, it's too late." Naomi scooted a box toward the narrow door leading to the woefully inadequate kitchen, where two large stewpots already simmered away for dinner.

"Couldn't you both simply. . .oh, I don't know"—Lacey's voice came out a bit muffled, what with her head half buried in a steamer trunk clearly belonging in the "upstairs" section—"simply pretend not to have heard the last little bit?" She emerged with a triumphant sound, waving an airy scarf at them. "Or let them know you ignored it, as beneath your attention?"

"No." Evie and Cora answered as one, with emphasis.

"Oh." Lacey blinked. "I, for one, ignore most of what Braden says to me. I find it makes life much more pleasant."

"Well, Mr. Creed isn't the sort of man a woman can ignore," Naomi offered. "There's a certain quality about him. . . ."

"Arrogance." Evie didn't like the look in Naomi's eye. "The quality Mr. Creed possesses is arrogance. Can you imagine the nerve, telling us all we need to be making better decisions?"

"I don't know, sis. He only said something to you." Cora's amusement didn't douse the anger still burning beneath it, fueling her abrupt movements and keeping her from more tears.

Some things, an older sister knew all too well. Mostly because Evie learned, after years of failure, there were some things she couldn't fix. There were times when words offered little comfort, and logic could only make things worse. Time, prayer, and love were the only way to wear away deep hurt.

But laughter smoothed away the ragged edges. *If nothing else, I'll forgive Creed's interference because it gives Cora something to think about, a way to tease, a reason to smile.* Evie fought her own smile at a sudden, ironic realization. *Maybe that's the first of my "better decisions"—to not resent them. Actions over words. . .*

"I'm the first one he found the opportunity to speak with," Evie shot back. "Seems as though he could've made the same comments to any one of us, from where I'm sitting. I took the insult personally, but I'm also offended on your behalves!"

"My behalf feels wholly fine." Cora thumped a box onto the ground as though to squash her own terrible pun as they groaned.

"Oh, that wins as worst of the trip." Naomi shook her head. "For what it's worth, although I dislike Mr. Creed's high-handed manner, I'll admit to a nagging sense there's some truth behind his observations. We can't handle this on our own, ladies."

"That's why we advertised for husbands!" Lacey stretched the scarf between her hands. "We knew we'd need help with the entire sawmill venture, or it would fail before it began."

"But now we need help with hiring your husbands. I know I'm not really in any more of a position to say anything than your Mr. Creed, Evie, but—" Cora's comment ran into a delay.

"He isn't mine!" Evie protested immediately. "Don't try to pawn him off on me, as though I should be the one to deal with the one man so headstrong he tries to take over an entire town the very night he arrives! I don't claim Mr. Creed."

"Not yet," Naomi teased. "But you have to admit, he knows how to surprise you. I knew the moment he pointed to your sign and swept the hat from his head that we were looking at the stranger who'd made such an impression on you in Charleston."

"That's another thing!" Evie tried to push a crate of books into the corner and failed. It was one of many—not one of them had been willing to part with a single work of literature. "How on earth did he show up here? No one knew of our plans!" *Not that he would have followed me, in any case.* She'd considered the glorious, far-fetched notion and discarded it the moment she'd seen him the night before. A man like that could take his pick of women. *And he wouldn't pick a foolish one.*

"You won't claim Mr. Creed." Lacey helped her wrestle the books out of the doorway, where they'd hitched on an uneven floorboard. "Perhaps he's come all the way here to claim you."

Evie's heart thumped in her chest, a result of moving too many heavy boxes, to be sure. *Only ninnies go giddy at the idea of opinionated men striding into town to sweep them off their feet.* Unfortunately, the stern reprimand did nothing to quell her inner ninny, who chose now to make her presence felt.

"Like Evie said, he wouldn't know who placed the ad, which puts paid to the notion he followed her to Hope Falls. Honestly, so many men trickled through her café it would be a wonder if she never ran into any." Cora walked over, frowning.

"Even if he didn't know Evie placed the ad," Lacey insisted, "anyone could tell he was pleased to see her here!"

"That's true." Naomi joined them, looking at the stacks of crates holding their assorted volumes with something akin to awe. "I don't remember bringing quite this many books."

"When she had to give up the house after Papa's death, Evie

refused to give up any of his books, even if they crowded our rooms." Cora shrugged. "So there will be more than you brought."

"Naomi refused to leave behind a single volume from Lyman Place," Lacey commiserated. "She packed up every tome from the study to bring out here. Added to your books, and the novels we purchased to read on the journey, we could start a library."

"Precisely!" Naomi's exclamation made them all jump. "Ladies, these crates contain the Hope Falls Library! A bit of knowledge, education, and culture to civilize the wild."

"That's a wonderful idea." Evie caught on to her friend's enthusiasm. "We'll simply choose a building and have the men move the books there. After things settle and we've time, we can go about unpacking and organizing the library."

"Good—at least that's one section of crates that won't be underfoot!" Lacey peered around. "We've boxes and luggage all through the parlor and study down here, creeping into the kitchen, and nothing but our carpetbags in the bedrooms. Have you three sorted out what you'll need in your rooms, and what you'll put in the third as storage until. . .needed?"

Even Lacey, the originator of the entire Hope Falls scheme, faltered at putting the end result into words. She and Naomi would share one bedroom, Evie and Cora the other one that was outfitted with a bed. The third, they'd designated as storage for all the household goods they'd brought to set up their homes—once they each chose a husband and married him.

"Now that we're here, and the men are already here, it's going to be much faster than we planned." Naomi's voice lacked the enthusiasm from when she talked about the library.

Which just goes to show there's something very wrong—or very foolish—about all of this. Evie sighed. *We can make the best decisions possible from here on out—not because Mr. Creed wants us to, but because it's what's best, and the Lord bids us to seek out wisdom.* She sighed again. *No matter the source.*

"Plans change. So do people." Cora snatched a hatbox from

one pile and shifted it to another. "We can adjust accordingly."

"We agreed no one would rush into any wedding," Lacey reminded her cousin, "and that much stays the same. If he's the right man, he'll wait until you're certain of it, too."

"I think we should wait until we've all chosen our grooms and then share one big wedding." Evie seized the opportunity to propose the idea. "With so many men here, it's not safe for us to leave this house one by one, and it sends the message we aren't going to be in a hurry." *By then, hopefully, Cora will have gotten through to Braden, and they'll join us!*

"I like that idea!" Naomi's agreement came a breath before Lacey's but several beats before Cora's slow nod. "But I'd like to add something on to it—we should have the approval of at least two of the others in whomever we choose."

"Absolutely." Cora supported the suggestion almost before Naomi finished giving it. "That's the best decision yet."

"We haven't made it a decision!" Lacey's brows came together. "While your opinions matter to me, I didn't escape the strictures of society and travel all the way out here to require anyone else's *approval* or *permission* regarding my choices."

"But that's exactly what you've done, Lace. Your husband will have more of that sort of power than society ever did. Since we know you better than any of these men possibly could in a couple months and have only your best interests at heart, why not see it as a precaution against choosing some sort of tyrant?" After five years as her companion, Naomi knew how to best soothe Lacey's nerves and coax her into listening.

"What if only one of you will agree to the man I choose?" Lacey saw them exchange amused glances. "It's best to prepare for such contingencies! Look what happens when we don't think ahead." She peered out the window, where she could see their workers already fashioning walls for the storeroom.

"Don't borrow more trouble than we've already found, Lace. If he's the right one, you'll fight to keep him until you win."

Everyone knew Cora didn't just refer to Lacey's future love. "If he's the wrong one, we won't regret it when he catches a train."

"So long," Evie grumbled as she caught sight of a familiar lean figure heading toward a cluster of three men she couldn't make out, "as you don't let him have the last word!"

"Then there's nothing more to say." Jake uncrossed his arms—the better to reach his pistol, should the need arise. "I'm sure you three can catch the train before it pulls out if you hurry." He judged it worth the odds to send them out of Hope Falls. Only one of the men before him fit the description of Twyler, and that just happened to be the one who talked too much.

"I've plenty more to say." Williams proved him right. Shorter than his companions, with thinning brown hair and a bristling demeanor, he had the look of a man used to giving orders. His speech marked him as intelligent and possibly educated, but despite that and the coloring, Williams didn't match up with the depiction of a nondescript man who faded into the background and vanished into the night. If this was Twyler, the man mastered disguise to a degree Jake hadn't prepared for.

"We don't need words here." *Unless they're confessions.* Jake scrutinized Williams more closely, trying to discomfit the stranger. When shows of confidence faded, the real man stood for evaluation. "If you won't pitch in like everyone else, the rules are you get back on the train and ride on."

"I want to talk to the ladies who wrote the ad. It was an open invitation, and I don't see how you have any authority to retract it." Williams's confidence might not be a facade, or if it was, he'd built it high and strong. "Where are they?"

"Have you found troubles this fine morning, Mr. Creed?" The brogue sounded pleasant enough, but the newcomers' expressions showed that Rory "Bear" Riordan didn't look very welcoming.

"These three men came in on the train. I offered to show them

to the bunkhouse before they started working, but they refused."
Jake didn't bother to glance behind him. He knew when Bear
reached his side. "At that point, I suggested the train."

"Work or leave—that's the law of the ladies."

"Where are the ladies?" Williams repeated, this time directing
the question to Bear, whose size apparently didn't intimidate the
smaller man enough for him to shut his mouth.

" 'Tis no' your concern." Bear's ham-sized hands folded into
fists. "As you won't be working to win your keep nor their hands,
you won't be needin' to make their acquaintance."

"I work hard when there's something to work for." Williams
took an ill-considered step forward. "But I don't work for nothing.
How do we know this entire scheme isn't a hoax?"

"Do you think over a dozen men would work for nothing?"
Jake kept his tone amused but his hand near his holster. This
Williams character had enough brains to make him suspicious and
enough pride to make him dangerous—a volatile combination.
The sort of man who might hold a grudge or seek revenge.

The irony of that judgment pinched at the sides of his jaw,
where Jake clenched his teeth against finding himself guilty of
the same. Yes, he hunted a man he'd never met, but this was no
petty offense. A thin line divided justice and vengeance, and it
all depended on which side the murder fell. Jake knew where he
stood. Question was, where did Williams?

His assessment cost him the man's response, but Bear's reaction told Jake all he needed to know. Either he'd overestimated
Williams's intelligence or Twyler would go to any length to keep
his identity hidden. Even anger a giant.

Bushy brows slammed together, forming a furious red curtain.
"Just turn those boots an' meet up wi' the train."

By that point, most of the other men noticed the disturbance
and circled around. Speculative murmurs and hostile glares made
no impact on three strangers standing their ground.

"What'd they do to rile Bear?" someone wanted to know.

"We asked where the women are." One of taller men spoke up before Williams, suddenly keen to keep the peace.

"I asked what kind of gargoyles these women are, to have to hide away when men come calling." Williams's challenge both explained Bear's ire and incited the same in several others.

"Don't you talk about our women that way!" someone yelled.

"Now, Bob," another talked over him. "If they're so smart, let them hop back on that there train and ride the rails more."

Kane. Jake dredged the name from his memory. The man lobbying for the loggers to go along with their assumptions so others left town wasn't above manipulating circumstances to rid himself of competition. He also happened to be one of the half dozen men sporting brown hair and brown eyes.

"It's never smart to insult a lady," Gent intervened, his ever-present top hat skewed to the left. "If a man can't think of a kind word, he speaks none." He cast a sweeping, meaningful glance at what Jake began to think of as the "regulars." "No matter how stooped, old, spotted, or hideous the woman in question, a gentleman never remarks upon it."

"Hush, Gent." Dodger caught on quickest. "Such talk would hurt their delicate feelings, and you know it."

"We've seen enough tears this morning," Jake added, beginning to enjoy the new strategy to route the interlopers. "Seems the doctor couldn't improve their situation."

"Situation?" Williams, whose belligerence wavered in the face of rising doubts, asked with something akin to dread.

"Yep, Craig here was joking about the women being gargoyles," one of the others explained, glancing back toward the train. "That was before all this talk. What situation?"

"Deafness," rang Miss Thompson's too-sweet reply, "so that twenty men somehow manage not to hear four women approach them."

Jake's shoulders tensed, but he wouldn't turn his back on Williams, whose gaze turned right-down predatory as he realized the trick they'd played. . .and why.

"Finding yourself surrounded by men determined to frighten off any other would-be grooms could count as a situation." A second feminine voice carried above a cacophony of groans.

"We been caught right an' proper," someone confessed.

"There's nothing proper about what you men just did." He couldn't be sure without looking, but Jake pegged that as Miss Higgins. "You ought to be ashamed of pulling such a stunt."

"They ought to be ashamed for making these men think we're gargoyles!" Indignation dripped from Miss Lyman's exclamation—the same indignation from when she'd defended her poufy sleeves.

"They should be ashamed for making light of those in need of medical care." The quiet outrage had to belong to the younger Miss Thompson, who'd been distressed after visiting a patient in the doctor's care. Her tears gave way to dignity now, at least.

"But most of all"—the cook's voice gathered strength for the final feminine invective—"they should be ashamed of their own hypocrisy!"

FOURTEEN

Bull's-eye. Evie bit back a triumphant grin when Creed's shoulders, already tense, went completely rigid. *Good to see he knows that was aimed at him, judging other people's decisions. Humph. At least he can't argue with my evaluation of him in return! A more presumptuous man never drew breath before me.*

But he still didn't face her. He and Mr. Riordan kept their backs turned while every other man in Hope Falls—minus Mr. Draxley, whom they'd left placing orders with someone on the train, and, of course, occupants of the doctor's or post offices—changed positions the moment she spoke. That they did, indeed, feel shame didn't seem enough of a reason to explain their odd behavior. Evie pondered it as she made a path through the other men, her sister and friends following.

She reached the new arrivals with an apologetic smile, as any woman would. Or at least, she came close to reaching them. Evie found her way blocked by none other than the maddening Mr. Creed, who somehow collaborated with Mr. Riordan to make things difficult. The two guardians didn't block her entirely, merely angled their bodies so the group had to form a large circle—the new men on one side, the women on the other, with the guardians slightly inward so they didn't form simple rows.

They're being protective. The realization drained away some of her indignation. *Only Creed and Riordan refused to turn their backs on the unknown. While every other man sought to placate us, they made sure we stayed safe.*

Gratitude on behalf of her sister, Lacey, and Naomi won out over the obvious logical conclusion that strangers wouldn't get to them before the others intervened.

Because now, if these two men hadn't interposed themselves, Evie and her friends would stand toe-to-toe with the newcomers, with the men who'd already accepted their terms too far behind to step in. She'd fully planned to storm up here, have the women introduce themselves, and establish the town rules fully under their own power. *Pride makes poor decisions. . . .*

"We are the women of the ad," she began, sliding a glance at the others and raising her right hand to rub her forehead. They'd established a few signals last night before turning in—a glance before rubbing one's forehead meant "wait and listen," to be used in case someone planned something unexpected.

"In usual circumstance, we'd introduce ourselves and welcome you to Hope Falls," she continued only after seeing faint nods of understanding. "But these circumstances are most unusual, and so we'll be doing things a bit differently."

"I'm Craig Williams." The man she pegged as the leader of the three stepped forward in what she instinctively recognized as a territorial move. When he came forward, Mr. Williams all but closed his men from the circle, upsetting the balance.

He wants to see if Mr. Creed and Mr. Riordan will step back, giving up ground to let his men in. It's a test!

Women played the same sort of game with seating arrangements. For the first time, Evie wondered what other subtle rules dictated interactions among men—and if all of them were so complex and nuanced as polite feminine rituals.

"Step back, Williams," Creed growled, reclaiming his territory and ending Evie's nonsensical notions. Men were blunt.

"What if I don't?" The shorter, more muscular man didn't seem concerned. "Seems I traveled here to be near the ladies."

"If you don't, the pleasantries end here." Evie made a show of turning toward her cohorts. "We'll return to the house and let these gentlemen return you to the train, where you'll be more comfortable until you find a town more to your liking."

Cheers sounded behind them, reminding Evie of the more than a dozen ornery men who hung on every word. She'd all but finished the job of running the newcomers out of town for them.

A great, bellowing laugh sounded over the cheers as Mr. Williams threw back his head in a show of mirth Evie suspected was more show than mirth. But respect shone in his eyes when he looked at her and took a step back—a smaller one than he'd taken forward but a concession nevertheless. "Very well, ma'am."

"What made you change your mind, Mr. Williams?" Naomi's voice, usually throaty and full, sharpened with suspicion.

"Things might not be usual here in Hope Falls," he explained, "but at least they're interesting. I don't plan on leaving until I learn more about it—and about the beautiful women who rule it." Somehow he managed to include all four of them in an admiring glance while his men nodded their agreement.

Grumbles and mutters sounded from behind them as the men realized they'd been thwarted—newcomers would be welcome. Evie wondered how many of them realized they'd all forfeited dessert that night—a boon, considering she'd be cooking from the house kitchen, which simply wasn't equipped for mass baking anyway.

"In that case, allow me to introduce"—Evie raised a brow in silent acknowledgment as she named their champions—"Mr. Creed and Mr. Riordan. Should you have any questions, they're the ones to ask. Direct any requests regarding supplies to them, and they'll bring the matter to our attention if need be. They'll also instruct you in town rules. And, should you decide not to follow those rules, they'll escort you from Hope Falls."

"With our assistance," the Gent swiftly seconded, with rousing support from the remaining men. No one wanted to be left out of the opportunity to toss someone else out of town.

A grudging nod from Williams preceded two more congenial ones from the pair behind him, who seemed almost like a set of matched horses. Perhaps they worked as a team? Less pleasant were the measuring looks given Mr. Riordan and Mr. Creed.

She refused to look at Mr. Creed, refused to let him think she'd admitted defeat in accepting his help, refused to seek any support for her decisions from the man who'd belittled them. His opinions on what was best for the other women mattered. His opinion of her did not. *I won't let it.*

"We've set things up as follows." Lacey took over, as she should. The town belonged to all of them, and every man who wandered through needed to esteem them equally. "We'll provide room, board, meals, and the opportunity to further our acquaintance until we've chosen our husbands."

A glower from Mr. Creed silenced a swell of hopeful murmurs about lunch when Lacey mentioned meals, making Evie glad she'd baked ten pans of corn pone that morning while the men ate, then set two massive pots of Brunswick stew to simmer at the house. Better still, she'd had the foresight to lock the pie safe so none of the men might try to steal a snack before dinner.

Once things quieted down, Naomi added the final stroke. "In return, we ask you to help lay the groundwork for the Hope Falls Sawmill Company. Every other man knows these conditions and has agreed to them. The question is. . .will you?"

The pair behind Williams glanced at each other, shrugged, and each gave a single nod, but Williams took longer to make his decision. His gaze ran over everything in town and evaluated the trees beyond before taking stock of the people around him. The men didn't seem to concern him much. The women did.

"Four women standing here, so why do only three of you want

husbands?" It seemed he'd noticed a lack of wedding bands during his scrutiny. "And which woman isn't available?"

"One of us"—Cora lifted her chin as she answered—"already has a fiancé and thus isn't looking for a husband. Which one of us that happens to be shouldn't make a difference to you."

"It matters very much, ma'am—you'll forgive me for not using proper address, as we've yet to be introduced. No man wants to set about courting a woman when she's taken." Craig Williams shook his head. "And some men know right away which women they're willing to court and which they won't be." His eyes ran down the line of them once again. "I'm one of those kinds of men who knows his own mind and doesn't change it."

Incredible! He's saying that if the woman he most likes the looks of isn't available, he's not interested in any of the other three. Evie stewed, refusing to name Cora. *Doesn't he realize it's not for him to waltz in and choose but for us to wade through and select which man we'll accept? He doesn't deserve Naomi or Lacey!*

"In that case, it's best you move along." Clump stomped forward, his irate appearance causing her to wonder where he'd been before. "Mr. Draxley's still talking with the conductor, so the train's still here. I know 'cause I went to see about getting you some milk, Miss Thompson. I remembered what you said last night about making shortbread instead of somethin' else on account of having no milk. Hoped they might be carrying some, but they didn't have any on board today. Sorry 'bout that."

"Thank you for your thoughtfulness, Mr. Klumpf." Evie favored him with a smile, hoping to ease his disappointment. "And for mentioning Mr. Williams has time to catch the train."

"Oh no." A wolfish smile gleamed her way. "See, *Miss Thompson*, Mr. Klumpf over there wouldn't be trying to bring you any gifts if you already had a fiancé."

"Miss Thompson does have a fiancé!" Dodger—Evie could already tell it was Dodger—shouted that bit of information. No one added a single word of clarification either.

Evie couldn't stop a smile over his clever phrasing—a smile that made Mr. Williams's brow furrow as he began to rethink.

"My brother proposed before we journeyed out here." Lacey jumped in, making it obvious that, for all her words about independence, her friend wasn't above meddling. "Braden Lyman? He's the principal investor in the mill, you see."

"I see. Your brother, Miss Thompson's fiancé, and. . ." Williams turned a questioning eye to Naomi, then Cora.

"Miss Higgins, cousin to the Lymans." She offered no other explanation or attempt at conversation. Then again, Naomi didn't approve of falsehoods in any form. Leaving out the relationship between Evie and Cora in an attempt to fool a man into thinking the wrong sister was engaged counted as one. Somehow. . .

"And you're related to all this in what way?" Now less than amused, Mr. Williams's tone took on a demanding tinge as he spoke to Cora. He suspected something, and Evie almost respected him for possessing enough intelligence to discern that much.

"I'm Miss Thompson's sister." Cora's eyes narrowed.

"Yes, that makes all of us related in some way," Evie agreed. "But that's as it should be. Family supports each other and stays together. No matter where it leads."

Her words struck him with the force of a falling redwood. Jake closed his eyes to lash down the memories jarred loose, but one tumbled free in spite of his efforts:

"Why don't you come with me this time?" Edward invited, flipping his favorite good-luck talisman in the air. "It's a good-sized profit we stand to make if this contract goes through, but the company owner's skittish. Someone double-crossed him on the last deal, so he'll need persuading."

"You're the persuasive one," Jake joked. Eyes on the copper piece as it spun upward, he waited to snatch it out of the air just before it

hit Edward's waiting palm. *"That's why you stick with the business contacts, and I handle operations."*

"So why is it you're the one who's made a fortune of his own in side investments?" Ed watched as Jake removed the matching piece from his own pocket and began juggling the two small squares until they blurred into a single streak. He reached forward, but not to make a grab and see which one he wound up catching, as they'd done since their school days. No, this time Ed jostled one of Jake's hand's, neatly seizing both pieces and examining them before tossing one back.

"You cheated!" Jake plucked it from the air and checked the side not embossed with a crown and fleur-de-lis. Sure enough, nothing but a surface worn smooth from centuries of use stared up at him. "You never cheat. Hand over the lucky one as forfeit."

"Sometimes you try a new trick to get what you want." Edward shrugged and tucked the lucky coin weight, its blank side marred by the gash of an axe blade, into his pocket. "You won't come with me, and I've got a feeling I'll need all the luck I can get on this trip. Besides"— his brother grinned—"we're family. You can win it back the next time you see me."

"All right, but you won't keep it for long. Good-bye. . ." Jake couldn't resist throwing one last jab at the older brother whose virtues so far outweighed his vices. "Cheater!"

The last thing he'd said to his brother, if only in jest. And now, thanks to Twyler, the way Edward would be remembered if Jake didn't find justice for him. Only one part of Jake's taunt that day had been true—Edward didn't keep the piece long. The scarred metal square, passed to the firstborn Granger through generations, hadn't been found among his possessions.

And now, here stood Miss Thompson, reminding him that family stayed together. *I didn't go when Edward asked. I waited too long with Mother and Father, making pointless inquiries while the trail went cold after his death.* "No matter where it leads," she says, and she has no idea how right she is.

Craig Williams's eyes slitted as he looked from one woman to the next—too clever to be allowed near them and too much of a suspect for Jake to let out of sight.

Family. . . Miss Thompson said it herself. There wasn't really a choice to be made. Jake could have kicked himself for how close he'd come to putting Williams on that train—and betraying Edward in doing it.

"So there are not one but *two* Miss Thompsons." The man read people well and thought too fast on his feet to be trusted.

"Yep." Jake slid a glance at Evelyn, who stiffened.

"And only one of them's spoken for," the intruder prodded.

"We've already explained that, Mr. Williams." Evelyn—Jake thought it suited her better than "Miss Thompson," which belonged to her younger sister—made a dismissive gesture. "At this point, you've managed to insult three of us and are still speaking in circles. Don't you think it's time to move on?"

Jake knew why a lot of the regulars began clapping. Her ability to avoid an outright lie and still address the pertinent issue deserved applause. More to the point, he itched to set Craig Williams on that train, where he couldn't so much as look at any of the women. But Jake couldn't let that happen.

"Yes, I do. I think it's time to move to the point of all this, Miss Thompson." Brown eyes gleamed with anticipation. "I notice everyone here's very careful not to mention which Miss Thompson happens to be engaged, but they're mighty eager to see the back of me. I'm thinking it's your sister who's taken."

Jake could see the battle between her conscience and her will as she stood there, silent. Defiance flashed in her amber eyes, consternation showed in the way she nibbled her full lower lip, and pride kept her chin up as she made her decision.

"But you won't lie. I like that." Williams leaned forward—too smart to take a step but too brash to do nothing. He stayed put even when Jake shifted farther into his path. "And I like a strong woman who needs an even stronger man. You're worth accepting the terms. I'm staying."

"No, you aren't." Braden rubbed a hand over his eyes and stifled a groan. "You can't stay because I won't allow you to."

"Well, at least you've moved on from the asinine nonsense about not *wanting* me to stay." Cora leaned over to balance the tray across his lap then removed the plate she'd set atop the soup bowl—most likely so nothing spilled while she carried it.

If I had even one good leg, I'd kick myself. Braden groaned. *No matter how long I live, I'll never understand women.*

"I won't allow you to stay because I don't want you here. They're connected, but if one won't oust you, the other will." *So help me, heaven. Because, to be honest, Lord, I think I'll need all the help I can get if I'm going to convince Cora to leave me behind and move on. It's even harder than I thought.*

"No, it won't." She cheerfully—*cheerfully*—dug a spoon from her apron pocket and handed it to him. "Because you do want me. You just don't want to admit it because you're too stubborn."

That hit close enough to make Braden bend the spoon handle. *Not quite, but what can I say? "Actually, Cora, I don't want you here because I want you here too much?"* He snorted. Loudly.

"For pity's sake, if you want a hankie, just ask for one." She pulled one from another pocket and pushed it toward his other hand. Then the daft woman picked up what looked to be corn bread, split it in half, and began slathering it with butter.

When Cora drizzled honey on top, he reached for it. "Hey!" His jaw dropped when she smacked his hand.

"Fix your own." She nodded to the three other pieces sitting on the tray before sinking her teeth into hers. "You don't want me here, you should pretend I'm not. In fact"—she gave the tray a considering glance—"you shouldn't eat that at all. Evie made it and I carried it in, so it should be part of your protest. If you don't want us, you don't want our food."

"Lunch can stay." Braden held the sides of the tray in a death grip, silently daring her to try to wrestle it from his hands. "You can't. And this is *my* tray."

"Very well." Cora set down her piece of corn bread, stood up, and dusted her hands in a show of supreme unconcern that didn't fool him enough to relax his grip one bit. "Keep your tray, Braden Lyman." In a flash, she grabbed the soup bowl and plate of corn bread and flounced toward the door. "Enjoy it!"

FIFTEEN

I changed my mind." Lacey saw Cora come stomping out, sloshing stew from one hand and trailing corn pone from the other, and made an instant decision. "Telling Braden isn't something I should do alone. Truly, it isn't." *Especially when he hasn't been softened up by a good meal first, like we planned.*

"We're running out of time, Lace." Naomi waved her hands to encompass the entire town. "Look at this place—men everywhere! The doctor may be prudent enough not to say anything to Braden for now, not wanting to overset him until we explain, but he's bound to notice all this activity and begin asking questions."

"I know. Twenty men do make an awful racket." Lacey felt surrounded by noise and eyes. Men in the house moving boxes, men in the diner knocking doors into walls, men outside the diner building on rooms, and men in what used to be a saloon, of all things, carting in crates of books for the library. "We're dreadfully outnumbered, though it pains me to say such a thing."

"Five men to every woman," Evie mused. "That's what Mr. Creed mentioned to me as part of the reason we've so many responses. With the three arrivals today, and if you count Mr. Draxley and Braden, that's twenty men to the four of us."

"Don't count Draxley and Braden," Cora directed. "Draxley isn't courting anyone, and Braden's already taken. So am I." Her eyes widened. "That leaves eighteen men to three of you."

"Six men to each woman." A giggle crept from Naomi before she stifled it and gave a penitent shrug. "I'm sorry, girls. I just never thought an old spinster like me would see such odds!"

"You're twenty-seven, Naomi." Lacey dropped into the familiar scold with ease. "Hardly ancient. Besides, you know you look far younger than your years. Don't ever call yourself a spinster."

"None of us will be spinsters, and any man would be blessed to have either of you. Now, Cora"—Evie changed the subject—"may I ask why you brought back Braden's lunch? With no tray?"

"He spouted some hogwash about not allowing me to remain, then got testy when I pointed out at least he wasn't pretending he didn't *want* me here." Cora rolled her eyes. "So I told him if he didn't want us, he didn't want our food. Braden said I couldn't take his tray and held on to it like a drowning man."

"So you took the dishes." Lacey began to giggle at the image of Braden clutching a suddenly-empty tray as Cora left.

"Of course she did." Evie patted her sister's shoulder, the show of closeness sending a pang of regret through Lacey.

Braden was a good brother, usually, but still a brother. *Worse, my only sibling acts like an utter heel from the moment we arrive in Hope Falls. Braden may be a man, but that's no excuse for his boorish behavior.*

Lacey remembered comments about poufy sleeves and Mr. Williams's bluntness over how he only cared to court Evie. *Well, it's a very poor excuse at least.*

Besides, Braden hadn't always been such a cad. Back in Charleston, they'd gotten on quite well in most circumstances. He'd treated Cora as a priceless treasure, an amusing and charming way of showing his affection. It would have driven Lacey mad to be treated as a delicate china shepherdess. Indeed, many suitors made that mistake back home, forcing her to refuse them. A pretty face didn't erase a healthy curiosity after all.

But it did tend to put a woman in danger, her brother often pointed out—the very reason he'd insisted she, Cora, and the others wait until he'd established Hope Falls more fully. Braden wanted the town to be not only prosperous but far more civilized before they arrived to take their rightful places.

Which was why he'd been so put out when they showed up. Now, more than ever, Hope Falls lacked any sort of order or civilization. *And he doesn't even know the half of it.*

"He's not going to handle this well," Lacey warned in what just might be the greatest understatement of the century.

"He doesn't get a choice." Cora's lips compressed into a thin, determined line. "Braden can't give orders all his life."

"We'll all go in." Naomi clasped Lacey's hand in hers. "Together."

Alone, Braden stared at the empty tray he grasped. It still held a small pot of honey, a butter crock, and the spoon he'd set down to stake his claim on the tray. So really it wasn't empty. It just didn't have anything worth keeping anymore.

Useless. His hands were clenched so tight his knuckles went pale. *Like a man who can't walk or provide for his own bride.* He had more in common with that almost-empty tray than Braden ever would have believed possible.

"We both need Cora back to make us complete again," a treacherous voice whispered.

"No!" He shouted the denial as his tray slammed into the wall, shattered crockery sticking to globs of honey as everything else clattered to the floor. *I don't need her.*

"What on earth is going on?" Lacey plowed through the door, drawing up short as she caught sight of the mess to her left. Cora, Naomi, and Evie raced in right behind her, until all four clustered around his bed wearing expressions of shock and anger.

"I take it back. It's not that I just don't want any of you here."

He directed his gaze at Cora, refusing to wince when her eyes widened in hope. Braden wouldn't change course now, not when gentler means failed. "I don't want your food either!"

"Oh, you. . .you. . .insufferable. . ." She started spluttering at him, searching for words vile enough to describe him. "Lout!"

"I'm much worse than that, sweetheart." He tucked his hands behind his head and forced a sneer. "Want me to sully your ears with a few more colorful descriptions, or will you *leave*?"

"You should slap him, Cora." His own cousin turned on him.

"If you don't, I'd be happy to." Evie's hand twitched, and Braden hoped she'd go ahead and do it. Maybe it would ease some of the guilt he felt and help hasten this entire process.

"We can't hit him. He's injured." As they so frequently did, Cora's eyes showed two different emotions. The left, brilliant blue, blazed with the heat of anger. The right, a more faceted hazel, swam with sorrow, hurt, and resignation just before she reached out and yanked the pillow from under him.

Braden's shoulders and neck jerked back without the familiar support, only the cushion of his hands keeping his head from smacking against the mattress. It didn't matter. The move jostled his still-healing shoulder and jarred him clear down to his legs, sending shooting pains upward. He sucked in a breath and held it until the room blurred—and so did the intensity.

This is why they can't stay. A pillow. A single blasted pillow moves, and I'm down for the count.

As the pain cleared, so did his thoughts. No more worrying about their feelings or even considering them. As far as Braden was concerned, Cora, Lacey, Naomi, and Evie no longer owned emotions. They owned only themselves—and he'd pay whatever price it took to pack them up and ship them home to safety.

"I think that might've been worse than slapping him." Evie's quiet comment reached him now. "Did you know he dislocated his shoulder, too, Cora? We can't jar him like that."

"He deserved it." Again, his fiancée's eyes showed separate

emotions—conviction she'd been right warred with horror at the unexpected severity of her punishment. "But I didn't mean it."

You should mean it! he wanted to yell at her for daring to look overwrought at giving him *less* than he deserved for treating her so terribly. She didn't know it was for her own good. *I'm not worth your tears.*

"One of us means what he says. Get out. All of you. Wire me a telegram when you're back in Charleston, and don't return."

"I mean everything I say." Cora glowered at him afresh.

That's my girl. He bit back his smile. *But not anymore.*

"I didn't mean to cause you so much pain when I moved your pillow. All I wanted was to give your brain enough of a thunk to knock some sense back into it!" She railed at him; the entire time she tenderly tucked his pillow back beneath his head.

"Try that little maneuver on your own selves," he barked. "Let me know when the four of you combined manage to scrape together enough common sense to match what I already possess. You don't belong here, this is no place for women, and you need to pack up what I'm sure is too much stuff and head home!"

The jibe about packing too much hit pay dirt, Braden could tell. Evie bit her lower lip, Lace inspected her nails, Naomi cleared her throat, and Cora harrumphed in the sort of way she did when she couldn't deny something but really wanted to. He'd give them this much—they rallied in a blink.

"We belong here as much as you do, Braden!" His sister made an expansive gesture he took meant Hope Falls. "Each of us owns a part of this town, same as you, and that makes this our home."

"And our livelihood." Evie raised a brow. "Lacey's mercantile, my café, and Naomi's mending shop all represent substantial investments we can't afford to see lost or sold for the ridiculously low current market value, Braden."

"The low market should tell you any business situated here will fail, and you're better off concentrating on the café in Charleston. Lacey and Naomi are well taken care of with Lyman Place and other investments, so you're not choosing wisely."

"You're here." Cora's simple statement cracked the foundation of his defenses. "So we came to be with you."

Me. He pinched the bridge of his nose. *That's the bottom line. They discovered I survived and couldn't be moved, so all four of them packed up their lives and moved out West. For me.*

It humbled him, the strength of their devotion. It also made him want to yell until his voice went hoarse.

"I'll join you as soon as I'm able to travel." He gave the last-ditch, polite concession they absolutely couldn't ignore.

"You won't have to." Lacey's chipper assurance made a muscle in his jaw begin to twitch. "We already came to you."

"But you're leaving," he insisted. "End of story."

"No, we aren't." Now that he'd left behind tray-throwing, shouting, and offering to instruct them in vulgarity, Naomi seemed to have regained her typical regal composure.

"I won't allow you to stay." Braden sucked in a dry breath. "If it comes down to it, I'll have the doctor telegram the authorities, and they will remove you from Hope Falls."

"You can't do that." Lacey looked completely unconcerned, but then, she'd mastered the art of ignoring anything unpleasant long before she'd started putting her hair up for company.

At least the others seemed uncomfortable, shifting about.

"Yes, I can. Half the mine and surrounding land belong to me. Even the properties you call 'yours' are under my name." Braden knew he'd sunk lower than a snake in a ditch, but without his normal abilities, fighting fair wouldn't yield results.

"You wouldn't." His fiancée grasped the corner of the pillow, thought better of it, and released her hold. "No."

"I would." He leaned forward slightly, in case she changed her mind and decided to rob him of his headrest again. "I will."

"Legalities pose the only reason your name holds our properties." Evie spoke as though biting off the words. "Ethically, you know they belong to each of us, and would on paper if single women bore the right to own property."

"Lawmen uphold the law, not murky morals. Names on paper mean more than a pathetic protest. Make it simple and leave under your own steam, or earn yourselves an escort." Braden set his jaw. "Either way, you will leave Hope Falls and not return."

"I don't think so." Naomi eyed him. "You won't do it."

"Try me."

"No need." Lacey's smile could have dripped syrup, so sweet was the look she gave him. "You won't have to waste your time."

The words should have filled him with relief, with even a hint of regret, but suspicion pooled in Braden's gut. He knew that sugary smile. Lacey wore it whenever she planned to spring something so incredibly devious, the victim never suspected the trap until he or she fell headlong into it. *Not good.*

"Don't let that worry you, sis." He gave her the smile she knew promised retribution should she pull anything out of line. "I don't have much else to do with my time."

"Fixing your attitude looks to be a Sisyphean task." Evie folded her arms. "That should more than keep you busy."

Cora gave the little snort that always escaped when she tried not to laugh but couldn't quite manage to keep it inside. His sister and cousin both grinned, though whether at Evie's saucy comment or Cora's reaction to it, Braden couldn't say. It didn't matter. The point was they weren't taking his threat seriously, if the four of them could smile and joke.

"I'm finished with this conversation." An all-too-familiar weariness crept over him. "And I'm having you four removed."

"You can't." This time Lacey reached out and clasped his hand. "I know you would if you could, Braden, but you can't."

"I've already explained—it's my right under the law." He didn't pull his hand away—he knew it would be a long time before he felt a caring touch again. "I can, and I will. So go."

"No, you can't. You were declared dead. Your assets shifted to me, held in trust by the family solicitor." Lacey's grip tightened in response to his own clench as her words sank in.

"Upon news of my survival, Mr. Rountree would have cleared up the matter, Lace." *He had to. The old fool may be wrapped around my sister's little finger, but he dots every* i *and crosses every* t. "It reverts back to me. Don't fool yourself."

"It reverts to you, yes." Her gaze hardened. "But the physical limitations and emotional trauma of your experience have persuaded Mr. Rountree to recognize me as head of the Lyman fortunes. While I used my position to buy the rest of the mine so you do own the entire town, and not just the majority share, you can't act on it. Until your doctor agrees you've made a full recovery, you don't have the right to order anyone from Hope Falls."

SIXTEEN

The string of curses pouring through the open window of the doctor's office stopped Jake in his tracks. If not for the vulgarity of it, he might have admired the sheer variety of colorful phrases as a stranger vented some rage. Jake usually bore a healthy respect for creativity. Not this time.

Oh, he'd worked alongside loggers for too many years for coarse language to shock him any. A man shouting such things in reaction to the sudden pain of a broken arm or the like happened fairly often. Such things, in the midst of a forest, with none but other lumberjacks around to hear, could be accepted.

A man yelling words like that around women absolutely could not. And from the gasps and reprimands flowing between and around the fellow's litany, he'd chosen to indulge his vice around none other than the four women of Hope Falls.

Too bad it didn't sound like Craig Williams. Jake wouldn't mind a chance to haul the cocky fellow off to the train. . .and wrangle the answers to a few key questions out of him. With a man like that, the blunt approach would probably work best. Blunt meant straight questions paired with right hooks.

For now, he needed to find out whose temper needed a trip down an icy flume before it burned any of the ladies. Two steps, a hand braced on the sill, and Jake vaulted through the window.

He landed on his feet, knocking into one of the women. Reaching out to steady her, he ignored the softness beneath layers of clothes and the curtain blocking his view and his hands. When blows began raining about his head and shoulders, Jake moved to free himself from the curtain caught on his belt. "Stop that!" He barked, batting the fabric from his face.

"Oh, Mr. Creed." Miss Lyman stopped pummeling him to put a hand to her heart. "What are you doing, jumping in windows?"

"At a guess"—Evelyn's voice held a note he couldn't place, but suddenly he knew which woman he'd almost bowled over—"I'd say he heard your brother's tirade and our displeasure over it, and assumed we were in danger." She didn't look any the worse for wear, almost amused at the entire incident. Only a shadow of apprehension dimmed her smile.

"Who are you?" The reason for her apprehension—at least Jake thought it a safe assumption—lay in bed, bracing himself on one arm and glowering as though *Jake* were the threat.

"Your brother's tirade. . ." In an instant, it all came crashing together. The tension that left when he knew the women weren't in immediate danger came rushing back. Hadn't he wondered what type of man let the women of his family wander out West alone? *A man injured in a mine collapse, of course.*

"Jake Creed." He reached out to shake the man's hand. "I'm going to go out on a limb here and say you're Braden Lyman." *Please tell me I'm wrong. Please say you're another brother.*

"That's right. What's it matter to you?" Pride and suspicion didn't cancel out Lyman's need for information. "Why are you in Hope Falls? How do you know my sister?"

Oh, this keeps getting better. Jake ran a hand over his face before looking each woman in the eye to make sure he hadn't gotten it wrong. *Nope. They haven't told him what's going on.*

"It matters to me because these women made it all the way out here and are flitting around without any sort of protection." He met Evelyn's gaze, remembering the moment when she'd named him and Bear, establishing them as their protectors. "Except me and another man. Riordan." Truth was truth. "We knew Miss Lyman's brother and Miss Thompson's fiancé owned most of this town and wondered when he'd make an appearance."

"I won't be appearing anywhere but this bed for weeks yet." Lyman's scrutiny ended. Apparently the man judged him an ally, because he relaxed against the pillows. "Which is why I've ordered the women to leave Hope Falls and return to Charleston. I'll pay well to see they make it safely, Mr. Creed."

What a mess. Even if the others would let me take the women, I couldn't be the one to do it. I have to find Twyler.

"We aren't going anywhere." Miss Higgins put one hand on her hip. "Braden doesn't have the right to send us away."

"Doesn't sound like he agrees with that, ma'am. And if he owns the town, the law won't take your side either." Jake decided to stick with the facts and make no enemies either way.

"He might not agree, but he knows it's the truth." Miss Thompson's grin could've rivaled that of a cat in cream. "Lacey's in control of Lyman properties until Braden recovers."

"She informed him of that pertinent detail a scant moment before you jumped into the conversation." Evie's tongue-in-cheek explanation brought him up to speed on Mr. Lyman's behavior.

"Hence the explosion of obscenities," Jake deduced.

"It's a technicality," Mr. Lyman spat out. "It's beneath them to abuse the situation to overrule my wishes."

"The same way it should have been beneath you to claim ownership of the town to have the authorities run us out." Evelyn showed the man no sympathy. "You would abuse the fact our land and businesses are registered under your name, which was done solely because single women cannot own property!"

"That's different!" the bedridden man protested. "I'd make you leave for your own good. It's not safe for you women here."

"It's no different." Miss Thompson fussed with her fiancé's

pillow for a moment. "We decided to stay, and you would have manipulated your position to overrule our right to Hope Falls."

"I'm thinking clearly and should control my assets. You women don't have the sense God gave a goose and need someone else making decisions for you. *That's* the difference." Braden Lyman turned his gaze to Jake. "Get them out of here, safe and sound, and I'll make you a wealthy man, Mr. Creed."

"I appreciate your confidence, Mr. Lyman." Jake slid a glance around the room. "But it's not a simple situation."

"Yes, it is," Lyman ground out. "Ignore whatever qualms you may have. You'd be ensuring the safety of four henwits who can't plan beyond the next day. You can take them back to Charleston. How could it be any less complicated than that?"

"Well, Mr. Lyman, for one thing, these women have planned a lot farther ahead than tomorrow." Jake let out a long breath and let the truth fall. "For another, there's the eighteen men they invited here to try and win their hands in marriage."

SEVENTEEN

T attletale!" Lacey's hiss faded beneath her brother's renewed vigor for words Evie had never heard before.

She blocked out another string of invectives from Braden, pushing back an urge to rush around the bed and clap her hands over Cora's ears. Cora needed to see the worst in her husband-to-be before she stepped up to the altar, and Evie wouldn't shield her from that. *Sickness and health. . .*

The news of Braden's death painted her sister's memories with the golden glow of treasured moments and dreams left forever perfect. Now, the reality of his life—and lack of health—would tarnish her image of him back to the truth. Worse than the truth of the old Braden, it would be the man she'd live with when things went wrong and days wore long. *'Til death. . .*

Of course, some men meet their Maker sooner than others. Evie looked at Jake Creed, who still stood between her and Lacey. *There's a man who's angling for an introduction quicker than most— challenging entire crowds of men, insulting the woman who cooks his meals, jumping through windows—all in less than twenty-four hours. Not to mention the way Lacey's looking at him right now for spilling the beans to her brother.*

163

"Not with ladies present, Lyman." Creed's voice cut through Braden's rant. "Throwing a tantrum won't get you what you want."

Braden stopped cold. So did everyone else, waiting for him to order Creed from the room, start yelling again, or something of the sort since he couldn't reach anything more to throw. "What will?" His quiet response, when it finally came, took them all aback. "What will it take to get the four of you home?"

"It's too late, Braden." Lacey put a hesitant hand on his shoulder, as though bracing her brother for the worst news. "Cora and Evie gave up their rooms, and Lyman Place has been sold. There's no place for us in Charleston now. Hope Falls is where we all are, and now we've brought everything we need."

Including future husbands in a passel of loggers willing to create a sawmill you know nothing about. Evie kept her lips closed tight around that comment, knowing the coming conversation would reveal everything as it unfolded. No sense rushing it with blunt statements sure to cause panic.

Mr. Creed missed the accusatory glance she shot him. *Not that he'd admit he shouldn't have blurted out anything about the men, anyway.*

She bit back a sigh as Braden groaned and raked a hand through his hair. *Why is it men enjoy the luxury of flat rolling-pin conversation, when women must resort to cookie-cutter comments? If something could raise hackles, we sort out the least offensive scraps and attempt to mold them into a more pleasing shape. It's a bothersome way to communicate.*

Just look at Lacey, trying so hard to tell Braden about the sawmill scheme. She couldn't overset him last night, and this afternoon she parcels out unpleasant bits of the story so it doesn't overwhelm. Mr. Creed no sooner jumps through the window than he spews out the worst in a single, uncensored sentence.

"So I cannot send you back, and even if I could, there's no place to send you?" Braden began tugging at his beard. "Do I have that much right, before I go any further?"

"Yes." Four women chimed the single word.

Joined by a "Sounds that way" in Mr. Creed's complementing baritone.

"And they've invited men up here to court them?" He directed this new line of questioning at the other male present.

"We didn't precisely invite men to come here," Lacey hedged, ignoring her brother's grammar to try to guide the conversation toward a more flattering perspective.

"When are the suitors supposed to arrive, Creed?"

"The seventeenth." Creed showed enough discretion not to offer more information than Braden requested. "Tomorrow."

"I can't send the women away, and it's too late to stop the men from coming here." Braden pulled so hard, Evie began to wonder how he kept his beard at all. "So I'll have to ask for your help, Creed. We'll send the men away as they arrive."

"You can't do that either." Cora tugged his hand away from his abused beard. "Even if you had the power, Mr. Creed wouldn't agree to it. He's one of the bachelors, you see."

"All the more reason he'd want to get rid of the others." Braden rose up to address Creed. "What do you say?"

"It's not for him to say at all." Evie couldn't quell the objection. "Neither of you make the decisions here."

"We can stop new men from coming in, but that won't do much." Creed shrugged. "Besides, the men here came for the women. No one wants to get on their bad sides, Lyman." The half-smile he sent her did nothing to ease Evie's indignation.

"No one." Braden fell back against his pillow. "That means more than just you and that other fellow you mentioned are already here. How many of the eighteen sit in town right now?"

"Eighteen." Naomi rubbed the back of her neck. "And they aren't going to escort themselves to the train, Braden."

"What kind of men did you invite that they all showed up early?" Braden began yelling again. "Where did you even meet that many men who'd be willing to come out West? Evie's café?"

"Don't you go insulting Miss Thompson's café." Creed's warning took her by surprise. "It's a fine establishment."

"Lacey already told you we didn't actually issue invitations." Cora shared a glance with her best friend. "And Evie's café didn't have a single thing to do with it, except Mr. Creed stopped in a few days before we left Charleston."

"So you just let it be known you'd be waltzing out West, and any men interested in you and your property could follow along?" Braden began knocking his head against his pillow in a series of rhythmic, muffled thumps. "You four need keepers."

"We do not!" Evie refused to take any more of his skewed assumptions and derogatory comments.

"Some might disagree." Creed's interference reaffirmed Evie's earlier thought about his meeting his Maker early. *Very* early.

"Evie's right. We don't need keepers. What we need," Lacey proclaimed, sticking her nose up in the air, "are husbands!"

"Oh, Lacey. . ." Evie groaned at that brilliant declaration as Cora and Naomi made similar sounds of frustrated disbelief, and Creed, reckless fool that he was, began to laugh. So she did the only thing a refined woman could to control the situation and discreetly demonstrate her pique. She elbowed Creed between the ribs.

He stopped laughing. Creed pivoted just enough to look down at her, his blue eyes somber. "You have my attention."

"I don't want it!" Evie snapped, unaccountably disconcerted by his perusal. "All I wanted was for you to stop laughing."

"I see." Creed raised a brow. "Someone mentions three women in the room needing husbands, and you're the one to nudge me. Does that mean you want to be serious, Miss Thompson?"

"No!" The gasp wheezed from her before Evie could blink.

"Serious suits me just fine." Braden's irritable voice spared her any further taunts. "Would someone tell me how it is that eighteen men came here if no one invited them?"

"We asked for responses care of the postmaster," Naomi began to explain, "expecting letters from interested men. From there we wanted to correspond and then perhaps invite a few."

"But things didn't quite go as planned," Lacey blithely tacked on, "and so here we are, with six prospects apiece."

"You mean to say you arrived in town to find eighteen lonely men you don't know from Adam?" If Braden looked any more grim, the reaper would get jealous. "Men who came here in response to something you sent out. What, exactly?"

"Nothing, really," Lacey assured him. "A simple ad."

"An ad," her brother echoed. "You placed an ad for prospective husbands?" His volume increased with each word.

"That's what it boils down to, yes." Evie spoke over Lacey's convoluted explanations and Naomi's elaborations.

"And what, may I ask"—he obviously tried to control his yelling, as he gritted out the words—"possessed you four to come up with such a harebrained, far-fetched piece of idiocy, much less *follow through* with it?"

"We need men to protect our claims and help save the town." Evie summed it up as best she could without making Braden feel guilty for being unable to help protect those claims.

"It was my idea," Lacey confessed with some pride.

"Who else?" Braden's lips compressed, his color an ashen sort of gray with a thin line of white around his mouth. He wouldn't admit that he was tired and hurting, but Evie could see it as he extended a hand. "Show me this ad you placed."

"No." Lacey shook her head. "It'll make you angry, and it's not important. All you need to know is we placed one, and men came, and we have things completely under control."

Dumbfounded, Evie could do nothing but stare at Lacey. Until Creed began to laugh again, pulling a piece of paper from his pocket. He handed the creased square to Braden, and Evie lost what little was left of her composure.

This time she stepped on his foot.

Jake didn't stop the laughter springing up at Miss Lyman's confident declaration that the women had "things completely under control" for more than a few reasons. First, it'd been too long since he'd laughed so much, and it felt good. Second, if someone didn't throw a distraction or two his way to keep him afloat, Braden Lyman would drown in anxiety over his women.

It didn't take a doctor to see the strain of the situation showing around the wounded man's eyes and mouth. He needed rest, and instead all he got were more worries. The Good Book said laughter did good like medicine.

Now, I may not think much of a lot of folks who claim to follow the Word, but that doesn't mean it's not good in and of itself. People agree to take sound advice every day, then go back on their decision and ignore it. Give their own word, and don't follow through. . .

But the final reason clinched it. Jake knew his laughter would provoke Evelyn Thompson. Evie, they all called her.

I knew it. It suits her spunk. In fact, he liked that spunk enough to want to see what it would do when he laughed at another one of Lacey Lyman's naive comments. Last time, after Evie had bemoaned the comment with a small, disbelieving cry, she'd gone ramrod stiff. Without a word, without a glare, without moving so much as an inch, she'd simply lifted her elbow and jabbed him in the side with unerring aim. Right where it hurt.

Then she lowered her arm and, with great dignity, set about pretending she'd never done any such thing. Until he'd called her to the table for her sneaky maneuver and she'd blushed that rosy color he liked so well. Evie's impulsive streak intrigued him enough to bait her with his question about getting serious.

Almost a pity she said no, but she needs to learn to be less impetuous around other men. The thought stilled his laughter just as her heel came down on the toe of his boot.

The boots he ordered special-made from a cobbler he'd known

for a decade. The boots with two layers of leather hiding a thin piece of steel between them to guard his toes. Jake witnessed too many ax accidents caused by carelessness or an unforeseen back-strike not to take any precaution he could dream up.

So he felt her stomp on his foot, but it didn't hurt any. Worse, he couldn't make a joke about her trying to bring him up lame because Braden Lyman lay in the bed before him. Lyman's hands, arms, shoulders, and neck all seemed in working order, but Jake hadn't seen the slightest movement of the sheets to indicate the man could use his legs. Which meant Jake didn't say a word about Evie's second attempt to curb his amusement.

And from the gleam in her eye, she'd known he wouldn't.

Clever minx. A realization jolted him. *It's not the first time she's shown discernment. She knew Dodger would steal a biscuit when she made that deal, and she took Williams's measure in a few moments. That's why she named me and Riordan and went along with the "Miss Thompson" gambit—she didn't like Williams. Evie has good instincts and the ability to read people.*

He eyed her with new respect. Now that Jake knew about Mr. Lyman, the entire situation made far more sense. He'd been right about her following her sister to her fiancé's side but wrong about the necessity of them moving out here. He sided with Lyman in believing the women belonged back in Charleston and had landed themselves in a heap of trouble. But now he respected Lacey for coming to her brother, Naomi to her cousin, Cora to her fiancé, and Evie for staying with her sister. Family first.

I'd do the same, and would expect no less from any man. Jake looked down at Evie's oh-did-I-do-that? smile, that dimple as bewitching as ever. He fought to forget how soft she'd been when he almost knocked her over through the window. . .and failed. And that right there was the entire problem in a nutshell.

She's a woman. Worse, she's a pretty woman. Worst of all, she's a pretty woman who cooks the best meals I've ever eaten. No wonder

Lyman's desperate to get them back to civilization. Out here, single women like this will start riots.

"Get out." The first words he spoke since seeing the incredible ad, and Braden Lyman sounded as though he expected defeat before he fought the fight. Well, maybe he should. He'd already lost this battle a few times over. "All four of you, get out but don't go far. I want a word with Mr. Creed. Alone."

"Absolutely not," Evie squawked, the first of dismayed clucks all around. "He shouldn't have barged in here at all!"

"No," Miss Higgins fretted. "Mr. Creed doesn't have a say in how we run Hope Falls. You should talk with us, Braden."

"We haven't even discussed the plans for the mill!" Miss Lyman's plaintive wail hit a shrill note. "You'll want to—"

"Speak with Mr. Creed," Lyman reasserted. "Now."

"You can talk to him with us present." His fiancée set her jaw. "We've set this in motion, we know the plans, and we're the ones who will see it all through. Speak with Mr. Creed if you like, but you won't try to make decisions without us present."

"Seems to me you four made a few decisions without him." Jake wanted to know what Lyman had to say. Besides, he upheld that ancient, unspoken code to stand alongside his fellow male when the so-called "gentler" sex started to run roughshod. "We all know it, so none of you can argue the point now."

"You obviously don't know them very well." Lyman snorted. "They'll argue anything."

"That's not true, and you know it!" His sister reached out and pinched his upper arm. "You take that back, Braden."

The man on the bed dissolved into laughter. "Are you arguing to try to prove you're not argumentative, Lace?"

"You tricked her," Evie broke in. "If she said nothing, she agreed she argues anything. If she disagreed, she proved she argues. It's like flipping a coin and declaring, 'Heads I win, tails you lose!' Either way, *you* come out ahead."

"There's always another option." Jake found the one-sided

piece in his pocket, rubbing his fingers over the familiar squared edges. "She could tell him he's entitled to his own opinion and leave him to talk it over man-to-man."

"Or"—Evie reached behind and pulled back the curtain— "you could hop back out the window and work with the other men. Please notice that we are willing to compromise, Mr. Creed, so if you fancy a change, you're welcome to try the door."

EIGHTEEN

Looks like someone attacked that door earlier." He'd noticed the tray and broken crockery, coated in clumps of butter and globs of honey, heaped at the base of the wall by the door.

For now, Jake found it difficult to keep his eyes off Evie. *She's not going to forgive me for this anytime soon.* He realized he'd overstepped his place with their earlier conversation, but she'd been wise enough to listen and take his advice to heart. *Somehow I don't think lightning will strike twice. One livid woman's bad enough, but now I've got four on my hands. And the best of the bunch looks in the worst temper.*

"I wanted my lunch, and she stole it." A guilty grumble confirmed Jake's suspicions that Lyman didn't confine his tantrum to shouts and profanity. "Rotten thing to do to a man."

"Oh, I forgot about that!" Evie's sister sprang forward to start cleaning the mess, righting the tray and placing broken bits atop it to be carried away. "It'll be gone in a moment."

"Here, Cora, let me help." Miss Higgins abandoned her post by the bed, pulled a towel from her apron, and began scrubbing the wall until it became evident she'd need stronger measures. ·

"Lyman, I know they've tried your patience, but you and I need to have a talk about the way you act around women." Jake curled a hand around Lacey Lyman's elbow and pulled her forward, trading places so he stood at the head of the bed. "I won't let any of the other men use foul language or violence." As he spoke, he placed his hand at the small of her back and nudged.

"That's right, Braden. You've forgotten your manners!" his sister twittered at him, either unaware or uncaring of the steps leading her toward the door until Evie halted their progress.

"Yes, Miss Lyman, your brother needs some time to consider all the news and collect himself before he's fit company." Jake put his free hand at the small of Evie's back and tried to guide them both toward the door. One of them resisted.

"I need some water," Miss Higgins murmured and slipped out the door, presumably to go wet her towel and return.

"It's not safe for her to wander alone," Jake directed Miss Thompson, who already stood with the tray in hand.

"Right. I need to dispose of this anyway." With that, she bustled after the other woman, leaving the room half empty.

"Stop pushing me toward the door." Evie dug in her heels.

"You women need to stay together, and Mr. Lyman wants a word with me before he passes out from exhaustion. Don't make it any harder on him or anyone else than it has to be." He knew the whisper carried to Miss Lyman, because she threw a glance over her shoulder as though surprised by her brother's fatigue.

"It's Lacey's place to speak with Braden, Mr. Creed."

"That's true." Miss Lyman looked torn. "But he's tired. . . ."

"And you yourself put me in the position of answering any questions the men had, bringing requests before you, and taking care of problems," Jake said, reminding Evie of her previous trust, then lowered his voice. "Let me answer his questions, so he'll be more comfortable, and bring his concerns back to you."

"All right." Miss Lyman headed for the door. "Braden, we'll let you two alone this once, but if your behavior doesn't improve, you won't be allowed any other visitors until it does."

"I'm not a child asking for a tea party, Lace." Lyman nearly ruined Jake's victory by snarling at his sister.

"You've got your work cut out for you, Mr. Creed." With that, Miss Lyman sailed from the room.

"Now you're stuck, Evie." Lyman laughed. "If your position is that Lacey owns Hope Falls until I heal and it's her right to inform me of how it's run, you have to respect her decision."

When cornered, animals become most dangerous, and Jake knew firsthand humans could outdo them all. Since Evie boasted more fight than most, he braced himself for her reaction to hearing the trap spring shut. *This should be interesting.*

She went still. "You're entitled to your opinion," she said, parroting Jake's advised response for when someone found herself in an impossible conversation. "I'll leave you to discuss it." With that, she raised her chin and swept from the room in the most dignified exit Jake ever had the privilege to witness.

He followed in one step—and shut the door behind her.

The man had the nerve to shut the door. Evie whirled around to find wood blocking her view of the room. More importantly, the thick barrier blocked her plans to eavesdrop.

Her fingers crept toward the handle as a plan formed. *Maybe I'll open it a crack, so slowly they won't even notice a difference.*

The snicking of lock tumblers sliding into place stunned her. *How low will that man sink? What does he plan to discuss that he's so determined not to be overheard? And what sort of suspicious mind expects to have someone listen in at all?*

A rather brilliant one, Evie begrudgingly admitted. Then plucked a hairpin from her bun and set about trying to coax the lock open. But really, the last thing she planned to do was admire anything about the devious, double-crossing Mr. Creed.

"What are you doing?" Cora's question made her jump, snap her hairpin in the lock, and lose all hope of opening it.

"Ssssshhhhhhhh!" Evie straightened up. "Lacey's defection after you two went for cleaning supplies forced me to leave or admit Lacey didn't have the right to make decisions for Braden. Then Creed shut the door on me." She paused for Cora and Naomi to take that in before adding the *coup de grâce*: "And locked it!"

Naomi gave a satisfactory gasp. "The nerve of that man!"

"Lacey, you didn't agree to leave them alone?" Cora took up the most important issue, if not the most timely.

"Braden's tired and Creed will explain the town rules," Lacey faltered. "So I went after you two to wait for them."

"Leaving Evie alone to stop their plotting, until they forced her into the hallway," her sister moaned. "Where they shut the door and locked it, adding insult to injury."

"The sheer gall"—Lacey recovered from her regret to indulge in righteous rage—"to assume we'd eavesdrop!"

"Presumptuous men," Evie agreed, and promptly set about trying to retrieve the other half of her hairpin from the lock. "Now be quiet so we can hear them better, will you three?"

Giving up the hairpin as a lost cause, and furthermore deciding it served Creed right if he had to jump back out the window if the lock jammed, Evie pressed her ear near the doorjamb. The other three joined her until they lined up almost like a show in the circus, with her crouching at the very bottom and the others leaning over her to try to catch any hint of the ensuing conversation. She hoped they had more success.

When Lacey disentangled herself and tiptoed down the hallway to the doctor's study, her murmurs to the doctor further canceled out any chance of hearing Mr. Creed or Braden. She tiptoed back with two water glasses. She set one down and promptly leaned the drinking side of the other against the door panel, pressing her ear against the bottom of the glass. "That's better," she mouthed, then covered her other ear as though to better concentrate on the conversation only she could properly overhear in this thoroughly improper spying attempt.

A brief tussle ensued over possession of the other water glass. Evie made a grab for it with one hand, pulling Cora's arm away from the prize with her other in a bid for victory. Her sister used much the same tactic in return, leaving the field open for Naomi to swoop in and claim the piece instead. A smile bloomed across her features as she copied Lacey's posture, apparently with the same results.

When her smile faded, Cora jabbed Evie between the ribs in silent retribution.

"That was your fault!" Evie hissed. "I stayed in the room the longest and tried to listen in first. That glass was mine!"

"Sssssshhhhhhhh!" Three women shushed her before two went back to their glasses, no longer smiling. Apparently the conversation had taken a turn for the worse.

That does it. Evie rose to her feet. She'd sunk from her crouch into a kneel once the others joined her, and now her knees ached, anyway. *Creed closed the door, but I doubt he'd go so far as to shut the window. With those curtains, they won't even see me so long as I'm quiet.*

She headed out of the building and around the corner, finding the window wide open, the low timbre of male voices carrying the conversation to her ears. *No water glass needed.* Evie inched closer until she stood beside the window. She stooped slightly. Her eyes peeked over the frame. One never knew when a stiff wind might blow back the curtain.

Thanks to Mr. Creed's dramatic earlier entrance, the curtain slid back, revealing a slice of the room. When she shifted, she could almost make out Creed's profile as he spoke to Braden. A foot to the left, and she'd have a better view, but the office was built on a hill. The top of her head would bump the sill, but she wouldn't see anything at all over there.

Hmmm. . .perhaps if I scoot a bit forward and step on this muffin-shaped rock. Ooops! She hopped off, looking at the now-sideways stone before gingerly pressing her toe on it then testing it with more weight. *I'll just grip the windowsill with my fingers and raise up on tiptoe, like this, and—*

"This is much better!" Cora's murmur ended in a muffled *oomph* as Evie landed on top of her sister, whom she hadn't noticed follow her outside. "Get off me! We're missing everything!" The barest breath of sound, Cora's voice lost no urgency as they struggled to their feet.

As usual, it took her sprightly sibling less time to recover. Cora didn't bother to brush off the dust coating her skirts, merely glanced about to make sure they hadn't been spotted and hopped into place atop the rock where Evie so precariously perched the moment before Cora startled her.

"That's my spot! Find your own!"

"I like this one, and you lost it!" Cora peered into the room. "Now be quiet, Evie, or they'll hear us and—"

Her sister didn't get the chance to finish that sentence, as Evie grabbed Cora's apron strings and tugged her off Muffin Rock, leaving her standing beneath the window while Evie reassumed her rightful position. Smug smile still playing about her lips, she turned to look through the window.

And found herself eye to eye with Jake Creed.

Her exclamation of outrage when he shut the door made Jake smile…and decide to lock it before beginning his discussion with Lyman. They didn't say a word before the other man pointed to the base of the door, where shadows played and a thin scrap of green flirted with the floorboards. The same green Evie wore.

Jake stopped wondering if he'd become overly suspicious. The women were spying. At least, they were trying to. He and Lyman watched and waited, and sure enough, the faint sounds of footsteps and even what sounded like a small scuffle pushed through the barrier to their ears.

When it became clear they'd not hear anything, Jake turned to his unlikely ally.

"I've got a few questions of my own, Mr. Lyman." He kept his voice low. Not a whisper, but low enough that it couldn't carry past the room. "But you go ahead and ask yours first."

"Can you and this Reary fellow you mentioned keep them safe?" Lyman kept his priorities in order at least.

"No one man can watch over four women, Lyman. Even two won't manage that task every hour of the day, and it'll be worse once we start heading into the timber, and I can't account for all the men at any given time." Jake didn't hold back. "Then we'll be splitting into about four teams. Riordan and I can only monitor half. If any from the other crews double back to town. . ."

"Can you enlist two men you trust to lead the other crews?"

They know me as Granger. Jake hesitated. *They're smart men; they won't slip up. If they do, better my identity is lost than one of the women.* "I can. We need to choose the site for the mill and clear it, from what I can see. That will buy us time. Wouldn't hurt to have a day or two of rain to hold things up."

And speed up my hunt for Twyler so I can give this more focus. When the rain falls, trees and mud aren't the only things to make a man slip. Boredom loosens tongues like little else.

"I'll pray for rain then." A muted thump outside the window halted Lyman's next words. The men exchanged glances.

Not even a peep for the next moment, and then a muffled cry and thudding bump, accompanied by a series of not-so-quiet whispers. Finally, a stifled *oomph* before scrabbling at the windowsill.

Lyman turned his head, trying to hide his chuckles. *If the government employed these women as spies, we'd still belong to the British.* Jake crouched and pulled back the curtain, not surprised to find a pair of golden eyes staring back at him. They widened in surprise before darkening in irritation long before either of them said a word. "Next time you decide to take up jumping through windows, I'd be happy to teach you better technique, Miss Thompson."

"Why, you lousy—" She reached for him, only to lose her purchase on the windowsill and make a hasty grab for it.

Curious, Jake leaned out the window to see the cause of her troubles. Aside from Cora, who gave a sheepish wave, the construction of the building left too much distance between the window and the ground for such a petite woman to cover. Evie balanced precariously on an uneven stone, clutching the windowsill to maintain her perch. He guessed she'd slipped twice and downright fallen at least once, if the dust coating her and her sister's skirts was anything to go by.

"Lousy what?" He moved back into the room and gave her a grin. "I make a far better spy than you and your sister here."

"I'd expect that, from a double-crossing sneak." A lock of brown hair, threaded with cinnamon strands and dusted with, well, dust, escaped from her pins. She tried to puff it away from her vision and failed, looking adorably thwarted.

"Double-crossing?" Jake wouldn't protest the sneak part of her insult. He'd let everyone believe he'd come to Hope Falls to win a bride. "How have I double-crossed anyone?"

"Despite your presumptuous, arrogant, high-handed summation of my choices, I listened to you." Her chin jutted out. "I took your advice to make better choices. Not because of you, but because I'll do whatever it takes to do right by my sister."

"Even yank her by her apron strings to take her eavesdropping rock." Cora's mutter explained the thump.

"Reclaim her rock, more like." Evie spared a glare for her sister before turning back to Jake. "But when I decided to accept your assistance and set you in the position to help us, you turned right around and sided with Braden instead."

She thinks I've betrayed her trust. It stymied him. "You entrusted me with your protection, Miss Thompson. Have I done anything to endanger any one of you?"

He waited for the reluctant shake of her head.

"In that case, perhaps you need to reconsider your concept of trust. Look to what I do—not what you think you hear."

With that, he closed the window. And the curtain.

NINETEEN

"Have you done anything to earn it?" Lyman started talking the moment the window hit the sill. "Their trust, I mean."

"Has the doctor done anything to stop the epidemic?" Jake countered. "Eavesdropping seems to be spreading like butter on Miss Thompson's corn pone." His stomach rumbled at the memory, but he ignored it. Another line of fabric peeked under the door.

"Corn pone?" Lyman perked up. "Is that what it was? I guessed corn bread. Did it taste as good as corn bread?"

"I'd say it's about the same." Jake lowered his voice a bit with each step he took toward the door, so the women wouldn't catch on. "Seems Miss Thompson's making do without milk, but we'd never know it by the meals she sets on the table."

He set a hand on the doorknob and one on the lock, turning both at once. Something snapped inside the mechanism, but it worked regardless. The moment he opened the door, Miss Lyman and Miss Higgins tumbled into the room in a heap of cotton and blushes.

Jake helped the women to their feet before reaching down and plucking two water glasses from the floor. *Impressive.* "Which one of you knew this little trick?" He held one up, the light catching on a hairline crack spidering down the side.

"An old friend taught it to me at boarding school," Miss Lyman admitted as the two Miss Thompsons edged their way into the room behind everyone. "Though I never expected to use it."

"You shouldn't have needed to," Evie defended her friend.

"Nor should you have had to lurk outside windows, only to have them slammed shut in your face," Miss Higgins commiserated.

"Lurk? I did not lurk," she objected. "I. . .hovered."

"Until she fell on me," her sister helpfully chimed in.

"One o' the lassies fell?" His shadow preceding him, Bear filled the doorway as though unsure which woman to help.

"All of them," Jake informed him. "Two toppled into each other beneath the window, while the other two met the floor when I opened the door they'd been eavesdropping against."

The women spluttered—though they didn't deny it, Jake noted. Lyman began demanding to know the name of the giant, and Riordan looked at them all as though they'd sprouted antlers.

For his part, Jake judged Riordan to have the best grasp on things. "Rory Riordan, meet Braden Lyman." Jake didn't say more. Let Riordan work out the connection for himself.

"Ahh. . ." Riordan caught on quick. "Miss Lyman's brother and Miss Higgins's cousin what owns the bulk o' Hope Falls. We didna know you been injured in the mine collapse, Mr. Lyman."

"We didn't think it best to mention that detail until we had the situation more settled." Evie stepped closer to Mr. Riordan to confide that fact. "It seemed prudent to wait."

"Indeed." Green eyes searched the room, lingering on Lyman as though to note that the man didn't rise from the bed. "Though I'd go so far as to say it would hae been still more prudent for you lassies to wait to come here a'tal. 'Tis no safe when your man canna watch o'er you proper in these parts."

"We'd been told Braden died. When we heard he'd survived but couldn't travel, we took the only choice." Miss Lyman's sudden anger took them all aback as she defended her position at her brother's side. "What else could we have done?"

"You could have hired a caregiver and corresponded," Lyman burst out. "You could have waited for my recovery. For heaven's sake, you could even have made a trip out here with armed men accompanying you to protect your safety and then returned to Charleston. You could have done *anything* other than sell our home and advertise for a horde of strange men to descend upon the town with no way to manage them or protect yourselves!"

"Aye." Riordan nodded. "Any one o' those would hae done."

"Corresponding is what left us believing you dead, Braden." Miss Thompson slipped past Jake to stand by her fiancé's side. "And we had no way to know. . ." She fished around in her apron for something as she spoke. "Had no way to know if you'd recover at all or if you'd contract some wasting disease and truly"—a deep breath steadied what Jake strongly suspected shaped up to be sobs—"died before we saw you even one more time. Oh, where is my handkerchief?" She apparently gave up searching for it.

"Here." Lyman pulled a folded square from his sleeve. "You gave it to me when you brought lunch—just before you stole it." The fact he'd saved his fiancée's hankie before hurling the remains of his lunch tray at the wall spoke volumes. "Now you see I'm recovering and plan to stay among the living."

"Thank you." Miss Thompson accepted her hankie to dab her eyes before glaring at her beloved. "Though I begin to suspect you hang on to your life simply to make mine more difficult."

"A worthy cause." If Evie's smile seemed strained around the corners, it didn't stop everyone from joining in. "Don't deny the man whatever motivation keeps him among us, Cora. It'll brighten his days when you find ways to get even with him."

The hairs on the back of Jake's neck prickled. Not from Evie's words, but from the fact she looked at him when she said the part about getting even. *And I'm about to make her angrier.*

A smart man stops while he's ahead. Any fool knows to quit when he's behind. So what does that make me, when I'm not only behind but plan to stay there and enjoy watching the sparks fly?

"I was wantin' to know what the lassies want done with their furniture and such," Riordan was saying. "Another train's come in, and things won't fit in the ladies' house."

"Sounds like something the women need to oversee." Lyman grinned. "Mr. Creed and I need to discuss a few things, but I think I can trust Mr. Riordan to watch over the ladies."

"O' course." Riordan gave Jake an arched look—quite the accomplishment for a shaggy lumberjack the size of a mountain. "Not a single lass will fall on my watch, Mr. Lyman."

"I don't mind falling, Mr. Riordan," Evie mentioned as he ushered them out the door. "So long as I take a stand first."

Jake Creed let out a low whistle as he shut the door for a second time. "Rare to see a woman with that much spunk."

"Cora's one in a million," Braden agreed, looking at Creed with narrowed eyes. *Who's this stranger to notice? He's only known her for a day. Not nearly long enough to appreciate her. Maybe I should wait and talk to Riordan instead.*

"I meant the other Miss Thompson." Creed sauntered back toward him. "Not that your fiancée isn't a rare woman, but her older sister beats her for spirit and sass."

She's not my fiancée. You're wrong about her spirit. And I'm not enough of a fool to tell you so, with nearly twenty men running loose in town. Braden shook his head. *Besides. . .* "Evie's caught your eye, has she?" As though he needed to ask. He'd seen it in the way Creed looked at Cora's sister, spoke to her more than anyone else, waited for her reactions.

"She's a pretty woman." Creed's noncommittal response told Braden everything he needed to know. "Any man too blind to see it can still taste her cooking and figure some of her worth."

Some. Braden would have laughed if he hadn't been in the same predicament over Cora a couple of years back. A man who met a Thompson sister and couldn't get her out of his head qualified as walking wounded. But the man in front of him couldn't yet guess he'd been dealt the blow to bring a man down. . .on one knee.

Wish I still qualified as walking wounded. He stared at his legs, encased in casts and strapped down so they wouldn't move. *Instead, I'm worthless. Unable to keep Cora safe from her own choices or other men, I have to sit here and do nothing.*

No. Not nothing. He eyed Creed, deciding not to press him about Evie. It wouldn't do any good, and he had bigger problems. "You were saying you could enlist two other men to lead the timber crews, after they cleared the sawmill site. Men you'd trust to look after your own sister or wife?" *Or Evie, at least.* Braden couldn't say how much Creed's interest in her put him at ease when it came to Cora, Lacey, and Naomi. When it came to Evie herself, well. . . *Evie's the strongest, and Creed strikes me as honorable. This, and prayer, is the best I can do.*

"Yes, I would trust Lawson and McCreedy. They're good men and better bosses." Creed sank down into the high-backed wooden chair beside the bed, steepling his fingers. "There's something I need you to know before they arrive, Lyman. You're trusting me with your family, so I'm going to be straight about mine."

Braden didn't say a word. Didn't make any promises. If Creed revealed something that made him a danger, he'd have to be removed from Hope Falls. One way or another.

"My name isn't Creed. It's Granger. I had a falling out with my family—my father in particular—about four months back. I left the name and family business behind, but these men will know me as Granger. They're smart, but if they slip up, I don't want it to take you by surprise." His piece said, Creed stopped.

"Granger." The name floated through his mind like a dust mote, catching a beam of light but fading before Braden could catch it. Then, "Like in Granger Lumber? Montgomery Granger?"

"My father."

"I'm sorry to hear about your falling out." The loss of his own father, a five-year-old wound, gave a sudden ache. *Dad would tear his hair out if he knew I'd gone out West and left Lacey alone. If he knew Lacey sold Lyman Place and broke our legacy...* Braden winced at the thought. "Never easy to break ties."

"Sometimes a man has to walk away." Creed's stoic shrug hid a world of pain and reasons Braden could only guess at. The only reason he knew they existed was because he'd told himself the exact same thing about letting go of Cora.

"I'll want to meet each of the men, put names to faces, learn where they're from, what they do, and which woman they're interested in." Braden set his jaw. "If we both agree he's no good, I want you and Riordan to see him out of town."

"The women should be here for those interviews, Lyman. They have a say in who goes and in who they're willing to have court them. Besides"—Creed started to chuckle—"I don't see how we can chase all of them from the room whenever you meet with someone. You'll need to discuss the idea with them before planning it, but I'm glad you're asking me to be present if the meetings occur."

"They'll occur." Braden shot him a look. "You want to size up the competition or just hope they make fools of themselves?"

"Size them up." Something flashed in Creed's eyes, a sort of determination too intense for the situation. It left in a blink. "Not just as competition, but as workers for the outfit."

"That's the last issue." Braden leaned forward, unable to conceal his interest. "A man of your background and experience wouldn't be wasting his time if he didn't see at least a possibility for success, which is more than I would have believed if my sister approached me with this scheme. My question is how slim are our chances of making it work?"

"To be honest, Lyman, I can't answer that." Creed rested a boot on his footboard. "You've got the land, you've got the forest, and you've got a snake-off of the Colorado River to help you transport trees to the mill. The railroad already runs through town to carry lumber to buyers. Pretty much an ideal setup if you've got the capital to get it up and running."

"So, aside from the start-up investment, you're saying Lacey's dreamed up an entirely plausible business proposition?"

"And a lucrative one, at that. Lumber's at a premium, with New England forests suffering over a century of harvesting. A lot of places out West run into trouble with the transport. That's why the river and the railroad put you in an optimal position." Creed gave a slow nod. "I don't know about your finances, or how much of that the ladies managed to plan. The figures run high, but a lot of that is the land. If you run dry in start-up, you could consider taking on investors."

"After the failure of the mines, none of my contacts would invest in another venture associated with my name." Braden rubbed his forehead. "We don't have contacts in lumber."

"I do." Creed paused. "And I say it's a sound investment."

"It relieves my mind to hear you say so." The streaks and shoots of pain starting in his legs couldn't be ignored much longer, but Braden needed to finish this. "As much as it shames me to admit it, I don't know the state of our finances. I don't know what all Lacey's done in the past month. . .aside from sell the house and buy the rest of the mine. I couldn't say what price she paid for the mine, or how much it takes to begin a mill or pay the workers. Lacey and I will have to talk."

"For now, your workers are taking their meals as payment. That and the chance to court your sister, cousin, and Miss Thompson. They'll eat a mighty amount of food, but that's always included aside from pay, so you're coming out far ahead." Creed appeared to think for a moment. "Then again, considering the cooking, everyone's coming out ahead in the bargain."

"So they're lounging around town, eating like horses, doing nothing until they're organized?" The headache that hadn't completely left came roaring back. "That can't last, Creed."

"It seems like the mining company emptied the cookhouse and the sheds before selling the land, so they weren't functional. The diner wasn't equipped for supplying and feeding a logging camp, so today the men are building a storeroom onto the back. They're also redistributing the goods the women brought along."

"No need to tell me they brought enough to sink the Ark." Braden almost smiled at the thought. "Or overburden a train."

"They made it here yesterday just fine, by all accounts, but had been sending things ahead for a few days. Today's the last of what they sent from Charleston, but they have Draxley making orders right and left for the mercantile and diner."

"Any other men should arrive tomorrow, you said?" Braden saw the nod and dared to ask, "Think any more will arrive?"

"I'd stake my claim on it, Lyman. Spring's the slow season for logging. Rains make it worse than foolhardy to work with saws and axes, and mud ups the danger for days afterward. Even during dry days, running sap makes for harder work and lots of cleanup and wear and tear on tools. There'll be loggers available to come."

"We have long winters here. Spring doesn't show itself until May. That's why you're finding sap a problem so late in the year," Braden agreed. "So even though we're coming up on summer, that means eighteen would be a low number? Will we need more workers at this point, or is this a viable reason to send some away in the first few days before they eat us dry?" *Fewer men make it easier to watch over the women, safer for everyone.*

"It depends on the finances, Mr. Lyman, but I can tell you there'll be enough work for two dozen men to clear the site, construct a working flume, and build the mill itself."

"Building a mill doesn't take that long, Creed! I've seen it done by two men in a matter of weeks with brick and mortar."

"A small, rural mill, perhaps. An industrial sawmill, built from lumber hewn from your own trees, as it should be, will take longer." Creed's boots hit the floor. "You'll lose standing if you order precut lumber from another mill, Lyman. If you don't stand by your own product, your competitors will broadcast it."

"Understood." Braden leaned back, more relaxed than he'd felt since he spotted his sister the afternoon before. "So we can actually turn Hope Falls into a sawmill town."

"Those women got in over their heads with that ad." Creed got to his feet. "But the mill could keep you afloat."

TWENTY

Sinking into a nice, soft feather bed—the dream dogged Evie's every step after the busiest week she'd ever spent. She'd thought the time after Father's death would rule as the most hectic time of her life. Moving herself and sixteen-year-old Cora while Evie struggled to set up the business took every ounce of energy and ingenuity she scraped together.

This time, it isn't simply Cora, the move, or the business. It's the men. Evie gave a bone-weary sigh. *If Mother had survived, she would have warned me about how exhausting they are, always needing something, constantly wanting attention and praise.*

And food. Merciful heavens, the amount of food these men packed away boggled the mind. She'd run through the supplies she'd brought along and almost half of the first order she'd put out the day after their arrival. Worse, the dairy cows had been held up in a freak spring storm, leaving Evie fantasizing about all the recipes she'd create if only she had milk and cream.

You'd think I'd find better things to dream about, with prospective husbands around every corner. But somehow, hard work and compromise pushed any hint of romance from the air. Even with two dozen would-be grooms underfoot, they'd accomplished more than she'd imagined possible in the past eight days.

Her diner now boasted a storeroom twice the size she'd envisioned—which she now feared would still be only half as big as she'd need. They'd gone tramping up mountains and through forests to survey trees and sites for two days before choosing ground for the mill. Erstwhile suitors provided steady arms at every turn, while others cleared their paths of any obstacles.

Light rain showered them throughout the second day, but none of the men's protests could convince them to let a little water wash them back to town and leave such an important decision to be made by others. The perfect uphill spot, it sat within sight of town, near both the river and the railroad. Best yet, Cora pointed out, Braden would be able to watch the progress from clearing to construction through his window.

Mr. Williams insisted on another area, which seemed equally advantageous, but Mr. Creed and Mr. Riordan stayed firm on their choice, to the unanimous approval of the other men.

She still hadn't determined whether the men voted to be closer to the food or to thwart Williams. The man proved Daddy's old advice, "A man who shares many opinions keeps few friends." To be fair, Creed held easily as many opinions as Williams, and the other men seemed to respect him. Not necessarily like him, but still recognize him as a man of honor and intelligence.

Much the same way I do. His superior attitude and assumption of power never failed to irk her, but Evie couldn't say where they'd be now without Jake Creed. He kept the men in line, worked with Riordan to oversee labor, and, most importantly, alleviated the worst of Braden's worries. *Though I doubt I'd approve whatever else he does on Braden's behalf.*

Today she'd find answers to some of the questions she and the other women carried about Creed's collaboration with Lacey's brother. They already suspected he reported on the other men and the progress made so far with the mill, though when he found the time Evie couldn't imagine. Creed kept just as busy as she did.

"All right, ladies." Evie dried the final pan and set it on the proper shelf. "Before we meet with Creed and Braden, I need to find Draxley and set up a standing order for foodstuffs."

"He keeps himself well hidden in the telegraph office," Naomi reminded. "We've precious few telegrams, but coaxing him from that room is nigh unto impossible since that first night."

"We need to speak with him about other things, too." Lacey frowned. "Do you know he went to Braden to discuss an 'increase in salary due to onerous demands placed upon his time and as befits the change in business practice and his position'?"

"That's absurd." Cora gaped at her friend. "When the mine operated, he received and sent far more telegrams and spoke to the train conductor daily. I kept all of Braden's letters describing the town. He's keeping his room and board, and now that we arrived, Draxley eats meals the same as our other men."

"He asked me just yesterday if we'd be so kind as to take trays to his office, so he wouldn't need to 'abandon his post' any more than necessary," Naomi threw in. "I hesitated to mention it, as I told him he was welcome to come fetch his meals and bring back the tray if he felt uncomfortable spending time away from his desk, but we couldn't bring it to him."

"He's not given me the lists of suppliers I requested, nor the ordering catalogs for the latest season." Lacey frowned. "Evie, what would you say would be the cost for his food?"

"Twelve dollars a month." Evie heard the women gasp and knew the tabulations running through their minds.

"But. . .with thirty people, and thirty days, that's five hundred dollars in food every month!" Cora went pale at the sum.

"It's more than worth it." Evie and Lacey said almost the same words at the same time. Evie looked at Lacey in surprise.

"Their labor is worth more than three times that," Lacey elaborated. "Some of them are worth nearly nine, depending on their position, experience, and skill. Mr. Riordan, Mr. Creed, Mr. Williams, Dodger, and Bobsley would be some of those."

"I knew that they'd earn forty-five dollars a month, but how do you know the rest, Lacey?" Evie asked the obvious.

"Before I ever suggested this idea, I read up on the industry. What types of trees would be there, whether the wood would work, how much it takes to build a mill, what the pay scales for workers are. . ." Lacey blinked at their expressions. "Well, you didn't expect I'd suggest we uproot our lives and hie off with no specifics to ensure our success, did you?"

"Of course not, Lace," Cora hastened to assure her. "We simply had no idea you'd gone so far in depth as all that."

"How is it the men you listed are worth more than the others?" Naomi's curiosity matched Evie's on that point.

"Riordan, Creed, and Williams are camp bosses, crew leads, whatever you want to call them. They know every job and can do most. Dodger and Bobsley high-climb to the tops of tall trees to saw off the upper portion and make it safer to chop down the rest. Bobsley also does rigging up there for mechanized engines."

"I wouldn't have guessed that," Evie mused. "Dodger swims in so many layers of clothes tailored for a larger man, I'd think he'd find it dangerous to scramble about so high."

"Lacey Lyman, are you telling us you actually understand all that blather the men spew about beasts in the timber and felling bucks without hunting?" Cora planted her hands on her hips. "And you didn't mention it before or explain?"

"They've explained what they do when we've asked them." Lacey blinked. "Every single one we've asked to join us at dinner."

"But it hasn't made any sense! It's nothing but a bunch of nonsense nicknames and such to us, Lace. And you can explain." Naomi beamed. "What, exactly, is a timber beast?"

"They're all timber beasts. It's a silly term for any man who works in the woods, felling or hauling lumber. Fallers are men who chop down the trees. Buckers take a felled tree and cut it into more manageable lengths for transport. Bull of the forest is the nickname for the bosses like Riordan and Creed."

"That fits. He's stubborn as an ox," Evie muttered.

"Mr. Riordan's quite amiable!" Naomi protested immediately, making Evie wonder whether her friend liked the same man she herself felt something of a partiality toward.

"She meant Creed," Cora interjected. "Not Riordan."

"Mr. Kane"—Naomi moved on to mention a man quick with a compliment and flattering smile—"he's a faller?"

"Why?" Lacey's eyes narrowed. "Are you falling for him?"

"Worst pun goes to Lacey, now Naomi." Evie saw the light of battle in the sudden tension lining Lacey's chin.

"No." Naomi blushed. "I'm wondering if fallers work in teams. Those two who came with Mr. Williams—they're fallers, and Mr. Kane has that other fellow who follows him about like a shadow. They're roughly the same height and size, though Mr. Kane somehow seems larger than Mr. . . . I can't recall."

"Fillmore." The name sprang to Evie's lips. "I noticed it, too. He's the same size as others but seems to shrink around the other men. I keep thinking he should fill more space."

"Yes, fallers work in teams. It takes two to fell a large tree, trading off for rest periods." Lacey must have memorized several articles on logging. "It's best if they're roughly the same height and strength if they man a whipsaw together."

"That makes sense. In fact, a lot of things make sense now." Evie added lemons to her list and tucked it in her apron pocket before heading out the door. "Let's go find Mr. Draxley."

With that, they headed for the telegraph office to find the door closed and no one answering their knock. Evie pushed it with her fingertips until it swung open to reveal the office.

Two neat piles of paper, edges perfectly squared, bracketed the telegraph machine. A breakfast tray—plate clean, napkin precisely folded, and cutlery crossed neatly over the top—lay on a side table. If one thing could be said about Mr. Draxley, it was that he possessed a penchant for order.

Or, Evie added to herself, *that he didn't wash and return his dishes.* But both of those faded next to the significance of the sight monopolizing the middle of the room.

"Do you know," Naomi whispered, "I do believe he's asleep."

"Do you know"—Cora giggled—"I do believe his mustache twitches even while he sleeps. Yes, there it goes again!"

"Do you know?" Lacey didn't whisper. On the contrary, she raised her voice a few notches. "I don't find it amusing when a man who asks for an increase in salary due to his hectic schedule is found sleeping in his tidy little office."

"Hmm? What? What, now?" Draxley didn't startle awake so much as hop to his feet. Adjusting his spectacles, he blinked to find all four of them crowded before him. "Oh, I say. Er. . .well, yes, madam. In the normal way of things, I'm quite alert. I can assure you of that. It's only due to the increased demands on my time and abilities I find myself somewhat drained, in spite of my valiant efforts on your behalf. I'll endeavor to improve."

"What efforts would those be, Mr. Draxley?" Naomi lifted the edge of the tray with her forefinger then let it fall back to the desk with a small clatter. "Certainly not your dishes."

"Nor overseeing the men or helping organize the mill," Cora observed. "In fact, I've only spotted him during meals."

"It's an interesting question, Mr. Draxley." Lacey tilted her head as though confused. "Would you enlighten us as to what extra tasks you've taken on with our arrival? Aside from placing orders, which falls under typical telegraph duties, of course."

"The luggage and seeing the men settled." Peeved, his mustache stopped twitching, showing more personality than the man attached to it. "Coordinating with the conductor. . ."

"Those were either before or the day after our arrival," Evie objected. "What of the week since that point? Unexplained fatigue is a matter of medical concern, Mr. Draxley."

"I'll rally, madam." The mustache bristled. "This will not happen again, I promise you that. Now, is there a particular reason for the unexpected pleasure of your visit this morning, or did the four of you ladies merely drop by on a whim?"

He would have to imply we've no reason and operate purely on whim. After we find him asleep at his post, no less. And I'd planned to be gracious about the entire issue.

"We've a few matters to discuss. I'll leave the matter of your salary to Miss Lyman to address, as that decision rests in the hands of herself and her brother." Evie didn't smile, simply met his gaze with a steady one of her own. "My opinion happens to be that a man who sleeps on the job should consider himself fortunate to still be in possession of it, but perhaps you won't be in possession of it at all. That's why she'll go first."

"You won't be receiving an increase in salary, Mr. Draxley. If you find this unacceptable, please tender your resignation and we'll hire someone to fill your position." Lacey waited.

"In light of the most unusual and humbling circumstances this morning, I cannot argue." Though his still-bristling mustache told them all he'd like to. "What may I do for you?"

"We'll need to place a standing weekly order for these items." Evie slid the list from her pocket and passed it to him. "Please quadruple the first order, so we've laid in a good supply against inclement weather or railroad strike, et cetera."

"I say." He peered at her list. "Is this the quadrupled order, then a quarter of the same for each following week?"

"No, Mr. Draxley. That's to be the weekly order, with four times those amounts ordered for this first shipment." Evie didn't blame the man for his mistake—it made an enormous order.

"You are aware, Miss Lyman, that Miss Thompson requests"—Draxley adjusted his spectacles and began to drone in a reedy voice—"twenty-seven pounds of flour, twenty of cornmeal, eighteen of sugar, six of butter, ten pounds each of venison, beef, and chicken, five of pork, fifty in fruits and vegetables, and no fewer than seven dozen eggs?"

"Oh, Evie." Lacey drew in a deep breath. "That much?"

"Per week," she affirmed. "Though he left out coffee. I've

included a section at the bottom I'll be reordering periodically, separate from the rest, but it needs doing now. An assortment of spices, various preserves and airtights, condensed milk, molasses, raisins, peppermint sticks and honey. . ."

"How much will all of this cost?" Even Cora, who'd helped in the café, seemed staggered by the sheer volume of the list.

"Somewhere in the neighborhood of five hundred dollars a month. Perhaps more, considering transportation costs." Evie drew a deep breath. "Which is what I told you—twelve dollars a man, apart from the cost to lay in a supply against contingencies."

"That's true. Very well, Mr. Draxley. Place four times the order, plus the additional requests today, then work out a standing weekly order for everything else." Lacey sighed.

"Thank you for your time," Evie called to Mr. Draxley, ushering the others out the door and down the single step. "We'll be back regularly!" She shut the door behind them.

"So later we can check on his nap time, but for now we can join Braden before he and Mr. Creed plot anything without us." Cora knew her far too well for comfort.

"Does anyone get a sneaking suspicion they already have?" Evie couldn't point out anything in particular, but she somehow knew Creed wouldn't be content ordering around the workers. *No, that man wants to know everything that goes on here.*

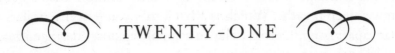 TWENTY-ONE

He needed more information. Jake needed time to ferret out the information. But somehow this week kept him the busiest he'd ever been in his life. He'd worked ten-hour days alongside logging crews since he graduated. It wasn't the work, the town, or even the time of year. It was the women. *Dad warned me not to let a pretty face get in my way, but he never prepared me for anything like this.*

In all fairness, Jake figured no man could have prepared another for a situation like this, even if it had a precedent. And he was all but sure nothing like Hope Falls existed before.

None of the complaints he'd heard about women seemed to fit the ladies who'd decided to carve a niche out of these mountains. They didn't complain about circumstances or pout to get their way. Jake could have handled that. *Instead, I find what no man bothers to warn others about—a woman who works hard and doesn't bother pouting when plotting serves her much better.* Which meant, of course, he had to watch her even closer.

Jake struck the final undercut blow into the trunk of a proud old Douglas fir and stood back to judge his own work. The angle, the depth. . .just right to let Robert Kane and Chester Fillmore team a whipsaw to bring her down. He motioned them over, mind working full-steam ahead.

With all the work to be done and the women to watch over, he'd done precious little fact-finding. Thus far, he'd narrowed the suspects down to ten men—which made nine too many. Jake's best hope lay in convincing the women to agree to Braden's scheme about interviewing the men one by one and asking questions.

After a cool drink of water and a swipe of his bandana along the back of his neck, Jake consulted his pocket watch. *Perfect.* He started walking, reaching the doctor's office a solid ten minutes before the appointed meeting time—the better to steal a word with Lyman before the women arrived.

He'd planned to show up even earlier, but that last tree proved more stubborn than most. He'd needed to clean the resin from his ax twice before carrying on. In most areas, spring came around about March, but the San Juan Mountains held a longer winter season. Running sap meant slow going. Not that it mattered. Women always showed up late.

Except "always" didn't always manage to be the case. All four women sat around Braden Lyman's bed in a cluster of chairs. Those chairs hadn't been there when he'd poked his head through the window to say a good morning earlier that day. Once again, they defied his expectations and set him at a disadvantage. Evie's smile as he entered the room told him who planned it.

I wonder if I'd grow accustomed to her, and she'd become as easy to read and anticipate as everyone else. Jake shook away the thought. Nothing about that woman, from her tiger eyes to the tips of her toes, managed to be mundane. *How could it? She's one of the first women to try to run a sawmill.*

He gave her a genuine smile in return for her smug one, before realizing they hadn't brought in a chair for him. Not that he expected women to haul furniture around for his benefit, but Jake didn't intend to stand around while everyone else sat back and chatted. He held up a forefinger and left the room.

A swift search of the doctor's study turned up no extra chairs. Neither did the other patient room. The best Jake found was a curious wheeled stool. It'd have to do. He wheeled it into the room and maneuvered to be near Lyman's side. Men stuck together. . .especially against a quartet of troublesome females. Most especially when wedging his stool up there edged Evie into less prominence, eliciting an irritated little huff.

He liked that huff, and he liked sitting next to her. *She smells like cinnamon and warm woman—the kind of smell a man could get used to.* If he planned to stick around. Jake shifted so he sat farther away from her and her tempting scent. He had other things to focus on, things that meant he'd be leaving.

Something in him stalled at that idea, but this wasn't the time to consider it. Jake could buck that log after he felled the tree. For now, he'd undercut the troublemakers and chop away suspects until the time came to take Twyler down. Hard.

In the meantime, the women would need a softer approach. "It's good to see everyone in this room with no one glowering, arguing, or refusing to let others pursue a conversation." He grinned, seeing tight smiles in return.

Only Evie refused to play along, her eyebrow shooting upward. "I'd say it's good to see everyone in the room without anyone trying to push them through the door and lock it." Her rejoinder told him he'd hit the right note. They accepted each other's presence, but she stayed on guard. *Smart girl.*

"Let's not dredge up the past." Miss Higgins stood and shuffled around another chair toward a side table bearing a teapot, pitcher, and now-familiar mugs. She poured some coffee, added sugar, and passed it to Lyman. "Coffee, Mr. Creed?"

"Thank you." He held completely still as Evie got up to help pass cups around. When she stood, her skirts brushed his legs in a sudden caress—an unconscious retribution for his decision to force his way between her chair and Miss Lyman's.

He didn't breathe easy until everyone was served and seated.

"First order of business," Lyman started in, "is a frank discussion of finances. Creed tells me it takes about twenty-seven thousand to build a sawmill, but that's taking into account lumber, labor, and land, which we already hold in hand."

"The labor isn't entirely free," Evie spoke up. "Lacey asked me before I placed a standing weekly order this morning. It comes to twelve dollars a man, per month. An excessively low price for the work, but something to take into account."

"Five hundred dollars a month," Miss Lyman clarified.

"Negligible compared to typical wages," Jake approved. "So what you're looking at is hardware materials and the machines."

"Wait," Miss Lyman reminded. "I've read that the costs to build an operational flume can be staggering. Those men building the Sanger Flume estimate costs of over five thousand dollars per mile. Even if we start short, that's a large investment."

"Smith and Moore's costs run so high because they're buying their precut redwood. Right now they're building at a decline of over three hundred feet per mile. That's steep going and slows things down considerably." Jake alleviated some of her concern. "You won't need to buy your wood or deal with inclines of that grade, and you'll only need to build enough of a flume to carry the logs to the river in any case. Much simpler."

"This sounds like it will take time," Evie pointed out. "We can't rely on free labor indefinitely or even beyond a few weeks at best. We'll choose our husbands and need to pay the rest of the workers good wages to keep them in Hope Falls."

Something in his chest began to snarl while the other women nodded their agreement. Jake drained his coffee in one gulp, the hot liquid a slight distraction. That Braden didn't look pleased either did nothing to quell his rising irritation.

"You three don't need to get married to make the sawmill work. It's foolish to chain yourselves to men you hardly know, who don't match you. Pay the men decent wages, and they'll stay on for the food, I guarantee it. If the outlay looks to be a problem,

I'll help you rustle up investors." *I'll invest.*

"We aren't getting married to save on labor, Mr. Creed." Evie's glower could have burned through a sequoia. Twice. "I, for one, am offended you think we're marriage mercenaries."

"The ad called for written responses," Miss Higgins corrected him. "When the men showed up in person, we adjusted. The four of us couldn't route them from town, nor could we leave them loitering about, idle and underfoot and causing trouble."

"You set out to hire husbands," Lyman broke in. "If that's not mercenary, I'd like to know what you'd call it."

"Practical." Evie all but pounced from her chair with the answer. Jake felt her tense and lean toward the bed. "Logical. We came out here to begin new lives and establish a business, and sought partners for both ventures. We're offering a lot, and any man who wants a chance should bring something to the table."

"Gingersnap?" Miss Lyman passed around a plate of crisp, spicy cookies, starting with her brother and ending with Jake.

"This isn't the type of thing I meant when I said bring something to the table." Evie's dimple made a shallow indentation, but he spotted it as she passed him the plate. While everyone else munched, she didn't take any cookies.

That's when he noticed it. The sharper angle of her jaw, the more pronounced hollow at the base of her throat. "I'm not taking one unless you join us." He held the plate out to her. *She's either not been eating enough, or not sleeping enough, or worrying too much, or all three.* "Take one, please."

"No, thank you." Her dimple vanished, and Jake suddenly wondered if it would leave forever when her cheeks lost their beguiling, cheery roundness. "I'm not hungry, Mr. Creed."

"You should be." He pushed the plate into her hands. "Take more than one, Miss Thompson, because I'm only having as many as you do, and I've got my heart set on a minimum of three."

"Then take them all." She pushed the plate back. "There's no connection between whether I partake and how much you enjoy."

"But there is." Jake scowled at her. Surely she wasn't one of those namby-pamby females who tried reducing regimes to be fashionably thin? Evie had more sense. "I can't properly enjoy your fine baking when I see you looking like that."

"Excuse you?" She rose to her feet. "If the sight of me so offends your delicate appetite, perhaps you should leave the room, Mr. Creed." Her offense made him realize his mistake a moment too late. "Better yet, why don't you leave Hope Falls?"

"I meant I can't enjoy it when I see you not eating with us, woman." He stood to look down at her. "Don't look for offense when there's none to find. So sit down and eat up."

"You don't tell me what to do or when to eat, Mr. Creed, and I'll thank you to remember it. Furthermore, I didn't look for an insult. You flung one my way with your ill-considered words. Next time, be more clear about what you mean."

"Fine!" He scooted her chair forward so it nudged behind her knees, forcing her to sit; then he shoved the plate into her hands again. "I'll be clear. I don't like it when a woman stops eating. You're working too much not to need the strength."

"Are you saying I look sickly?"

"You aren't sickly at all, Evie, considering you can outwork most men I've known. But Creed's observant." Lyman shook his head. "He wants you eating more, and now that I look at you, I can see what he noticed before any of us. Eat a gingersnap."

"I don't want to." She set the plate on the bed and folded her arms. "But tell me what you think you see, Braden."

"You know, Evie." He stared at his fiancée's sister, who stared back in complete incomprehension. Then Lyman shot a glance at the other women, whose wide eyes and silent smiles offered no assistance. "It looks as though you. . ." He waved a hand up and down as though to indicate her frame. "That is to say, the work up here seems to be taking something of a toll on you."

Creed watched as Evie's hands flew up to check her hair. She looked down as though to make sure her clothes were in order.

None of the other women spared her the uncertainty. Instead, all three kept their gazes locked on him, heads cocked to the side as though encouraging him to enlighten their friend.

"Oh." Understanding flickered in a normally sunny gaze, clouding it over with a foreign sadness. "I believe I know what you're all too polite to say. It's true there's been more work to begin than I expected, but that's no excuse for my poor temper or being quick to take offense. My apologies to everyone. No need to press sweets on me to improve my disposition."

"No!" Three women and Lyman burst out their denials.

But Creed had had enough. Delicate manners caused the misunderstanding and hurt in Evie's eyes, and he wanted them gone. "You're not a fool, so stop acting like one, Evelyn Thompson." He held the plate out to her one last time. "Truth is everyone's too polite to be blunt, but I'll do it. You're losing heft and I don't like it. Now eat your cookies."

"Heft!" Evie could only be thankful her friends' cries drowned out her own screech, or at least relegated it to part of a chorus instead of a full-fledged solo. It wouldn't have flattered her already paltry share of feminine graces.

Then again, she decided, *I'd really rather not hear that word. Ever. For as long as I live. Having it surround me doesn't minimize its impact at all.* Then she realized two terrible things. First, Braden started laughing and hadn't stopped since Creed uttered the loathsome word. Second—and far more unforgivable—she was eating one of the accursed gingersnaps.

Why, oh why, do I always eat when I'm upset? She pushed the plate at Creed, who refused to take hold of it until she let go, forcing him to catch the entire thing. *And I was doing so well with ignoring my sweet tooth. It's all his fault!*

"I can't. . ." Braden wheezed between hoots of laugher. "Can't believe you, Creed." He drew in a deep breath only to start off on another round again. "As good as call a woman. . .hefty."

"*Yes, dear*"—Evie fantasized about the conversation she'd have with her sister later—*"it's a terrible thing to lose your fiancé again. But we both know he more than had it coming."* Then her sister would sigh and completely agree that smothering Braden Lyman had been a necessity. Not even Lacey would argue.

"Lyman, I know you've been through a lot, but if you ever say something like that about Ev—Miss Thompson again, I'll make sure you regret it." Creed's low growl interrupted Evie's reverie. "Even if I have to be tied down to make a fair fight."

"You said it first." She poked him in the chest with one finger. "Don't threaten Braden." *If anyone gets him, I will.*

"I did not!" Creed's blue eyes went icy. "But if you're going to hitch on exact words, I said you're losing heft, not that you're hefty. And I said I don't like it." He surveyed the plate, selected the biggest cookie, and held it out to her. "Here, eat this one next so you don't get scrawny."

"Scrawny?" This time the echo came out in a sort of squeak. *Did a man just say I'm in danger of being* scrawny?

"That's what he said," Cora yelled three feet away.

"I heard it, too!" Lacey and Naomi verified the event.

"Don't you start getting your feathers ruffled over being called scrawny," Creed warned. "You're not that far gone, and I aim to make sure I don't have to see it happen, but even a woman can't get her dander up over being called two opposites." He brandished the cookie at her in both threat and invitation.

"My feathers are fine and don't need you evaluating them." Perversely, now that she knew she looked thin enough to eat a cookie, she didn't want one. In fact, wouldn't touch it.

Contrary as she felt, Creed had her beat. He raised a brow then looked her down and up in a slow, assessing glance that left her feeling the blush from her ears down her neck. An appreciative smile tilted higher to the left of his face. "I've reevaluated, Miss Thompson." His words sent her mood plummeting. Of course it'd been a mistake for him to think she needed feeding up. "I was selfish, claiming three." Creed moved so he handed the plate to her. "Let me keep this one instead."

"Oh no, you don't." Evie couldn't believe the way the rascal dared to tease her in front of everyone. "Mr. Creed, you take that back right now." She waggled the plate.

"Yes, ma'am." A hangdog look crossed his face. Quick as a flash, he dropped his one cookie atop the mound on the plate. "You're right. The way you're wasting away, you need every one." With that, he sat back on his stool, which somehow turned to leave her staring at nothing more than his back while he resumed conversation with everyone else as though nothing had happened.

Leaving her standing there with a plate of gingersnaps. And the memory of a man who'd said she looked almost scrawny. If she wasn't very, very careful, Evie realized, she might just end up liking Creed.

And then where will I be?

TWENTY-TWO

Facing the same conversation she'd started three weeks previous, Lacey fought the urge to bury her face in her hands. Giving in to frustration over everyone's doubt in her grand vision wouldn't win any confidence from them, she reminded herself.

Why is it that men are the ones credited with common sense and good instincts, when they're completely incapable of the most basic daily tasks? She watched as Braden ignored Cora and Creed smothered Evie with orders, both of them too obtuse to carry on so much as a decent conversation. When Braden and Creed both insulted Evie, Lacey almost left the room in disgust.

How Evie withstood it, I'll never know—unless she secretly returns Creed's interest. That kept Lacey in her seat. *For all his domineering ways, at least Creed's protective and kind underneath. He shouldn't have said "heft," but how many men would notice that Evie's dropped weight? He's only known her a sennight! Better yet, he liked her the way she was.* For that alone, Lacey would approve Creed if Evie chose him as her husband. . .despite his inexplicable loyalty to Lacey's own brother.

As for Braden's own behavior toward Cora. . .well, that would be Cora's dilemma. Not that such a technicality stopped Lacey from wondering and watching. Nor would it stop her from involving herself if Braden didn't shape up. In a very real way, Cora's presence in Hope Falls was Lacey's fault.

In fact, all of their presences in Hope Falls could be laid squarely at her door—a circumstance Lacey hoped she'd one day be proud to proclaim. For now, she had her hands full trying to keep it from devolving into a catastrophe. At least she had it figured out what to do if this endeavor became a spectacular failure. After all, she'd been doing it since she was old enough to talk. *Blame Braden.*

And this time it wouldn't even be a lie. Braden chose to invest a healthy portion of his own inheritance and all of Cora's dowry into the mines, then encouraged Lacey, Naomi, and Evie to do the same. Braden insisted on moving out here alone to oversee things, insisted on personal involvement with the business. Braden's own decisions led to his being trapped underground in that terrible mine collapse, breaking his legs. That's what pulled them west to the ghost of a town they'd planned before.

If the sawmill succeeded, that meant Lacey's glorious ambition saved the town and provided for them all. *My dream.* She held that close to her heart. *Not Braden's, mine. Not Evie's café. My mill will be the way to redeem Hope Falls and renew Braden's spirit.* She could already see it working. He had more color and vitality than even the first time he'd yelled at her.

Well, the first time he'd yelled at her since she'd come to Colorado. Lacey couldn't really remember the first time he'd yelled at her back when they were both children. It's part of what made her so good at ignoring him whenever he disagreed with her. Years of practice afforded a woman a great degree of skill in defusing unpleasant situations. An increasingly useful skill, Lacey found, when one was surrounded with uncouth men.

Especially men who didn't appreciate how incredibly fortunate they were to enjoy her presence. Braden pestered her and Cora about coming here. Creed took it upon himself to irritate Evie over the same matter. And neither one bothered to consider the fact he wouldn't be enjoying the opportunity to harangue anyone if the women didn't brave the wilds of Colorado.

With appreciation in short supply and men in overwhelming numbers, Lacey was almost tempted not to defend her entire idea to advertise for husbands. Almost. If it weren't for the basic, unchanging principle that Lacey was always right, and Braden always wrong—unless, of course, he wisely agreed with his sister—she would let the matter rest.

But Lacey Lyman had undergone more than enough change in the past week. So this two-way conversation between Braden and Mr. Creed about simply paying her suitors instead of allowing them to work for meals and the chance to court them would end now.

Lacey waited only for Evie to reclaim her seat before breaking in. "We advertised for husbands instead of workers because we need husbands instead of workers." She kept her tone even. "It isn't a matter of money but because women are, as you two have taken every opportunity to point out, vulnerable in Colorado."

"Yes, you're vulnerable." Creed's habitual scowl returned as he warmed to the subject. "And even more so with your brother unable to get his feet under him for the next few months. But with me, Riordan, Lawson, and McCreedy, you'll be looked after well enough you needn't rush into wedlock anytime soon."

"Lawson and McCreedy?" Naomi's brow grooved into deep lines Lacey hoped never showed up on her own forehead. "Why don't I recall those names? Are they any of our workers?"

"You haven't met them yet." Braden brushed away her concern. "They should arrive today. One's an engineer to help design and construct the building and flume and operate machinery, and the other will make the fourth team boss."

"What?" Lacey yanked the coffee mug from her brother's hand. "You two went behind our backs and hired additional men?"

"Give that back." Braden made a swipe for his drink and

missed. "We sent for extra eyes Creed can trust, and who fill specific positions we need. Did it the first day we met."

"You didn't tell them?" Creed showed the decency to look displeased. "So they don't know about Martha or Arla either?"

"They're bringing wives?" Cora perked up. "More women can be nothing but a blessing in this town, to tell the truth."

"McCreedy's bringing his wife, Martha. Lawson's bringing his newly widowed sister, Arla Nash." Creed's hesitation warned Lacey she wouldn't like what came next. "She's in the family way, with the child due within the next month or so."

"This is no place for a woman with child!" Naomi's wrath made Lacey jump. She'd never seen her cousin so angry. "She shouldn't be subjected to the journey, much less the harsh realities of Hope Falls as it stands. What of the child?"

"It's too late to object," Evie pointed out. "If they arrive sometime this day or the next, we make the best of it."

"Lawson wouldn't leave her behind, with no other family to speak of." Creed's explanation accounted for the decision. "Same reason the four of you came out here to be with Lyman here."

"No, it's opposite. We came to him. He's making her come along." Lacey refused to be lumped along with such selfishness.

"Whatever the case"—Cora pushed aside her objection—"we'll need to make arrangements for their housing. Ms. Nash will need the third room in our house, and the McCreedys should take one of the homes abandoned by a mining family. You would tell us if they planned to bring any children, wouldn't you?"

"They've no children," he assured her. "Just themselves."

"Mr. Creed, after this discussion, we'll need men to empty out the final upstairs room and move the second bed from the first room to the third, so there's one bed in each." Evie's direction made it so she'd share a bed with Cora—a selfless act, in Lacey's estimation. She knew Cora kicked in her sleep.

"The four of us will find and fix up a house as best we can this afternoon, given the short timetable." Naomi didn't waste a glare, and Lacey wondered if it was because they did no good. "We will welcome these four, but you two men may not invite anyone else into our town without our agreement. Understood?"

Creed and Braden exchanged looks as though reluctant to make any such vow. As though they had a choice, really.

"Either that, or we send the McCreedys back." Lacey mimicked the steel-and-starch tones of her former headmistress. "We'll do to them what Braden threatened with the four of us. Give us your word that you'll pull no more of these quick changes, and we'll take you on your honor as gentlemen."

"Agreed." Creed made the decision for Braden, but Lacey took it. He gave the right answer, which was the important part.

"You also need to stop sending men away from town without our consent." Evie's addendum shocked Lacey and the other women.

"What?" Naomi's and Cora's disbelief assuaged her pique. At least they'd all been left in the dark about this little trick.

"Haven't you noticed that no new men have arrived since the seventeenth?" Suddenly, Evie's observation was painfully obvious. "Men step off the train but never stay in town."

"The ad itself listed the seventeenth," Braden defended. "The men who arrived on time have the right to send latecomers packing. Otherwise, you'll have trouble among your workers."

"Besides which, we don't need more men right now, and you four are stretched to feed us all and keep things going." Creed's logic couldn't be refuted. "We've two dozen workers, and that's men aplenty for clearing the site and starting construction. Any more and they'll get in each other's way so much that you won't be able to control the fights and such."

"The issue isn't whether or not the decision makes sense. The issue is you made that decision without us." Cora frowned.

"Every one of your workers made that decision," Creed revealed. "I couldn't have naysayed them even if I wanted to." The look on his face clearly said he hadn't wanted to.

"If that's the case, what makes you think they'll accept these men you two have hired, Mr. Creed? They're bound to protest some sort of favoritism. Particularly as I assume you've promised them competitive wages to convince them to uproot burgeoning families and come here. None of the others are paid."

"The men will accept them for the sake of the women." Evie answered Miss Higgins in a blink. "McCreedy isn't bound by the same deal as he's already married, and no one would oust a woman in the family way. That ensures Lawson's tolerated presence. If he's the engineer, they won't be able to object his salary."

"Well done, Miss Thompson." Creed's nod told them Evie assessed the situation correctly. "Those are the reasons I chose McCreedy and Lawson before I knew about his sister."

"That, and to increase your pack of watchdogs," Lacey accused her brother. "It doesn't change the fact we need husbands. The security I spoke of isn't just for ourselves, Braden. It's to hold our property and defend against claim jumpers who'll try and take what we build once it's of value."

"Not to mention expansion," Cora tacked on. "More men mean more claims, and married women are allowed to own property now. The more land we hold, the stronger our position against those who discover our success and seek to move in on it."

"Besides"—Naomi waited a breath behind Cora to speak her piece—"there's the issue of propriety. If we aren't married, people will assume that the only sort of single women to live in a logging town are of. . .loose morals. A house full of us won't be secure indefinitely with dozens of men around—particularly as time wears on and the business grows to include more workers."

"That leaves only one option." Evie made up in certainty what she lacked in enthusiasm. "A husband."

A wife. Corbin Twyler couldn't believe he'd sunk so low as to need a wife. Worse still, he'd returned to his roots in logging.

He'd sworn never to come back to this sorry, scrape-bait existence. Little more than a boy, he'd seen no opportunity in the muzzle-loaded bunkhouses of the lowest logging outfits back in New England nor in the flasks of cheap ale passed around to pass time.

Until the Game.

At first, he'd ignored even its call, blind to the beauty of battered cards dealt and flipped until their marks faded to fond memories. The young Corbin lost his pay and his pride with capricious dice he now knew had been weighted against him. But the Game didn't take luck so much as patience. And skill.

The annoying habits that so irritated him about his fellow loggers suddenly served a purpose other than to send him straight to a book after supper. Tapping fingers, a blink too many, a red nose or itchy neck—they signaled a change in fortune when Corbin tried his hand at the Game. Winning too often raised suspicion, so he lost occasionally, enough to placate the roughest workers. A few beatings taught a man awfully fast.

All the while, he saved his cache in a hinged flask. Men searched his boots, his bunk, his bedroll, and his laundry, but none found his freedom flask. Then one payday, he left to try his luck elsewhere. Without the familiar mannerisms, against other cardsharps, he fared worse. Better bluffs, more experience, marked decks, and his own desperation stacked against him more than the cards themselves ever could.

For a good bit, he steered clear of other inveterate players of the Game. Corbin could read common folk and fleeced them regularly while he cultivated the skills used against him. It worked its way into his dreams, his very soul. The Game called to him. The thrill of the stakes, pulse pounding as he turned a card, the exhilarating fear of being caught with a marked deck. . .nothing pumped the blood like the Game.

Nothing made the Game better than a worthy opponent. That's why he needed the stake for big games. He couldn't test his worth anywhere else. Without the shared passion, the consuming drive to win at any cost, the honed senses precisely tuned to determine the other player's thoughts and moves. . .the Game withered. And without the Game, Corbin had nothing.

So what were a few petty thefts, a minor robbery here and there, if it kept a chair open for him? Cheating didn't count as a matter of dishonor but as the best sort of bluff, the ultimate level of conning another player. Either they knew the score when they sat down, or they'd learn. Even when a man suspected he'd been cheated, he usually had too much pride to announce the fact. Corbin counted on it when he underestimated a mark. That didn't happen too often now.

It happened just over five months back. He chose the wrong mark, in the wrong place, at the wrong time. If the Granger boy hadn't caught on, or had kept his mouth shut, he'd have lost a bit of walking-around money and that funny coin he flipped around. No more harm done. But he did catch on, showed every sign of raising Cain right in front of the men Corbin fleeced two nights prior. From there, things went bad. Real bad, real fast.

He'd been running ever since. And when he ran out of funds and friends, he found that ad and headed for Hope Falls. Corbin Twyler could live through logging for a little while. He'd survived worse for less. After all, who needed Dame Fortune when a man nabbed a wealthy wife?

The Game waited.

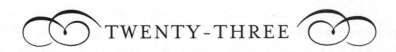 TWENTY-THREE

Evie needed a miracle to keep up with the ravenous appetites of two dozen hardworking men who put away enough food to feed a small city, and enough coffee to wash all of it down. Sure, Cora helped out as she'd done ever since Evie judged her old enough to boil water, and Naomi could manage basic tasks and even a few more complicated skills, but that wasn't enough.

So she prayed for a miracle—and God sent Martha McCreedy. A sturdy Irishwoman whose lilting speech patterns closely mimicked those of Mr. Riordan, Martha no sooner rode into town on the iron horse than she took a post behind one of Evie's iron stoves.

God bless the Marthas of this world, Evie rejoiced time and time again over the next few days as Martha's name proved no mistake. Not that Mrs. McCreedy in any way lacked a heart for resting in the Lord's will and teaching, but Martha's busy hands and servant's spirit made her a welcome addition in Hope Falls.

Mrs. Nash, the grieving widow expecting her firstborn, made for a more cumbersome, if no less welcome, addition. She stepped from the train with a watery smile and gracious, "Thank you for your kind welcome. I'm so pleased to be here," before subsiding into the sort of gut-wrenching sobs best indulged in private.

Of course, it made the transition far easier for Mr. Lawson and the McCreedys. One whiff of a weeping woman and almost every timber beast made for the forest. Or, at the very least, the luggage. In either case, they swiftly maintained a wide berth between themselves and the new arrivals. By the time the men realized a single man had been included in the bunch, even the most curmudgeonly didn't bother to grump about the situation.

Evie highly suspected Mr. Creed threatened them with spending time looking after the good widow if they made trouble, which would have been a violation of their agreement not to create or enforce punishments without first consulting the women. As she wholeheartedly approved of the results, Evie made it a point not to question this particular method. It worked.

Better yet, it kept the men from upsetting Arla Nash. Or getting close enough to discover a lovely and more even-tempered young woman than she initially appeared. After a difficult day rounded off by a porter bearing an uncanny resemblance to her deceased beloved, Arla withstood a poorly timed warning from her brother about the uncertainty of her welcome in Hope Falls.

Apparently he hadn't seen fit to concern her with the detail earlier for fear of oversetting her, so he sprang the news upon her mere moments before she faced dozens of now-unfriendly faces. It seemed Braden Lyman and Jake Creed weren't the only men incapable of exercising good judgment.

In any case, Arla made herself as useful as possible. She swiftly volunteered to peel any vegetables needed, freeing Lacey from the monotonous task she so often deplored. Since Lacey proved herself adept in only two other areas, she managed beverages and baking bread. Not biscuits. Not muffins. Not corn bread nor cakes. Bread, and bread only, came out correctly when Lacey took to baking. No one could explain it, but they accepted it after a while and their days settled into a rhythm.

Evie woke up earliest, used to sunrise hours from getting up at dawn to head for the café. Once she washed up and dressed, she nudged Cora until her sister emerged from beneath the covers like a disgruntled hedgehog from the zoo, fine wisps of ginger hair spiking around bleary eyes.

By the time Evie carried the tea and chocolate upstairs, Cora had accomplished the unenviable task of coaxing everyone else awake. Cups of warm fluid braced the women before they wrapped themselves in cloaks warm enough to ward against the biting chill of each spring morning.

Mrs. McCreedy somehow managed to meet them en route to the diner. "I canna believe that Mr. Draxley o' yourn still hae not managed to obtain proper milking cows." Mrs. McCreedy tsked a familiar lament as she scrambled panful after panful of eggs.

"The men didn't mind an extra team of oxen to pull logs away from the felling site." Naomi tried to look at the silver lining. "And everyone enjoyed the fresh meat from butchering the others. Besides, it gave Evie a reason to request a smokehouse."

"We'll be ordering more condensed milk, I take it." Lacey looked up from where she diligently worked bread dough. "Those cows arrive by tomorrow, or Mr. Draxley pays for them himself."

"My babe fancies a glass of fresh milk," Arla admitted as she peeled another mound of potatoes to tax the patience of Job. "Tea and chocolate are all well and good, but some days there's nothing like a fresh bit of milk alongside your breakfast."

"I fancy some of whatever it is Evie's up to at her stove." Cora looked up from where she cut long, even slices from a wheel of cheese before dividing them into squares. "Fried corn mush?"

"That's it exactly." Evie took two loaves from the oven and slid two others inside. A few moments, and she tapped the cooling loaves from their pans and refilled them with more batter before slicing the baked mush and lightly frying each side in a hot, buttery skillet. She filled platters with them.

"Since I've never heard of it, I've never eaten it." Lacey wiped an errant strand of hair from her forehead with the back of her hand. "But I do know it takes twice as long to bake this bread with you using all of my loaf pans, Evie Thompson!"

"*Your* loaf pans?" Evie cocked an eyebrow. "How's that?"

"I use them at least three times a week." Lacey gestured toward the six loaves cooling on the windowsill. "Although, come to think of it, why is it that I bake so much bread these days? It seems as though that's all I do when I enter this kitchen."

Evie exchanged guilty glances with the other women. Truth be told, they all conspired to make sure Lacey did precious little besides bake bread. "You also take care of the coffee and help serve, same as the rest of us."

"For the most part, all I do is peel potatoes and such." Arla sounded downright cheerful. "It's good to have something to occupy your hands and ease the burden for everyone else."

"Thank you, Arla." Naomi gave the woman's shoulder an encouraging pat. "We're glad to have you and Martha with us."

"I wish I could say I'm glad to be here." Arla looked down at the lumpy, half-peeled potato in her hands. "Truth is I miss my Herbert something dreadful and want nothing more than for him to have never choked on that fish bone. He'd be such a wonderful father, and I'd still be in my own house. . . ." Her voice trailed off, eyes shining with tears she wouldn't let fall. "But since I can't have that, I'm grateful to have found friends."

Evie's own vision went a bit misty, so she nearly burned the next piece of fried corn mush. "It's selfish of me to say so, but I'm glad you and your baby are here. You'll be the one to make Hope Falls a real town, Arla. Until a place sees a baby, it's only an outpost at best." She heard the others agree with her, except the part about her selfishness, but Evie knew.

She knew how much she'd ached for a little baby, though she'd given up hope of ever holding her own son or daughter as years passed by and no man showed the slightest interest in proposing to her. Evie accepted awhile ago that Cora would be the closest she'd come to having a daughter and convinced herself to be content in her role as an entrepreneur and chef.

Lord, why is it that whenever I feel comfortable with the path You've set me on, the road takes a sharp curve? I resigned myself to the entire scheme of advertising for a husband, but it snowballed out of control before we even arrived in town. To be honest, Jesus, I'm almost afraid of what will happen when I resign myself to choosing a husband from amongst these strangers. What strange turn will You bring then? Give me faith to trust You, and some sign that the husband of Your choosing wants me for more than my property or my cooking, but myself. . .

". . .shoot him." Lacey finished saying something Evie wished she hadn't missed. "Of course, it takes more than just aim. I'd imagine you need great courage and determination to fire."

"Don't hesitate, lassies." Mrs. McCreedy covered another platter of scrambled eggs and planted her hands on her hips. "Once Miss Lyman teaches you to shoot, pull the trigger the instant you know you're in danger from any man, you ken?"

"Yes, Mrs. McCreedy," Evie chorused dutifully along with the others, but she couldn't help thinking of a pair of changeable blue eyes. Laughing one moment, icy with rage the next. . .

There's more than one kind of danger to guard against.

The sound of gunfire made Jake's blood run cold. Without another thought, he dropped his end of the saw he'd been manning with Gent and took off running toward the sound.

Praise God, it's not coming from town. He barely noticed the prayer. Jake rarely prayed. He believed in the Lord, didn't believe most people bothered to live up to what He laid out in the Word, and washed his hands of paying lip service to any of it long ago. But he'd accepted the truth, and those sorts of thoughts slipped out in intense times.

Jake hoped God saw it as a good thing—that he did the best he could and handled most of what came his way as he saw fit, but didn't hesitate to call for help when he needed it. And if the women were in trouble, Jake would take any help available.

Pistol drawn, he slowed, taking cover behind trees as the haphazard shots grew louder. Closer. From the sounds of it, he'd circled behind the shooters, which meant they fired *away* from town. Good. That meant everyone might just survive this.

Then he heard it. A feminine shriek. *The only women for miles are ours.* Jake threw caution to the winds and ran toward the bloodcurdling sound, heart pumping so loud in his ears he almost missed the next sound. This one stopped him cold.

Giggles? Jake canted his head toward the cheerful sound breezing toward him. No doubt about it—girlish giggles filled the forest. Right before another shot rang out.

"Did I hit anything this time?" Evie's call made him blink.

Did she. . . Then he understood. The women were practicing their marksmanship, learning to shoot as a precaution against the many threats surrounding them. *That's my girl.*

"Wait and let me go check. I didn't see any of the cans move, but perhaps you scratched one." Miss Lyman's voice sounded farther and farther away as she presumably went to check a target. A few moments later and, "Well, I'm sure you hit something, Evie. But not in the vicinity you aimed for."

"Razzlefrass," Evie muttered. "I should be good at this."

Jake paused in the act of creeping toward the stand of trees guarding the voices, easing into a better position rather than rushing now he knew the situation. He snickered silently into his sleeve at her assertion she should be good at shooting, as though everything came easily to her. Then. . . *Razzlefrass?*

"Razzlefrass?" Miss Higgins repeated the strange phrase. "That sounds like a berry jam, Evie. A tart one, I think."

"I used to wonder why my sister can't say something simple, like fiddlesticks, when something irks her." Miss Thompson's amusement carried to him. "Now I enjoy the words she concocts."

So do I, Jake decided. *I wonder what others I've missed.*

"*Peduncle* remains my absolute favorite," Miss Lyman mused. "There's something so whimsical about saying it. You cannot help but smile when you do. Try not to...peduncle..."

"I've told you a thousand times, Lace, I didn't make that one up. A peduncle is the stem of a piece of fruit. I've offered to show you in the encyclopedia several times!"

"But that's less fun to believe, Evie. Now why don't you try again, but this time, squint at the target when you fire." Miss Lyman seemed to be the one directing firing practice.

Jake took advantage of the noise to steal forward the last bit he needed to see them all clearly. Sure enough, the four women stood in a long, clear expanse. At the end, they'd balanced several cans atop a broad rock. From here, Jake could make out more than a few holes in the beaten metal. *So at least one of the women can shoot accurately. Maybe more.*

"I'll go check for myself this time." Evie stalked toward the end of the field, determination lengthening her stride and emphasizing the sway of her hips. She was a sight to behold. Right up until she counted the number of bullet holes in the cans and a frown furrowed her brow. She counted again and let out a strange, unfeminine sort of frustrated sound.

"Don't worry, sis," Cora called out. "You'll get it."

"This is our second lesson, and Lacey had no trouble teaching you and Naomi. Shouldn't I be doing well by now?" She nibbled on her lower lip, obviously distressed over not being good at something she'd set her mind to excel in.

It's about time. I was starting to wonder if there was anything Evie set her mind to that she didn't master. Jake caught himself grinning and immediately frowned. *An imperfection in no way makes her perfect,* he chided himself. Stupid notions like that got a man in trouble. Jake watched as Evie took aim again and missed by a mile.

This time he couldn't stop the grin.

 TWENTY-FOUR

The grin abandoned him by the time he sat next to Braden Lyman for the first of the "interviews" the women agreed to. Everyone sandwiching into one room made for a tight fit, so Jake removed the dresser and washstand for the meeting and brought in a bench for the men to sit on. It took up less space than chairs and had the added benefit of seating two if the women decided to speed things along by taking them in pairs.

Jake saw the benefit in that but also wanted the opportunity to take a good, close look at each suspect individually, without having to divide his attention. If two suspects were questioned together, he'd be more apt to miss some small sign to indicate that Twyler's disguise had slipped.

Every one of Jake's instincts told him he'd tracked Twyler to the right place this time. The feeling grew stronger the less he wanted to leave Hope Falls, spurring him toward his real purpose. The proposed mill made for good cover, and nothing more. The women made for a constantly aggravating diversion.

But, ultimately, the entire setup would lead him to Edward's killer. Smiling faces hid treachery, and the longer it took Jake to find Twyler, the longer it gave the vermin to get close to Evie. Or one of the other women, he supposed, but by and large, the men paid Evie the most attention.

Jake couldn't blame them. He could see why some were put off by Miss Higgins's cool reserve when Evie's warm smile provided such contrast. And Evie's shirts with their simple lines made a far more approachable picture than Miss Lyman's fussy frills and overblown sleeves. Even if Miss Thompson weren't engaged to Braden, the men would most likely prefer her older sister. So Jake couldn't blame them. But he didn't have to like it.

He sat in what he'd begun to think of as his customary place between Evie and Miss Lyman, near Braden. Sure enough, the women all agreed they should send the men in pairs. If need be, they decided, they could always speak with one in private. For now, their main concern was speeding things along.

Robert Kane strolled through the door first, his coloring and build placing him squarely on Jake's list of suspects. Most loggers carried more muscle after years on the job. His unctuous smile and ingratiating air whenever one of the women happened to be nearby put him in another category. That one didn't reflect well on the man either.

A second man trailed in his wake. If Kane strode with an overabundance of confidence to make himself seem taller than he truly stood, Chester Fillmore's retiring nature made the man smaller. The same height, build, and coloring as Kane, Fillmore shrank into himself. And away from scrutiny, Jake noted.

Lyman began with the basics—what jobs the men performed, how many years of experience each had, whether they'd worked with ponderosa pine or Douglas fir before, or anything larger.

"We're fallers, the pair of us," Kane answered for both. "I've put my hand to some bucking work when whipsaws will do and, all told, done about seven years in the woods. Two in Puget Sound, five farther east. Douglas fir's about the largest I've brought down." He named two lumber outfits he'd worked with.

"I'm a faller, as well, with four years. Three in Oregon, so I've gone up on springboards to take down coast redwoods fourteen feet across if they were one." Fillmore's voice came out quiet enough everyone strained to hear him. He didn't name any companies he'd worked with, but then again, Lyman hadn't asked. Kane volunteered that information, and Fillmore didn't seem the type of man to use three words when a nod would do.

"Where'd you put in this past winter?" The crucial question, from where Jake sat. It'd take some time to make inquiries and follow up whatever answers the men gave, but this provided the starting point to sniff out a liar. It came closest to the real question on his mind: *Where were you in January, when some coward fitting your description shot my brother?*

Kane named a small outfit in an isolated area, not likely to be well known or listed by any others in town. Nevertheless, his response made Jake's back tense in recognition. If he didn't misremember, that's where McCreedy had spent the season. He could verify or debunk the smooth talker's story that very afternoon. He didn't let any of his racing thoughts show in his expression, keeping it bland. *Even if Kane left for Christmas and didn't return, that's a strong sign he's hiding something.*

Loggers typically came back for another two months in the strongest season. Snow didn't stop the lumber business. In fact, cool, dry weather made for better conditions than hot summer. Snow facilitated moving the giant logs across short distances in areas where they hadn't upgraded from skid roads to the new compact steam engines for hauling. Donkeys, they were called.

Late spring through early autumn, several camps closed or greatly slowed while many of their loggers went home to farms. Late fall through the start of spring, it went full-speed ahead. If a timber beast vanished in the middle of the season, it would be noted. Twyler started running across the country in January.

"Truth be told. . ." Fillmore's hesitant opening nabbed Jake's attention. "I didn't join any outfit this past year. Heard of all the success in mining and decided to try panning for gold. I planned to come back, but an early blizzard snowed me in. Turns out I'm a better timber beast than silt-sifter any day."

"I'm sorry that didn't pan out for you." Miss Thompson's statement elicited a round of groans from her friends. More suspiciously, it earned the sort of cleared throat sound from Lyman that a man made when stifling a chuckle.

"Cora reclaims worst pun," Evie announced. "I'm sorry, Mr. Fillmore. It's something of a game amongst the four of us."

"But that one was unintentional!" her sister protested.

"I cannot believe"—Miss Lyman giggled—"you manage such an abysmal turn of phrase without any effort whatsoever."

The lighthearted banter gave Jake time to sort through his impression of Fillmore's answer. *Getting snowed in would explain his slighter build. He wouldn't have the provisions or constant workload to maintain a faller's strength.* A simple, believable reason, as so many men succumbed to the lure of gold fever.

But it's too neat and tidy. He didn't name the company he usually worked for, and Fillmore doesn't seem the short-stake type. A story about a freak blizzard can't be verified or looked into. There are too many solitary miners in too many places. It'd be the perfect cover for a man like Twyler, if he suspected someone might bother to check a false reference.

Fact was he'd walked into the room with two suspects, thinking to eliminate at least Fillmore. Instead, he'd follow the lead on Kane and keep a closer watch on the mousy man who followed him. If anything, Jake's list kept growing.

Evie's store of patience shrank as the conversation wore on. Too many things ran through her mind, too much to do for her to be sitting still. It seemed a waste of time to question the men's logging credentials when they'd all been out working for almost two weeks now. Couldn't Creed judge their competence firsthand?

Of course he can. Really, this entire exercise is more for Braden's benefit than anything else. The thought kept her from fidgeting. If being unable to get things done for a mere hour made her itch to get moving, how much worse must it be for her sister's fiancé? Suddenly, she didn't begrudge the time spent. *Besides,* she cautioned herself, *you're supposed to learn as much as possible about the men you or your friends might marry.*

Except. . .Evie didn't care for either Mr. Kane or Mr. Fillmore, and she rather doubted Lacey and Naomi did either. Surely Naomi's question about the pair the other day only had to do with her curiosity over the way they worked in teams. Unease crept through as she recalled Naomi's blush and the competitive glint in Lacey's gaze as she asked if her cousin had "fallen."

Perhaps I'm only halfway correct. Neither evinced an interest in Mr. Fillmore, but maybe the more forward Mr. Kane caught at least one eye. She looked at him afresh. He did count as one of the better-looking possibilities, Evie supposed—if one ignored the sense of something sort of. . .oily. . .about the man.

"When did you two meet?" She looked from one man to the other, wondering at the bond between them. Perhaps distant cousins? They shared the same coloring, if not mannerisms.

As expected, Kane answered. "En route to Hope Falls."

"From what I've seen, I assumed a long, strong friendship." Naomi admitted the surprise Evie shared.

"We get on well, match up for a whipsaw." Kane glanced at his companion and shrugged. "Fillmore makes for good company since he's not a hothead or given to talking anyone's ear off."

Fillmore gave a shrug and seemed ready to leave it at that, but rethought and added an eloquent, "It works."

Cora inquired as to age, finding them well-matched there, too. Both claimed twenty-eight years, twenty-nine in the fall.

Evie breathed a sigh of relief—that had been the last question the six of them planned to ask, unless the conversation led to others as a matter of course. Just in time. *The train with my dairy cows should pull in within the next hour or so.*

"I've one last question for you, gentlemen." Lacey rubbed her right hand over her forehead—the old signal for "wait and listen" when one of them changed plans. It didn't bode well. "At this point, we'd like you each to specify which two of the three of us you'd choose to direct your attentions toward, and why."

Evie's stomach dropped to her shoes. She entertained the brief, fanciful notion that if she stood, she'd squish it underfoot like grapes for wine. *Little wonder Lacey didn't mention this question when we planned the interviews. She knew good and well we'd never agree. It's an embarrassment!*

From the corner of her eye, she saw Naomi shoot an alarmed look her way, as though imploring her to find a way to end this dismaying turn in conversation. But Evie could think of no method to save them from hearing the assessment of their would-be suitors, straight from the horses' mouths. So to speak.

Lord, I know I fall short in many, many ways and one of them happens to be humility. But did Lacey have to ask for both names and reasons? I don't want to listen to a man explain why he'd choose other women before looking my way. Especially not with others listening, and most especially not with other men within hearing distance. If I must be humbled, and being sent into a situation beyond my control is not sufficient, could it not happen at some time when Jake Creed isn't watching?

"A man would count himself fortunate to win the hand of any lady in the room, Miss Lyman." Kane's slick response left Lacey shifting irritably and Evie hoping for a way to avoid this.

"You're right, Mr. Kane. Thank you both for your patience." The words spilled in such a hurry, Evie could only be thankful they formed coherent thoughts. "We're glad to have you here."

"Why don't you answer the question, Kane?" Braden eyed the faller with undisguised hostility, and Evie belatedly realized he wondered about Kane's evasive response. "Any lady in the room" included Cora, and despite Braden's obstinacy in insisting he'd dissolved the engagement, he hadn't suggested or allowed anyone else to suggest Cora remained free to wed.

Another time, his protectiveness would gladden Evie's heart. *But the numskull would choose now to be possessive!*

"The answer I gave happened to be sincere." The glint of battle appeared in Kane's eye. "Since you press the issue, I would narrow my selection to Miss Lyman and Miss Thompson. Miss Lyman appeals for her femininity, and Miss Thompson for her domestic abilities. I find I prefer a woman with more conversation than Miss Higgins seems inclined toward sharing."

Evie drew a deep breath, offended for not only herself and Naomi, but Lacey as well. No matter he'd pointed to Lacey as his first choice, Kane didn't see beyond her penchant for bright fabrics and dainty patterns to the woman beneath. Meanwhile, he only recognized Evie herself as a cook and housekeeper, and all but called Naomi a bore. *I won't approve of Robert Kane even if Lacey decides she'll accept his proposal. Naomi and Cora will have to be the two who allow it. As far as I'm concerned, Hope Falls could do better with another worker less self-absorbed.*

"This sort of question does no good for any man or woman involved, but as the ladies make the decisions here, I see no alternative but to answer." Mr. Fillmore showed the good taste to present a mild objection. "I'd select Miss Lyman, for her foresight in recognizing the lumber after the mines collapsed. It seems a good characteristic in a wife, that she look ahead and find the best in each situation. Although I agree Miss Thompson shows great creativity and skill in the kitchen, I differ from my friend. Miss Higgins, with her more demure ways, would make a more fitting companion for me. Still waters run deep, or so they say, and I like to believe it true." With that, Mr. Fillmore sank back onto the bench, looking as though he'd exhausted himself by speaking more words in that one speech than he'd voiced during his entire stay in town.

Much better. Evie sent him an encouraging smile. Not because he'd chosen her—he hadn't—or even noticed anything about her beyond her cooking—as far as Evie could see, men never did—but because Chester Fillmore's quiet personality hid a discerning nature. He'd understood and appreciated some of her friends' fine qualities. In particular, the well-spoken miner might make a good match for Naomi. Never mind that he, too, listed Lacey first.

"Thank you, gentlemen." Cora signaled the end of the conversation, and Braden leaned forward to shake each of their hands in turn before Mr. Kane and Mr. Fillmore departed.

"Lacey, what were you thinking to throw that last bit in?" The words blurted from her mouth the minute Evie thought the men left hearing distance. "We never discussed anything like that!"

"If we discussed it, you wouldn't have let me ask." Lacey gave an unrepentant shrug. "All those details about their work history and logging make for a fine work interview, but that part interests Mr. Creed more than it pertains to us. We need to learn more about the men themselves, and which one of us they plan to ask for. With so many about, it's difficult to guess."

"That may be, but to put them on the spot like that smacks of poor taste." Naomi's eyes remained as wide as they'd been since Lacey asked, and Evie found herself wondering whether her friend had blinked in the past quarter hour. "An ambush."

"If you catch a man off guard, you're more apt to get an honest answer." Creed's observation did little to soothe her nerves. "Notice how much more polished Fillmore made his response than what Kane scraped up. Forewarned is forearmed."

"So now the other men know what to expect, there's little to be gained in asking." Evie gladly followed his logic.

"Wrong. Those two won't warn anyone." Braden shook his head. "They're competitors and won't hand out an advantage."

"From now on, we call them in singly." Creed looked out the window, sunlight illuminating his profile. "Kane answered for both too often, and Fillmore reaped extra time to think. We'll see more of a reaction if we talk to them one at a time."

"Drawing things out seems unwise." *And painful.* Evie swallowed. *How many times will I sit here and either not hear my name or be lauded for nothing but my meals? Do any of the men see me as more than a cook? Do any of them even want me?*

Jake wanted her to stop looking as though someone shot her dog. He saw the doubt in Evie's expression and wanted to tell her that not all men would be idiots. Some saw her kind smile and the brave heart behind it. He wanted to tell her the two men who walked out of the room a moment ago were nothing but fools.

But one of them might be so much more. Even if Kane and Fillmore turned out to be clean, one of the men walking so freely around town wore the stain of murder on his soul.

Seeing her hurt made him want to go find one of those sequoias he'd seen photographs of and fell one with nothing but an ax, but Jake knew he'd rather Evie stay gun-shy than moon about with stars in her eyes. Better she be wary, stay on guard against the men surrounding her and her friends than let any one of them fall into the schemes of scum.

After all, it's only a matter of time before I carry the filth away.

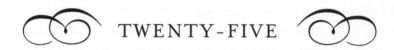

TWENTY-FIVE

T hey're here!" Clump pushed his way past the line of loggers
snaking toward the washing tubs the next day. His heavy, uneven
gait more pronounced than ever as he ran toward the women, he
made better time than Jake guessed. "The cows is come home!"

He bellowed that last as he burst into the kitchen, Jake just
behind him.

Jubilant whoops sounded before Evie came bustling out
the doors, apron strings streaming behind as she headed for the
train. Needless to say, everyone followed. At least, everyone who'd
already washed his dishes. Those who hadn't sulked in line while
faster men chased after the women.

If that wasn't some sort of commentary on the entire setup of
Hope Falls, Jake didn't know what was. Nor was he entirely clear
on what that commentary said about any of them. He just shook
his head and kept close watch as the tableaux unfolded.

He tried to guide the women away from the train so the men
could unload the livestock, but Evie insisted on seeing her cows
first thing. The other women took one look at the bulk of their
suitors keeping a distance and wisely accepted the arms of Clump,
Gent, and Riordan. Only Evie remained resolute in her position.

So Jake stuck directly beside her as they rolled open the doors to the livestock car, took a deep breath, and held it.

"Mercy." Eyes like sunshine began to water as the stench rolled over them. Evie coughed and rocked back a step as the workers set up the unloading ramp for the cows to walk out.

"Here." Jake closed her fingers around his bandana and raised her hand to her nose to block the scent of cow patties, methane, and livestock. He held her elbow to keep her steady and led her to the other women, away from her precious acquisitions.

"Those can't be *my* cows," she moaned from behind his bandana. "Nothing as wholesome as milk could come from anything smelling like *that*. Mr. Draxley erred again, I'm sure."

"If quilts need to air before use after they sit in trunks, cows need heavy winds after being crowded in trains." Jake saw no reason to hold back a chuckle and heard a few more from the men who caught his comment. "These are no oxen, I'm sure."

"Nah, Miss Thompson." Clump gestured toward the five bovine culled from the cargo. "You can see those there ain't ox nor even bulls, but honest, live, milking cows. It's easy to see."

"How can you tell?" Miss Lyman looked at the animals with great interest. "They look much the same to me, Mr. Klumpf."

"That's easy. See, it's the ud—er. . ." Clump hit the realization he'd stumbled into an indelicate topic of conversation, and his ears began to turn red. "Small horns."

"Oh." Evie lowered the bandana to reveal that fickle dimple of hers. "I wouldn't have noticed such a slight difference. Thank you for your expertise, Mr. Klumpf. Have you had much experience with barnyard animals, or ranching, or some such?"

Suddenly, Jake saw Clump with new eyes. The compact logger with sturdy legs and an inability to keep anything to himself never mentioned his own past. *Why is that? And how is it that a logger knows anything about dairy cows and how to identify them?*

"M' family settled in Kansas, where we claim a good-sized farm. But Klumpfs believe in being fruitful. We multiply somethin' fierce, and there's only so much land to go around. I left to set up a homestead but started logging along the way." Clump shrugged. "You could say I know plenty about a barnyard."

A Kansas farm boy found logging in the Colorado mountains? Jake might find it suspicious if it weren't so ludicrous. Farmers usually remained farmers, no matter if they uprooted. They just set back down and planted somewhere else. On the other hand, Clump would be a fool to lie with five cows waiting.

Then again, he had no business making that comment to Evie about Klumpfs being fruitful and multiplying. It went too far, was too bold. The fact Clump used a biblical reference to boast of his family's virility worsened the offense. *I never thought to hear the Bible used when a man tried to flirt.*

"Let's take our cows to the 'barn.'" Miss Lyman drew a deep breath.

"We'll give Mrs. Nash a fine surprise with supper," Evie planned as they led the way to a surprisingly well-made shanty behind the café, off to the side. "She's craved milk for days."

Now partitioned with four barriers to make five stalls, the structure smelled of fragrant hay. Various men led the cows in one by one until each stall housed an antsy occupant. They lipped at the straw, slurped up water from their trough, and gave resonant lowing sounds as they restlessly moved about.

With the cows inside, Jake sent the loggers back to work digging out the stumps of trees they'd felled the week before. No need for over twenty men to loiter underfoot and gawk over the women, as they tended to do whenever given the chance.

"They don't look happy." Worry creased between Evie's brows. "Don't they stop giving milk if they're not happy?"

Miss Lyman rolled her eyes. "Whoever heard of happy cows?"

"They need milking," Clump instructed. "It pains them."

"The books say to milk in the morning and evening, not the afternoon." Evie looked surprised at the very suggestion.

"Usually 'tis so," Mrs. McCreedy affirmed. "But in this case,

Mr. Klumpf tells it true. More than likely these poor dears had no morning milking, and they're long overdue."

"Very well." Evie rooted around in a corner and emerged with three short stools. Pails hung on pegs in the wall. "I've read about the method behind milking. Now I'll practice."

"They're not looking very friendly," her sister warned. "Perhaps we ought to wait until they've settled down?"

"Discomfort makes anyone testy." Miss Higgins chose a stool after Miss Lyman took one. "I doubt they'll settle as is."

"Come along." Mrs. McCreedy took the two toward the closest animal. "I'll show you two how to go about it. 'Tis simple."

"The tracts seem straightforward enough." Evie headed for the farthest stall and began murmuring to the beast. The soothing sound of her voice carried as Jake followed to find her patting the cow's side while lowering herself to the stool.

Placing her cheek against the same place she'd had her hand, Evie reached under and began pulling. First one hand, then the other, she tugged in a rhythm that matched the sound of milk squirting into a tin pail. Only trouble was the sound came from across the makeshift barn. Perplexed, she drew back, glanced down, repositioned herself, and tried again. Same results.

Jake bit the inside of his cheek to keep from laughing as her confidence faded to confusion then irritation.

Meanwhile, Miss Lyman moved on to another cow while Mrs. McCreedy showed Miss Higgins the way of things. The sound of milk splashing into pails filled the structure. . .and none came from Evie's efforts.

She went so far as to get up, giving the cow's hindquarters wide berth, and settle on the other side. Still nothing. Finally, Evie gave an exasperated huff. "This one doesn't work."

"I'll try." Clump shuffled over, distinctive tread muffled.

Yet again, Jake noticed how thick the soles of the other man's boots must be for the entire uppers to remain visible when each step sank into so much hay coating the ground. Could Clump's characteristic stomp be an adopted mannerism? *Does he wear those boots as protection in the woods and for stabilization in the mud, or to make himself taller?* It wouldn't be the first time a short man elevated his shoes.

Clump squatted beside Evie. Oblivious to her doubtful glance, he reached in and had milk pouring into the pail in about two seconds flat. "There she goes, Miss Thompson."

Bewilderment gave way to outrage. "I talked to her, patted her side, rubbed my hands together so they weren't cold, and tugged firmly but carefully with alternating hands like all the tracts directed. That cow did this on purpose, Mr. Klumpf!"

Jake couldn't hold back his laughter anymore, earning himself an evil look. He didn't care. The expression on Evie's face when Clump succeeded had been so incredulous.

"Stop laughing this instant, Mr. Creed." She gave the order but didn't bother to see if he followed it. Instead, she watched as Clump repeated what he'd done before, protesting that she didn't see any difference. In fairness, neither did Jake.

But Evie didn't need to know that. Her annoyance whenever she didn't master something amused him. It was as though she expected to be good at something simply because she wanted to be. And on the rare occasions when determination and preparation didn't produce results, the idea anything remained beyond her control was treated as a personal insult. It made Jake's day.

Until Clump slid his hands over Evie's to demonstrate what he described as "rolling your palm while you pull." Then the entire scene didn't seem so funny anymore. Especially when she smiled that way, flashing her dimple at Clump. *At Clump.*

Jake stopped laughing.

A sense of humor was God's greatest gift to mankind, Braden Lyman decided during the dozenth interview with one of his new workers and his family's prospective suitors. Maybe he should list those the other way around, since the men came to Hope Falls for the women and worked as a secondary pursuit.

Either way, Braden figured he would've gone mad weeks ago if he hadn't been granted a keen appreciation for the ridiculous. And Lacey's ad certainly managed to attract a few improbable characters. Clumpy Klumpf and Bear Riordan were distinctive men with amusing names, but Braden had other favorites among the workers he'd met thus far.

Salt and Pepper, he nicknamed the two tall Nordic fallers who'd apparently arrived with the man now answering Creed's questions about his work history. The pair split one personality between them, but at least their dependence on each other made for a point of interest.

Dodger brightened Braden's day when the shifty fellow tried to make off with his pen. When Evie caught him at it, Dodger gave a merry wink and tossed it back, claiming he liked to borrow things from time to time. Since he possessed fine taste, Braden should have been flattered. Instead, Braden was amused. He gave Dodger the pen as payment for the entertainment he provided then told him he'd be out of Hope Falls the moment he tried anything like that again. Strange how the men who made their way through his door seemed so much more full of life than the stuffed shirts he'd known back in Charleston or even when he did accounts for the mine.

Take that fellow with the overblown manner and patched top hat who went by "Gent." Sweating from the start, Gent's brow and neck bore charcoal-colored trickles of nervousness. No one mentioned the telltale evidence that Gent blackened his hair, but Creed pressed the man about his age. Gent admitted to a stately thirty-seven, a mere two years over the request. No doubt he shaved a few years from that figure, but the man worked hard and made a good influence among the men, so Gent remained.

So a man in his forties roamed the forest, chopping trees and trying to nab a bride half his age, while Braden lay stuck in bed.

His sense of humor kept him going when hope couldn't. Time stretched thin, days passing in dark drips of unfamiliar shadows creeping over too-familiar walls.

"You know I'm a bull-of-the-woods." Bullheaded Craig Williams spoke now. "Creed knows the outfits I've worked for. I've been at it for twelve years. I can do everything from bull-whacking to falling to bucking and even make a passable engineer when called to man a donkey engine. My work speaks for itself."

But that doesn't stop him from flapping his gums. Braden wondered how quickly they could get the pompous logger out of his room. *Going to be a long time if we wait for him to pause.*

"That's not the real reason you're calling all of us into this room one by one. So why don't you skip easing into things by asking about my profession and move to the important questions?" Suddenly, Williams sounded a lot smarter.

It made Braden trust him even less. None of the other men challenged the way they chose to conduct the interviews. That Williams felt comfortable enough to do so said a lot about his character. Or lack of it.

"All right, Williams." Creed didn't shift from his chair, where he sprawled to take up as much of the room as possible. If he leaned forward, it signaled interest. If he leaned farther back, it indicated he'd given up ground to Williams. That Creed knew the rules of staking territory and didn't hesitate to use them was just one reason Braden kept the man close. He made a good ally, but Creed would probably make a far worse enemy. "If you've got everything figured out, why don't you just tell us?"

Braden arched a brow in silent challenge, relieved to notice that, for once, none of the women interrupted. His sister had a way of barging into situations without understanding them—the entire town had become a prime example of that—and his fiancée and her sister didn't do much better. In fact, Evie might just give Lacey a run for her money when it came to being outspoken, but that wasn't Braden's problem.

From the way he'd seen Creed eyeing Evie, he'd be glad to take on that burden when the time came. And when the time came, Braden wouldn't object. If nothing else, Creed could match his fiancée's sister for stubbornness. Besides—it amused Braden to watch the byplay between the two of them. They each kept so busy not acknowledging their interest, it became comical.

"You're trying to make sure I'm good enough to marry one of your women." Williams mimicked Creed's posture—knees bent, boots facing outward, and shoulders down and back as though relaxed. Only trouble was, the shorter man looked boxed in, as though keeping all his energy leashed. "I never attended a university, don't come from a prestigious family, and don't regret either one. What I do have is years of experience, a history of hard work, and the ability to protect what's mine."

Braden tensed. He hadn't imagined the way Williams's gaze flicked toward him when the cocksure lumberjack said that last bit. "The less you own, the easier it is to guard."

Williams drew in a deep breath, too smart to rise to the bait. "That's true, Mr. Lyman. And if it's easy to guard a little, it's difficult to protect a lot. You and your family here possess too much to safeguard without help. That's the reason you put forth the ad, and the reason I'm here."

"I respect honesty, Mr. Williams." *Doesn't mean I like you.*

"I'm an honest man. Ask whatever questions you want."

"My grandma always told me to beware a man who says he's honest, because he's either lying to others or lying to himself. No one manages to tell the truth about everything." Naomi smoothed her hair and gave a winsome smile. "Do you believe my granny's advice, Mr. Williams?"

Braden closed his eyes. He knew if he met his cousin's gaze, or saw Lacey's startled glance, he'd start laughing. *I never heard Grandma Lyman say that.* He shook his head. *Only Naomi would twist a moral question to trap an opponent like this. It's why I never argue or play chess with her.*

"Although no one succeeds every time, I believe a man who attempts honesty can be called an honest man." Williams gave a catlike grin. "But, all told, yes, I believe your granny."

"Now that's an interesting answer, Mr. Williams." Evie tilted her head. "By such logic, a man who attempts piety should be labeled pious, one who attempts to gain wealth would be rich, and so on until everyone on earth could be anything."

"You twist my words, Miss Thompson. That isn't my meaning."

"Do you suppose"—Cora twirled a lock of red hair about her forefinger as she speculated—"that means he was dishonest?"

"It's a moot point," Lacey broke in. "Our granny never gave any such advice, so Mr. Williams shouldn't have believed it. Naomi was giving one of those peculiar lessons of hers again, trying to show us it's a mistake to assume *anyone* is honest."

"How clever!" Cora beamed at his cousin. "But what do you suppose Mr. Williams makes of your ruse?"

"I'll tell you what I think." Williams got to his feet. "I like a woman who uses spunk to fight her battles and spirit to enjoy life. These sneak attacks and silly lessons don't work. My first decision was best. I'll take Miss Thompson."

"And I'll take your apology, Mr. Williams, for acting as though I'm a horse for auction." Evie jumped from her chair.

"I apologize when I'm wrong, but I've not treated you as a horse, Miss Thompson." He rose from his bench. "Though I admire your spirit, I've not so much as asked to see your teeth."

She resisted the impulse to bare them at him, something warning her he'd take it as encouragement. Strange man.

"Insult the lady again, Williams, and you'll lose a few of your own teeth." Creed didn't bother to stand when he made the threat, but somehow that made it all the more ominous.

"Since when does a woman find it insulting that a man wants to marry her? Miss Thompson's a spirited woman with enough fire and wit to keep a man from slipping into boredom." Williams eyed her as though trying to piece together a puzzle. "I like what I see and chose her from the bunch as soon as I got off the train. If she doesn't want a husband, why advertise for one?"

Good questions. Even worse, Williams answered whether or not there's a man in town who wants to marry me for more than my cooking. He chose me before he knew I could make more than gruel and says clearly to anyone who asks that he admires my spirit, strength, feisty ways, or what have you. So why, Lord, does my stomach capsize at the very thought of wedding him?

"Because she wants the *right* husband." Cora began tugging on the lock of hair she'd been twirling. "My sister and friends went about selecting their spouses this way so they'd find partners. Evie chooses which man she'll accept."

"She did the choosing when she listed her requirements in that ad. I fulfill them, and I've come to claim my prize."

"She's a prize, to be sure, but not yours to claim." Catlike reflexes silent and sudden, Creed stood beside her.

Braden held up a hand to stop Williams from moving forward. "You can't pick her up and carry her off, Mr. Williams."

He could have said that some other way. Evie refused to blush as abandoned plans to wreak vengeance upon her sister's fiancé sprang to mind. *First Braden said hefty, and now this.*

"I could with strength to spare." Williams cast an appreciative gaze her way, squared his shoulders, and made the muscles in his arms jump beneath his sleeves.

She let out a squeak of horror. Firstly, the idea of a man picking her up and slinging her around like a sack of potatoes meant he'd know exactly how much "heft" she had. But secondly, the entire image reminded her too much of the Sabine women carried off by Roman soldiers and wedded against their will.

I have more will than most. Evie squared her own shoulders. *And heft, if it comes to that. It might do me good for a change.*

She also found it comforting that Creed looked ready to use

his fists if her overly determined suitor came another step closer. *No, wait. Creed's starting toward Williams. That's a mistake.*

Without another thought, she reached forward to curl her fingers in Creed's sleeve, snagging him and halting his movement before it could start a brawl. Or, if not precisely start one, as Williams' own belligerence held more fault for that, at least exacerbate the situation. Either way, Evie wouldn't allow it.

They'd made strict rules about no fighting in town, and she wouldn't let Creed be the one sent away from Hope Falls for it. Particularly not over a cretin like Williams.

"Don't make mischief, Mr. Williams. Any smart man knows you don't claim a prize like Evie." Naomi's wit defused the situation before it escalated to fists. "You have to win her."

Eyes narrowed, Williams looked from Creed to Evie and back again. "So be it. Let the game begin."

TWENTY-SIX

The Game played before him—a paltry example, to be sure, but Corbin expected no more from a logging camp bunkhouse. Not even one so outlandish as this, with its strange assortment of workmen at odds with themselves, the season, and each other.

The long room unrolled into levels of function. Two layers of bunks lined the walls, outlining the half-log deacon seat benches boxing in the center fire pit. Lanterns hung at intervals on pegs above bunks wherever occupants wanted, and none said a word about it so long as they went out at a decent hour. With generous quarters, they didn't chafe for space.

Groups of men huddled on or around the benches, telling stories, throwing dice, whittling whatnots as they passed time before sleep. Those didn't interest Corbin. High in his perch on the top bunk in the farthest corner, lamp wick pushed barely high enough for a faint glow, he ignored the pages of his book. As he'd done for two weeks, he turned an odd square coin over and over between his fingers, watching the men who played the Game. Memorizing their faces, their movements, the tells that would betray them when Corbin left his corner at last.

He never began the Game. Corbin considered it a sacrilege to demand her favor. Instead, he bided his time, tested his strength by resisting the unworthy. He stayed faithful, knowing the Game would call him once again, give him the opportunity to prove himself the accomplished player he'd become.

He'd allow himself the small pleasure of an occasional round with the men. He'd win most often but throw a few hands occasionally to stay beyond suspicion. Already he'd come close to overplaying his disguise. Too little left him vulnerable with Granger tracking him, but too much left him less desirable to the women. They'd already shown more shrewdness than expected, setting up those probing interviews of theirs.

Not that the questions posed any trouble for him—Corbin had his background set up long before anyone asked. Always did as a matter of course, and it never failed to be useful. Situations changed, stories changed, but how to play the Game never did. Because the rules of the Game were taken from life—where people like these foolish women begged to be played.

If anyone remarked on his ability with the Game, or identified him as a follower, the women would ask uncomfortable questions. The ad specifically listed "God-fearing" as the first requirement for prospective husbands, and Corbin dealt only in the solid truth of here and now. Things he could manipulate.

The Game provided means for survival, offered constant challenges, and rewarded him for success. He didn't fear some vague notion of anyone else's god. Corbin feared losing the Game. Maintaining the facade that he cared for anything else took every ounce of the skills he'd honed over the past decade.

But Corbin judged it worth the effort. By the end of this match, Corbin Twyler planned to win the richest hand he'd ever played for.

"This isn't some amusing diversion, Lacey." Her cousin scolded her as though she herself hadn't toyed with Mr. Williams two days before. "These days will shape the rest of our lives."

"I'm well aware of that, Naomi." Lacey carefully stacked three cans atop the now-familiar target rock at the far end of the clearing, also aware that all three of her friends had followed her. "Why do I have a feeling you three planned to discuss something more than shooting during today's practice?"

"High intelligence?" Cora offered the compliment as a sop.

"Or she knows us very well." Evie's dry response probably came closer to the truth, but Lacey liked Cora's answer better.

"We can chitchat at any time." She made for the other end of the clearing at a rapid pace. Not running, but not lollygagging either. If they hoped to nab her in an unpleasant conversation, Lacey planned to make them work at it.

"Not in private, with just the four of us. Men plague us everywhere we go except the kitchen or the house. Mrs. McCreedy spends as much time in the diner as Evie these days, and Arla only leaves the house in our presence." As always, Naomi wielded logic like an infallible weapon. "When can we speak alone?"

"Not now. Now is the time to practice marksmanship and ensure we can all protect ourselves if need be." Lacey darted a meaningful glance in Evie's direction, raising her eyebrows.

"Don't you do that, Lacey Lyman." Evie shook a finger at her. "Don't you look at me as though I'm the only reason we come out into these woods and fire bullets into stacked cans."

"You're right." Lacey's patience frayed like the edging of an old satin ribbon. "You're not the reason we fire bullets into those cans, Evie. How could you be, when you've never hit one!"

"That was uncalled for, Lace." Cora sprang to her sister's defense. "Every single one of us needs the practice."

"Some more than others, and Evie's the worst of the lot. Stop looking at me as though I've committed some terrible grievance by being honest about it! Right now, your sister would be lucky to hit the broadside of the bunkhouse at ten paces." She knew she should stop talking. Knew that the anger surging in her chest and venting through her words shouldn't be aimed at Evie, but Lacey couldn't hold it inside anymore.

Nothing, but *nothing*, had gone right since they arrived in this town, and something needed to change. Since Lacey couldn't magically make the men into husband material or whip up a functioning sawmill as easily as a loaf of bread, the only way to ease the pressure in her chest was to cry. And Lacey Lyman didn't cry over trivialities. She cried when her parents died, then waited five years before tears swamped her over Braden. In between, not a single salty speck marred her record.

Which meant she had a solid four years and ten months to go, at the very minimum, before indulging in another bout. Or until she had a child. Either/or. But neither one of those options allowed for standing in the middle of the woods, surrounded by friends she'd just insulted, while two dozen lonely men waited for them to hurry up and get hitched.

Maybe, Lacey considered, *I need to rethink my terms.*

In the meantime, her three closest friends all stared at her as though she'd donned a dress four years out of date. Their shock should have spurred her to make amends, but it only brought up her defenses even more. What right did they have to judge her?

"Lacey, what's gotten into you?" Cora reached out. "None of us is good at everything. We accept each other's shortcomings and pool our talents to make the load lighter for everyone."

"I'm tired of carrying so much," a voice sounding suspiciously like her own snapped at her best friend. "Who bakes bread three times a week? Lacey. Who has to keep Braden in line? Lacey. Who teaches you to protect yourselves, or thinks to ask the men what they're looking for in a wife while everyone reprimands her? Lacey!" She threw up her hands. "For pity's sake, you three can't even *eavesdrop* properly without me!"

The more things she listed, the tighter her chest constricted. Why did everything have to be so difficult?

"That's enough, Lacey Danielle Lyman." The stern note

in Evie's voice put the old headmistress to shame. "You'll stop indulging in this morass of self-pity right now."

"It's not self-pity." To her horror, she felt tingles running up her nose, the precursors to unsheddable tears. "All three of you know I'm telling nothing but the truth!"

"A very small part of the truth," Naomi chastised. "We're all working hard. Evie does the lion's share of all the cooking and planning even with Mrs. McCreedy here. Before she ran herself ragged cooking and figuring what supplies we'd need to keep the town going, I suppose you didn't notice how hard she worked to keep the men in line? Mr. Creed contributed to that success, but he's been a difficult one to rein in on his own account, and we have Evie to thank for that, too."

"That's true." Lacey gave a great big sniff. "I know you do a great deal, Evie. It's not that I don't appreciate it. I—"

"And if you think you've managed to keep your brother in line, you need to open your eyes, Lacey." Evie drew a comforting arm around Cora. "My sister never complains over the way Braden continues to treat her, but I see the way it wears. It's between them, but she takes the most care of him and reaps the worst of his temper in return. And she washes most of the pots and pans!"

Evie's outburst, coupled with the misery Cora didn't hide for a few moments, weighed heavily on Lacey's conscience. *I did this. I brought them here and convinced them to place the ad.* Sniffling wasn't slowing down the tingles very much anymore.

"Naomi's the one who steps in to keep peace or put someone in his place without starting a fight." Cora took a turn now. "She's the one to look after Mrs. Nash, and she does most of the milking, too. Even now, she pumps most of the water we need when none of the men are around to take on the task. Each and every one of us does our part, Lacey. It's shameful to hear you imply that we leave the worst of the work to you."

"That isn't what I said, and not what I meant," she protested. "It just seems as though you three don't notice what I do, or think

I fool around and don't contribute or take everything as seriously as anyone else. And that's not true!"

Evie spoke softly after a long silence. "We notice what you do. And I think you see your own plans more than you see the larger picture. Since we came to Hope Falls, you've slowly stopped involving us in your decisions, Lacey."

"I'm thinking of all of us. How can you say otherwise?"

"Small things, at first." Naomi wet her lips. "You didn't think to help us understand the logging terms when it would have helped so much, and you knew we had no chance to read the books."

"You waited until Naomi and I left the room to change your mind and allow Creed and Braden a chance to plot together." Cora's nostrils flared. "That put Evie in the position of stopping the men from scheming or supporting you. She chose to support you because we're a team, but you don't think that way."

"Of course we're a team!" Lacey looked from one upset face to another, reading the disappointment in each one.

"Then you shouldn't have asked the men to narrow down their choices when you knew the rest of us would object." Evie shook her head. "With each day, you're acting more like your brother, Lacey, choosing what you think is best for all of us instead of letting us decide how we want to proceed. We don't like it."

If asked, Evie felt confident she could list quite a few things she didn't like, but Lacey's increasingly self-centered attitude happened to be one she could help change. Or at least try to.

The incredible growing laundry pile back at the house would wait until the next day they found some spare time. The four of them needed to band together again before everything fell apart. Because, loath as Evie was to admit it, Lacey and the laundry just might be the only two things on that list she could fix.

Not that Lacey needs fixing, Evie corrected then glanced at her friend. *And perhaps her nose,* she added. *I've never seen one turn precisely that shade of crimson before.* Then again, she'd never seen Lacey cry. Or even come close to crying. A sudden surge of sympathy for the youngest member of their group had Evie drawing Lacey into a hug.

"Well, I don't like it either." Lacey's nose brightened another shade. "Especially since I didn't know I was doing it."

Naomi fished one of her never-ending store of embroidered handkerchiefs from a pocket and passed it to her cousin. "We know, Lace. If you realized, you would have stopped."

"I don't even like it when"—she paused to rub her nose, adding the luster of a polished apple—"*Braden* acts like Braden. That's not the sort of thing I ever aspired to, you know."

"Everyone's tired and trying to settle into an unfamiliar place." Cora patted Lacey's shoulder. "Making the best of things sometimes brings out the worst in us, I think."

Evie stared at her little sister, who'd grown up and gained wisdom when she hadn't been paying close enough attention. Perhaps Cora could brazen out Braden's recovery, after all.

"The entire plan collapsed before it started," Lacey moaned. "It's just like the first time I visited a dressmaker's shop with Mother and wandered out of sight. I found the most beautiful gown draped over a dressmaker's doll—an absolute vision of a dress in gold and cream—and nothing would do but I try it on. They warned it wasn't finished, but I begged and pleaded and cried until Mother insisted and they agreed."

Spoiled little bratling, Evie couldn't help but think.

"The moment they put it on me, dozens of pins jabbed me and it fell apart before I got to the mirror." Remorse filled Lacey's voice. "I feel as though I put each one of you in that dress when I convinced you to write the ad and come here."

"It's not the same, Lace." Naomi rejected the comparison.

"Yes, it is. I forced you into something that didn't fit. It jabs and pokes, and it's all falling apart before any of us gets the chance to see how beautiful it should have been!" She crumpled the handkerchief, her nose fading to deep pink.

"Lacey, you're a persuasive woman, but you couldn't have forced me to take part in your plan." Evie took responsibility for her own choice. "I said no once and could have again. All of us did. Not one woman who stands here was dragged across country, kicking and screaming against the injustice of it."

"If you ever question how willing we were, just look at how much we packed." Cora's giggle sparked a round of chuckles.

"It's true," Naomi joined in. "We brought along a library and a diner, sent ahead enough to stock a mercantile, and packed up everything needed to begin four homes and families. How many women can claim they carry an entire town when they travel?"

"Only four that I know of." Lacey cracked a smile.

"So we've encountered a few obstacles and made mistakes along the way," Evie acknowledged. "That doesn't mean we can't make it right."

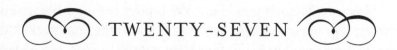

TWENTY-SEVEN

Something was wrong. Jake felt it low in his gut, the same way he'd known when Edward found trouble. The air lay thick in the room but thin in his throat when he breathed deep, his pulse thrumming in anticipation.

Sleep would elude him if Jake reached for it, but he didn't close his eyes. Tonight called for readiness. He didn't speak a prayer—God, in his opinion, was bigger than mere words. Wasn't the Creator of all a God of action? One who saw into hearts, listened to thoughts, and heard hopes? So Jake lay in wait, thinking of what might be needed—of Him. . .of the Lord who watched over His own.

He waited to see if he'd be part of that protection, if that was the reason raw energy filled his mind instead of rest. He prepared, wordlessly, for whatever would disturb the quiet of the bunkhouse. Quiet, in this case, a relative term. It may be the dead of night, but silence found no home here.

Snores and grunts punctured the peace at regular intervals, joined by assorted thuds and thumps as restless limbs bumped against wooden walls. Several slept in their boots. Outside, wind whistled through sharp branches, forcing its cold inside to tickle the flames of their fire.

When Jake could lie still no longer, he slipped his boots onto his feet and walked outside. A circle of the women's house revealed nothing amiss. No lights flickering, no cries of distress, no windows or doors flung open to indicate intruders.

But the feeling remained. So Jake did what any man of sense would. He scaled the nearest tree positioned between the house and the men's quarters and kept watch. If no trouble showed itself, he suffered no more than a sleepless night. But if—

Jake's thoughts ground to a halt as he heard the sound of footsteps. He shifted, ready to jump at a moment's notice. That's when he spotted them. Four men, bundled in jackets and hats as they crept toward the house, whispers carrying on a suddenly subdued breeze. It was as though the entire mountain listened along with Jake as the mysterious figures spoke.

"Pretty little Lacey Lyman's mine, and no switching. Once we make women out of 'em, they have to marry us."

"No need to get shackled when you can enjoy someone else's. Engaged girls know what's what, and she'll need a real man now that her fiancé's an invalid." Snickers met the crude comment.

Jake gripped the branch so hard his hands bled, but it wasn't time to leap. They weren't close enough. Yet.

"I don't think any of 'em is decent women. Only trollops prance around these parts without a man, but the best ones know we like a little chase. Prissy Higgins is mine."

"We'll know the truth after we take their hair down and let loose." The first one rubbed his hands together before he added, "Creed's not abed, so you might have to wait, Tom. Plain to see which woman he fancies, though I can't see why."

"After chopping logs all day, some of us don't want twigs in our beds. There's nothing better than a nice, soft—" The fourth man never got a chance to finish.

Jake leapt from his perch and slammed the man's head into the trunk. He crumpled without another word. By the time Jake planted his fist in another's face, the other two got over their surprise. A punch to the stomach made Jake double over, so he plowed his head into the man's gut and took him down.

From that point, he stopped thinking. Jake couldn't say how long the fight would have lasted—until they'd taken him down or he'd finished beating them so bloody they'd never touch another woman, most likely—if they hadn't made such a racket they woke up half the town. Which, in turn, woke up the other half.

Several things happened almost simultaneously. First, the windows to the house opened, and a cacophony of female shrieks and wails rent the night. Right after that began, but while it continued—because the women didn't stop caterwauling until long after the fists stopped flying—Riordan came barreling over in his bare feet to do battle alongside Jake.

Jake pulled back his arm and smashed the full force behind it into the heel of his palm, connecting with the nose of the opponent before him. As the man went down, blubbering, Jake saw Riordan simply lift the final fighter into the air and send him crashing into a nearby wall before trotting off to retrieve him. With that, the brouhaha ended as swiftly as it started.

Or it would have ended there, but every man circled around, suddenly keen to be a valiant protector. Questions abounded; boasts of how others would have handled things filled the air until not even all the knives in Evie's kitchen could cut through the bluster. Scuffles over who threw a better punch started to break out until Mrs. Martha McCreedy arrived.

"Get back in the bunkhouse, the whole lot o' ye." She assessed the situation in a single glance. "Creed and Riordan took care o' matters. Mr. Klumpf will kindly fetch the doctor."

No one moved. Jake felt fairly certain, since only one of his eyes was swelled shut. "You heard her," he yelled. "Get to bed or you'll all be worthless tomorrow, and we'll have four fewer workers as it stands. Besides"—he resorted to blackmail—"if you keep the ladies awake any longer, you'll be making breakfast for yourselves." That got them moving, if slowly.

For a pleasant change, the women didn't rush headlong into the melee. Instead, they waited until the men cleared out before bustling Jake into the house. He only went because two of the four offenders remained unconscious, one of them the man who'd had his eye on Evie. For that reason, Jake let Riordan truss up the criminals while he withstood the doctor's fussing.

Withstood, shooed away. . .what difference did it make? "I've had worse," Jake assured the women when the doctor slammed his black bag shut and stormed out the door. "Split knuckles, a black eye, a few bruised ribs—pass me some witch hazel, and I'll be fine in a couple days." *Unlike the men on the other side of those knuckles.* He indulged in a grim smile.

"I won't ask if you're all right." Evie's face entered his line of vision. "Obviously you'll be fine since you're as stubborn as ever, refusing to let the doctor look at that eye." She scolded and fussed the entire time she smoothed his hair back to lay a cool compress over that very eye.

Though she, like the other women, had donned a dressing gown over her night rail and was swathed from neck to foot in layers of fabric, there was something far too intimate about the gesture. Especially at night, and especially when her hair swung down her back in a long, saucy braid whose tip curled lovingly along her arm. Evie looked far too inviting.

Jake circled a hand around her wrist when she looked ready to adjust the compress. He thought only to stop her. Instead, the contact stopped his thoughts. Aside from the day they'd met, and the time he'd jumped through the window and gotten tangled in the curtain, almost knocking her over, he'd never let himself touch Evie. Not once.

And he never should have.

She shouldn't have touched him. Evie knew it the moment her fingertips brushed his forehead to whisk an errant lock of hair out of the way. The heat of him nearly burned her. But like a moth to a flame, she fluttered back, only to be caught.

And when the strength of Jake Creed's long fingers closed over her wrist, unintentionally pushing up the sleeve of her dressing gown, Evie feared she might hear a sizzle. Awareness of the contact streaked through her, scrambling her thoughts and holding her captive long after he released her.

In fact, he let go so quickly, Evie wondered whether he felt any of the same reaction. Warmth flooded her cheeks at the idea until she turned to hide the telltale blush. Fumbling, she passed him the witch hazel he'd requested, along with a towel.

It gave her just enough time to recover before Mr. Riordan and Mr. Klumpf strode through the door. Riordan looked none the worse for wear despite having joined Jake in the fight.

Everyone adjourned to the dining room, the only room with enough chairs to accommodate all of them. Evie could only be thankful Mrs. McCreedy insisted on taking Arla home with her for the remainder of the night—there'd been too much excitement for a woman in her condition already, and none of them was willing to wait to learn the details of what had happened. Before the brawl itself, naturally. They saw that firsthand.

"Where are they?" Creed directed the question to Riordan.

"Ach." The Irishman's face went thundery. "I trussed 'em good an' tight and tossed the lot in an old privy shack, then barred the privy door from t' outside. I found it fitting."

Evie choked back her laughter. *Until I know what these men did to deserve their fate, I shouldn't laugh at it.* She could almost imagine standing before an enormous blackboard, chalk in hand, writing the same sentence over and over again. *"It's not amusing to lock someone in the privy."*

Creed held no such compunction. He threw back his head and roared at Riordan's punishment. When he caught his breath, he clapped the other man on the shoulder. "That should hold them." As swiftly as it came, his amusement fled. "Though they deserve far worse. We'll need to call the authorities. Press charges."

"I dragged Draxley out of bed to send a telegram." Mr. Klumpf gave a satisfied nod. "Those men will be gone tomorrow."

"Lucky for them." A dark gleam lit Creed's eye. Only the one, since the other remained swelled shut and would for much longer than necessary since the fool wouldn't hold his compress over it. "If they stayed any longer, their fellow loggers would want to go a round or two before handing them over for lawful justice."

"I assumed as much." Riordan's voice rumbled low enough to mimic an earthquake. "When the lassies shrieked like banshees, I feared the worst. 'Tis glad I am you intervened, Creed."

"Banshees!" Lacey's screech didn't give lie to the label.

"Aye. 'Tis said they wail and scream a terrible warning." Riordan's green eyes took on a teasing light. "And can appear as uncommonly beautiful women if they take on the notion."

"Oh, well, that's not so bad." Lacey settled back.

"Irish superstitions aside"—Evie wanted to direct the conversation back to the events of the evening—"could someone tell us why you and those four were out wandering tonight, Mr. Creed? And what did they do to deserve such a sound thrashing and"—she paused, quelling another inappropriate chuckle before managing to finish—"unconventional form of imprisonment?"

"They came for you." Creed answered two questions in four words, none of them yes or no. In another situation, such a feat might have been deemed impressive. But not now. Creed seemed to sense that they awaited more of an explanation, as he generously doubled his response. "So I stopped them."

Perhaps, Evie wondered, *when a man resorts to using his fists, he temporarily loses the ability to express himself through words? It's either the visceral or the cerebral? But if he gives no reason, he's broken the law and has to leave.*

"We noticed that you stopped them, Mr. Creed." Cora gave him a bemused look. "We even assumed it had something to do with their proximity to the house?"

His nod verified the assumption but added nothing more, forcing the women to pry further.

"Did you originally make up one of their party, and something went wrong?" Naomi took a wild guess as to why, of five men strolling through the dark, only one still stood.

Or at least retained his ability to stand, in any case. The hope behind her question made Evie wince. Apparently she wasn't the only one desperate for any reason but the worst.

"Nope."

"Mr. Riordan, can you explain?" Lacey's exasperation shone through her attempt at making it a polite request.

"Well, miss, I only joined in after the wailing began, so I ken that the four o' ye saw more than Rory Riordan." He frowned.

"Oh, for pity's sake." Evie abandoned trying to be polite. It was late. She was tired. Four battered men slumped in an outhouse somewhere nearby with no explanation, and Creed needed to start talking. "Stop being vague and tell us what happened!"

Everyone's eyes went big, but smiles bloomed around the table.

"You know what you need to." Creed's jaw thrust forward. Or maybe it, too, was swelling. Either way, he wasn't talking.

"I know you and four men were involved in a brawl. I know we've given you the opportunity to explain yourself, and you've declined." Evie planted her palms on the table and stood. "I know I'm to look at a man's actions. The laws we set down for Hope Falls state that any man brawling in town will be escorted to the train, and since you've given us no reason to make an exception, it must stand." *Words are important, too.* She kept from saying this last by a slim margin.

The other women started to gasp, recognized her intent, and began setting their expressions. Nods, crossed arms, and regretful sighs circled the table as Mr. Creed looked about. If he thought he'd find a soft heart to sway, he'd underestimated their curiosity. Evie knew her friends better than he could.

Riordan and Klumpf stared at them all, incredulous, but held their peace. Whether they waited to see which side gave way, or to be given the order to escort Creed to the train, Evie couldn't say. Either way, it worked in her favor.

"Especially after an upset like this, every effort must be made to maintain order," Lacey chimed in. "You understand."

"I couldn't sleep, so I walked around to see if anything looked out of the ordinary. Nothing stood out at first, but over by the tree I heard footsteps." Creed's good eye narrowed, and the swollen one seemed to darken into a more livid bruise. "All I needed to hear were a few comments to know what they planned."

Silence reigned again as Evie, along with everyone else, waited for him to explain just what the four men planned. *Please tell me it's not what I think. Give me another reason.*

But Creed snapped his jaw shut.

"That explains why you were there," Evie prodded, "but not why the others were, nor the reason behind your actions."

"Some things a man doesn't like to mention to ladies," Mr. Klumpf broke in, darting a glance at Creed. "I suspect that's the case here, and Mr. Creed's doing right not to offend you."

"Is that the way o' it?" The question came on a breath, the answer a ghost of a nod between Riordan and Creed. "So be it." Riordan turned to them. "Those men planned to harm you ladies. Sneaking around in the middle of the night, heading to your home while everyone slept, 'tis the logical conclusion, and I lend my support to Mr. Creed. I assure you the other men would agree."

"But we don't." Lacey huffed. "What if Mr. Creed took offense at something they said, and things got out of hand?" She looked at him. "Did you overhear them insult any of us?"

"All of you." Creed's answer made Evie's blood run cold.

Four men. Four women they didn't respect, defenseless in the middle of the night. No alternate reason after all. *Braden's worst fear made real if not for Mr. Creed's vigilance.*

"The other men will suspect the cause immediately, will they not?" Evie held his gaze until he gave another short nod. "Do you believe any others think the same way, or will tonight's events abolish any doubts as to our virtue?" *Will we be safe?*

She ignored the horrified resignation on her friends' faces as Cora, Naomi, and Lacey were forced to face the cause of all the ruckus. They'd suspected as well as she but not accepted it until now.

"There should be no other doubts." Creed's assurance lent little comfort, despite Riordan's and Klumpf's hasty agreements. "But even amongst these four, they debated the issue."

"That makes no sense," Lacey all but whimpered.

"What Mr. Creed is saying"—Evie closed her eyes—"is that not all of those men believed us to be loose women. Even if they all know we're virtuous, our reputations won't protect us."

"On the contrary." Creed cracked his split knuckles as though to underscore his point. "A man knows that if he dishonors one of you, you'll have no choice but to marry him. They counted on it."

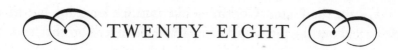 TWENTY-EIGHT

A man couldn't count on anything these days. Corbin stalked past the others, noisy crows cawing over the night's adventure and causing enough racket to make sure anyone sensible couldn't catch a wink of sleep. He flung himself onto his bunk.

Fools. He turned his back on the lot of them, facing the unfinished wood of the bunk wall. *Cretins.* Hope Falls had been settling into a familiar, plodding routine. Wake up, eat breakfast, work, eat lunch, work more, eat dinner and socialize with the women, and go back to the bunkhouse. If it weren't for the women—and their admittedly superior food—it would have been exactly the same setup Corbin abandoned a decade ago.

He despised the routine, but it served a purpose. Routine lulled the dull-witted and optimistic into a sort of drowsy contentment. It made men lazy, and women more appreciative of small gestures designed to woo and win. Corbin had bided his time, waiting for the routine to assert itself.

And four fools undid in forty moments what had taken weeks of patience to establish. Excitement ran high tonight, but tomorrow wariness would replace the thrill. Men would eye their fellow workers with new suspicion, the women withdraw to reassess their judgment. Something shattered never became whole again. At best it mended. But Corbin couldn't wait for time's healing touch.

Granger followed him across three states to Charleston, and he'd gotten word the man came as far as Colorado. Corbin didn't know whether the tenacious hunter tracked him to Durango, but he couldn't take the risk he'd get that far. Granger was to be avoided at any cost.

Except the Game. Corbin would sacrifice anything but that. He pulled out the piece he'd lifted from Granger's brother, square copper emblazoned with a crown and three fleurs-de-lis on one side and naught but an angry slash on the other. Rubbing it between thumb and forefinger, Corbin considered his next move.

Originally, he'd thought to pursue the cook. Miss Thompson appealed to him at first for the additional revenue to be earned from her café, but he'd quickly realized she'd be a difficult woman to control. So he settled on Miss Higgins, whose more biddable demeanor suited his purposes. If worse came to worst, a widower's inheritance could be worth more than a wife after all.

Miss Lyman, owner of the mercantile and sister to the principal mill investor, would make the richest wife but also the most closely watched. She'd never been a possibility for the simple reason that a wealthy heiress involved too high a risk.

But the situation had changed, and the Game called more strongly than ever. Corbin flipped the piece, pondering his options. He'd thought marriage would be the ultimate bluff, but now things were becoming clear. . . .

The longer the women stayed, the more muddled everything became. Before they arrived, Braden knew exactly what he had to do. He sent Eric and Owen home to proper hospitals as soon as they could be moved and wrote to free Cora. But the moment his featherbrained sister whisked into town, packing luggage to the sky and headaches to hide them, everything became a negotiation.

Battles couldn't be chosen because every single one could be the turning point, a weakness leaving Cora and his family exposed to even more danger. So Braden waged war with every word he spoke. Every pang of pain he ignored so the doctor wouldn't drug away his scant ability to protect the women.

And I failed. Braden's hands clenched into fists, nails breaking the skin of his palms as Creed summarized the events of last night. *Cora was in danger, and I slept through it. Blasted morphine.* The doctor would never force it on him again. Never.

Creed gave the bare bones of it, but they both knew the gravity of what could have been. Braden didn't trust himself to demand the details yet. He didn't trust himself to speak. If he opened his mouth, he'd yell himself hoarse before he could do anything useful. And it would scare Cora even more.

She walked into the room with the others, back stiff and chin set as she prepared for the conversation to come. But Braden knew her too well to believe her unaffected. Cora finally feared what he'd dreaded the moment he saw her in this accursed excuse for a town—that she'd need the type of protection he couldn't provide. And, for the first time, she might understand why she needed to find another man to build a life with.

But she wouldn't do it. She had to leave town to be safe, but he hadn't been able to force her from his side. Cora's loyalty ran as deep as an ocean and could drown any force but the woman's own stubbornness. Or Braden's.

There's only one way to be rid of her. Lord, forgive me for what I'm about to do. What other choice do I have?

Too many options. Robert Kane left town in a blaze of bruises, but Jake hadn't thinned his crowd of suspects nearly enough. Kane's story hadn't been cleared, but Jake could live with that. The odds Kane and Twyler were the same man sank low. For one thing,

Twyler wasn't stupid, and five suspects remained.

Even if Jake was wrong, Kane would remain in custody—safely tucked away from the women he'd planned to accost and easily within reach should word come back he hadn't worked where he claimed.

In all honesty, Jake didn't truly suspect Gent either. Despite his intelligence and the bootblack, Gent's age precluded him. All reports of Twyler put him at no more than thirty, too obvious a difference for someone not to have mentioned.

Which left four men fitting Twyler's description. Dodger, the high-climbing thief whose too-large clothing concealed more than Jake could guess; Williams, whose cocky attitude made him enough of a character it could be a disguise; Fillmore, the unassuming shadow who'd shown enough backbone not to accompany Kane the night before; and Clump, whose unusual background and raised boot-bottoms made him an oddity if nothing else.

Any one could be Twyler. Or none of them. Theories and questions chased themselves around Jake's skull until they tangled tighter than a logjam. It took him nowhere in a hurry while Evie and her friends faced growing danger. If Twyler panicked or changed his plans, the women might pay the price.

"We need to set guards to watch the house at night," he told Lyman the next morning. "I only trust myself, Riordan, and Lawson to do it. McCreedy, too, but he's got a wife to look after already, so he's out. Things can't stay as they are."

"Stand still or sit down, Creed," Lyman barked at him, obviously unable to marshal the fury coursing through him. "I can't believe I slept through the entire thing. Morphine takes away the pain but steals the time from a man's life."

"No harm done." His fiancée reached out to clasp Lyman's hand, but he pulled away. "Mr. Creed and Mr. Riordan kept everything under control, and we're none the worse for wear."

"I am." Jake gestured to his left eye, which only opened a fraction of an inch. "But keeping the women safe is all that matters." *And finding Twyler is a part of that. Edward's death deserves justice, but a crafty criminal who shows no remorse when it comes to murder needs to be caught more for the sake of the living. It shouldn't have taken a black eye for me to see it.* He cast a glance toward Evie, who didn't say much.

"A guard won't be good enough." Lyman stuck his hand beneath the sheet and glowered at his fiancée. "I was right when I said it at the start—Hope Falls is no place for a woman. You four need to leave. We'll find investors for the mill and use our resources to set you up back East, in safety."

"No." Evie shook her head. "Even if we could be sure that would work, it's too late. I gave my word to those men to make them meals while they worked here. Besides, I won't leave Mrs. Nash. She can't move now, with the babe so close."

"We can hire another cook." The moment he said it, Jake wanted to bite back the words. He made it sound as though Evie could be replaced, exchanged, or some such foolishness. Anyone who'd spent more than three minutes in her company knew better. And that was before tasting any of her food.

"Men consider it a matter of honor to keep their word." Miss Higgins looked at them incredulously. "Why would you imagine we'd go back on ours over an isolated bit of idiocy?"

"*Most* men consider it a matter of honor." Cora Thompson stared at Lyman with such intensity, Jake suddenly wondered what had passed between the two of them since her arrival. "Some make promises and become all too willing to break them."

"And some women are too blind to see when circumstances change," Lyman snapped back. "If it comes down to your well-being or being thought well of, there is no possible comparison."

"He's right." Jake threw his support behind Lyman before the women could quibble about the wording or some such. "I chose to shield you from the crudeness of what the men said, but I dislike the consequences. Words aren't actions, and I spared you both since the worst didn't reach your doorstep. But it came close—too blasted close to ignore."

"Language!" Miss Higgins fixed him with a gimlet eye.

"It's worth worse, and if that offends you, believe me when I say you'd faint dead away had your ears been sullied by the speculations made about the four of you last night." Jake refused to apologize. If one little "blasted" brought home the seriousness of the situation, he'd count himself blessed.

"You do offend, Mr. Creed." The hint of hollows pressed beneath her cheekbones, mute testimony to Evie's perseverance. And the fact she still wasn't eating enough. "Not only with your swearing but with your low opinion of us."

"Low opinion?" He was reduced to parroting her, unable to make sense of the statement. *I've never met a woman I think more highly of, and very few men.* "Aside from your determination to put yourself in harm's way, I highly regard each of you."

"They can also be bossy," Lyman added in. "But their stubborn ways overtake that. Paired with an inability to exercise critical thinking, stubbornness becomes dangerous."

"Lyman?" Jake waited for his so-called ally to look at him. "Now would be a wise time to stop talking. Before you win the ladies' argument for them." *Or I gag you for insulting Evie.*

"The one time Braden's outpouring of negativity can work in our favor, and he stops it." Miss Thompson rolled her eyes. "But the damage is done, Mr. Creed. It's foolish and dishonest to claim you hold any one of us in esteem when all you do is denigrate our decisions and order us about like children."

"All the while accusing us of selfish and shallow reasoning," Miss Higgins tacked on. Only a woman could manage to sound both triumphant and aggrieved in the same sentence.

"Selfish and shallow have no part in it. Nonsensical, I'd more than agree with." Jake searched the gaggle before him for any hint of solid reason and found only indignation. "We wouldn't bother trying to keep you safe if we didn't value you."

"Then you must value vapid fools who care only for what other people think." Evie's words hit too close to home.

All the way back to Jake's parents. "That's the last thing I value." Not that they were vapid, but the rest came within a splinter of describing his family. None of it came anywhere near depicting Evie or her friends. Or their worth.

"The Bible specifically tells us we can't speak out of both sides of our mouths, Mr. Creed." Miss Thompson fingered a golden cross hanging around her neck. "You can't claim to think both ways on a single issue, or you've ruined your own credibility."

"Would you believe he looks confused?" Miss Lyman shared glances with the others as Jake tried to dissect where they'd gone wrong, because obviously the women were the ones confused.

"I'd believe he judges us so trivial as to put the opinion of other people above our own safety." Miss Higgins furrowed her brow in mock concentration. "Yet he clearly claims he doesn't value petty people who think like that, so how can he value us?"

"They're doing that female thing again, where they ask a question with no good answer." Lyman's warning told him nothing new, only validated a long-standing suspicion that women took logical conversations and warped them into terrible traps.

"Every question possesses a good answer," his fiancée snapped at him. "It's just a matter of men not doing that male thing of refusing to admit how wrong they've been!"

"Hold it." Creed held up a palm to stop the squabbling and return to the issue at hand. "Lyman's a man who forgoes shovels to dig himself into a hole with nothing more than his mouth. That much is evident to anyone. But there's no denying you four took a solid conversation and chopped it to kindling. So instead of trying to undo the damage, let's go back and start again."

"We'll take that as an admission that men go about things backwards and graciously go along with it." Miss Lyman's capitulation—and the dig behind it—bought smiles from the women.

"Only because if men always go ahead, it means we can't look *after* you." Jake emphasized his point. "So you find danger. Now here's where things stalled. We place importance on your safety because we find you worth protecting. You four place more significance on what the men think about you than you put on your own security. That has to change."

"It's gratifying to hear you find us worthy." If a certain dry humor laced Miss Higgins's remark, Jake could overlook it.

"But far less gratifying to hear you disparage both our actions and our motives." Evie had stayed quiet since her comments about fools who cared only about what others thought. The grace period ended as she fixed her stare on him. "We don't deliberately put ourselves in danger, nor do we choose to remain in a precarious position out of a misguided superficiality. Simply put, Mr. Creed, we don't only keep our promises for the sake of the men. We keep them because we owe it to ourselves."

"You don't owe it to anyone to stay!" Lyman shouted. "Foolish decisions reflect poorly on you and your planning!"

"If a man's words are worthless, so is he," Evie threw back at him. "It's no different with women. We uphold our pledges because it respects the men we made them to and shows we value our judgment and promises enough to act on them. That you and Creed dismiss that reflects poorly on the two of you!"

"All that would be so, if not for one thing." Jake met her gaze with a fierce look of his own, standing so close his boots almost touched hers. "You're wrong when you say you didn't deliberately place yourself in danger. The moment you wrote that ad, the four of you brought this down upon Hope Falls. You set it in motion, and now you need to rectify your mistake."

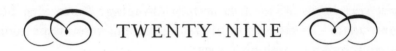# TWENTY-NINE

I t wasn't our mistake!" Miss Lyman slapped a hand on her brother's mattress for muffled punctuation. "We did not invite all these men into town in person and put ourselves in peril!"

"She's right." Miss Higgins sighed. "The ad may not have been the wisest idea, but, as written, it didn't invite danger."

"Since you've had over forty men come into town, despite only two dozen being allowed to remain, I'd say the general public disagrees with you, ladies." Jake silently dared them to refute that bit of evidence—a mistake.

"Of course they side with you. The general public of Hope Falls is male," Evie burst out. "They're the ones who misread or willfully disregarded the print and ruined our plans. Face it, Mr. Creed. This entire situation isn't because the four of us rushed headlong into danger. It's because men"—she paused as though to savor her next point—"refuse to follow directions!"

"You four are ones to speak." Lyman's roar muted to a thunderous growl. "Refusing to follow a single order since you arrived. No matter your intentions, no matter your plans, at least we can all agree that the outcome placed you at risk. Which means you need to abandon this failure and return East."

Four feminine heads gave mutinous shakes.

"Stop acting as though you need to stay. Safety and common sense overshadow some misguided principle here," Jake coaxed.

"Then we have different definitions of honor, Mr. Creed." Evie's remonstrance, a perfect echo of his parting words to his mother, robbed him of the ability to continue the conversation.

Honor is what brought me here. Honor is what keeps me spending time protecting you women. Honor is the bark that binds together the loose rings of my life. And she defines it as though I'm lacking. The irony roared in his ears until the sudden stillness of the room broke through to grab his notice.

"You don't mean that." Miss Thompson's brittle voice shattered the unnatural quiet, but no one moved.

"I do." Lyman's tones came out hollow. False. "If you won't leave, you have to marry. As soon as possible."

As Jake realized that his friend's alternative was to force the women into hasty weddings to gain the protection of husbands, his temples pounded in rage. *No. They'll marry the men they choose. Evie won't be given away to just any man so Braden Lyman can rest easy.* He opened his mouth to start objecting, but Lyman kept going.

"Even Cora."

Especially Cora. Evie leaped from her chair, intent on reaching her sister's former fiancé. *Cora will need another husband more than any of us once I'm jailed.* Her hands curved, pulling Lacey and Naomi away from where they tried to block her path. She couldn't tell whether the pair sought to protect their kin from her wrath or tried to beat her to him so they could let him have it first. They probably knew her well enough to know that there wouldn't be much left of Braden Lyman once Evie finished with him. Old adages claimed blood ran thicker than water, but Evie figured men thought that one up.

Battles didn't always leave visible bruises, friends became extensions of families when distance and time left loved ones lonely, and women knew well the wounds inflicted by words. Men shed blood together; women shed tears. Evie knew which made her stronger and believed she knew which bond Lacey and Naomi upheld now.

But it didn't matter why they blocked the bed. No matter their good intentions, her friends were in her way. So she barreled through. *I can't hit him. I can't kick him. I can't smother him with his own pillow.* She ran into the solid, unmoving obstacle that was Creed as she pondered just how she'd exact retribution on Braden for trying to throw her sister to the wolves. *I'll do worse than any of those. I'll sit on him!*

"Oh no, you won't." Creed slid to the side to block her when she tried to maneuver around, taking up far too much space.

Evie stopped. "Did I say that out loud?" Mortification swallowed surprise in a blink. Then she shrugged it away. If Creed stayed in the room, he'd see her act on the words.

"You didn't say anything." An inappropriate chuckle lightened his voice. "I could guess at a slew of possibilities by the look in your eye, but I'm not going to let any of them happen. So I don't see the use in giving you any extra ideas."

"Feel free." She leaned right then darted left, only to be brought up short by one rock-hard arm suddenly encircling her midriff. Evie gave a strangled yelp and jumped away from the contact. The heat surprised her. His speed caught her off guard. The idea that he felt, however briefly, how wide across she measured was unimaginably awful. That mortified her more than if he'd heard her plotting vengeance against Braden.

Braden, who still sat hale and hearty—or at least as hale and hearty as he had five minutes previous—in his bed. Which meant Lacey and Naomi remained behind her, most likely consoling a bereft Cora.

The man will pay. Creed can't guard him forever. Evie clenched her fists so tightly they cramped, the pulse in her fingertips matching the pounding at her temples and in the sensitive place behind her jaw. That Braden would stoop so low as to renege on the engagement, she'd suspected. That he'd throw her sister to a pack of lonely loggers without a word or any sort of arrangement for her protection, she'd never imagined.

Lacey, Naomi, and I came alone, knowing we'd find men. Agreeing to that plan. Cora came for Braden. Evie began to shake as she considered all that Cora had given up for the ungrateful brute. *He may not be able to stand, but he could have stood by his word. The simple title of fiancée offered Cora a certain measure of protection. The men didn't swarm around her equally.*

"Home or husbands." Braden started talking again. "You have to be protected, and either one will do. There aren't any other options, and each one of you will need to make her choice."

"They'll choose their husbands in their own time, Lyman." Creed's snarl jerked Evie's attention back to the man who blocked her path. "Marriage is for life, and, as you've so aptly illustrated, a woman can never be too careful about what sort of man she chooses to give her hand—or her heart—to." Blue eyes, blazing with heat, stared into her own as he said this last, making Evie almost believe Creed urged her toward caution rather than reprimanded Braden for being unworthy of Cora.

Either way, she fought a sudden, strong urge to hug him. Or bake him a pie, which was just as good and far more proper. "Thank you." She then rose on tiptoe to peer over Creed's shoulder.

The man unbent enough to champion them about not rushing to the altar, but he showed no sign of moving.

"Braden Lyman, you're no longer allowed to give any suggestions, offer any opinions, or make any demands regarding our safety," Evie declared. "Of all the men in this town, you've demonstrated that you, who should care for us and cherish Cora, Lacey, and Naomi the very most, instead value us the least. We aren't burdens to be given away."

"That's not what I—"

"Do. Not. Say. Another. Thing." Creed spoke as though each word was a sentence, a proclamation unto itself.

Lyman obeyed.

"We've arranged for Mrs. Nash's brother, Mr. Lawson, to move into the study below stairs. After last night, we all agree we'd feel safer with the added protection, and he's the only male relative any of us boast in town." She didn't tell them to assuage their concerns, merely to inform them of the decisions they—the women—had already made. "With the babe so close to term, it's wise to have him nearby in any case. These are the measures we've taken for our own security and to maintain propriety."

"Why did you four. . ."

Evie didn't listen to the rest. She spun on her heel and walked the few steps to where her sister still sat in her chair, shock freezing her in place. "Cora-mine"—she whispered the old nickname, the play on Coraline's full name—"you'll not be courted by the others. It's too soon and wasn't the plan."

"No," Lacey assured her. "We won't put about word that your engagement has ended. No one need know. Creed won't mention it, and if Braden does, he knows full well we'll move Mrs. Nash and her brother to another house. He's said more than enough, and it's time he learned to keep his fool mouth shut."

With that tirade, Evie knew she'd been right about the strength of the friendship shared among the four of them. Even though they'd faced Lacey in a sort of fight the very day before, she stood ready to deny her own brother for their sakes.

"There's nothing for him or Creed to keep secret." So strident were the words, Cora might have been marshaling troops. Or, perhaps, the formidable reserves of a woman's strength. "I'll not discuss it now beyond saying this: Braden can deny me as many times as he likes within the hearing of the four of you." Here, she gave a nod to include Creed. "Because we know that the truth of the matter is the engagement stands."

"Now, Cora," Braden tried again. "See reason. You need to marry another man to be safe. It's the only logical thing."

"I'm nothing but logical, my love." Bitter determination tinged the endearment. "You proposed, kept me to a long engagement, accepted my dowry, and invested it in this town." She gave a strange laugh, ruefulness mixed with determination as she looked at her fiancé. "You didn't think of that, did you, Braden? That I can sue you for breach of promise? That Lacey holds your estate and would support my suit?"

Evie sucked in a breath. *Lord, please don't let my sister force a man to wed her. Please look after her tender heart, and don't let her determination and the memories of the man who used to be her beau ruin her future. Please. . .*

"None of you thought of it, but I considered that this might happen. The other three placed an ad, Braden." Now Cora drew a deep breath. "But I knew, if worse came to worst and you became bullheaded, I could always point out one unchangeable truth. Out of all of us, I've already hired my husband. . . . You."

"Me?" Braden snorted, as much to keep the howl of despair jammed back in his throat as to sound amused. "I hope you realize how fortunate you are, Cora, that I've released you from a bad bargain without asking to see the bill of sale."

Stubborn, brilliant, beautiful Cora. She waits for me to reclaim her, and when I refuse, she rolls up her sleeves and comes for me instead. God, grant me strength to keep pushing her away until she stops pulling me close.

"Joke all you like." She folded her hands in her lap. "But I've not released you from our bargain and have no intention of doing so. You might as well resign yourself to your fate and make a wise decision—for a refreshing change—to be pleasant about the situation." The smile she gave him looked nothing like Cora. It looked like something with no heart wearing a tragic mask of Cora's smile.

Braden wanted to throw it away and bring back the real thing. *But I can't. Until she accepts that I've cast her aside and demand she weds another, she'll never leave Hope Falls. Cora won't be safe until they go back East. I have to make her believe. I have to make it even worse.*

"A man can't be bought, darling. Everyone knows that." Braden raised his arms and nestled the back of his head in his stacked palms, as though bored. "We're too smart for such a practice. Men use commodities and make the most of them. We aren't the goods to be made use of. The world runs on that truth, and the four of you need to accept it."

Creed made a low warning sound deep in his throat, but Braden ignored him. Now wasn't the time to explain the ploy to his odd ally. Now was the time to make sure it worked.

"You took my money; I took your hand. That's an exchange of goods." Cora pointed out the simple business. "That makes you a commodity I found to be worth a certain amount. Of course, you used to be far more pleasant, so it seems I made the common mistake of overpaying when I signed over my dowry. But all that is past, and we move onward."

His sister and hers tried, unsuccessfully, to hide chuckles at Cora's assessment that she'd overpaid. But it was no laughing matter.

Can't they see it's true? I'm no longer worth what I once was. No longer worthy of her. "Such naïveté for a budding businesswoman." Braden tsked. "It's not a matter of whether or not my worth matched your dowry, little Cora. Dowries are merely incentives. You know what incentives are, don't you?" He raised a brow.

"Lyman, I might let her sister get to you." Creed breathed the threat.

Braden knew that his friend was letting him know where he was headed. And, more importantly, that it was despicable enough to be effective. *Good.*

"When the goods are not up to par or don't match to the value being exchanged, something is added to make them more desirable. It's commonly accepted that women, in and of themselves, lack any particular value. Thus, the invention of the dowry to persuade men to part with their freedom. It helps even out the trade, so to speak. Your dowry was compensation for my sacrifice in taking you." Braden twisted the knife.

"Is that so?" The travesty of a smile took on the fine gleam of a sharpened knife.

"You've seen enough of the world now to begin to understand." He sliced away at every sweet memory they shared as he reduced their love to dollars and nonsense.

"I'm beginning to see that you admit you were compensated, and I'll hold you to the job. Better yet, I've been learning to get the most for my money." That sharp smile edged to the faces of the other three women as Cora spoke. "Since you seem so certain you'll be unhappy with me as a wife, I see no reason we should both be miserable. So I'll be happy. Which means you'll have a lot of work to do to pass muster from here on out."

"Cora, stop this." It had gone on far enough. "Lacey will return your dowry, plus interest. You're free to find another." He managed to say the words without wincing and ruining it all.

"I know I could be free." The smile vanished, leaving a grim, tight line in its place. "But you won't be. I won't accept my dowry in return, even if Lacey would give it to me. Which I'm certain she wouldn't, as her heart is set on having me for a real sister. Isn't that true, Lace?"

"Absolutely." Lacey nodded. "It'd be a shame for Braden to lose everything he owns in a lawsuit over such a thing."

"Send for the lawyer, Lace." He wasn't playing this game. "If I lose, I lose. But I'd rather lose my money than my life."

Because that's what will happen if anything happens to Cora while I'm trapped in this bed. She has to be safe. At any cost.

THIRTY

It's not worth it!" Lacey protested but knew she could only blame herself. Whether it was a matter of speaking before she thought or a simple case of packing everything she owned—and quite a few extra purchases to supplement her possessions before traveling west—Lacey Lyman created this entire mess.

And it looked like she'd have to unpack all of it. Today. For no good reason but a persistent need to make other people happy. *Or, at least, not* un*happy with me,* she acknowledged. Unfortunately, that admission didn't make her any happier with the task before her. And behind her. And in the next room over...

"It's more than worth the effort." Cora started to open a crate. "The rain won't let up anytime soon, and we aren't equipped to handle another day of so-called 'courting weather.'"

"I'd thought yesterday couldn't get any worse, after that confrontation with Braden." Naomi's mutter made Lacey wince and look at Cora, afraid of her friend's reaction to the reminder.

"It didn't." Cora's lips tightened. "But while Creed kept Braden alive, I accepted a few things. I expect Braden to adjust to his situation—proverbially lay in the bed of his own making. So I can do no less when it comes to my own circumstances."

"You don't have to stay with him." Evie dropped a box with a satisfying thud. "Wait until you're ready then find someone new. There's no rush for you, sis, and you don't deserve the way you've been treated. Leave Braden to his own miserable griping."

"In any other case, I'd say my brother should get far worse than his own way." Lacey unlatched a trunk and began rifling through paper-wrapped packages. "But this time, it'd serve him right to have things his own way. There is no greater punishment than losing Cora."

"Yes, there is—being outwitted and trapped in the engagement. For me, I deserve the strain of hearing how little he wants me. He threw me over in the letter telling us he'd lived, but I dragged Evie out here with me anyway. I came for myself more than I came for Braden, and now I'll pay for it." Cora moved to the next pile. "I just plan to make him pay more."

"Then you should have Mr. Riordan drag my brother's bed in here so Braden can make himself useful. Make him dig through trunks and crates in search of a tiny little box of cribbage pegs." Lacey shut the lid of the trunk she'd just searched. "Honestly, I never imagined being courted would take such work!"

"Don't you dare let any one of those men step foot in here, Lacey." Evie craned her neck around another pile. "Then we won't be rid of them until the sky clears. You may bemoan all the goods loaded into this mercantile, but I celebrate each and every reason for the four of us to enjoy some peace and quiet!"

"It's true. I don't care how many hog pens, chicken coops, and cribbage boards we have to set those men to making. An afternoon in their company is more than enough. The morning belongs to us!" Naomi sat back with an exhausted sigh.

"I never thought to see such a thing as arm wrestling." Cora shook her head. "Much less imagine they thought we'd find it impressive or appealing to see them twist and crush each other's hands to slam their opponents' arms atop Evie's tables."

"They do all have such lovely strong muscles." Lacey couldn't help but notice. "Strange the way I never noticed how the men in Charleston seem so. . . Well, scrawny sounds unkind."

"Big arms, big appetites, big, stinking cigars." Evie wrinkled her nose. "I can't believe they dared try to smoke those inside my diner. Did you ever consider whether you'd marry a man who smoked cigars or chewed tobacco? I doubt I could."

"So long as he limits it to his study or outdoors, it wouldn't matter to me." Naomi shrugged. "Not regularly, of course. Habitual smoking leaves an odor and stains clothes."

"And I'd imagine it makes a man less pleasant to kiss." Lacey sidled through a narrow space toward a long case lining the back wall. Shocked gasps followed her progress, making her stop and turn around. Well, try to turn around, give up, and back her way through to eye her disbelieving friends once more.

"Oh, do stop gaping at me! I know it's not precisely proper to think of such things, but we're not conventional anymore. Let's not pretend otherwise." She gave a righteous sniff. . .and promptly sneezed. When she recovered, the other three wore small smiles. "Now admit it. Whether or not you can stomach the thought of kissing a man should be an indicator of whether or not you might be willing to marry him. Don't you agree?"

"I agree." Evie and Cora eyed each other as though unsure how to handle their own accord. Both blushed the same shade.

"What do you mean, you agree?" Evie planted her hands on her hips. "We've never discussed any such thing, young lady."

"Oh, stop looking so appalled." Cora rolled her eyes. "I'm engaged and have been for quite a while. Did you never think—"

"Ugh!" Lacey broke in. "Of course we didn't think about that. Braden's my brother; you're Evie's sister."

"I thought about it." Naomi's quiet declaration took them all by surprise. "You may not have given it much thought, but I endeavored never to leave the two of you alone behind closed doors for more than five minutes, Cora. Not because I doubted either of you, but for the sake of your reputation. A woman can never be too careful. And now, more than ever, I'm glad I did."

"Oh." Cora's blush returned, deeper than before. "Now that you mention it, I do recall Braden being rather short with you in the month or so before he left Charleston for Hope Falls."

"He didn't appreciate my efforts." Satisfaction laced Naomi's tone. "Kept insisting I was a companion, not chaperone."

"We're all each other's chaperones now." Lacey gave her cousin a hug. "But putting that aside for just a moment. . ." She fixed a smile on Naomi, then Evie, before asking what she'd been dying to know for days. "Now that we're discussing the men, which amongst our contenders do each of you find acceptable?"

"For marriage or kissing?" Cora's teasing widened Lacey's smile. If her friend could joke, Braden hadn't crushed her.

Which means my brother might survive the coming weeks. "Both!" Lacey thought a moment. "Though if you're only willing to admit to a kissing curiosity, so to speak, rather than proclaim men marriage material, that is your prerogative."

"Kissing curiosity?" Evie's squeak sounded less like outrage and more like guilt. "Are you trying to say we're supposed to evaluate whether or not we'd like to kiss each man and then discard him as a potential husband accordingly?"

"Not at all." Lacey frowned. "Hopefully you won't be discarding every man, or even the majority, based on that."

"I take it to mean you haven't excluded them all." Evie's eyes sparkled. "And since you've given this the most thought, you should go first!"

Kissing was the last thing on Evie Thompson's mind. Until Lacey brought it up. Then the conversation pulled her thoughts into previously untraveled territory. The sort of thinking that got a woman in trouble, when the first man who sprang to mind needed clouting—not kissing. *When did I take such a violent turn?*

Now that question had an easy answer. Evie could trace her

dismaying urges to raise her voice to unladylike levels and shake sense into dense skulls back to her arrival in town. *No. That's not true. It's not fair to blame an entire town for my sudden surge of temper. Hope Falls isn't at fault.* Evie's eyes narrowed as she mentally caught the culprit. *It's the men!*

Oddly enough, she found the explanation soothing. What woman wouldn't be driven to the brink of brandishing cast-iron cookware after an arduous journey rewarded with nothing but oblivious, ogling, or—even worse—order-spewing men just like—

"Mr. Creed?" Lacey's sly inquiry, or the very end of it, dovetailed with Evie's ruminations. Except Lacey was supposed to be listing the men Lacey wouldn't mind kissing. Could it be that her friend developed a tendre for the man who increasingly preoccupied Evie's own thoughts? And why wouldn't Lacey notice Creed, whose innate authority and commanding presence kept even the most unruly loggers in line. . .or walloped them into submission on the one night four of them tried to cross over that line.

"What?" Evie tried to dislodge the lump blocking her throat at the idea of Creed and Lacey. *It shouldn't bother me. In fact, it's almost laughable I didn't see it before. He always sits beside her, and Lacey would have the good sense to notice him before any of the other men around here.* But she hoped for another reason why Lacey mentioned his name in conjunction with kissing, all the same. If only because. . . Well, she didn't have any good reason at the moment, but it didn't feel right.

"I said that none of us could fail to notice the four men who stepped forward that first night." Mischief sparkled in Lacey's eyes. "Gent, Mr. Riordan, Mr. Klumpf, and Mr. Creed."

A bizarre wave of relief washed over Evie at the explanation, receding slightly at the implication these men had won her friends' favor. "So you're saying you've considered kissing all four of them and remained there?"

"No. Gent's age makes him a poor match for me." At eighteen, Lacey's decision made good sense. "And Mr. Klumpf doesn't seem a good match for my interests, though I think he's very good-hearted and fulfills all the requests on our list."

"I agree, although Gent's age doesn't bother me." Naomi seemed hesitant to add her opinion. "I would preclude Mr. Creed as overly forceful for my tastes. And I wouldn't take Mr. Riordan for myself. I find his strength somewhat intimidating."

"Truly?" Evie blinked in astonishment. "He's a sort of gentle giant, Naomi. The only time I've seen him utilize any of that force was when he came to Creed's assistance that night."

"You'll each find different traits appealing," Cora pointed out. "It's a good thing you won't have all the same men on each of your lists, though I expect some crossover, of course."

"Do any others catch your eye, offhand?" Evie wondered.

"I'll admit that Mr. Fillmore's answer pleased me best." Naomi blushed. "Though his taste in friends, considering Mr. Kane led that troupe of men determined to accost us, gives me pause as to his ability to read character. So I don't know."

"Consider him with caution, Naomi," Evie urged, recalling the man who'd withdrawn even more since Kane's departure. "Does another man stand out, Lacey, or merely Riordan and Creed?" *Please let there be another, or I'll be left with only the kindhearted but somewhat overeager Mr. Klumpf.*

"Not one of our suitors, so that's all," Lacey hedged.

"Lawson!" Cora crowed. "Oh, I thought so. He's smart and mannered and keeps to himself enough to make Lacey curious. Besides, he's the best dressed out of every man in town."

"Stop teasing. What I want to know is why have both Lacey and I revealed the names of three men while Evie's managed not to say anything beyond a defense of Mr. Riordan? Which is not the same as choosing him." Naomi turned the conversation around.

"Snickelfritz, Naomi!" Evie leveled a scowl at her friend. "You weren't supposed to notice, much less draw attention to that. But since you have, I'll say I think Riordan one of the finest of the lot, and Mr. Klumpf would make a very good husband." *For someone else.* She didn't speak the last part aloud, but that didn't change the truth of her statement.

"Oh no, Evie Thompson. We each named three men. Pick your third." Lacey wouldn't let her squirm away. "So long as it isn't that awful, brazen Mr. Williams, we won't mock your choice."

"There's something to be said for a man who truly wants you and is willing to proclaim it to anyone within hearing." Evie pretended to consider the notion. "Flattering, you could say. He also fulfills the requirements on the list, so. . ."

"Stop joking, sis." Cora shuddered. "It's not amusing."

"She doesn't need to name her third, in any case. We all know it without Evie bothering to admit it." Naomi laughed. "Mr. Creed caught her attention that first night and never lost it."

"If something catches on fire in the kitchen, it takes my concentration, too. Creed's much the same way—untended, he can wreak havoc." Evie shifted uneasily, realized she was shifting, realized her friends noticed her shifting, and wondered why this entire topic made her so uncomfortable in the first place.

Creed. He walked in, took on the role of our protector, and set about exasperating me so thoroughly I stopped thinking of him as one of the others. The thought of marrying him made her uneasy. This sudden curiosity about kissing made her neck and arms feel prickly. *Is that a good thing or a bad thing?*

"Fire fascinates, warms, provides a means for you to do what you love, Evie." Cora tilted her head to the side. "Any man you marry should be able to do the same, and you can't deny Creed manages to strike sparks with you. I like him, sis."

"We strike sparks because we argue. He's constantly telling me what to do or what poor decisions I make. The only thing he likes about me is my cooking." A dull ache settled in Evie's chest. *Just like most of the men.* "Creed won't choose me."

"What?" Lacey shook with laughter. "Did you never wonder why we asked every man but Creed which two women he'd be most interested in, Evie?" She gulped in air as though to speak more.

"To be honest, I stopped thinking of him as a suitor and more as a partner in the mill." Evie shrugged. "But I'd assume if, after all he's done to earn a stake, he still wants to marry one of us, he'd choose you, Lacey. Why else didn't you ask?" The ache grew into a throbbing pain, sliding down to tumble in her stomach as she spoke the words aloud. *Creed would choose Lacey.* It was worse than riding the train days on end.

"Because he already chose you, Evie." Cora tossed a bundle of material at her head. "Don't pretend you're a half-wit. Our family intellect runs far too strong for you to insult it."

"All of us noticed it, Evie." Naomi peered at her. "We took it for granted you did the same. The only reason I've held Lacey back from interrogating you about whether or not you returned Creed's interest was I thought you hadn't decided."

"What interest?" It took an effort to keep from shrieking the words. "Mr. Klumpf follows me about. Mr. Williams all but tried to stake his claim. *They* have shown interest—not Creed." *I would far rather it be Creed than Williams, for one thing.*

"He always sits beside or across from you, Evie." Cora made the first point. "But even before that, he swept his hat from his head and pointed to your sign the moment he walked into the diner and recognized you. Mr. Creed remembered and paid you a compliment before he spoke a single word to anyone in town."

"He complimented the cooking," Evie muttered. "That's all."

"Did you see the look on his face when Mr. Klumpf tried to call dibs on you?" Lacey giggled. "Pure outrage. He disallowed that in an awful hurry, Evie. Then he chose to talk with you about making decisions, so you'd be protected. Not any of us."

"But all of that pales in comparison to the moment when all three of us knew Mr. Creed watched you more closely than the rest." Naomi's smile grew wide as though savoring it before uttering the single, unforgivable word: "Gingersnaps."

"When he mentioned my *heft*?" Evie could be forgiven for one tiny, disbelieving shriek. Or even a not-so-tiny one.

"When he said you were *losing* your heft," Cora corrected. "And he didn't like it! So he wanted you to eat more. The man did everything but force-feed you those gingersnaps to stop you from losing more weight, because he *didn't want you to change*."

"He'd known you only a few weeks, but he noticed the difference." Lacey all but bounced on the trunk she'd chosen as a seat. "Between your motion sickness for days on the train and all the running around you've done since we arrived, you'd started shrinking. We knew, but a man who didn't pay extremely close attention wouldn't see it—or care."

"Creed likes you as you are, Evie." Naomi's eyes softened. "Not just your cooking, but the way you look. And if you listened to him yesterday, he clearly values you, even when he disagrees with the decisions you make. Your safety is important to him, more than the rest of ours. It's the reason why he argues the most with you. I can't believe you didn't realize it!"

"I never imagined Creed might want me," Evie admitted. *So I never allowed myself to think about wanting him. Why borrow the pain, when I knew I'd be choosing after Lacey and Naomi?*

"You need more confidence." Lacey sniffed. "I never understood why you seemed to think men wouldn't clamor around you if you gave them the least encouragement. It's not that men won't want you, Evie—look at Klumpf and Williams if you need more proof of that—but that you made it seem like you didn't want them to! So don't doubt that Creed likes you. And it won't hurt to admit it," Lacey prompted.

Evie let out a shaky breath. *You can't make an omelet without breaking a few eggs, and I can't make the most of what's before me if I'm not willing to leave my own shell behind.*

"I like him, too."

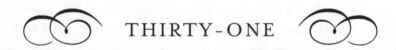# THIRTY-ONE

I don't like her much, to tell the truth." The words floated into the kitchen from the dining room, where men bored holes into cribbage boards. Unable to distinguish the speakers from where he'd just tightened the outside pantry door hinges, Jake took two steps.

And stopped.

Because, by opening the inside pantry door leading to the kitchen, he caught sight of four women. Mrs. McCreedy had left to look after Mrs. Nash, leaving only the four original females of Hope Falls to prepare the midday meal. Jake thought they'd all adjourned to the mercantile for a futile search for cribbage pegs. But before him stood the proof they'd returned earlier than expected. Earlier, it seemed, than anyone had expected.

How on earth did they manage to find such a small item amidst the epic disarray inside that store? I imagined they'd be kept busy for at least another hour before having to give up.

Reality replaced expectation yet again. The four of them clustered to the side of the swinging doors to the dining room, where the wall would hide their skirts from any man wise enough to glance back. From the sounds of the conversation going on in the next room, Jake seriously doubted any of the men speaking possessed that wisdom. Or rudimentary survival instinct, if he wanted to be particular about the entire mess.

Unfortunately for those men, the more they talked, the more particular Jake felt like getting. It hurt their case even further that he could see the women's faces and reactions to the foolish assessments spewing into the kitchen.

"What do you mean you don't like her?" One dumbfounded dummy yelled. "You've eaten same as the rest of us, and everyone knows she's the cook. Ain't a man alive who shouldn't like her!"

Jake's hands clenched, but he didn't move. If he budged an inch, he'd keep right on going and bust up the conversation before the women got to hear frank appraisals undiluted by threat of punishment. He owed it to them to allow the ladies an unfettered glimpse of the men they might choose to marry—but hopefully wouldn't.

"I like her cooking just fine, but the Lyman gal's prettier. Always took a shine to blonds, so you keep the chef."

"Don't go givin' any of the women away, now, Bob." Another speaker identified one of the fools. "I'll give Earl a run for the cook. She may be round as a biscuit, but I bet she keeps a man warm as anything she bakes fresh in the oven."

Feminine hands slapped over mouths to hold back outraged gasps, but that didn't concern Jake. Aside from a powerful fury at the thought of any man warming up next to Evie, he wanted to take away the dejection widening her golden gaze at the poorly phrased biscuit comment. The same dejection he'd seen when he'd fumbled over a way to protest how she'd started wasting away.

"She and the Lyman gal have spirit to spare," someone added in. "For me, I'd take the Higgins woman. She's more settled, knows her place, so it wouldn't take much to keep her in line."

"I like a high-strung filly." There was no mistaking Williams's strident tone. "And the rest of you can stop talking about Miss Thompson. Any man who tries to cozy up to her will have to go through me, and he won't make it in one piece."

Dodger's reedy, nasal whine cut through the jeers. "Stop your jawing, Williams. Everyone knows which woman you want—same as everyone knows she doesn't want you. Leave her be."

The first twinge of respect for the shifty high-climber niggled at Jake's mind. Even if Dodger turned out to be Twyler, at least he'd had the decency to tell Williams off—which would mean every man had at least one moment of usefulness.

"I'll gladly leave her be," someone chortled. "No appeal in a pudgy woman, but she holds true to the old adage about good cooks and housewives. The rest of you are welcome to Thompson."

Jake bit back a growl, his hand on the door before he stopped himself from barging through. Evie's horror would only be worse if she knew he'd been listening. *Never mind her own practice in the fine art of eavesdropping.* The stray memory almost made him smile. But not now, not over the rhyme of. . .

"It's a little too little to save,
And a little too much to dump,
And there's nothing to do but eat it,
That makes a housewife plump!"

A roar of laughter met the recitation, but tears clouded golden eyes as Evie spun on her heel and made for the door. The pantry door.

Jake stepped out of the way, pressing himself to the side of the shelves as she swept through as though determined to burst outside into the rain and keep walking until she'd left behind everything she'd overheard. Instead, he snagged her elbow, the speed of her own motion swinging her to face him.

"You!" Livid blinks kept her gorgeous eyes afloat in unshed tears Jake saw all too clearly. They hadn't built the pantry wide enough for two people, so she stood close enough to kiss, all but nestled in his arms. "Let go of me right now, Creed!"

If a man could call a squirming, arm-slapping fury of a woman the nestling type. *Wonder what it says about me that I think a woman like that's worth holding, so long as the woman is Evie.* Jake didn't take the time to ponder that thought before her elbow landed in his midsection and her heel stomped on his instep—just beyond the steel lining his boot, so it hurt.

The second he let go, she whirled out of his arms and through the door. Which she also managed to slam in his face, courtesy of those newly tightened hinges. Not exactly Jake's idea of thanks for a job well done.

I'd rather take that kiss, he decided as he jerked the door open and raced after her. Needles of rain stung his forearms, hands, and face where his hat didn't protect him. Wind pushed against him, a cold chill doing its level best to bite through his jacket. Jake bit back, his stride eating away at the distance between himself and Evie.

She didn't stand a chance, hampered as she was by long skirts and those confounded contraptions women strapped themselves into to look thinner. Men weren't supposed to acknowledge the existence of corsets, much less mention the fact they made it difficult for a woman to breathe when she laced them too tightly. But for all her good sense in other areas, Jake knew Evie didn't allow herself so much as an extra inch.

Some people never know when to give themselves some slack.

"Evie!" He bellowed her name, watching as she scampered even more quickly toward a thick stand of trees. Jake caught her in three paces, snaking his arm around her waist and tugging her beneath the protective canopy of the densely packed trees.

"Leave me be, Jake Creed!" She wriggled like a rabbit in a snare, water streaming down her face. Whether tears mingled with the rain or not was impossible to tell. Evie gave a great big sniff, the tip of her nose glowing an affronted red.

Tears, too, then. Jake scowled. "I'm not letting you hie off into the mountains because some idiot recited a nursery rhyme. Now

don't move. If I have to chase after you again, I'll carry you back."
He waited for her to gulp an acknowledgment of that threat
before regretfully slipping his arm from her waist.

Actually, he wouldn't have minded a reason to carry her back.
She felt warm and soft and needed some comforting. Maybe—

*Maybe I should hurry up and shrug out of this coat before I do
something stupid.* He whipped off his wool-lined leather coat and
wrapped it around her, frowning to feel her shivering.

"Thank you." She clutched the lapel, threading her arms into
the sleeves before wrapping her arms around herself—as much
to ward him away as to keep in warmth, he guessed. Good idea.
She looked far too alluring with her hair straggling in streams of
cinnamon and coffee around her fresh-scrubbed face, the rest of
her tucked into his coat.

It didn't quite close in the front—God made her too womanly
for that—but the leather hung far past her hips. Evie's strength
often made him overlook how small she was, but now, with her
golden eyes dimmed to dark amber, her nose red as she huddled
outside in the rain, it hit him anew how much she took on. And
how much thinner she'd become over the past month.

"You're not plump," he blurted out before thinking.

Her eyes widened, and Evie stared at him, saying nothing.
She tilted her head, looking for all the world like a curious little
owl as she blinked and waited. What she waited for, Jake didn't
know. He only knew he didn't plan to say more until he knew it
wouldn't be the wrong thing this time. *Which means I'll most likely
have to go mute around women.*

He blinked back, watching as she nibbled her lower lip the
way she did whenever she thought something over. Jake liked the
way she did that. Especially now that no other men could see it.

"Yes, I am."

"No, you aren't." Jake's—Creed didn't suit him, and Evie had never understood why—jaw set in that stubborn way of his.

"Oh, but I am." She rocked back on her heels and lifted her own chin. "In a pinch, Cora, Naomi, and Lacey could exchange clothes. A few quick alterations, tacked-up or let-down hems and so forth, and they'd manage." She looked down to where Jake's coat—a man's coat, cut wide across to accommodate his broader shoulders—didn't close over her own chest. "But not me."

"So?"

Evie let loose something sounding perilously close to a growl. "So, it's because I'm plump. I'm larger than other women, far more than fashionable."

"There." Relief lightened his blue eyes to an almost crystalline shade as he reached out and flipped the coat collar up to warm her throat. "You said it yourself, Evie. You're not plump or round or anything else you think of as bad. You're more than most women ever manage, in a lot of ways. Don't regret it."

Her eyes closed as though to imprint the memory forever. Evie fought not to think, not to ruin his admiration by analyzing what it might mean. What the words should mean. But she couldn't help herself. In a moment, she choked out, "More hefty, more bossy, more difficult. . .yes, I'm more of a lot of things. And I regret most of them. But I'm less, too, Mr. Creed. I'm less unkind, I'm less quick to judge, and I'm less likely to ignore someone when needed. Trouble is"—she finally trusted herself to open her eyes and almost faltered when she saw the anger in his expression—"others tend to see the more instead of the less. I don't know how to change it."

"It's not your job to change the way others see you." Jake took a step forward, a step too close, forcing her to back up. "It is your job to see yourself more clearly instead of muddying things up with all your doubts. The way people see you does not matter. The Bible tells us not to judge according to appearance, that man looks on the outward appearance, but the Lord looks on the heart."

"I found the Lord when I was young, Jake." Evie snapped

her mouth shut when she heard his name slip out then decided to forge ahead. "Here, in Hope Falls, I'm trying to find a man. You heard them as well as I did. They aren't looking at my heart. They're looking at my appearance and finding it lacking."

"Then choose a man who sees all of you, Evie!" When he rumbled her name, her heart beat faster. "One who sees that you're not bossy so much as protective of your loved ones. You're not difficult; you challenge others to be their best. And"—he stepped closer, eyes blazing blue fire as though he meant every word—"you're not round or plump or hefty."

She held her breath as he reached one calloused hand to tuck a soggy strand of hair behind her ear.

"You're soft and sweet." With that, he bent a breath away, sliding his forefinger lower to lift her chin.

My first kiss. Evie almost forgot to breathe. Forgot her anger at the men in this town and her distress over the one before her. In fact, she forgot everything but the one thought thrumming through her mind until it squeaked past her lips before he reached them.

"You." She swallowed. "I choose you."

He froze, hand still sending warmth from her chin down her throat. Jake's gaze searched hers, asking whether or not she was serious. A deep breath lifted his shoulders, his voice the lowest she'd ever heard as he responded to the single most important declaration she'd ever made. "What?"

Back to the monosyllabic replies. Evie fought the urge to scowl. After all, she'd just accepted a man's unspoken proposal. A man didn't want his new fiancée glowering at him. That would tarnish the memory of the day she agreed to make him the happiest man on earth or some such twaddle. So she smiled.

Which may have been a mistake, because he reached up to trace her lower lip with the rough pad of his thumb.

And her thoughts stuttered. *Oh my. . .*

 THIRTY-TWO

M*ine.* Something primal roared its satisfaction as Jake waited for Evie to repeat what she'd said. Now wasn't the time for any misunderstandings or strange twists of feminine logic to rob him of what she'd just promised. *No. Now is the time for her to be sure she knows what it means to choose me. To be* mine.

He felt her swallow, though his gaze remained fixed on the progress of his thumb teasing its way back and forth across the softness of her lower lip. Soon, he'd press his own lips there.

But until then, he kept his hand as a barrier, so he wouldn't rush things. Because Jake suddenly knew one thing with a certainty he'd never felt before. *Once I kiss her, there's no going back.*

"I said I choose you, Jake Creed." Evie's affirmation doused the fire in a flash. "I'll be Mrs. Creed, your wife."

"Evie." He dropped his hand as though it turned to lead, his chest tight with the sudden realization. "You can't be Mrs. Creed." *How do I explain what I've done, and how can I make you accept that I'm the same man you trust, when I've deceived you?*

"What?" She stumbled, her back pressing against an unyielding ponderosa pine as she tried to scramble around it. Away from him. "I thought. . .I didn't. . .I must have misunderstood."

Desperate to evade him, she tripped over a rock and would have fallen if he hadn't caught and steadied her. But Evie, who'd leaned into his embrace moments before, proclaiming her willingness to become his wife, fought him like a wild thing.

"Stop!" He planted his palms against the trunk of the tree on either side of her, pinning her in place. "You'll hurt yourself if you take off again, and I won't allow it, Evie."

"Miss Thompson, to you." Her hiss told of battered pride; the redness returning to her nose tattled of something far worse. "And it doesn't matter what you will or won't allow, Mr. Creed. You have no say over me or over what goes on in this town. I'm sorry I mistook your kind words for personal interest, but I assure you I won't do so again. Now. Let. Me. Go."

Never. "No." He straightened to give her more space but kept his arms as they were. "Not until you hear me out, Evie." Jake wasn't going to give up the newfound freedom of saying her name aloud. He'd been thinking it for far too long to lose it.

"There's nothing to hear. If you want Lacey or Naomi, that's between you and them. For me, I'll go back to the diner." She shoved at one of his arms, her tiny hands covered by the sleeves of his coat. Evie's effort couldn't even bend his elbow.

"There's plenty to hear. And no matter how much you don't want to listen and I don't want to tell it, we're both going to do our part in this conversation." He made a sound low in his throat when she tried to duck under one of his arms. "Try that again, and I'll step close to keep you in line until I finish talking." *Go on,* his gaze challenged her. *Try it. I'll like it.*

"A gentleman doesn't trap a lady against a tree, Mr. Creed." Her scowl could have sizzled the morning bacon.

"Most likely not, but I never claimed to be a gentleman." Jake took a deep breath. "More important, I'm not Mr. Creed."

"Yes, you are." The fierceness of her denial touched him. Evie shook her head as though rejecting the very notion he could be anyone or anything other than she believed—and she believed he was the type of man who deserved a woman like her.

Which made him, supposedly, the best kind of man.

"No, I'm not. My first name is Jacob, but Creed isn't my real surname, Evie. I left my family earlier this year and adopted the name, but I couldn't tell you or anyone else here." Silently, he willed her to understand, to decide that the name didn't matter so long as the man behind it remained the same.

"So. . ." She looked him up and down as though surveying an unknown insect and finding it both creative and faintly repulsive. The sort of thing that might well need squashing, but she hadn't decided yet. "Not Creed? May I ask why you chose that particular name? To be honest, I never thought it suited you."

"You never thought it suited me?" Unaccountably insulted, Jake looked down at himself then at her to demand, "Why not?"

"I never could put my finger on it. The same way Dodger's clothes are too big for him, the name Creed feels too small for you." She shrugged. "The only way I remember names is by how people break them in. A good name gets worn like a favorite shawl or pair of boots, until you almost can't imagine the person without it. Most folks grow into their names that way. You're one of the few I couldn't reconcile. Now I know why."

"Is there anyone else whose name doesn't fit?" He leaned closer, urgent now. "Think, Evie. It's important."

"Step back, whoever-you-are." Ice frosted her tone. "I don't know your name, and I don't know you. You have until the count of ten before I begin screaming fit to bring the forest down and all of Hope Falls running to find the commotion."

"Jacob Granger. I'm Jake Granger." He hastily offered what should have been the first thing he told her. "Ask Braden, McCreedy, or Lawson if you need to verify the truth of it."

"Lies." She all but spat the word. "All lies. You said you couldn't tell anyone in town, but you told *Braden* your name?"

"Not initially. Only when we decided to bring McCreedy and Lawson into town for your protection. Those two worked with me for years and know me under my real name, but they keep it to themselves and will continue to do so." Jake could have kicked himself for forgetting about Braden. "I wouldn't have told anyone at all if it wasn't for the fact that keeping you safe outweighed the risk of ruining my cover."

"You tell me not to concern myself with appearances, but everything you've done, everything you've been since the moment you stepped foot in town, was lies! You said look at actions, not what I heard, but do you know what?" She started shoving at his arm again. "Words count. What you say has to match what you do, and you've said one thing and done another."

"Try to understand the reasons, Evie." Her accusation sliced through him—too true to ignore. *Lies aren't just something we say. They're something we do to others.* He looked down at the woman still pushing fruitlessly at his arm, wondering if he might have lost her. *And ourselves.*

"I don't trust that you need a false name. I don't trust you brought McCreedy and Lawson to keep us safe. And I can't believe I was foolish enough to believe everything you said about me being more than most women and thinking you came here looking for a wife! You never saw me as more than an obstacle to some sort of grand, secret plan and I don't—"

No. I won't lose her. He swallowed a laugh as her eyes crossed, trying to track the finger he placed over her nose to stop her from speaking. "You're going to be thoroughly kissed if you don't stop spluttering and start listening, Evie. That's a promise."

"You wouldn't dare." Slightly muffled, she blinked to gather herself and glare again.

"I would. In fact"—he lowered his voice to a whisper—"after you're finished listening, you still might be thoroughly kissed. But that's only with your permission, so listen."

"Either way, you'll be thoroughly slapped. And that's a promise." She poked him in the chest, but Jake noticed she wasn't sidling away. Or slapping him, which showed potential.

"You never fail to surprise me, Evie Thompson." He gave in to the grin. "When I told you I'd taken a false name, the last thing I expected was for you to tell me I chose poorly."

"Well, you did," she defended. "And I called you a liar. And threatened to scream and have promised to slap you at some point in the future when I'm still furious but not so curious."

Curiosity, Evie decided abruptly, could be a curse. Because, really, any sensible woman when faced with a situation like this would— *Be honest, Evie. No sensible woman would be faced with a situation like this. How is it you just accepted a proposal never made by a man who never existed and stand trapped in the forest with a proverbial stranger about to spin his life's tale? After threatening to kiss you senseless, no less?* She gave up an inner struggle to pretend nonchalance. Especially *after he threatened to kiss you senseless.*

Well, for one thing, Evie obviously already counted as senseless since she'd abandoned good sense at some point in the past few weeks. For a few others, *he's not a stranger; he's still Jake. He's just a sorry, lying excuse for a Jake.* She harrumphed over that for a moment. *For another, it's not that I was wrong about him wanting to kiss me, after all, and that goes a long way toward mending my tattered pride.* Though if her good sense hadn't gone missing, that would most likely alarm her more than convince her she should stay. *Besides, it means I was right about Creed not really fitting him. And Braden knows about his name change, so it's not a deep, dark deception.*

Just one he kept from her. Evie started scowling again. *Good thing I kept the right to slap the man, at least. . .*

"We received news of my brother's death a month after it happened back in January. He'd been out of town on business and never returned. They kept things hushed due to an investigation into the circumstances surrounding Edward's death. He'd been accused of cheating in a poker game and drawing his gun on another player who called him on it. The other player, a man named Twyler, was a quicker shot, or so the story goes."

"Oh, I'm sorry to hear about your brother." Evie patted one of the arms imprisoning her against the tree trunk before pulling back as if he'd scalded her. Impossible, really. Despite the protection of the thick trees above them, the rainy weather permeated everything with its chill. And Jake didn't have his jacket any longer, because he'd given it to her. Her heart did an inappropriate little flip before she calmed it.

"Not as sorry as those who knew him would be." His face hardened, grief and rage blending into a heartbreaking mask.

"Would be?" Evie echoed the tacked-on phrase in question.

"My parents—great believers in appearance on earth then forgiveness in heaven—decided not to announce Edward's passing." Jake's hands fisted against the tree, fingers digging into bark until Evie winced. "I sent queries regarding the so-called facts surrounding his death, and assumed Father conducted his own investigations. All the while, they denied his death to me and never mentioned him to the outside world. By the time I did the unthinkable, looking through my father's papers for any clue about Edward I'd missed, two more months had passed. Two months in which I could have been searching for Twyler."

A chill having nothing to do with the weather crept down Evie's spine. "Never say you seek revenge on a man whose only crime was to protect himself when your brother drew his gun."

Lord, what do I know about this man? Where did I go wrong, believing his sweet words to be Your answer to my prayer for a loving husband? Have I misread everything and put myself in danger, only to dismiss the concern in favor of anger and curiosity? Give me wisdom, Father. I desperately need it now.

"Anyone who knew Edward should know he wouldn't cheat at a card game or try to swindle anyone. More importantly, he'd only draw his weapon to defend others first and himself last— never to threaten an innocent man. Never." A muscle in Jake's jaw twitched. "Edward carried a large sum of cash on him the day of his death, along with a French coin weight. The twin of one I carry." He pulled back to dig in his pocket, drawing out a square copper piece imprinted with a crown and fleurs-de-lis. "Neither the money nor the token—which has passed through our family for generations—were found on Edward after his death nor in his rooms. Twyler did it."

Evie stared at the piece as Jake pressed it into her palm, its slight weight a much heavier burden than she expected as she passed it back to him. "Twyler. Twilight. Liar. It's a name for a thief or a man who lives in darkness." She traced the small crown with a fingertip. Understanding flooded her. "Creed means belief, but it also means watchword or token. You chose the name because you believe in your brother's innocence, and you carry the token you hope will prove it when you find its match."

"Somehow Twyler murdered my brother, robbed him, and not only escaped but ruined Edward's name in the process." Jake's fist swallowed the weight. "The papers in my father's study—he wasn't tracking my brother's killer. He paid off officials and witnesses to cover up the ugly incident and pretend it never happened." Jake's voice went gruff. "My father. . . Evie. . .he even paid Twyler to keep the secret. Our father betrayed Edward by believing the lie and disowning my brother in his death."

"Oh, Jake. . ." Evie could find no words to comfort the man before her. "I see now why you left your family name." *Your father needs a few lessons in what it means to be a family, and what it means to be decent, for that matter.* But it was Jake's father, so she held her tongue.

"Not forever. Only until I find Twyler. I don't know his face, only that he's of average height, with brown hair and eyes." Determination straightened his spine. "I don't look like Edward, but the name would ruin my chances. So I became Creed. Twyler knows I've hunted him all the way to Colorado, Evie. I believe he came here."

"To Hope Falls?" Evie's hand went to her heart as though to keep it from leaping through her chest. "*That's* why you came here?" She made as though to back away from him, to find the tree behind her a cold reminder she couldn't hide her hot blush.

Was there ever such a fool? Humiliation lanced through her in hot stabs. She closed her eyes and let the back of her head thump against wet bark. *Of course a man like Jake didn't come here to woo a woman from an ad. The only man we didn't ask which bride he'd choose was the only man who would've told us he didn't want one at all, and here I went and. . .* Her eyes snapped open so wide she felt the strain clear to her hairline, but she couldn't blink.

"I proposed to you." Evie choked out the words, unsure if they were meant to be a confession or an accusation. "You let us think you came for a bride, and I convinced myself you chose me, but that wasn't true at all." *You never wanted me.* She couldn't speak the worst hurt aloud, but the anger poured forth easily.

"It's not why I came, Evie, but—" He reached to touch her face.

She slapped his hand away, talking over him. "You told me not to doubt myself, and you were right about that much. All along I should have been doubting you." The realization freed her from one weight even as her humiliation kept dragging at her. "People may not like what they see when they look my way, but I've never hidden my identity or my purpose."

His breath hissed in as though her words slapped him. Perhaps they did. "Try to understand, Evie. I have an obligation to my brother, and to protect others."

"Protect. . ." Now was her turn to fight for breath as his meaning dawned. She turned and hit his arm as she headed for the diner. "Let me go. I have to find Cora and Lacey and Naomi. And Mrs. Nash, now." Fresh rage flooded her. "You knew Twyler was here, and you allowed Lawson to bring Arla in her condition? How could you!"

"How could I not, when he told me after they were en route?"

She shoved at his arm and shoulder, which wouldn't budge, tried to duck beneath, and found herself hauled back up against the tree. "How could you not tell us of the danger?" She fought to get past him. To Cora. And she didn't get so much as half an inch until she made good on her threat. *Crack!* The sound of her palm striking his cheek split through the sound of rain falling and wind weaving between trees.

But still he didn't let her get past him. "I deserved that. I deserve more than that." The gruff edge to his voice grew more ragged. "But you four wouldn't leave on your own terms, and if I'd told you, Twyler would have known I'd gotten this close. Then I'd never catch him."

"But later, you should have warned us!" Even as she screamed it, Evie knew that if he'd told them, Lacey would have let it slip to Mrs. Nash, who would have told Mrs. McCreedy, and so on and so forth until Twyler slipped into the night like the criminal he was. "You disparage your parents for caring about appearances, denouncing hypocrisy when everything about you is a lie," she yelled at Jake anyway. "The Word promises there is nothing covered that shall not be revealed, Jake. Twyler's time will come, and you can't put others in jeopardy to hasten it! Now let me go, or you will regret it."

"I already regret more than you can imagine, Evie." He ignored her command, continuing to block her. "But you can't tell anyone about Twyler. He'll notice if you all act suspiciously, and he'll run away only to come back and remove anyone he sees as a threat. You have to keep it secret."

"I'll protect my own, Jacob Granger," Evie promised. Then she pulled out the only weapon left in her arsenal. She'd elbowed, kicked, stomped, scratched, pushed, shoved, pulled, pummeled, and slapped. Since she didn't carry her reticule with the tiny pistol Lacey had given her, Evie took him down the only other way she knew how.

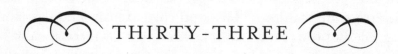 THIRTY-THREE

She cried.

Jake froze as his strong-willed, take-charge Evie dissolved into a series of sobs and sniffles to strike fear into the heart of Paul Bunyan himself. *And it's all my fault.*

Before him stood a woman who sold her family home and began her own business to provide for her sister after their father's death. A woman who packed up and headed West for the sake of her family, agreeing to marry so her friends could be secure. Evie could rise at dawn, feed an entire lumber camp, charm a contingent of loggers, and still have enough energy and determination left to console her sister and chastise a bullheaded Braden.

But I made her cry.

It was enough to paralyze a far better man than Jake knew himself to be. So when she made a watery request for a handkerchief—and Jake couldn't give her his trusty bandana, which covered the back of his neck and already held enough rain to fill half a glass—he did what he could. Which was thrust his hands into all his pockets in frantic hope he'd turn one up.

He didn't even realize he'd been tricked until his back end skidded into the mud, the memory of Evie's hands pressing against his chest fading in the cold air. Jake didn't recover in time to stop her as she stepped over one of his sprawled-out boots and beat a hasty retreat back to the diner.

Pulling himself from the mud with a sickly slurp, Jake started after her, ready to call her out on that piece of trickery. *Of all the underhanded things a woman can do,* he fumed, stalking down the mountainside after her, *crying has to be the absolute lowest. I never thought Evie would be so treacherous, adopting a pretense to get her way when I—*

The air rushed from his lungs when Jake realized exactly what he'd done. *I did all that and more. At least she showed the decency to warn me I'd regret not letting her through. Instead of giving her some sign to be on guard, I insisted she trust me.*

Her charge of hypocrisy hung heavier than the rain beating down on him. The memory of Evie insisting they had different definitions of honor wedged into the tree of his ideals until it was stripped of its branches and ready to crash to the ground.

Jake had, indeed, told Evie not to doubt herself, but she'd never pretended to be anyone other than exactly who she was. She didn't keep secrets or hold grudges against people who made wrong decisions on her behalf or the behalf of those she loved. If Evie didn't bear the gift of forgiveness—or at least tolerance—Braden Lyman wouldn't still be drawing breath.

But she'd never doubted him—because he'd shown the arrogance not to doubt himself. He'd fallen into the same trap as his parents—living out one life before the entire town but privately hiding an entirely different person. *No more. No cause overpowers walking upright. It's not seasonal work.* Aside from keeping the name Creed until he caught Twyler, Jake wouldn't allow any more shadowed truths.

Clear Edward's name, be proud to claim my own, then offer to share it with Evie. That's the new plan. Jake straightened his shoulders as he neared the doors to the diner...and heard the unmistakable sounds of a brawl in progress.

In one second flat, he burst through the door, ducked out of the way as another man flew past and out into the rain, and stiff-armed some fool who came running at him for no reason. Pandemonium reigned, but it didn't take Jake long to catch the reason for the brawl as blustering boasts, dire threats, and wheezing protests flew through the air along with punches.

While Jake took after Evie, someone else took offense at the conversation and started to "handle" matters inside. From an occasional yell, he could even gather who'd been the one to stop the talking and start trying to remove the offending parties.

"Clump, what in tarnation were you thinkin'?" Dodger shrilled, air whistling through what Jake suspected was a newly broken tooth. "Cain't try to force three fools to the train on yore lonesome. Shoulda waited for Bear or— Oh, hey there, Creed!" A judicious duck accompanied the welcoming wave.

Slight change in the plan. First check to make sure the women are safe. Then come back, track down Bob and Earl, and give them good reason to want to board the next train Clump sees. After that, I'll get back to the entire Twyler issue.

Jake cracked his knuckles and headed for the kitchen, making it three-quarters of the way before Earl came blundering into his path. A smile spread across Jake's face as he eyed the other man, whose brows smashed together and head lowered in imitation of a charging bull trying to decide on a target.

Shaped like a rectangle, shoulders squaring up clear down to his feet, Earl was built like a brick, with all the accompanying agility. But for all that, he had sturdiness on his side when Clump rushed him, shouting a defense of Evie's honor and beauty the entire time it took for him to bounce off the larger man and through the swinging doors into the kitchen.

From the sounds of the worried clucks and anxious questions barraging their way toward Clump, the women fared none the worse for wear. Jake assumed they'd decided on discretion instead of venturing into the fray in hopes of restoring order.

A wise choice, Jake approved just before he jerked his chin toward Earl in unmistakable challenge. Sure enough, the fool lowered his head and rushed him. Jake sidestepped, slamming one fist into the man's gut—where he presumed Earl got the gall to call Evie plump—before bringing the force of his weight down on his elbow to the man's back. Earl hit the floor just about hard enough to bounce then showed the idiocy to rise. Jake popped him one in the nose, not bothering to watch the other man hit the floor a second time while he continued toward the kitchen.

Jake got one boot past the swinging doors when something caught his eye. A small square piece of copper lay on the ground. Directly between the door and where Clump now stood amid all the women, Edward's coin weight stared up at him.

"Put him down!" Lacey swatted at Jake's hat as though trying to dislodge a willful butterfly. "Mr. Klumpf stopped those men from saying such awful things. Don't blame him for their vulgarity!"

"Hush, Lace." Evie's warning came out sharper than she'd intended as she herded her sister and two friends across the kitchen. Away from Mr. Klumpf, who even now dangled in the air, caught by Jake's grip on his suspenders. "There are other things than just the brawl out in the dining room. Trust Jake."

Trust Jake. Now that was sketchy advice. *Why do I feel it's safe to trust an admitted liar bent on vengeance?* Evie fretted along with the others as they watched Jake interrogate the hapless Mr. Klumpf, who'd gone slightly purple in embarrassment. If the man were more round and less boxy, Evie considered the idea he'd bear a striking resemblance to a blueberry as he protested Jake's treatment of his suspenders.

"These are good suspenders, and you need to let go of 'em, Creed. Iff'n you're of a temper on account of how I decided Earl, Bob, and Mason needed to hit the train and not look back, believe you me, they deserve it. Just ask the ladies." Klumpf's babbling sounded as sincere as always to Evie's ears.

"The piece, Clump." Jake released his grip on the suspenders, dropping the shorter man to his heavy boots. He held a square copper coin in his hand. "Where did you get this?"

"That? If you take a fancy to it, you can keep it, Jake." Klumpf adjusted his collar and straightened his shoulders. "Just a trinket I won in a poker game is all. Nothing important."

Evie let out a breath she didn't know she'd been holding at Klumpf's explanation. She hadn't been able to believe the worst of the good-natured, sweet man whose signature stomp added to the rhythm of Hope Falls. Klumpf was one of their own, really.

"To tell you the truth, I most likely would've forgotten and not noticed it fell through the hole in my pocket if you hadn't picked the thing up." He put a hand in his pocket, and Evie could only assume he fingered the unraveled seam within it.

"Poker game?" Jake's throat worked. "With who? Who put this in the pot, Klumpf?"

"I don't remember who threw it in. But it was just me, Draxley, Dodger, and McCreedy who was playing." He scratched his head. "Sorry I can't recall any better than that, Jake."

"Evie? Call Dodger in here, please." Jake kept his tone perfectly controlled. Evie took it to be a sign of how uncontrolled he really felt.

Dodger scuttled inside in response to her summons so quickly it almost made her feel guilty for luring him in to face Jake. Until she reminded herself that this might well be the man who'd murdered Edward and could threaten each and every one of them. Dodger would be fine so long as he wasn't Twyler.

And if he was. . .well, Evie would have to wrangle pity for the man when it came down to that. At the moment, she couldn't dredge up any sympathetic feelings for such a mangy cur. So she watched, tense as could be, while Jake circled to keep himself between them and the petty thief.

"Dodger, Clump tells me he won this off of you in a poker

game." Jake held up the coin weight and lifted a quizzical brow. "You never struck me as coming from a French background, and it's an unusual piece. Where did you run across something like this?"

"It's mine." Dodger plunged his hands into various pockets, fiddling with the contents before moving to the next pocket. "Or was, until I lost it to Clump there. If someone says I lifted it, they's lying sure as the sun shines after a rain, Mr. Creed."

"Take your hands out of your pockets, Dodger." Jake's hand hovered over his own holster as Evie kept Lacey and Cora from leaning forward. Thankfully, Naomi had the wisdom to refrain.

"I took what Mr. Lyman said to heart, I did." Dodger gave a virtuous nod. "Seeing as how if I help myself to little pretties, I'll feel the boot quicker than I can snatch a farewell present. That there flattened coin-y is mine, fair and square. Especially the square part, in this case. It's why I like it."

"Why's that?" Once again, Evie's curiosity got the better of her.

"Round places got no corners, Miss Thompson. Can make a man nervous." Dodger gestured around the room. "So it's the first time I saw a square coin instead of round. Liked it better."

I imagine you did, Dodger. You're a sly one, liking dark shadows and places where sticky fingers don't go noticed for a good while. Evie tapped one finger against her chin in thought.

"It only makes a man nervous if he's trying to hide something." Clump crossed his arms from the other side of the room, apparently having decided to side with Jake again.

"I'm going to ask you one more time, Dodger." Jake flipped the weight into the air, watching the other man as he watched it fall back into Jake's outstretched hand. "To whom did this coin belong before it found its way into your hands?"

"He wouldn't put it on the table." Dodger began to babble, backing up until he bumped against a counter. "He knew I'd taken a shine to it but seemed awful put out I'd noticed it at all. Don't go telling Mr. Lyman I light-fingered the thing, Mr. Creed. It's just a little coin. I figured it can't be worth much. And, in all fairness, it don't seem like Fillmore's missed it any—"

Evie watched as Jake charged through the swinging doors and back into the mass of fighting men.

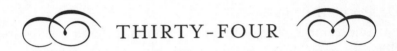

THIRTY-FOUR

Fillmore. Jake's pulse pounded in time with his boot steps as he paced around the dining room, eyeing men slumped on benches or down on the ground, steering clear of those still up and fighting as he searched for the one man he'd traveled so far to find. *Twyler.*

His nemesis hid himself deep within the faded background of Fillmore's identity, so unobtrusive that Jake wasted the bulk of his time focusing on more obvious choices like Williams, Kane, Dodger, and the like. When all along he should have expected Twyler to be so crafty he poked about like a turtle—content in a slow, steady pace where he could observe everything and retreat to safety at a moment's notice.

Which is why Jake wasn't surprised when he didn't find Fillmore in the diner. Out of concern for Mrs. Nash and Mrs. McCreedy, he looked in on them at the house before proceeding to the bunkhouse. That's where he expected to find him, perched in the top back bunk, hunched around a book like an overgrown crow. Because that's what Twyler was, whenever he shed Fillmore. A crow. Sharp and greedy, with a wicked intelligence to get his way no matter who he hurt in the process.

But Fillmore didn't lurk in the bunkhouse either. Fingers

of dread tickled the back of Jake's neck as he raced back to the diner—to the women he'd left under the care of Klumpf and Dodger, neither of whom would manage to outwit the likes of Twyler.

He burst through the dining room doors, vaulted over a groaning bucker with a swelling shiner, and barged through the swinging doors to find Clump—and two women. Naomi and Evie's sister sat at the same table where he'd left them, with Dodger nowhere in sight.

Evie came rushing out of the pantry, pale as a snowdrift. "They're gone, Jake." Her lips trembled. "Lacey went to find Dodger a peppermint stick for his upset stomach—he claimed he's nervous about you and Braden kicking him out of town since he swiped that token from Fillmore. But Lacey couldn't find them, and he wandered over to the mercantile while she checked again. . ." Her voice died off as Jake rushed past her to check things while she finished explaining. "But neither came back, and now Lacey isn't in the pantry and the door's wide open."

Dodger! Tracks crossed the mud beyond the door—a clear set of footprints marred by long stripes and deep heel scuffs—the imprints of a woman dragged away against her will. Mercifully, the sun replaced the rain clouds as Jake ordered Evie back inside and began tracing the tracks back up the mountain. He hurried, knowing he'd made a grave mistake—the same mistake he'd resented his parents for making.

I erred, Lord. I judged by appearance, letting my knowledge of Dodger's petty thievery color my judgment until his flawed caricature of a cover worked in his favor. Just as he'd planned. Now he has Lacey, and I pray for her protection. I ask for peace when I confront my enemy. Let me seek justice instead of the vengeance I'd planned before. Help me see Your way rather than let my own decisions hurt Evie's friend. Let Lacey be all right. . . .

"Here's your jacket." Evie's whisper made Jake want to pound a ponderosa into the ground with nothing more than his fists.

She panted from the exertion of running to catch up with him, swathed in her own chestnut cloak as she held out his coat.

"I told you to get back inside," he ground out. "I don't have time to send you back." A worse thought occurred to him. "Twyler might have doubled back. You can't go alone." He snatched the coat from her outstretched hand and shrugged into it.

"You'll notice I went inside to fetch your coat and a few of my own things." She patted her reticule with a smile. "Now hush and do keep going. Lacey wouldn't be in danger if you'd handled things differently, and griping about me going along to help the pair of you will only slow us down, Jacob Granger!"

Now wasn't the time to notice she'd said his real name. Jake noticed anyway, even as he twined her right arm into the crook of his left and plowed ahead as swiftly and quietly as possible, following the disturbed mud, moss, and ferns underfoot. It looked as though Lacey hadn't gone easily. Quietly—Twyler must have gagged her to avoid any ear-splitting screeches to sound the alarm—but not docilely.

Good girl. She's spent a lot of time with my Evie. The thoughts fled as he heard a male voice a few yards ahead.

"Don't test my patience." Less nasal and lacking the whine, Dodger's thin voice resonated through the forest. "I said I'd tell them your location. I did't promise you'd be alive. So you can climb on in and they can find you snug and spitting mad, or I can waste a slug and cram you down there so they find whatever the bugs leave behind."

An angry murmur responded, too muffled to be made out. Jake shared a glance with Evie and nodded. That had to be Lacey.

"Let her go, Twyler." Jake edged out from behind the uneven row of trees concealing him from view. "She's no good to you." The sight that greeted him wore his considerable store of patience very thin indeed. "You can't shove a full-grown woman into a hollow tree stump, Twyler. And there's no reason to anyway. Drop your gun, set her free, and we'll go back to town."

"I'm not going back to that place," Dodger snapped, all hint of mischief abandoned. "Miss Lyman here is going into this empty stump—it'll make for a tight fit, but we both know how large ponderosas are, and luckily she's a tiny thing. You and Miss Thompson will be tied around the same while I catch the next train from Hope Falls."

"We can't allow that, Twyler." Evie edged forward, standing level with Jake. "There's nothing to be gained by it, in any case."

"Ransom, my dear." An evil smile spread across the face Jake once considered simple-minded. "I'll reveal your location, as well as the location of Miss Lyman, after a substantial sum is wired to me. By then, I'll have the means to move on, and the time in which to do so before Mr. Granger decides to follow me yet again. Pity it's unwise to kill him outright, but after the unfortunate incident with his brother, it's a risk I'd rather not take. I'm more than happy, however, to take the additional ransom the two of you will provide."

"That's not going to happen." Jake shook his head. "We both know you won't leave us to be found in the woods so near town, so easily. And we've only run across one large hollowed-out tree stump for you to use, Twyler."

"Ah, ah. Dodger, now. I must say, I'm pleased how well my little ruse worked. What better explanation than that I'd stolen the piece, should Granger show up and discover me? Simplest thing in the world to get 'caught' swiping other trinkets. A smart trickster is always one step ahead with a solid contingency plan behind him. Like this." With that, he hauled his hostage against him, pressing a sharp blade against her delicate throat. With his free hand, he pointed a pistol at Evie.

Jake struggled against the hot rage surging inside him, urging him to do something to protect Evie. *But not at the expense of Lacey. Not in anger. . .* A small measure of calm steadied him. *It's not about my vengeance. It's in the Lord's hands now. He can't play upon my weaknesses.* "One ruse worked, Twyler. No more. Give up—now."

"This is no ruse." A thin red line inched across Lacey Lyman's throat, though she did nothing but wince. "I suggest you drop your weapon, Granger, if you want both—or either—of these ladies to see another sunrise. Your one shot might just as well hit Miss Lyman as myself, but I'm guaranteed success with at least one of my targets." Satisfaction oozed from his voice. "And I'm quite likely to survive, if not go entirely unharmed. So let's get on with it, shall we? A stacked deck is a gamer's greatest ally."

"I wonder"—Evie's nonchalance warned Jake that she planned something outlandish—"whether that's not something like a woman with a well-packed purse. Because I do find, Mr. Dodger or Twyler or whichever you prefer"—she chattered on brightly as she rummaged through her reticule—"that it's best to be prepared for anything." In an instant, she pulled out a familiar dainty pistol with inlaid mother-of-pearl handle. "Don't you agree?"

Besieged with memories of Evie's complete inability to so much as wing a metal can at ten paces—memories she had no idea he possessed—Jake could only stare at the spectacle with something approaching awe. He noted, too, that Lacey made an abortive attempt to struggle, brought up short by the knife held to her throat.

Jake knew Lacey didn't want to be anywhere near the direction where Evie chose to fire, but Twyler would read her movements as an attempt to give her friend an even better shot. Despite her complete inadequacy when it came to shooting, everything about Evie's conversation and bearing indicated an intimidating level of expertise.

"You've proven more perceptive than most, Miss Thompson." A gleam of appreciation lit Twyler's gaze, inciting further fury from Jake. "A rare and resourceful woman could be a great asset, but I find myself unimpressed by your show of fashion accessories. Wield your toy as you please, Miss Thompson. This is between

Granger and me."

"Then let the women go." Jake jumped on the idea.

"We've come too far for that, I'm afraid. And time ticks away while you make idle chitchat. Throw down your gun, Mr. Granger, and admit that the woman at your side wouldn't be able to hit a target if I drew one three feet from her nose."

"Oh, that's absolutely true, Mr. Dodger." Evie's smile widened. "It used to be that I couldn't hit the. . .what's the expression my mentor used? Oh yes, I couldn't hit the broadside of the bunkhouse. But it's such a cunning little piece."

"Listen to her." Jake opted for honesty. "She won't be able to hit you, Twyler. There's no threat in letting her play along. It's not as though she'd shoot you." He gave a convincing scoff at the idea. Convincing more thanks to reality than his acting ability.

"No." Twyler's self-satisfied ooze dried up in a hurry. "You want me dead. You want me to ignore her purse pistol in hopes she wields it as well as she claims and ends my life." He darted glances around himself, edging farther out of reach. "She changes the game. Changes the cards, different value. . ." He degenerated into strange rambling mutters.

"Why did you kill my brother, Edward?" Jake needed to know the truth before the man in front of him slipped beyond the edge of sanity forever.

"He noticed me cheating and started to raise a fuss. Two men I'd fleeced a few nights prior sat just one table over, so I couldn't allow that. And I'd already marked him for carrying a large amount . of cash." Twyler clicked his teeth together repeatedly. "So I fired first, paid off the other players, and pocketed the profit. Double the windfall when your old man started paying off people to not besmirch dear Edward's memory."

Twyler's mocking laugh made Jake's trigger finger itch.

"And then you came after me, and I did more and more paying off of my own until I ran dry and needed a rich wife." Twyler's eyes narrowed. "But here you are again, forcing my hand. With two skilled shooters against only myself, I can't hope to make it out alive and carrying off my plan." He looked right at Evie. "So I can either take revenge on Granger here, before leaving this earth, or hope your misguided sense of feminine kindness precludes you shooting a man to death in the back."

With that, Twyler shoved Miss Lyman so she stumbled, falling downhill and forcing Jake to catch her. He halted her progress, sat her down, and took off running after his prey.

One shot. I only get one shot, Lord, and I can't shoot a man in the back no matter how despicable he is, or I become an opportunist like the man I chase. Justice over vengeance—let my aim be true.

He followed, waiting until Twyler hit an open area before Jake sank to one knee, steadied his hand, and took the shot.

A shot echoed in the forest, followed by a terrible cry. Then silence.

Evie huddled with Lacey, whom she'd unbound after the men went hurtling off through the trees.

"Please tell me you wouldn't have fired," Lacey said only after the silence became unbearable—and Evie handed over the pistol.

"Have a little faith, Lace." Evie scanned the horizon, anxious for Jake to come back. It hadn't escaped her notice that Twyler hadn't dropped his gun before taking off.

"Does that mean you would've uttered a prayer and pulled the trigger, or that I should have faith you wouldn't do anything so foolish?" Lacey blanched at the thought, which wasn't precisely flattering.

"We can do all things through faith, Lacey Lyman." *Even wait for Jake to come striding back through these trees. No matter if it's taking him forever and a day to mosey his way home.*

"In that case, I have faith that you'll never fire a gun unless faced with a man like Dodger or Twyler or whatever his name was, with absolutely no one else anywhere near the vicinity." Lacey rubbed her throat, where the knife had rested. "Thank you for coming after me. I couldn't have gone into that stump."

It was then that they heard it, the snap of twigs beneath boots as someone heavy headed their way. They froze, Lacey's hand tightening on the gun, until they made out Jake, with a prone form slung over his shoulders.

Twyler.

Evie's heart sank. *I'd so hoped he'd find justice and not vengeance, but Twyler forced Jake to choose between the lesser of two evils. Shooting an evil man in the back is the better choice than letting him go free to harm more people.*

Jake slung the other man's body to the ground, eliciting a wretched moan from the captured criminal. "Oh, my leg," Twyler groaned. "Why couldn't you let me go, Granger? Or let the woman shoot me outright, at least?"

"Because I can't shoot the broadside of a bunkhouse. We told you that, Twyler." Evie couldn't smile at the sight of blood soaking the man's right leg from the knee down, but she judged him a lucky man nevertheless. He deserved far worse.

"Brings new meaning to the term 'long shot.'" Lacey shuddered.

"Worst pun, Lace." Evie nudged her friend.

"Best threat, Evie. Pity we can't use it on the rest of the men."

"You mean. . .it was true?" Twyler gasped the words, starting to wheeze. If Evie hadn't heard only the one shot, she'd have wondered whether something was wrong with the man's chest. Until a bark of laughter escaped. "A double bluff, then. I was outdone by a double bluff from an amateur?"

"And an exceptional shot from a master," Evie lauded Jake. "He could well have ended your life, but he chose not to take revenge."

"The shot didn't matter. Only the bluff. Never the hand, only how it's played. . ." The wheezes stretched and thinned into a series of wispy cackles. "An amateur! I deserve my fate, then. I held all the winning cards and threw them away."

He kept up the steady stream of incoherent babble about

games and bluffs and the ultimate loss until Jake left him with the doctor, who mercifully put Twyler into the oblivion of drugged rest. Merciful for everyone—not just the man with the shattered knee.

"Evie, I'd like a word." Jake had washed up and taken off his jacket, so Twyler's blood no longer stained him. Nor did the memory of his brother's injustice or his father's betrayal, it seemed. He stood even taller than before, the lines of worry she'd never thought unattractive lessened until Jake seemed almost free. When she nodded, he led her into the doctor's study. . .and sat her down in the wing-backed chair.

"You know the worst of me, Evie Thompson. You've seen my quick temper and penchant for issuing orders. I've lied about my name and my purpose in Hope Falls, allowing you to think I came looking for a wife when I came hunting a killer." He paced during the entire recitation, as though unable to remain still. "I'm not as good a man as you deserve. I can't go back and start things over and introduce myself as Jacob Granger, or appreciate your sense of honor before you explain it. But I can do one thing—and I hope I do it right."

Is he proposing? He can't be proposing. Can he? Evie fought the urge to hop up and pace alongside him.

But it was a good thing she didn't, because the next thing she knew, he stopped right in front of her and stared down into her eyes with the same intensity she remembered from all the way back in Charleston—when he'd first taken off his hat. Her heart fluttered as he opened his mouth and professed, with touching sincerity, his deep and abiding need to. . .

"Apologize." Jake reached out those large, callus-roughened hands of his and cradled hers between them, an inadequate anchor when her heart fell like a cake.

Of course he's not proposing, she chastised herself, blinking furiously against unreasonable tears. *We've already gone through this once today. If he didn't accept it when I all but proposed to him, what sort of wigeon would I be to think he might be doing anything more serious than apologizing?* Although, of course, to a man that might just be a more serious and difficult matter than even a proposal.

"You can stop apologizing." She tried to end the conversation by standing, but he laid one large hand on her shoulder to keep her seated.

"No. I can't. You charged me with hypocrisy, for saying one thing and doing another—and it's true. I've a long way to go, Evie, starting with the trip home to bring Twyler up on charges. Before I left, I should have confronted my father and spoken with my mother, and now I need to make amends as best I can. Even if they don't see they were wrong, I have to own up to my mistakes. But when I get back. . ."

Her breath hitched as he dropped to one knee.

"Proverbs tells us that 'a false balance is abomination to the Lord'"—Jake pressed one of the copper squares into her palm as he spoke—" 'but a just weight is His delight.' With you, I find my balance, Evie.

"I'm asking you to be mine to delight in for the rest of our lives. Once, you were willing to take Jacob Creed. Now I'm giving you the only thing I can offer, besides myself. The greatest gift love ever gave was a choice." He paused, his gaze searching hers. "Could you choose to love Jacob Granger?"

"Jake, don't you know?" She clutched the square coin weight in one hand, reaching out to trace the contour of his jaw with her other. "I already do."

He stood at the same moment she did, sweeping her into his arms for an embrace to prove something Evie always hoped. *For every woman, there's a perfect fit.* Hers just happened to be a land as rugged as the mountains they covered, and a man relentless enough to convince her they belonged together.

"Although I should mention," she managed to gasp once

she'd somewhat recovered from his kiss, "you'll have to convince at least two of the other women to accept you as my fiancé. It's one of the rules we agreed upon."

"Oh?" For the first time, one of his short responses didn't bother her. Perhaps because he followed it with another searing kiss.

"Well, yes." Evie looked up at him, emboldened by the love she'd found. "But I'm sure we can do away with that. I can be rather determined when I want something."

"No." Jake tugged gently on a lock of her hair. "I'll never again ask you to break your word, Evie. You're more than worth running the gamut through your sister and friends."

"You'll win them over, Jake." She beamed at him.

"I don't mind winning them"—he leaned in for another kiss—"so long as I can keep you."

Life doesn't wait, and neither does **Kelly Eileen Hake**. In her short twenty-seven years of life, she's achieved much. Her secret? Embracing opportunities and multitasking. Kelly received her first writing contract at the tender age of seventeen and arranged to wait three months until she was able to legally sign it. Since that first contract five years ago, she's reached several life goals. Aside from fulfilling fourteen contracts ranging from short stories to novels, she's also attained her BA in English Literature and Composition and earned her credential to teach English in secondary schools. If that weren't enough, she's taken positions as a college preparation tutor, bookstore clerk, and in-classroom learning assistant to pay for the education she values so highly. Recently, she completed her MA in Writing Popular Fiction.

Writing for Barbour combines two of Kelly's great loves—history and reading. A CBA best-selling author and dedicated member of American Christian Fiction Writers, she's been privileged to earn numerous Heartsong Presents Reader's Choice Awards. No matter what goal she pursues, Kelly knows what it means to *work* for it! Please visit her Web site at www.kellyeileenhake.com to learn more.